PSALM

A Novel/Reflection on the Four Plagues of the Lord

Translated by
Andrew Bromfield

Cherry
Orchard
Books

Friedrich
Gorenstein

PSALM

A Novel/Reflection on the Four Plagues of the Lord

Translated by
Andrew Bromfield

CHERRY ORCHARD BOOKS
2026

Library of Congress Control Number:2026935494

ISBN 9798887198859 (hardback)
ISBN 9798887198866 (adobe pdf)
ISBN 9798887198873 (epub)

Book design by Kryon Publishing Services
Cover design by Ivan Grave
On the cover: Jean-François Millet, *Starry Night*
Source: Wikimedia Commons

Published by Cherry Orchard Books,
an imprint of Academic Studies Press

1007 Chestnut St.
Newton, MA 02464, USA
press@academicstudiespress.com
www.academicstudiespress.com

The translator and the Press would like to thank late Mr. Howard Turner, whose keen interest in this book and financial support made its publication possible.

Contents

Translator's Preface

Friedrich Gorenstein's novel "Psalm" is a highly distinctive literary text. Its narrative is structured in the form of a sequence of five "parables" that span the period of the earthly path traveled by Dan the Antichrist in the Soviet Union from the early1930s to the 1950s. It weaves together vivid stories of people's lives—which provide the narrative substance of the parables—with commentaries on religion and religious history, and numerous quotations from the Bible. The latter are used primarily, but not only, to represent the thoughts and spoken words of the Antichrist in response to various situations. The reader will gain valuable insight into the relationship of such a daringly multifaceted novel to the literature of its own time from a reading of Marat Grinberg's lucid afterword "The Soviet Jewish *Haftarah*: Friedrich Gorenstein's *Psalm*," included in this volume, in which Grinbeg places "Psalm" in the general corpus of Soviet Jewish Literature.

From the viewpoint of translation, two elements of the text are of special significance. The first of these consists of the numerous biblical quotations that appear on virtually every page. Gorenstein presents these in the language of the Russian Synodal Bible of the late nineteenth century, and I have translated them using the language of the English Standard Version (ESV), which in general is far more easily comprehensible to the modern reader than the King James Version (KJV) first published in 1611, and sits comfortably alongside the varied language of the narrative sections to produce the second significant element of the text, which is a unifying "biblical rhythm." In the process of translation, I was very much aware of this rhythm, and hope that I have succeeded in conveying it to the reader.

Andrew Bromfield

Dedicated to my mother

“You shall not fall in with the many to do evil,
nor shall you bear witness in a lawsuit,
siding with the many, so as to pervert justice,
nor shall you be partial to a poor man in his lawsuit.”

The Second Book of Moses, called Exodus (23:2-3)

“Following the thoughts of a great man is a most absorbing study.”

Pushkin. *The Moor of Peter the Great*

“I have heard of your paintings too, well enough; God has given you one face, and you make yourself another: you jig, you amble, and you lisp, and nickname God’s creatures, and make your wantonness your ignorance.”

Shakespeare. *Hamlet (Act 3, Scene 1)*

A Parable of a Lost Brother

"Ah, the thunder of many peoples; they thunder like the thundering of the sea! Ah, the roar of nations; they roar like the roaring of mighty waters!" So said Isaiah, son of Amos, eight hundred years before the Star of Bethlehem that proclaimed the birth of an infant child, a son, to his dearly beloved, stubborn and fractious nation, a nation languishing, exhausted by the roaring and tramping on all sides. So said the prophet, whose keen ear discerned the most menacing sound of heavy tramping from the north.

Yes, here below there is tumult and turmoil. But the closer one ascends to heaven, the more the tumult is hushed and the closer one approaches to the Lord, the less compassion there is for people. And this is why, to show his compassion for people, the Lord sends his messengers to earth. The Lord does not send them on His own account, He does not choose for Himself, but sends those who are chosen and designated by the prophets. The Lord granted this right to man at the beginning of existence, during the creation of the world. "Now out of the ground the Lord God had formed every beast of the field and every bird of the heavens and brought them to the man to see what he would call them. And whatever the man called every living creature, that was its name." In so doing, the Lord invested man with the power of a creator and initiated man into the mystery of art. The seventh day of creation was the day of art's birth, it was God's gift to man on the seventh day, and to this day the Lord has reserved it for his chosen ones. From among these chosen ones He has singled out seers and prophets, greater and lesser, and from among the prophets He has singled out only three: Moses, the originator of the Law of God, Isaiah, who foretold the Messiah, Christ from the tribe of Judah and Jeremiah, who foretold the Antimessiah, the Antichrist from the tribe of Dan.

On his deathbed Jacob, the founder of Israel, told each of his twelve sons their future, so that his sons would not merely be curious about their destiny, but devote all their energy exclusively to fulfilling the covenant. To his fourth son, Judah, he said:

"Judah, your brothers shall praise you, your hand shall be on the neck of your enemies, your father's sons shall bow down before you. Judah is a lion's cub, from the prey, my son, you have gone up. He stooped down; he crouched as a lion and as a lioness; who dares rouse him? The scepter shall not depart from Judah, nor the ruler's staff from between his feet, until tribute comes to him; and to him shall be the obedience of the peoples."

To his sixth son, Dan, he said:

"Dan shall judge his people as one of the tribes of Israel. Dan shall be a serpent in the way, a Viper by the path that bites the horse's heels so that his rider falls backward."

From the fullness of strength and gait of the lion, the Messiah Christ was born; from the Viper, the snake, who took the place of the deadly sword for ancient executioners and suicides, the Antimessiah-Antichrist was born. And on the great day of blessing and cursing, when Moses from the tribe of Levi taught the people to love God and fear calumny, they stood apart: the tribe of Judah on the mount of blessing, Gerizim, and the tribe of Dan on the mount of cursing, Ebal.

Time had then moved on a long way from the seventh day of creation, the sacred day of the birth of art. Already the agony of thought, that most appalling of earthly torments, which subsequently afflicted Shakespeare, a genius who huddled close against the earth and was spurned by the heavens (for he who is strong in human thought is always weak in the thought of God) already the agony of thought was tormenting man, and for this agony he was banished from Eden and cursed to eternal toil. Man had learned to turn even art, the Lord's sacred gift, against Him who gave it. And the first curse that was pronounced on Mount Ebal concerning the commandments of Moses, was this:

"Cursed be the man who makes a carved or cast metal image, an abomination to the Lord, a thing made by the hands of a craftsman, and sets it up in secret!"

But man, tormented by his desires and the shame engendered by the Tree of the Knowledge of Good and Evil, persisted in his ignorance of his own limits, knowing no fear. He no longer created idols in secret, but openly, he exalted to the heavens those exactly like himself, resembling himself in their sinfulness . . . In vain, like a voice crying in the wilderness, the great weeping prophet Jeremiah proclaimed:

"As for their tongue, it is polished by the workman, and they themselves are gilded and laid over with silver, yet are they but false, and cannot speak . . . And they become nothing other than what the artists wished to make them . . . When ye see the multitude before them and behind them, worshipping them . . . say ye in your hearts, O Lord, we must worship Thee."

However, for his prophecy Jeremiah received traditional treatment: he was beaten and imprisoned in the cellar of the house of Jonathan the scribe, which had been made into the public prison. But when Jeremiah's suffering became so great that he was likely to die, the king had mercy on him and had him moved to the guards' yard of the royal prison, where he was given bread.

"Then the king commanded Ebed-melech the Ethiopian: 'Take thirty men with you from here, and lift Jeremiah the prophet out of the cistern before he dies.'" Ebed-melech took with him some old cast-off clothes, and let them down on ropes to Jeremiah in the dungeon. "Then Ebed-melech the Ethiopian said to Jeremiah: 'Put the rags and clothes between your armpits and the ropes.' Jeremiah did so. Then they drew Jeremiah up with ropes and lifted him out of the cistern and Jeremiah remained in the courtyard of the guard."

Such were the sufferings of the great Jewish prophet, the prophet who foretold the Antichrist from among his own brothers in the tribe of Dan, and who conceived the legendary teaching of nonresistance to evildoers by means of evil and violence, which was appropriated from him seven centuries later, becoming renowned throughout the world. For every prophet sermonizes against the king and against the people and is persecuted and tormented by them. The Lord could not annihilate a multitude of many sinners by inclusive punishment, in case a few righteous individuals might perish, for life is His divine manuscript, and even an earthly author, if he does not work in the style of Socialist Realism, cannot annihilate that which is evil, leaving only that which is good, he can only emulate Gogol and fling the entire manuscript into the fire, annihilating it as a whole. Therefore the Lord, having abjured inclusive punishment since the time of Noah, created, in distinction from the punishments of kings and the punishments of peoples, the four terrible plagues of the Lord. These were recorded as follows by the prophet of exile, Ezekiel:

"The first plague is the sword, the second is famine, the third is the beast (which is construed as lust), the fourth is sickness, or pestilence . . ."

Sometimes these plagues come together, sometimes singly, sometimes one intensifies, sometimes another . . . But in the year when the prediction of the martyr-prophet Jeremiah was fulfilled and Dan from the tribe of Dan, the

Viper, the Antichrist, created not for blessing, but for judgment and cursing, appeared on earth, the second plague of the Lord, famine, intensified to the utmost. And what had been foretold by the prophet Ezekiel came to pass:

"And I shall send against you the deadly arrows of famine, arrows for destruction, which I will send to destroy you, and bring more and more famine upon you and break your staff of bread."

At that time there appeared on earth Dan from the tribe of Dan, the Antichrist . . . This happened in the fall of the year 1933, near the town of Dymytrov in Kharkiv Province. That is where the beginning of the first parable is set. For when the plagues of the Lord come, ordinary people's destinies assume the form of prophetic parables.

***

"The harvest is past, the summer is ended, and we are not saved," so said the prophet Jeremiah on a day as overcast as this one, as he gazed at the empty fields of the Promised Land, which in the fall twilight were as deserted and dreadful as the dark, menacing sky above them. "I looked on the earth, and behold, it was without form and void; and to the heavens, and they had no light."

And indeed, the window of the former tavern, now the People's Tea Room of the Red Plowman Collective Farm, offered a view of land and sky identical to those that had tormented the Jewish prophet's heart, the compassionate, aching heart of a pessimistic lover of humankind, a psalmist sorrowing for others.

We should note in passing that, while more than two thousand years of the present civilization have scarcely altered the character of the optimist at all, neither reducing the rapturous exaltations of his blustery lungs, nor increasing his wits, the pessimist has changed completely . . . Having lost his lyricism, he has acquired philosophical pungency and a haughty disdain for life . . . However of all those gathered in the People's Tea Room of the Red Plowman Collective Farm on that evening, only one had any idea at all about all this, and he was a youth, almost a boy in fact and, moreover, clearly not from those parts, and therefore the other customers kept glancing at him rather often at first. This boy was sitting apart from the general company, in the most uncomfortable spot, at a table by the window. He was dressed in town style and was clearly Jewish in appearance, but since a large number of mandated officials, including quite a few Jews, had come out from the town in this year of collectivization and crop failure, the other customers quite soon grew accustomed to the sight of the boy-youth and forgot about him. And in addition, there was a strong draft blowing from the window, which was partly boarded over with plywood, and none of the experienced customers used the table beside it.

The tea room's customers on that evening were from the most well-to-do section of the local population, as things went in those days: shock-worker tractor drivers, who had gathered together after a district convention. For the occasion of the convention, herrings and bread rolls had been delivered to the farm's canteen, and sunflower seeds and fruit-flavored sugar candies to the tea room. And so, from early in the morning beggars had started harassing the shock-worker tractor drivers. It would not have been so bad, if they came only from the local village of Shagaro-Petrovskoe. But they came from everywhere: from Kom-Kuznetsovskoe, and the Linden Trees settlement, and from the separate farmsteads . . .

"Lord have mercy! In the name of Jesus Christ . . . the Son of God . . ."

Since time immemorial this refrain, chanted now in a shrill, childish voice, now in a senile, faltering whisper, has accompanied the traditional Russian crop failure and famine. In the time of Boris Godunov, and in later times, described by Leo Tolstoy and Korolenko, in their ruinous impoverishment fathers and mothers, and the entire working population, became the idle dependents of their own children and old folks, their lives maintained by the name of Christ. Korolenko once said that in Russia begging was a mighty power of the people. Now, however, crop failure and famine had been augmented by fear and unrest, and that final power in the face of disaster had started to wither away. For its sins, the church had been reduced to ashes, and Jeremiah spoke long ago, with heartfelt grief, of a people without a shepherd:

"For my people are foolish, they know me not. They are stupid children, they have no understanding.

"They are wise in doing evil! But how to do good they know not."

Even in former times people had not given willingly, out of a kind heart, but out of the fear of sin. Now, however, all the sins of heaven had been abrogated by the new authorities, and as for the churches, where only recently priests, mumbling with indifferent lips, had transformed living truths into dead trinkets, nowadays these churches were filled with the smell of damp cellars and the spirituous odor of putrefying straw and badly stored potatoes. Jesus Christ from the tribe of Judah had been abrogated and replaced everywhere, removed from the walls in public places, scraped off and papered over. But people continued to beg in Christ's name, if only because nothing else had yet been invented for beggars. For in order to feed himself, a beggar, who from time immemorial has stood on the very lowest rung of society, can only use the most exalted of names to overcome his brothers' callousness. However if anyone were to hit on the idea of begging in the name of the Council of People's Commissars, he would surely have been taken for an agent provocateur, liable to punishment by the State Political Directorate! Therefore Christ's name had been retained for begging, as an anachronism, in a similar fashion to certain prerevolutionary brands of *papirosas.*

And so as evening drew in, when the usual refrain: "Lord have mercy! In the name of Jesus Christ . . . the Son of God . . ." rang out in the People's Tea Room, hardly anyone looked up from their conversations, or from drinking their carrot tea with fruit-flavored sugar candies, or from the din of the genuine feasting around the foreman's table, on which there was a large bottle of diluted grain alcohol and genuine, pink bacon fat lying on plates alongside salted herrings . . .

Shortly before this, they had given alms to two young brothers, who had sung and danced the "Gypsy Girl," then to an old man, then to a woman with a babe in arms . . . Poverty is importunate, poverty has no tact or conscience, its only desire is to snatch as much as it can for itself, ahead of its beggar-brother . . .

The little girl who had walked into the tea room was clearly not interested in knowing that the men were tired after their hard day, that what they were eating and drinking was their own, obtained by back-breaking labor, as well as through good luck and privilege, and that for them beggars were a tedious pest, like gadflies sucking the blood of a workhorse . . .

And in general there is something insolent and importunate in the poverty of children, unlike the poverty of adults, and especially of old people. Firstly, child beggars rarely cry in an attempt to move you to pity, and if they do cry, it is obviously phony, you can see that they have been taught to cry, they are not really crying for themselves. And secondly, they thank you for your charity without any satisfaction, and often don't thank you at all, but take it as their due, as if everyone around them owes them something, as if everyone around them is their mother or father. And apart from all that, there weren't any women in the People's Tea Room, and a man in a tea room is more likely to give alms if a beggar doesn't play on his pity but, on the contrary, makes him laugh, and so the men had given generously to the two brothers who danced the "Gypsy Girl." But the little girl had obviously only started begging recently, she didn't try to amuse the public, but simply walked between the tables, mechanically repeating Christ's name in a shrill little voice, like a children's nursery rhyme learned by rote. The little girl's face was typically womanish: calm, with a look somewhere between stupidity and kindliness in the gray eyes. And there was already a feminine kind of pout on her lips, something that she herself didn't understand, it was more visible to other people, but only to those with a tutored eye. Such faces are usually rounded and appear sated, even on very little, on a small piece of good bread and a slice of bacon fat, but even this "very little" had clearly been lacking for a long time. There were liberal amounts of this "very little" lying on the foreman's table, but she had been shooed away from that rich table, and at the other, poorer tables nobody had taken any notice of her, they hadn't even given her a candy or a handful of sunflower seeds. As we know, there were reasons for this: the people's life was hard, they were tired of beggars and were not afraid of sin. The little girl, having walked round all the tables, was about to approach the very last one, the one farthest away, where the town youth of Jewish appearance was sitting. But she suddenly halted indecisively. We should note here that none of the other beggars who had visited the tea room on this evening had approached that farthest table, probably out of wariness of the town stranger. The little girl also recognized him as a stranger, but this was not why she hesitated and halted. Her own people had not given her anything and she had made up her mind to ask the stranger, in the hope that he might. It was his glance that had stopped her, that brief flash, like a glimpse of interstellar light, from those dark eyes. Of course, she did not know that this was the glance of the Viper, the Antichrist foretold by the prophet.

No, not the Antichrist that Christian artists wax hysterical about. Not the Antichrist who is the enemy of Christ, and not that Antichrist with whom the modernist mystics amuse themselves, calling the Antichrist a Creator and setting him above God, but the Antichrist who, together with his brother, carries out God's business... One is sent for cursing and judgment, the other for blessing and love... One is from the mount of cursing, Ebal, the other is from the mount of blessing, Gerizim... It was only for a mere instant that Dan from the tribe of Dan, foretold by Jeremiah, gave in to his feelings, but the atmosphere in the tea room suddenly became oppressive, the murmur of voices fell silent and everyone, even the tractor drivers' foreman, a man of some consequence, pulled their heads down into their shoulders involuntarily and unawares, which is what happens when something heavy or sharp hurtles by, bearing death...

The reason for Dan's momentary failure to control his feelings was a homesickness as fresh as a recently dug grave. The miserable evening with rain, so rare in the Kharkiv region in the fall, rendered this yearning even stronger, and it had reached its apogee at the sight of these strangers' faces, the faces of people far distant from his heart, who, to make matters even worse, were being cheerful and amiable with each other, and this was the final drop that had set the stranger's cup of poignant yearning overflowing . . . All evening Dan, the Antichrist, as impressionable as all Jewish children, had tried to find some tranquil object on which to rest his eyes, the intelligent and bitter eyes of the Viper, so that his soul, if not gladdened, would at least be granted some respite. But if he turned his gaze into the interior of the People's Tea Room, the dark, ignorant heads of apostates were everywhere, and there was neither a trace of lyricism in the despondent faces, nor a trace of nobility in the brazen ones, nor a trace of intelligence in the kind ones. And if he turned his gaze outward from the People's Tea Room, outside the window lay the hopelessness of the provincial Russian fall, with wet poplar trees standing along the road, with dogs barking and two or three lights twinkling in the distance, and you could even shout out loud, or burst into tears, but nothing worked to counter all this except a glass of strong sugar beet moonshine. However this Slavic recipe was useless to the son of Jacob, who saw in oblivion the likeness of death. And death, so extolled in many Eastern religions and philosophical systems, was hateful to his people, whether physical death or the death in Buddhist contemplation . . . "For in death there is no remembrance of Thee: in the grave who shall give Thee thanks? . . . Turn, O Lord, deliver my life; save me for the sake of Thy steadfast love." So it says in Psalm number six. Death deprives a man of the ability to perform his duty to consciously love the Lord. In the Buddhist nirvana he does not love the Lord, he loves himself . . . No emissary of heaven who treads an earthly path, can avoid the human condition. Dan recalled this admonition, it was written in his tefillin texts, beside aphorisms from the Law of Moses, in the tefillin that were attached to his forearms. But during his first hours here, in the Kharkiv region, everything human was still alien to Dan, and therefore he turned his gaze inward into himself and saw his own City, illuminated with the sun of the month of Aviv.

The Sheep Gate, and the Fish Gate, and the Spring Gate by the Selah Reservoir, opposite the Royal Garden by the steps . . . And the Tower of the Ovens . . . And the Armory Tower on the corner, near David's Tomb. And the pond that was dug beside the house of Eliashib, the High Priest. And the upper Royal House beside the prison yard, where the great prophet Jeremiah suffered. And the Wall of Ophel. And the Horse Gate facing the Merchants' House. And the Water Gate on Merchants' Square, where the great scribe Ezra stood on a wooden dais and recited the Book of the Law of Moses from dawn until midday to a people that had lost its courage in

Babylonian captivity, and the ears of the people were captivated by the Book. Ezra from the tribe of Levi recited and the priests elaborated. Dan knew that Ezra had experienced the greatest happiness a prophet can experience: the rare submission of the people to the good. "And Ezra opened the book in the sight of all the people, for he was above all the people, and as he opened it all the people stood."

Dan recalled that, as they were acquainted with great matters while listening to the words of the law, the entire people began crying in happiness. That same people which, several centuries earlier, had burned the sermons of Jeremiah, and which, several centuries later, would reject its king, Jesus from the tribe of Judah. Dan knew that his brother Jesus dreamed of the success that had fallen to Ezra's lot, his brother had dreamed of ascending a wooden dais at dawn in the middle of the Merchants' Square and seeing joyful tears of repentance in the people's eyes. For he loved his people as passionately as the great scribe Ezra loved his people, despite the brazen stubbornness of its foreheads and the veins of iron in its necks, veins of defiance of the Lord. He loved his people so greatly that at times even his nobility of speech deserted Him. For after all, it was He, Jesus, the brother of Dan, who said that He lived for the sake of His own wicked children, and not for the sake of others' goodhearted dogs. This thought of His was expounded, very cursorily and incompletely, but in essence clearly, by the Evangelist Matthew, but nonetheless ignored by Christian preachers, beginning with Saul from the tribe of Benjamin, who was later the Apostle Paul . . . Dan's brother lived and fought for the sake of His own people and He died at the hands of those who cooperated with the Roman occupiers, those who in our present time are called collaborators. Just as His oppressed brothers failed to understand His love for them, so did the alien oppressors fail to understand His hatred for *them*. The story of the Roman Pilate's attempt to rescue Jesus repeats the story of Nebuzaradan, the head of the Babylonian king's bodyguards, who rescued Jeremiah from the prison into which he had been cast by his brothers as a defeatist. For both Jeremiah and Jesus pointed towards the path of nonresistance to evil, which seems idealistic only to those who do not understand the foundation of Jewish thought: an extreme practicality in daily life, together with an extremely metaphysical approach in heavenly matters. The path of nonresistance to evil in the face of a powerful evildoer is feasible, but with one important proviso, which was indicated by Jeremiah. It is essentially as follows: let the evildoer take everything, but you in turn must take your own soul as your spoils from the evildoer... This is the most important thing, that in the face of the evildoer you must preserve your own soul as your spoils, for sooner or later the evildoer will lose his own soul and will not be able to profit from your love, with which you love him for his evil. You yourself will profit from it. There you have it, the extreme practicality of Jewish thought concerning nonresistance to evil by force . . . But in the face of the modern evildoer, created by the advance of civilization, the prophet Jeremiah's proviso, that proviso which was known and relied upon by Dan's brother, Jesus from the tribe of Judah, Dan's brother from the mount of blessing, Gerizim, becomes ever less practicable.

Oh, how far Dan had wandered in his thoughts and his visions from the rainy fall evening in Shagaro-Petrovskoe village in the Dymytrov district of the Kharkiv region before the moment when the little beggar girl almost set out toward him in the hope that he would give her alms. For several seconds after he turned his gaze, still ablaze with otherworldly visions, toward her, she was badly frightened, so frightened that she would have cried out if she had had the strength to do it. But when the little beggar began to recover her strength, Dan was already holding out to her a piece of bread, which he had taken out of his shepherd's bag of coarse leather. This bread was the impure bread of exile, ordained by the Lord through the prophet of exile, Ezekiel. It was baked from a mixture of wheat and barley, beans and lentils. For the people's sins the Lord had instructed that this impure bread of exile should be baked on human excrement, but the prophet Ezekiel had solicited from the Lord the right to bake it on cow dung...

The little girl was frightened of both the giver and his charity, but she was hungry and she took the piece of impure bread from the stranger. A tremor ran through the people's tea room. The company was piqued. Something old and half forgotten stirred, first of all in the kindest faces, then moved on to the dismal faces, and then, in some peculiar fashion, also touched the brazen faces. These local people, her own blood, had refused the little beggar girl, whereas a stranger, a town Jew, had given her charity. First the closest man sitting over his carrot tea, who was not yet old, but already had no front teeth, which meant that he had to soak breadcrusts in hot water and afterwards not chew, but suck them, which was, in fact, more economical, first this toothless individual held out one such saturated crust to the little girl, then someone else a little farther away gave her two sugar candies, someone tipped out a handful of sunflower seeds and finally, from the very richest table, where the tractor drivers' foreman was sitting, "his honor" himself beckoned to her.

"Go on, you fool," the toothless man whispered to her, "don't be shy . . . Petro Semyonovich is feeling kind now. You ask for some bacon fat . . ."

And indeed, no sooner did the little girl approach the table than the foreman Petro Semyonovich, with the eyes of everyone there on him and in the same solemn manner in which a shock worker is presented with the reward for his efforts, either a bolt of cloth two meters long, or a pair of boots, presented her with a small piece of bacon fat on a sheet of newspaper . . .

"There you are now," said Petro Semyonovich, "and you go asking strangers for help . . . You never know, a stranger could be from the enemy camp, a kulak or a kulak sympathizer . . . You need to understand that . . ."

At that moment Petro Semyonovich, being in a state of inebriation, felt an urge to utter various political pronouncements. And the little girl, not daring to object after being frightened for the second time in only a short while, although for a different reason, took the bacon fat without saying anything and started wrapping it in the newspaper.

"But why don't you eat it, my little one?" Petro Semyonovich asked, suddenly struck by something new that brought tears to his eyes. "Who are you saving it for, and you so little? Could you really have children?"

"My brother Vasya's waiting for me on the porch," the little girl said timidly.

"Your brother Vasya," said Petro Semyonovich, "all right, then. But what's your name?"

"Maria," said the little girl.

"And why is it, Maria, that your Vasya sends you begging, while he takes it easy on the porch?"

"He's still little . . . he's afraid."

"There's nothing to be afraid of," said Petro Semyonovich, offended. "There aren't any wild beasts in here . . . These are your own people . . . It's your village . . . Outsiders are a different matter . . . You should be afraid of them, unless they have credentials . . . You're obviously local, if your father lets you go begging at such a late hour . . ."

"My father died last year," said Maria.

"And what was your father called?" Petro Semyonovich asked.

"I don't know," said Maria.

"Well, what can I make of that?" Petro Semyonovich asked in surprise. "Then what's your mother called?"

"I don't know," said Maria, "she's my mother, that's all."

"Um," said Petro Semyonovich, wiping the corners of his lips with his large forefinger, in Ukrainian fashion, "someone's taught you bad ways, kid . . ."

"Drop it, Petro," said a dark-complexioned man sitting on the foreman's right, "let her go . . ."

"No, hang on, Stepan," said Petro Semyonovich, "something's not right here . . . And what's your surname?"

"I don't know," the little girl said, almost crying by this time.

"Scram!" the man with no front teeth whispered to her almost inaudibly.

But Petro Semyonovich was suddenly excited, he had the bit between his teeth now and he had spotted the whisperer.

"I'll give you whispering," he said, grabbing the little girl by the hand, "keen to relocate to Siberia, are you? I know the families of lots of kulaks and kulak sympathizer are hiding on the farmsteads, to avoid moving to Siberia . . . You're from a farmstead," he said, moving his terrifying face, with a saber scar from the Civil War, close to Maria's.

"Yes I am," Maria replied, more dead than alive from fright now, "from the Meadow Farmstead."

"There, now you're talking sense," said Petro Semyonovich, calming down a bit, "now, continue your testimony in due order."

"Please, mister, I don't know my surname and I don't know what my father and mother are called, because our parents never looked after us, and they never had any time for us, because they were always busy with work at the collective farm, and now our father's dead, our mother's busy all the time in the house or at the vegetable garden, she has to keep things tidy, plow and sow, and do lots of other work, and so she hasn't taught us anything. I've got a big brother Kolya and a sister Shura, and my little brother Vasya, and Zhorik, he's still in the cradle."

"Well done," said Petro Semyonovich, "there, now you're not playing the fool. Only what do people call you all? Take me, for example, in my childhood, the neighbors called me Semyon's son . . . Look, there goes Semyon's son . . . But what do they call you?"

"We're the citizens' children," said Maria.

"What can I make of that, 'the citizens' children'? The 'citizens' are all in Dymytrov and Kharkiv. But we have the peasant class here . . . So why do they call you 'the citizens' children'? Does that mean your mother's from the town, then?"

"No," said Maria, hanging her head.

"You're lying," Petro Semyonovich said angrily. "You're lying, you're not looking me in the eye." His speech had suddenly shed its Ukrainian accent and Ukrainian words, becoming dry, Russian and formulaic. "Why do they call you 'the citizens' children' if you're not from the town?"

"Well, so that's what they call them," said the dark-complexioned man sitting on the foreman's right, trying to get a word in again. "You know what village nicknames are like, don't you, Petro?"

"You just keep quiet, advocate. Have you qualified as a lawyer, then? Ah, but you're not a Yid, they won't let you be a lawyer . . . Well, carry on," he said, turning back to Maria.

"Tell him, little girl, don't be afraid," the dark-complexioned man told her.

"Last year our father died, it was a hungry year."

"I've already heard that," said Petro Semyonovich, "go on . . ."

"My mother was left with us five children, each one smaller than the last," said Maria. "When our father was gone our house collapsed, and the collective farm management gave us another house, beside the Dymytrov road . . . And our mother stayed in this house, seeing as we're almost all swollen up and most of the children are sick in bed. We don't have a single scrap of cloth left to change into, only what we stand up in or lie down on is all, except for rags and tatters . . ."

Maria fell silent. Petro Semyonovich stopped talking too. Nobody spoke. This little beggar girl was talking about something they all knew, something many of them had experienced themselves, but somehow now, when it was uttered aloud in a child's voice, and under duress, it sounded like a prayer of lamenting for her hardships and sorrows. And perhaps because it was a long time since they had prayed, tears sprang to the eyes of many of them, and Petro Semyonovich sat there, pale-faced in sorrow and rage, except that his saber scar had become engorged with blood.

"That's what they do to us, those bourgeois leeches," he said in an agonized voice, through clenched teeth, "capitalist encirclement . . . But never mind, we'll tough it out . . . We won't allow them to gloat . . . We'll see them off, we'll be the death of them." Suddenly he raised his head abruptly. "And where's that youngster who was sitting by the window, the one who gave her the bread? Come on, show me that scrap he gave you," he said to Maria, reaching out to her an immense hand, with fingers like iron springs protruding from it, capable of squeezing a throat hard enough to kill in a second.

And the piece of impure, dark brown bread of exile, prepared according to the prophet Ezekiel's recipe, was placed on that palm, callused by instruments of labor and weapons.

"I knew it," said Petro Semyonovich, "it's not our bread, it's foreign bread . . . Ah, we failed to exercise vigilance . . ."

And true enough, the place at the window was empty. No one had seen the outsider leave.

"We should go to the village soviet with this," Petro Semyonovich shouted. "Stepan," he said, turning to the dark-complexioned man, "dart across to the village soviet and call Maxim Ivanovich, the State Political Directorate representative . . . And in the meantime we'll rummage around a bit here . . . Right then, five men come along with me . . . You, you, you, you . . ." As he walked he jabbed his fingers at the faces of customers in the People's Tearoom, selecting ones who were suitable for a search and pursuit . . .

And as he walked he also pulled out of his pea jacket a battered revolver with flaking paint, which had been repaired many times over by his own capable, self-taught hands. The pursuit group ran in a sparse line along the village street, through the mud and the puddles, along the row of dark huts with barking dogs.

Meanwhile the rain stopped, evidently to wait for the dawn before setting in again for the whole day, when hungry village residents would emerge from their houses on personal and public business. The moon appeared, the Ukrainian halfmoon, which here, in the Kharkiv region, where there was a strong admixture of Russia, was perhaps not as buttery as in the Poltava region, but nonetheless differed from the Ryazan region moon, being less severe in outline and more radiant and sparkling. By the light of this moon they ran out onto the "tamba," which for some reason was the name by which the high road that ran to Dymytrov town was known in these parts.

"Looks like he ran into the reserve," said the man with no front teeth, who had also ended up in the pursuit group, "and you won't catch him in the reserve, it's night . . ."

In local parlance "the reserve" was what they called the dark forest standing on the far side of the open field.

"What's wrong with you, Okhrimenko, demoralizing the people like that!" Petro Semyonovich exclaimed, clenching his jaw like back in 1918. "Never mind the reserve, if a contra hides under his own skin, I'll scratch him out of there with my fingernails. I've pursued plenty of them, and purged plenty of them from the socialist land . . ."

And it was true, in his time Petro Semyonovich, the present-day foreman, had indeed hunted down many men, including, as it happened, some of Denikin's highbrow soldiers, who had cruelly tortured Petro Semyonovich's best and only friend, his namesake the machine-gunner Petro Lushno, when he was their prisoner, and also Petliura's rough peasant soldiers, who had left that saber mark on his face until the day he would die. Petro Semyonovich recalled how, not far from Kom-Kuznetsovskoe village, or plain Kuznetsovka in common parlance, he had intercepted a Petliurite army convoy, piled high with looted Jewish junk from Dymytrov town. There and then, disregarding all their entreaties, he had hacked Petliura's men down with his saber: Petro Semyonovich liked slashing with his saber, he fired his pistol less often, and his carbine only rarely, he preferred hand-to-hand fighting. And so the saber first dealt with Petliura's soldiers, then it was the Jewish junk's turn. He let the down out of feather beds, shredded velvet dresses with lace trimming, shawls, bedsheets and short, fur-trimmed jackets of some kind or other, then he threw silver shot glasses and candle sticks in the river, because he wasn't mercenary and had no interest in wealth . . . One time, when a man in his detachment tried to purloin some Jewish junk, Petro Semyonovich had put him up against the wall in a flash. That horse louse had cried and pleaded too, but what's the point of a man like that living in the world? If you're a thief, and you don't know how to live honestly, steal your own kind of things, filch a sheepskin jacket or a horse. But what would a man want with a Jewish feather bed or a velvet dress with lace trimmings? Stuff like that only gave the house a bad smell, instead of smelling of unsoused apples and cow dung, it stank of sweet candy. That's the kind of man the foreman Petro Semyonovich was. He fought hard, but he adhered firmly to one principle: my hands may be bloody, but they're clean . . . And last year, when Mitka the kulak, the miller's son, set fire to the collective farm stable, Petro Semyonovich had pursued him, together with Maxim Ivanovich, the local State Political Directorate representative, and overtaken him in the reserve and grabbed him by the throat and when Maxim Ivanovich came running up with his usual "Hands up!" there was no one left to surrender . . . They drew up a report, had it witnessed by the village soviet and sent it to Dymytrov, and they released strangled Mitka's body to the old miller for burial. Petro Semyonovich had pursued many enemies and run down many of them, but never before had he run as he was running now, in pursuit of the Antichrist, under his Kharkiv moon, less buttery than in the Poltava region, but more radiant than the Ryazan region moon.

And in truth, its sparkling radiance was by no mean wasted, for Shagaro-Petrovskoe village was beautiful even in the fall season . . . And the Meadow Farmstead, where Maria, the little beggar-girl, lived, was very close by. Their new house, which the collective farm management had given them to replace the old one that collapsed, was on the outskirts of the farmstead, and opposite the house there was a garden plot, where various berries, wild strawberries and mushrooms were gathered in summer. If you went into that plot, you had to sneak in stealthily, taking a great risk, since it belonged to the sanatorium. This sanatorium stood on a knoll, and Maria's mother had told her that an old landowner's wife used to live in it, and after the revolution she had turned very cantankerous and kept trying to hit any peasant or peasant woman she saw with her stick, only her daughter, a softhearted, weepy young lady, always restrained her mother. But one day the daughter let her guard down and the old lady of the manor ran out through the gates with her stick and with that stick she struck the peasant Volodya Senchuk, who was walking past on his way from the tavern and, being drunk, he swung round and whacked the old woman back so hard that she gave up the ghost . . . After that the landowner's daughter went away somewhere and a sanatorium for workers from Dymytrov was set up in the house. The sanatorium had a large apple orchard that Maria often sneaked into, while there were apples, and she fed herself with those apples, and took them home. Right beside the orchard was a church, which was now the collective farm storehouse. Close by there was the collective farm club and the noisy watermill and the little river at the foot of the knoll ran off to a different village, Kom-Kuznetsovskoe. On the other side of the tamba was the reserve and beyond the reserve was Popovka village. Maria remembered that a very long time ago, when she was still very small, smaller than her brother Vasya now, and her brother Vasya was still sleeping in the cradle, like Zhorik now, and Zhorik wasn't even there yet, her mother and father, dressed up in festive style and in a cheerful mood, took her to Popovka to see her grandpa and grandma. First they walked through the open field, then through the reserve. Then they came to some kind of big yard, and a piglet suddenly darted out of a barn. Maria was frightened and cried out and her mother picked her up and calmed her down. Grandma had red-dyed eggs lying on a plate, because it was Easter. And grandma told her:

"Sweetheart, say 'Christ is risen,' and I'll give you an eggy."

Maria felt frightened and didn't say anything, but grandma gave her an egg anyway. That was all a long time ago. Maria had never been to her grandma's place again and she didn't know if her grandpa and grandma had died or moved away. Since then her father had died too, and the hungry times had come and her little brother Vasya had grown a bit during those hungry times. At first he had been cheerful and affectionate, and Maria spent all her time with him, because her sister Shura, her brother Kolya and her mother had things of their own to do. But then Vasya's belly had started swelling and his little legs had turned very thin and he started spending more time sitting than walking. He took one or two steps on the stove and then sat down. And he had turned very surly and bad-tempered: he didn't have the strength to pinch, so he bit her. But not always, when he ate a little bit of something he became affectionate again. Maria hadn't wanted to take him begging with her, but her sister Shura had said:

"Take him, he looks sickly, they'll give you more."

Maria hadn't tried to argue with Shura, her sister might have beaten her for arguing, but when she reached the tearoom she had left Vasya on the porch after sitting him on a little bench in the corner, taking off her headscarf and wrapping it round his face. The people had given well this time, although she'd been frightened twice, by that man from the town and the foreman. And, what was more, the foreman had taken the bread the man from the town had given her. But even without that she'd collected a lot: bread crusts and sunflower seeds and a few sugar candies and, best of all, the piece of bacon fat. Maria walked out onto the porch and her brother Vasya was still sitting where she'd left him as if he was sleeping, but he wasn't sleeping, he was watching and his eyes were open.

"Let's go, Vasya," said Maria, "it's late already, nighttime."

"I don't want to," said Vasya, "it's a long way to walk, let's sit here until morning instead. Snuggle up against me, Maria, it'll be warmer like that."

"Don't be silly," said Maria, "they'll shoo you away from here. And when we get to the house we'll eat what I've begged, and perhaps our mother or our sister Shura will give us something."

"What have you begged?" he asked. "Give me some bread, or I won't go."

"Well, Vasya, I begged something a bit tastier than that," Maria said proudly, showing him the bacon fat.

Vasya grabbed the bacon fat and crammed it into his mouth, the whole piece.

"How could you do that, Vasya?" said Maria, then she thought for a moment and didn't feel bitter. "Let him eat it," she thought. "He's suffering more than the rest of us."

Vasya ate the bacon fat, got up and said:

"Let's go home to the house now."

They walked along the dark street and across the open field, then they crossed the tamba and walked past the reserve. In the reserve wet branches rustled: that was some night birds or other trying to frighten them. But neither Maria nor Vasya were afraid of the night. The wolves here had been completely wiped out a long time ago, and why would any of the people be tempted to bother poor children? Except perhaps out of mischief, but in these hungry times even the dashing daredevils had given up playing mischievous pranks, they'd lost their brigandish idealism and become too practical: they preferred to give the foodstuffs commissar a bad beating or rob a grain depot. Although perhaps some office worker-intellectual, tormented by a desire to understand the idea of universal suffering and the reasons why God permitted it, some admirer of the Messiah Dostoevsky, perhaps he might kill innocent children out of doctrinaire considerations. But as a result of the revolution people like that had either become almost extinct or their appearance had been greatly altered, and even in their best times they used to be found in more hysterically inclined places, where there were plenty of icons, and they didn't stray into the boring Kharkiv region. So, owing to these circumstances, Maria and Vasya reached their farmstead safely, and then they could already hear the noise of the watermill's dam and see the fence of the sanatorium. They knocked on the door of the house, their sister Shura opened it and said:

"You've come . . . Mother was already getting anxious, but I told her: they'll be here."

Their mother hugged and kissed Maria and Vasya, and asked them:

"Did you beg anything, children?"

"Yes," Maria replied.

"Then sit in the corner, eat your supper together and go to bed, I have something to talk about with Nikolai and Shura."

"I begged some bacon fat, Mom," Maria said, "but Vasya ate it, the whole piece."

"Never mind," said her mother, "Vasya's weak, he needs it. You two have your supper; Kolya, Shura and I have already had enough."

Maria and Vasya ate the people's charitable offerings, lamented briefly that the foreman had taken the piece of bread given to them by the town stranger, climbed up onto the stove, nestled close against each other and fell asleep. And the mother and her older children carried on with their conversation.

"We don't have a cow," said the mother, "or any clothes, or any bread. This summer I earned ten kilograms of rye in the collective farm, and the potatoes are spoiled. There are only two ways things can turn out for us: either we'll die or we'll stay alive, but we'll be invalids... I don't have anything to feed you with, children, and I've decided to split you up. I'll take the young ones away from home and you, Kolya and you, Shura, will go to work in the collective farm field, you'll be able to feed yourselves."

"That's right," said Shura. "If we're stuck with Maria and Vasya and Zhorik, we'll never cope. Maybe some people will take them in, or the orphanage will, and they'll survive."

"And if they die," said their mother, "then at least I don't want it to be where I can see. I couldn't bear to watch them dying."

So they took a decision to send the little children away from home.

Day still hadn't broken when Maria and Vasya were woken by their mother, and by that time Zhorik had already been taken out of the cradle and wrapped in a warm red blanket. Of course, Vasya didn't want to get up.

"It's cold," he said, "and outside the sun hasn't risen yet." His mother replied:

"Children, let's go to the town fair in Dymytrov, perhaps I can exchange something or buy something and there'll be a present for you. Perhaps I'll buy a twig with dried plums, nuts and sugar candies tied to it. Remember the twigs they gave us at your father's wake?"

Maria not only got up obediently, she also started helping her mother, who was trying to make Vasya get up:

"Remember what the dried plums were like, Vasya?" Maria asked. "Only we have to hurry, because it's a long way to the town, and if we're late, the other peasants will come and take them all."

When they walked outside, the sky was still gray and empty. Following their usual route, they walked past the fence of the sanatorium, the church, and the watermill, and when they walked down off the knoll into the field, the sky turned brighter and a cool morning sun rose over the reserve.

Maria and Vasya walked along holding hands and their mother carried little Zhorik in her arms, bundled up in the red blanket, and he was the most comfortable of them all. While they were walking across the field, Vasya tried several times to squat down for a rest, since his little legs were so thin they could hardly support his body, but his mother and sister admonished and reasoned with him by turns, and when they reached the tamba, Vasya cheered up and started walking more steadily, without waddling. Meanwhile the sun had risen clear of the reserve and lit up the entire sky, a huge flock of migrating birds landed a short distance away in the hope of finding a feast of wastefully abandoned ears of grain, and an insect of some kind with shimmering wings flitted out from right under their feet, rushed away and disappeared into the roadside ditch. And they realized that the fall wasn't really so very near its end yet, that in previous, abundant years they had bathed in the river at this time of the season, and there had been summer visitors from Dymytrov town living in their dachas and making jam from country berries, which were brought to them by the children's mother and their sister Shura and the other women. Even Maria could remember how she went out berrying with her mother and sold the berries to the people in the dachas, how an orchestra had played in the sanatorium garden and a summer visitor with a little goatee beard had laughed and said something to her mother, and her mother had laughed too, and waved him away, and the summer visitor with the little beard had caught hold of her hand, and after her mother snatched her hand away and set off back home with Maria, she had smiled all the way there. Her mother's complexion was fair then and she used to cover her black hair with a bright-colored headscarf that she'd bargained for with millet.

The sun had grown warmer, and the day had taken a turn for the better, a windmill was indolently spinning its wooden wings close by and collective farm carts carrying sacks of grain were turning off the tamba toward the windmill, fulfilling the requirements of the state agricultural tax. And all this seemed to enchant Maria's mother, awakening pleasant memories. She sighed from her heart and started musing, without any sadness. And at that moment Vasya, who had been walking with difficulty for a long time, suddenly kicked out like a stallion on the early spring pasture and ran joyfully toward the ditch to catch a beautiful insect that had flown by and crush it. His breath was coming easily and his weariness had disappeared. And just then the first houses of brick and stone, not village houses, came into view.

"Here we are, Vasya, we've arrived," Maria said cheerfully. "We're in time for the fair."

"No, children," their mother said, as if she had awoken from a trance, "that's not Dymytrov town yet, it's the Lindens suburban settlement. Hold each other's hands, because there are lots of people here, you'll get lost."

The settlement was very crowded with people and carts, and they immediately started feeling hungry. In a square in front of a large stone building an immense red flag was drooping limply in the still air, and there was a strong smell of millet porridge with pork dripping. Vasya started sniveling that he wanted some porridge and bread, and Maria said:

"Don't be sad, Mom, or you, Vasya. I'll walk over to that house and start begging, and they'll give me something." But her mother said:

"We don't have enough time for that, children. It's a long way to Dymytrov, we'll be late for the fair. Let's walk to the back of the settlement, there's a well there with water so pure, if you just drink some of it you'll feel full."

And it was true, once they had drunk a bit, they stopped wanting to eat so badly and they walked on. From the Lindens to Dymytrov the tamba became even wider and they started coming across people more often, some on carts and some on foot. And suddenly Maria recognized one of the people walking along as the stranger who had given her bread in the People's Tea Room. He was wearing a threadbare coat with short, narrow sleeves, so that his bony wrists stuck out of them a long way, and on his head he had a little, round sealskin cap, that was also old and shabby, and his lace-up boots were nothing out of the ordinary, the only distinctive things about them were their robustness and the unusual thickness of the soles for those times, as if they had been made especially for long and frequent journeys. The coat, incidentally, had a velvet collar of the kind that was only worn by aristocratic dandies at the beginning of the century, although later many members of the intelligentsia, even those with low incomes, had started wearing them. In general, the stranger was dressed like someone who had seen quite a lot of life, yet at the same time he was an adolescent, still almost a boy. No matter how fast the foreman Petro Semyonovich ran, no matter how much experience he might have in pursuing and exterminating enemies of the socialist state, he could never have run down this outsider. Indeed, to his own great perplexity and extreme chagrin, he had failed to find even the slightest trace of him. For the Lord gives over many into the coercion of the wicked for their sins, and He even gave over into coercion the intercessor for the sins of others, the intercessor sent for benediction, but He never gives over into coercion the Viper, the Antichrist sent for malediction. For the Antichrist is the judge of the wicked, as he is the judge of all things. Although this is a heavy yoke for the emissary of heaven to bear, he treads an earthly path. It is not in his power to save and to help, but it is in his power to judge and to destroy. And as he walked along the road from the Lindens settlement to Dymytrov town early on this sunny fall morning, Dan from the tribe of Dan, the Antichrist, spoke with the Lord through the prophet Jeremiah, from whose spirit he was born, and who was his spiritual father. And the Lord said to him:

"Before I formed you in the womb I knew you, and before you were born I consecrated you."

"Ah, Lord God! Behold, I do not know how to speak, for I am only a youth," Dan replied.

But the Lord said:

"Do not say, 'I am only a youth'; for to all to whom I send you, you shall go, and whatever I command you, you shall speak. Do not be afraid of them, for I am with you to deliver you."

And here on this bustling high road, known in local parlance as the tamba, Dan felt something touch his lips and he heard this:

"Behold, I have put my words in your mouth . . . Lift up your head, look at the people who are walking around you, enveloped in their cares . . . They have spoken falsely of the Lord and have said, 'He will do nothing; no disaster will come upon us, nor shall we see sword or famine.'"

And the Lord spoke to Dan through another of His prophets, through Isaiah, from whose spirit Dan's brother, Jesus from the tribe of Judah, the Intercessor, was born:

"Behold, they have conceived chaff, and they shall give birth to stubble. Lift up your eyes and look around . . . Can a woman forget her nursing child, that she should have no compassion on the son of her womb? Even these may forget, yet I will not forget you."

Dan lifted up his head and saw Maria in front of him, holding out her hand to him as she had done the day before in the People's Tea Room, and a little distance away he saw a woman who was not yet old, but oppressed by hunger and poverty, holding an infant in her arms, and a little boy, her son, who was filled with dread and hope. Once again he took out of his shepherd's bag the bread of famine and exile, made out of a mixture of wheat and barley, beans and lentils, baked according to the instructions of the prophet Ezekiel, and handed Maria a large piece of this bread. And for the first time something touched Dan's heart, and he was gladdened by his own good deed, but the Lord admonished him:

"Do not rejoice in your good deed, Dan, for you were not sent for that. This people has broken a wooden yoke off its neck, but fashioned a yoke of iron to replace it. It has much to endure before its land will be married again."

And the Lord fell silent and Dan turned away from those to whom he had given bread, setting off with a brisk stride, and was soon lost to sight.

Maria was delighted and said to her mother:

"What a big piece of bread, we can share it. Divide it up into three, Mom, for you, Vasya and me, and we can wrap the soft crumb in your headscarf for Zhorik to suck on."

Vasya quickly held out his hand, so that he could pinch off a little bit above his own share when they started dividing up the bread. But their mother snatched away his hand and said:

"Throw that bread away, Maria. It's unclean, a bad man gave it to you, it isn't Russian bread."

"But why throw it away, Mom?" Maria asked. "When we're hungry and we haven't eaten anything today, only drunk water from the well . . . At least let Vasya and me eat a little bit."

"No, children," her mother said, "it's better to eat bulrushes than that bread. Bulrushes are edible and plenty of them grow on the river bank beyond the marsh. When we get back from the fair, I'll take you to gather bulrushes."

And Maria's mother took the bread bequeathed by the prophet Ezekiel and flung it far away from her, straight into the mud washed out from the collective farm field by the rain, and it startled a flock of birds, but even so they immediately started pecking at it.

Dan, the Viper, the Antichrist saw this although he was already far away and said, speaking through the founder of prophecy, the first prophet of the Lord, the Tekoite shepherd Amos:

"For that I gave you cleanness of teeth in all your cities, and lack of bread in all your places. And I also withheld the rain from you when there were yet three months to the harvest."

And since, like all Jewish children, Dan the Antichrist was easily offended and resentful, he harbored a grudge against the sinful woman.

It was already long after midday when the woman and her three children arrived in Dymytrov town. Maria had never been in Dymytrov town before, she had only heard about it, and Vasya had never been here either, but their mother had been here and she clearly knew everything here well, because she walked along without asking anyone the way, and reached where she wanted to go. She stopped near a large, beautiful building with an iron porch, entwined in wild grape vines. And nearby on the street, which was paved with cobblestones, there were many buildings just like it, and there were trees growing there, whitewashed halfway up their trunks in the way they whitewashed the houses in villages. Carts frequently drove along the street, which apparently led to the fair, and the cobblestones were generously scattered with straw that had fallen from the carts. The mother gathered up an armful of this straw, spread it on a small bench beside the building and said:

"Sit here and wait for me, children. Your feet are hurting and you're tired, and there's a crush at the fair, a whole crowd of people. I'll go and buy you some dried plums and sugar candies, and come back here."

Vasya didn't need any persuading, he sat down quickly and Maria also sat down with Zhorik in her arms. And their mother walked away quickly, without even kissing the children, so that they wouldn't feel suspicious at all that she was abandoning them and saying goodbye. At first it was pleasant to sit there on the soft straw, and the sunshine was baking hot, and it was good to think that their mother would bring them dried plums from the fair. But then a wind, the harbinger of evening, started blowing, and the carts started moving away from the fair, mostly empty, having sold all their wares, and then a scraggy dog come running up to the bench they were sitting on, frightening Vasya, and their mother still didn't come back from the fair and bring the plums. Vasya almost burst into tears several times, but Maria calmed him down by telling him that these were hungry times and it wasn't easy to get hold of good dried plums, it took a long time. However when little Zhorik started bawling in her arms she surrendered to despair herself. Zhorik was sick, covered in pimples, and he was hungry, he was demanding food, but Maria didn't have anything for him or for Vasya, her own insides were aching from hunger and she started crying too, because she couldn't take their mother's place either for Vasya or for Zhorik. They sat there and cried, and Zhorik started jerking his legs about and kicked open the little red blanket that he was wrapped in. And then the door of the building opened and a man in glasses came out and asked:

"Where are you from, children, and why are you sitting here crying?"

"We're from the Meadow Farmstead," said Maria.

"And where are your parents? Your father and mother?" the man in glasses asked.

"Our father died last year," said Maria, "it was a hungry year. And our mother was left with us five children. After our father died, our house collapsed, and the collective farm management gave us another house near the tamba . . ."

"I see, I see," the man in glasses said impatiently, interrupting Maria: evidently he found what she was saying boring. "And what's your family name, what's your mother called?"

"We don't know," said Maria. "We only know that the village nickname for us is the citizens' children."

At that moment a very beautiful woman, wearing a man's shirt and tie, glanced out through the door and asked:

"Pavel, what's happened?"

"Look here, someone's dumped these children on us . . . I'll call the orphanage straight away."

"Oh, invite them to come in," said the woman, "people are already peeping out their windows, they'll think we've done something to offend these children . . . Come in, children," she added, swinging the door wide open.

Maria, with Zhorik crying in her arms, and Vasya walked into the hallway, where there were lots of clothes hanging up and a delicious kind of smell. It was the smell of naphthalene, but to Maria every smell was delicious now, even the smell coming from Zhorik reminded her of something fermented that she had eaten or drunk at her grandma's house in Popovka village at Easter. From the hallway a very steep wooden stairway with banisters painted green led upward to somewhere. Vasya took two steps with his skinny little legs and immediately sank down into a squat, because his plump little belly hampered his movements. But Maria whispered:

"Let's go upstairs, Vasya, perhaps they'll give us something. Perhaps they'll give us some bread or feed us some of yesterday's borshch that they can spare."

An old beggar woman from Shagaro-Petrovskoe village had told her that in rich houses in the town they made so much borshch that what was left over had to be thrown out, and sometimes they gave beggars some of it, and the old woman had often eaten left-over borshch like that. But they weren't given any borshch, or any bread either. Probably before they managed to reach the top of the stairs, Vasya with his thin little legs and Maria with heavy little Zhorik, the woman had had enough time to take the borshch off the table and set out books on it. The man was calling someone on the telephone: Maria knew about telephones, there was one in the village soviet. Very soon, as if she had just come from the building across the street, an angry woman with short-cropped hair arrived, unwrapped the little blanket in a rough, indifferent manner, looked at Zhorik and asked what he was called and what his surname was. Maria told her what he was called, and instead of his surname she started telling her story about the house that had collapsed. But the woman didn't bother to listen, she just took Zhorik and left.

"Well, now go home," said the man in glasses.

"No, we can't go home," said Maria, "we want to go to the fair. Our mother's there. How do we get to the fair?"

"It's very simple," the man said brightly, "it's as easy as pie. Walk left along the street all the way, cross the square, and there's the fair."

And he quickly led Maria and Vasya down the wooden stairs, then locked the door behind them.

First Maria and Vasya walked toward the fair, and they found it, but they couldn't find their mother there, although they searched and searched for a long time. On the other hand, although it was already evening and little by little the carts were leaving, there was still plenty of millet in sacks and bundles of green onions, and an old woman with a face like the old beggar from Shagaro-Petrovskoe village, the one who had told Maria about her good luck in getting left-over borshch in rich houses, was selling dried plums that she had laid out in little heaps on sackcloth. And that was when the idea of stealing first entered Vasya's head.

"I'll grab a whole heap with both hands," he said, "and even though my legs are weak, the market woman won't catch me, she's old".

"God forbid!" Maria told him. "That's a great sin. Don't you ever let me catch you doing that! And you wouldn't get away in any case. The old woman wouldn't catch you, but she'd raise a hullabaloo, and other people would catch you. And do you know how hard they beat thieves? I saw them beating a gipsy in our village once."

"But why," asked Vasya, "didn't our mom buy us some plums, so we wouldn't have to steal them?"

"Probably here at the fair they didn't want to give her enough for the headscarf she brought to sell," said Maria, "and it's a beautiful headscarf, it's wool. Father gave it to her as a wedding present. It would be a shame to sell it for cheap. So she took it to the big houses to sell. Let's walk around the town a bit, Vasya, and perhaps we'll find our mom."

Dymytrov town was big and beautiful. There was a boulevard here too, closed off with a fence, but although the fence was made of iron, it was very low, and even Vasya could climb over it if he was given a leg up. And there were lots of little electric lights here in big glass windows with various kinds of goods lying in them, mostly clothes and shoes. But there weren't any food-stuffs, because this was a famine year, and food was issued to the townspeople on ration cards. And the people walking along the streets were all strangers they had never seen before, so when Maria recognized that outsider she already knew in the crowd beside the main post office in the very center of the town, she immediately whispered to Vasya:

"Look, there's the man who gave us bread twice already. Come on, perhaps he'll give us some a third time. Our mom's not here, and neither is the foreman, there's no one to take it away and we'll eat the bread, we're really starving."

In front of the main post office there was a fountain from before the revolution that had turned dark with age, with figures of naked little children sitting astride toad-frogs like horses, and there were jets of water coming out of the toads' mouths. And nearby there was an idol only recently carved out of granite and set up on a stone pedestal, so the heavy chunk of stone hadn't yet managed to attach itself to the ground on which it was set up, as happens with old idols in pagan cities.

In the short time that he had been here, Dan from the tribe of Dan, the Antichrist had realized that he was among pagans, who had only recently accepted this faith, or else were living through the heyday of this faith, for there were too many idols cast in metal, carved out of wood and sculpted out of stone, and also too many painted images on all sides. There were various different idols, but the one he came across most frequently was a mustachioed effigy with Asiatic cheekbones that looked like the Babylonian idols that the prophet Jeremiah had warned against worshipping . . . Two great prophets, two abhorrers of idols, Isaiah and Jeremiah, had admonished the people, but the people had not seen reason.

"All who fashion idols are nothing, and the things they delight in do not profit!" Isaiah had exclaimed bitterly. "The ironsmith takes a cutting tool and works it over the coals. He fashions it with hammers and works it with his strong arm. He becomes hungry, and his strength fails; he drinks no water and is faint. The carpenter stretches a line; he marks it out with a pencil. He shapes it with planes and marks it with a compass. He shapes it into the figure of a man, with the beauty of a man, to dwell in a house. He cuts down cedars, or he chooses a cypress tree or an oak and lets it grow strong among the trees of the forest. He plants a cedar and the rain nourishes it. Then it becomes fuel for the man. He takes a part of it and warms himself; he kindles a fire and bakes bread. Also he makes a god and worships it; he makes it an idol and falls down before it. Half of it he burns in the fire. Over this half he eats meat; he roasts it and is satisfied. Also he warms himself and says, 'Aha, I am warm, I have seen the fire!' And the rest of it he makes into a god, his idol, and falls down to it and worships it. He prays to it and says, 'Deliver me, for you are my god!'"

No doubt paganism and idolatry were not new in this land. In the local temple Dan from the tribe of Dan, the Antichrist had seen a crowd of old people kneeling down and worshipping a carved wooden image of an Alexandrian hermit-monk nailed up on a cross, tormenting his own flesh in his unbelief, and for some reason they had called him by the name of Dan's brother, Jesus from the tribe of Judah, who was as sturdy as his forbear, the founder of the tribe, the young lion Judah, and had blazing eyes like those of the Maccabee brothers, and had perished at the hands of the idolators of his own people and of others, even as the prophet Jeremiah had perished seven centuries before him. And standing there in the temple amidst the crackling of a multitude of candles, Dan from the tribe of Dan had thought bitterly through the prophet Isaiah:

"No one considers, nor is there knowledge or discernment to say, 'Half of it I burned in the fire; I also baked bread on its coals; I roasted meat and have eaten. And shall I make the rest of it an abomination? Shall I fall down before a block of wood?'"

Dan knew that during the first two centuries of Christianity even the early Christians, although they already had in them much that was pagan and not of the Lord, had never worshipped images and idols. The moment when they had begun worshipping the emaciated Alexandrian monk was the point at which a substitution occurred, and Christianity became the enemy of Christ. But whereas earlier they had replaced a Lord who possessed flesh, but no form, with elegant Greek idols of wood, ivory and marble, nowadays they had started replacing the Creator with crude Babylonian idols made from heavy materials, either metal or stone. This, however, was still one and the same process, which had already lasted for fifteen hundred years, and its essence remained the same. It was simply that the beautiful, elegant Greek idolatry, which still survived here and there among old people, had started being supplanted by Babylonian idolatry, with idols in public squares, idols around which throngs of young people jostled and which even children were taught to worship, for this evening there were many of them running around in front of the recently installed Asian-featured idol with high cheekbones and a mustache, and also around the fountain. For children are children, and when the initial fright at the menacing appearance of the deified face of stone had passed, they wanted to run about and frolic. Children's frolicking and games contain the rudiments of the lesson of the Lord that God taught man on the seventh day of creation, but extreme hunger abolishes childish frolicking and a hungry child is like a wise old man, he exists only because he thinks, and a hungry person's thoughts are always the same: about where to obtain bread. And so it was with precisely such thoughts that Maria approached Dan, holding out her hand for charity, and her arm was immediately seized by a representative of the authorities, whose post for the maintenance of public order was located beside the idol that had been installed, a place where all forms of begging, gambling and other disturbances of public order were forbidden.

"Whose little girl are you, then?" the militiaman asked sternly, but not angrily. "Where are your mother and father?"

"My father died last year," said Maria, "it was a hungry year. And our mother was left with us five children, each one smaller than the last. After our father was gone, our house collapsed, and the collective farm management gave us a different house beside the tamba. And our mother stayed in that house, because almost all of us were swollen up and sick."

"Let the little girl go, comrade militiaman," a soft-hearted woman said.

"Why, I'm not keeping her here," said the militiaman, "but where does she live? . . . Where do you live? Do you know the way home?"

"Yes," Maria said hastily. "Cross my heart, I know that . . . The Meadow Farmstead. You have to keep going straight along the tamba without turning off anywhere. When you get past the sanatorium and the church, then there's the club and the school, and then the river flowing at the bottom of the knoll and the watermill standing beside it. And nearby is the garden plot, where people gather berries and mushrooms. And our house is there, opposite the garden plot."

"Well, go home then," said the militiaman, who was already up to his ears in work without any child beggars. "Go home quickly and tell your mother that if she sends you here looking for charity again, both of you will be arrested."

"That's right," said an eager beaver in the crowd, backing up the representative of the authorities, "instead of working in the collective farm, they beg and thieve, like gypsies."

"Now don't you go talking like that about a nation, all nations are equal in our country."

"Sorry, my mistake," the eager beaver said hastily, retreating back into the crowd.

And Maria, who had been prevented for a third time from eating some of the bread baked according to the prophet Ezekiel's instructions, but was nonetheless glad to have been let go, took her hungry brother Vasya by the hand and walked away.

And watching all this, Dan from the tribe of Dan, the Antichrist licked his dry lips, and there was a bitter taste on his tongue. And he said through the prophet Jeremiah:

"Better a useful vessel in the house, which the master uses, than false gods, better a door in the house, safeguarding the property in it, than false gods."

And expressed in present-day notions, these words, spoken by a prophet who loved the Lord, signified the following:

"If the strength is lacking to believe in the Lord, better atheism than idolatry. Let there rather be a healthy, maternal atheism." But the atheism tolerable to the Lord can only be attained either by honest, hard-hearted toilers or, on the contrary, by inactive, wise contemplatives. In other words, genuine atheism is only accessible to a very few. And since time immemorial in this country and this people there had been as few atheists as there were genuine believers in the Lord. But there had been either indifferent psalmists or vehement idolaters.

And Dan said to himself:

"Your prophets prophesy falsely, and the priests rule at their direction, and my people love to have it so. But what will you do, apostates, when the end comes? Shall my spirit not avenge itself on a nation such as this? An appalling and horrible thing is happening in this land . . ."

And having said this, Dan the Antichrist went round the corner of the main post office into a side street feebly illuminated by sparse streetlamps and walked away.

But Maria and Vasya carried on wandering round the town for a long time that evening, afraid to ask anyone the way in case they might be seized again, until they found the tamba by themselves.

"Well, now we'll find our house," Maria said happily. "It's straight along the tamba, without turning off anywhere, right to the very end."

And once again the poor children set out at night, all on their own, and once again no one was tempted by their defenselessness, and once again the Kharkiv moon shone down on them from the sky. Only this time the road was very long, and they were worn out by the time they reached the Lindens suburban settlement. As usual Maria's brother Vasya started crying and pleading:

"Maria, let's spend the night in a hallway somewhere, on the stairs. Or let's find a little bench in an alleyway, where there's no draft. We'll cuddle up against each other and sit there until sunrise. As soon as it's morning, we'll go on."

"No, Vasya, don't be silly," Maria replied, "perhaps our mother has already got home, and if she doesn't find us there she'll be worried. Come on, we don't have to walk for very much longer. The same distance we walked across the collective farm field to get to the Lindens settlement, where mom threw away the bread the stranger gave us, you remember, that's how far we have left to walk across the field to our little river, and then there's the reserve, and the watermill, and the church, and the sanatorium. And when we reach the sanatorium, we'll see our house."

Maria managed to persuade her brother and they set off again, tired, hungry and defenseless. But at night everything seems different. The collective farm field was windier and they couldn't tell where the bank of the river ended and the water began, and the reserve was like a dark, impenetrable storm cloud, and they themselves, so little and all alone, were such a great temptation for an evildoer that if this had not been the provincial Kharkiv region, where reprobates wore boots greased with tar and didn't have pale, inspired, artistic faces, the children would almost certainly not have reached their house. But they did. They knocked at the door once, and then again. Their sister Shura unlocked it, gave them an angry look and asked:

"And where have you left Zhorik?"

"A strange woman came and took him away," Maria replied.

"You know what," said her brother Kolya, "our mom has signed up for work, she wants to leave us and go away."

"Where to?" Maria asked.

"We don't know," Shura replied, "but since you're here, lie down over there in the corner and sleep."

Maria and Vasya lay down on the earthen floor beside the cold stove, put their arms round each other, warmed each other as much as they could and fell asleep, worn out. In the morning, before the sun had even risen, someone shook them to make them get up. Maria jumped up in a hurry, thinking that Shura wanted to scold her for something, for she was afraid of Shura, but it wasn't Shura, it was their mother standing over them in a cotton-wadded jacket, holding a sack in her hands.

"Come on, children," she said, "let's say goodbye, I'm leaving."

She kissed Maria, she kissed Vasya, who was really drowsy, she kissed Shura, and she kissed Kolya, and she left. After that, Maria didn't sleep any more, although Vasya did. But as soon as the sun rose, Maria shook Vasya awake.

"That's enough sleeping," she said. "It's time to go and find something to eat."

When they walked out into the street, it was still chilly and the cocks in Shagaro-Petrovskoe village were still crowing to each other here and there. Maria and Vasya walked across the tamba, around the swamp, and down off the knoll to the river bank. Mist was still hanging over the water and the water was splashing in the mist, it was damp and unwelcoming here, but this was where the edible bulrushes grew.

"Pull them, Vasya," said Maria, "take a bunch of green leaves in your hand and tug like this . . ." And she pulled out a bunch of leaves. "We'll collect lots of bunches," said Maria, "as many as we can carry, because not everything in these leaves is edible, so part of them will be thrown away."

By the time Maria and Vasya had collected their bulrush leaves, the mist had dispersed and it had got warmer. They took the bullrush leaves back to the house and Maria started peeling off the inedible skin and removing the dry stalks, giving the edible parts of the leaves to Vasya and eating them herself. Maria and Vasya ate as much as they could, and when they were full they started pondering.

"I tell you what, Vasya," said Maria, "let's go to the railway station in Dymytrov, since we already know the way."

"Yes, let's," Vasya replied.

"Only we have to run all the way," said Maria, "because I'm afraid we'll miss mom . . . All right?"

"All right," Vasya agreed.

They set off at a run, and they ran all the way, and this time the road seemed shorter, perhaps because they'd eaten the bulrush leaves and they had more strength. They didn't even notice how the sanatorium, and the mill, and the church, and the reserve were all left behind them. Just before the Lindens settlement, in the collective farm field, they stopped to catch their breath and then ran on. They passed by the field where their mother had thrown away the bread that the stranger had given them, they went through the Lindens settlement . . . And then there was Dymytrov town.

"Please lady," Maria said to one of the town women, "how can we get to the station as quickly as possible?"

"What for," the woman asked with a smile, "are you late for a train?"

"I don't know what a train is," Maria replied, "but we need to get to the station quickly."

"But if you don't know what a train is, how do you know what a station is?"

"A station's where steam engines sound their whistles."

"So that's how it is," the woman laughed, "you don't know what a train is, but you know what a steam engine is?" And, still laughing, she showed Maria and Vasya the way to the station.

Maria and Vasya walked across the railroad tracks and saw their mother sitting on a bench beside her sack. When they ran up to their mother, she flung her hands up high in the air and started kissing them and crying, and she took them to the station buffet and bought them bread rolls. Maria and Vasya ate the bread rolls, and their mother said:

"And now children, run home quickly, before it gets dark."

Maria and Vasya immediately started crying loudly and begging her not to drive them away, so that people around them started asking what was wrong. Their mother said:

"Don't cry, children, sit here beside me, I won't drive you away." And she said to another woman, who was also wearing a wadded jacket, but had a trunk instead of a sack:

"I know it's forbidden, but I can't drive them away. My heart couldn't bear it."

"Yes," said the woman with the trunk, "a mother's always a mother for her children."

Maria and Vasya sat down beside their mother and cuddled up against her, and they felt good. But Vasya kept looking round, he was curious.

"Oh, what big mountains," he said, pointing with his finger.

"They're not mountains," his mother explained, "those are piles of sand on railroad platform cars. It's not like at the farmstead here, children, everywhere's dangerous here and you can be run over in an instant. We'll be boarding the train at night, so you keep an eye on Vasya, Maria. You get on the train separately from me, afterward, and we'll meet in the car. Or the recruiting agent will notice and forbid me to take you."

And it was true, when darkness fell, the station became a frightening place. There were lots of people, all jostling and running, and steam engines hooting, in short, a general hustle and bustle, with no one concerned about anyone else. And getting on the train was really scary. When the iron monster appeared, Vasya was terrified and he planted his little feet stubbornly, shuddering and refusing to get into the car. Maria completely wore herself out before she managed to shove him into the small vestibule, but in the car, even though it was packed with people, their mother found them straightaway, and she told Maria:

"You climb under the seat."

Maria climbed under the seat and it was even more comfortable there, there weren't quite so many people and there was a banging sound, like two hammers in a smithy, only not as booming as iron on iron, more like iron on planks of wood. The banging went on for a while, then there was hooting, and then there was hissing, and Maria fell asleep. She was woken by her mother thrusting a metal kettle under the seat.

"Have a drink of water, daughter."

Maria drank some water and went back to sleep. And then in her sleep she suddenly felt that something bad, something that was really frightening, was happening. She woke up and stuck her head out, and someone's fingers immediately took a painful grip on her and dragged her out from under the seat.

"So you're hiding them under the seat too," someone's disembodied voice shouted at her mother in the darkness, and her mother sat in front of the person without saying a word, hanging her head guiltily. "I warned you . . . I forbid you to take any children with you," the man said and walked away.

"Who's that?" Maria asked.

"That's the recruiting agent," her mother replied, "he was walking by and noticed Vasya sitting beside me. Oh, disaster, disaster," she groaned despondently. But she didn't drive Maria back under the seat anymore, and for the rest of the night Maria and Vasya slept on their mother's knees.

In the morning they arrived in Kharkiv city. And then, oh goodness, what a scene of luxury was presented to the children's eyes! Even if Maria and Vasya had been told about it, how could they ever have believed it? Dymytrov town was big and beautiful, but compared with Kharkiv, it was like a village or a farmstead. The children and their mother walked through what looked like a doorway, but they didn't find themselves in a building or out in a street. There was a glass sky above their heads, and odd-looking trees growing right there in wooden tubs, and between the trees there was a stairway of white, gleaming stone, and in general lots of gleaming and glittering on all sides, and in a single minute Maria saw as many people as she had seen in her entire life before. And Maria and Vasya immediately started reveling in all of this, they wanted to look at everything and touch everything. She took her brother Vasya by the hand, and they ran up the white, gleaming stairway, and when they reached the top there was a floor of crimson squares, as slippery as ice. Vasya, who loved sliding down an icy slope in winter, took a run up and fell, but he didn't start crying, he laughed. Maria took a run up after him and also fell, and she laughed too. They kept running and falling like that, and then Maria made up a new game of running away from Vasya and round a tub with a tree growing in it, with Vasya chasing after her. But we should note that, greatly as Maria was enjoying herself, every now and then she ran over to the railings, looked down and saw their mother sitting on a bench beside her sack. Every time she ran over, their mother was still there. But the last time Maria ran over and looked, their mother was gone. And Maria and Vasya ran down the stairs and started shouting and calling for their mother. Where could they have got the strength to shout for so long and so loudly, without a pause, when all day long until the evening they hadn't eaten anything but a bread bun in Dymytrov, and nothing else? But although they shouted for ever so long and ever so loudly, they still didn't find their mother. At the sound of shouting, people gathered round and stood in a tight circle, with their faces turned toward Maria and Vasya, and started reasoning with them:

"What we'll do is call the nice mister militiaman, he'll find her straight away."

The militiaman came, took Maria and Vasya by their hands and said in a soothing voice:

"Let's go and look for your momma."

Maria immediately took a liking to this militiaman, but Vasya scowled at him sullenly and tried to jerk his hand free, only the militiaman was holding it too tightly. He led Maria and Vasya across some railroad tracks and brought them to a railroad car standing on the tracks on its own, uncoupled. In the car there were a lot of children of both Maria's age and Vasya's age. Maria said to the militiaman who had brought them:

"Please, mister, stay with us until they find our mom and we go away from here, or else they might beat us."

"I don't have the time for that, little girl," the militiaman replied, stroking her hair, "and you scallywags," he said to the other youngsters, "watch out, leave these youngsters alone. They're not used to this kind of life. They're from the country. That's right, isn't it, you are from the country?"

"From a farmstead," Maria said.

"If there's any trouble, you call the lady attendant, she's right there, just behind the partition."

But no sooner had the militiaman left than the scallywags started mocking Maria and Vasya and mimicking the militiaman's voice:

"Call her, call her... The lady attendant, the lady attendant... She's just behind the partition."

For the most part, they were a dirty crowd, smeared all over with coal and other filth, who had long ago forgotten what the affection of parents was like, or had never even known it, whereas only that morning Maria and Vasya's mother had cuddled them and held them tight. Maria said to Vasya:

"Stay sitting close to me and don't look at them."

But an urchin about the same age as Maria, dressed in rags with a thick coating of greasy dirt, with a very dirty neck and dirty hands, scratched all over, showed Vasya a clay whistle and Vasya moved closer to him, forgetting about his sister. As soon as Vasya moved closer, the urchin flicked him on the ear with his finger, and the whole gang burst into laughter.

"I'm glad that happened," Maria said to Vasya. "That will teach you to listen to your sister. And I'll tell mom, when we find her."

And after that Vasya moved right up close to Maria and didn't leave her side again. Before long a man with a briefcase and a woman holding sheets of paper in her hands got into the car. The man looked round and pulled a face, obviously at the foul smell, since the ruffians had started loudly breaking wind and laughing, without the slightest embarrassment, and the man said:

"Somehow we have more people now, where shall I put them . . . there aren't any places in the orphanage . . . There'll be a row . . . Unless perhaps I could send them out into the region."

At this point Maria, who was a quick-witted little girl, said:

"Mister, we lost our mom today, we'd like to find our mom."

"There now, Kaleria Vasilievna," said the man with the briefcase, "we have lots of cases like that. They should all be sent back to their homes, and not take up the places for orphans."

The woman turned to Maria and Vasya:

"Come on," she said, and led them in behind the partition.

There was a table there and an iron stove that was lighted. The man put his briefcase on the table, took off his coat, took off his hat, hung both of them up in the corner and started asking Maria questions, and the woman wrote everything down.

"What's your surname?" the man asked.

"I don't know," said Maria.

"Then what are your mom and dad called?"

"I don't know that either, they're just our mom and dad, that's all . . . We called our dad father, but last year he died, because it was a hungry year."

"And do you two have brothers and sisters?" the man asked.

"Yes," Maria replied.

"Do you know what their names are?"

"Yes, we do," said Maria, "our brother's called Kolya and our sister's called Shura, and we had a little brother called Zhorik, but he's not at home now."

"Well all right," said the man, exchanging glances for some reason with the woman, who was writing everything down. "And do you know where you lived? Your village and the district, or region?"

"No," said Maria, "we don't know all that, but we know the village and the farmstead."

"What's your village called?" the man asked.

"The village is Shagaro-Petrovskoe, and it's the Meadow Farmstead," Maria replied.

"It's not likely to be far away," the man said, "not outside the Kharkiv region."

"But, Modest Filippovich," the woman said, "there are lots of villages in the Kharkiv region that are called Petrovskoe . . . I personally know three with that name."

"Well then, let's give them a guide, and give them some provisions, and they can travel round the villages, looking for their home. I think the Department of Education will approve of our initiative. The only outlays are for travel and the provisions. We'll select a guide on a voluntary basis from among the local activists."

And Maria heard all this and said:

"I'll pray to God for you for a hundred years if you get Vasya and me back to our house and we see our brother Kolya and sister Shura, and we know that Zhorik isn't at home."

"Now, Kaleria Vasilievna," said the man, "send them to the sanitary inspection center at the station."

At this point Maria once again demonstrated her quick-wittedness and said:

"Mister, please give me and Vasya some bread, in the name of Christ, because we haven't eaten anything since last evening, and you can't pull up edible bulrushes here, like you can in our village."

The man looked at Maria: sometimes her appeals could be very skillful, like that time in the People's Tea Room, when the foremen of the tractor brigade, Petro Semyonovich, had shed a few tears. And the man suddenly wiped his eyes with his handkerchief and said:

"Kaleria Vasilievna, pour these children a glass of hot water each and give them this." And he took something wrapped in greasy paper out of his briefcase and handed it to the woman.

"I'll have rations issued for them," said Kaleria Vasilievna. "But how will you manage without breakfast, Modest Felixovich?"

"Never mind," said Modest Felixovich, "give it to the children. I can see they haven't learned how to steal yet and they're actually completely dependent on other people, like little kittens. They're not hardened street urchins yet."

The woman took the tin kettle off the little round stove, poured some hot water into tin mugs and unfolded the greasy paper. Oh, the happiness that was placed in Maria and Vasya's hands! It was a fresh French bread roll, cut in half, and on each half there two slices of sausage with fat in it. Vasya swallowed his half in a minute and for another minute the memory kept him feeling happy, then he started looking greedily at Maria, who was being smart and eating her share slowly.

"You wash it down with hot water, Vasya," said Maria, unable to tear off even a crumb of her bread roll and a slice of sausage and give them to Vasya. And he wanted it so badly!

And afterwards she often saw an omen in this, and often reproached herself for it. But Maria didn't give Vasya even a little bit of her share, she ate it all to the very last crumb, after gathering them all up from her knees. Vasya saw that he wasn't going to get anything extra and started drinking hot water. Maria finished her hot water too, then she started feeling sleepy and her eyes started feeling heavy. After all, she had only slept in fits and starts, first under the seat, then on her mother's knees. But the woman didn't let her take it easy on the chair in the warmth.

"Now off to the sanitary inspection center," she said, "seeing that I've got other things to deal with apart from you."

She led Maria and Vasya back across the railroad tracks, and Maria was glad that she and Vasya had got away from the urchins, who could have beaten them, and from whom Vasya could have learned bad habits.

They arrived in a stuffy, wet room, with water sloshing about under their feet.

"Take everything off, that's all for roasting, to disinfect it," said the woman.

Vasya took his clothes off and his belly became even bigger, his little legs became even thinner and every bone was visible under his skin. But Maria's body, although it was gaunt, was well proportioned, and she had felt embarrassed to get undressed in front of men for a long time already, even in front of her brother Kolya. But she wasn't embarrassed in front of Vasya. There was no one in the sanity inspection center at that hour of the day and the children joyfully washed themselves in the hot water, which was a second joy after the bread bun with sausage, and it had come straight after it, too . . . Maria found a sliver of soap on the floor and lathered Vasya thickly, and he growled happily, like a grateful dog. They had been given a waffle towel, one for both of them. No sooner did Maria start wiping Vasya down in the dressing room, than she got a feeling that someone was watching. She looked round, and there was a young man peeping in. She screamed out loud and dashed back into the steam room. The young man laughed.

"What's wrong?" he asked. "I'm your guide, I've been assigned to you, and you have to do as I tell you."

"Close the door," Maria said from the steam room, "let me get dressed first and dress Vasya."

"Okay," said the guide, "get dressed." And he disappeared, smirking.

This guide looked a bit like Vasya would look if he grew up. Like Vasya, he was thin, with small, gray eyes, a long face and a slightly snub nose. Although he looked like Vasya, Maria immediately took a dislike to him, but Vasya, on the contrary, was drawn to him, so that for the first time ever Maria had a strange feeling that seemed to be one, general feeling, except that concerning Vasya it was dissatisfaction, but concerning the guide, it was hate, as if the guide had something for Vasya that she, his own sister, didn't have. However she couldn't openly express her dislike to the guide, since he had the basket containing the provisions: bread and bacon fat. In fact Grisha the guide didn't give them any bacon fat yet, but he did give them bread.

So they set off to travel round all the villages called Petrovskoe in the Kharkiv region. They arrived at a big village with lots of stone and brick houses and a white church on a square.

"There it is," said Grisha, "your Petrovskoe."

And to oblige the guide, Vasya said:

"Yes, that's ours . . ."

But Maria looked round and said:

"No, it's not ours . . . Our church stands on a knoll, with a sanatorium beside it, and there's a river at the bottom of the knoll."

"Okay," said Grisha, "if it's not yours, it isn't."

They got on a train again, then got off the train and rode along the local tamba on a cart. While they were riding in the cart Grisha kept whispering with Vasya all the time and Maria kept glancing at this disapprovingly, but she didn't say anything, since Grisha had the basket with the provisions. Maria noticed that for himself and Vasya, Grisha cut off bread and bacon fat, a bit more for himself and a bit less for Vasya, but he only cut bread for her, and only a small piece at that. "Well, let Vasya eat the bacon fat," Maria thought, "even if I don't get any of it, let him have some." And although she was annoyed for herself, she felt glad for Vasya.

Eventually they reached another village: a church standing on a knoll, with a river flowing at the foot of the knoll.

"Is this village your Petrovskoe?" Grisha asked.

"Yes," simple-minded Vasya replied to gratify him.

"No, it's not ours," said Maria, "although the church does stand on a knoll, with a river flowing by below it, where's the sanatorium? And I don't see the reserve that you have to walk through to get to Popovka village, where our grandma and grandpa had a house."

They set off again: first on a cart, then on a train, then on a cart again.

"Is this your village?" Grisha asked.

"Yes," said Vasya.

"If it's ours, then where's the Meadow Farmstead? And just try finding our house, Vasya, where Shura and Kolya live . . . Don't you remember that our house was separate from the others, and opposite it there was a garden plot where people gathered wild strawberries and mushrooms in summer?"

"Okay," Grisha said with a smile, "don't argue with each other, let's keep going."

They arrived at a small railway junction.

"There won't be any more trains today," said Grisha, "so let's stay here for the night. Night isn't the right time to look for Petrovskoe village, anyway. You can't even recognize it in the daytime."

But Maria replied:

"I'd recognize it even at night, if I saw it. A watermill on a little river at the foot of a knoll, and the river flows on to another village, Kom-Kuznetskovskoe, and the tamba leading to Dymytrov town, and the Lindens suburban settlement on the way."

"Tomorrow you'll find the place from those signs," said Grisha, smiling in his usual manner, "but right now it's time for supper." And he cut off a large piece of bread and a piece of bacon fat for himself, a rather smaller piece of bread and a piece of bacon fat for Vasya, and for Maria once again only a small piece of bread.

Vasya took a bite of bread and gave the bacon fat a lick, took a bite of bread and gave the bacon fat another lick, all the while whispering about something with Grisha. Eventually Grisha said:

"Why should we spend the night here at the junction? It's windy here and we won't be able to get to sleep, the trains rumble and clatter and the steam engines sound their whistles. I know this area well, let's go, there's a big barn not far away, left over from the former landowner, with lots of hay in it. We'll shout to drive the rats away and spend the night there."

Maria started to object, not because she liked it at the junction, but simply because whatever Grisha said, she wanted to object. But Vasya took Grisha's side.

"I'm cold here," he said, "I won't get to sleep. I want to go to the barn . . ."

What could she do, if Vasya wanted to go to the barn? They set out on foot from the junction, where there was at least an electric lamp glowing on a post, into pitch darkness, since that evening not even the Lenten Kharkiv moon was in the sky, and there were no stars. It was a dark night, but it wasn't raining, it was quiet, without even the sound of dogs barking, or any wind, and it seemed to have got a bit warmer. Maria wanted to take her brother Vasya by the hand, but he jerked his hand away and huddled closer to their guide, and Maria walked along on her own, dropping behind slightly. There wasn't any kind of road, nothing but humps and holes under their feet, and in general they seemed to be walking across an open field without any dwellings nearby. Eventually she thought she caught sight of something ahead.

"There's the barn," said Grisha, "only the door's locked, we have to move aside one of the boards that's been torn off."

They climbed in through the hole, and really did tumble straight into straw.

"Ooh, it's soft in here," said Vasya, "warm."

"There, you see, Maria," said Grisha, "and you didn't want to come."

"Come on, Vasya," said Maria, "lie down beside me, cuddle up close, that'll be even warmer. Even though there's straw here, by morning we'll start feeling the cold."

"No," replied Vasya, "I'll lie down with Grisha." He didn't call him "Uncle Grisha" or "our guide," but simply Grisha, as if he was his brother, like Kolya.

"Lie down wherever you like," Maria replied angrily, "you nasty boy . . ."

"It's you who's nasty," Vasya replied, and Maria was taken aback by that.

"Vasya," she said, "my little brother, who's been teaching you to talk like that? If our mom, or our sister Shura, or our brother Kolya heard what kind of boy you've become, they'd think I've been teaching you bad ways, since I'm the one who looks after you all the time. After all, you're still a little child, Vasya, you should obey your sister like your mother, now that we've got separated from our mother . . ."

"You're not my mother," said Vasya, "I'd obey my mother, but I don't want to obey you."

At this point Grisha intervened from out of the darkness.

"Okay," he said, "really, Vasya, don't be rude to your sister."

And as soon as he said that, Vasya stopped being rude. But this absence of rudeness didn't bring Maria any peace of mind, on the contrary, she only started feeling miserable. "If Vasya turns out to be a bad man," she thought, "neither my mother, nor my brother Kolya, nor my sister Shura will ever forgive me."

And with these morose thoughts she dozed off without her brother, who started snoring at the far end of the barn. And in her drowsy state she heard someone close by.

"Vasya," Maria said delightedly, half-asleep, "lie down as close as you can to me."

And someone really did lie down, pressing himself up close against her and her knees. She was sleeping on her side with one knee pressed against the other, and he thrust his hand between her knees. And Maria immediately realized that it wasn't Vasya. She pushed the other person's hand away and jumped up.

"What do you want?"

"Quiet," said Grisha, "you'll wake Vasya."

"What do you want?" Maria repeated more quietly.

"I've brought you some bacon fat," said Grisha, "you haven't eaten any bacon fat, only bread. So I've brought you your full ration all at once."

Maria took the bacon fat and she could feel that it really was a big piece. She took a bite to try it and it was good bacon fat, moist and soft. She bit off another little bit and felt the despondent yearning with which she had fallen asleep melting away little by little . . . And she thought to herself that everything would be all right with Vasya too, he was just being stupid.

"Is the bacon fat good?" Grisha asked and laughed.

"Yes," Maria replied.

"There, you see," said Grisha, "and you've been taking against me, over and over. If you just take a liking to me, you won't need any mother."

"What do you mean, I won't need my mother?" Maria asked. "She's my very own . . ."

"I mean it's obvious your mother deliberately dumped you and your little brother . . . To get rid of you . . . You don't need a mother, what you need is a boyfriend, because you're just the right age for real pleasure, but once you grow up a bit and you get breasts, and start getting pregnant, the pleasure of it's not the same at all."

It was only when Grisha said this that Maria finally understood what he wanted, although no one had ever taught her about this notion, and all this was happening to her for the first time.

"Go away, you lecher," she said, "I realized straightaway what you wanted when you were peeping at me with no clothes on."

"If you understood me, so much the better," said Grisha. And suddenly he grabbed Maria really hard under her arms, as if he wanted to sit her on something, and he parted her childish knees with his iron-hard man's knees, and she was left completely in his power, in a dark barn, with its door locked from the outside, in a remote spot in the middle of a dark, open field that ran up at one side to an isolated junction on dark railroad tracks. And on this night not even the lenten Kharkiv moon was shining.

There was only one living soul nearby, her brother Vasya, but he was gently snoring. And even if he wasn't asleep, what could he have done, after all, he was still a little child . . . There wasn't anybody to shout out to, she'd only frighten Vasya, because Grisha wasn't squeezing her mouth shut, the way they don't squeeze an animal's mouth shut when they slaughter it: let it bellow, who's going to hear it? Maria tried to defend herself without saying anything, but every time she tried to defend herself, Grisha twisted her arm and it was very painful, and when she stopped defending herself, Grisha let go of her arm. And Grisha got what he wanted from Maria, and in the process he moaned like a man with typhoid fever, but Vasya slept on and even when Maria cried out at the extraordinary and unfamiliar pain that Grisha inflicted on her for the sake of his own pleasure, and Grisha moaned especially loudly, as if his body was also being torn, in the way that he was tearing Maria's body, even then Vasya didn't wake up: Maria realized this after everything was all over. All she could hear was her own and Grisha's heavy breathing and Vasya's snoring. And Maria felt glad that Vasya hadn't heard anything and hadn't been frightened. Meanwhile Grisha's breathing had calmed down and he told Maria, who was still breathing heavily:

"Don't you get upset . . . With a life like yours, you'd end up getting raped by some old guy in any case . . . So it's better if it's me . . . Here, take this." And he gave her some bread.

Maria took the bread and quietened down, and Grisha crawled away from her to the far end of the barn and after a little while he started snoring like Vasya.

You couldn't say that Maria fell asleep, rather she fell into a delirium, since all the time she could see the roof trusses of the barn protruding into the darkness from behind her head, and feel the straw under herself. She had pain in her belly and below it, as if she hadn't gorged herself on bulrush leaves, but poisonous grass, like one of their neighbors at the farmstead, who had died on the same day as her father from intestinal poisoning. But the pain gradually subsided and when it became brighter in the barn and the roof trusses were clearly visible, the pain was insignificant, more like a hint at what had happened during the night. Maria lifted herself up into a sitting position and saw there was no one else in the barn but herself and Vasya, and the guide Grisha had disappeared. She felt glad about that, then immediately felt upset, because he'd taken the basket of provisions with him. But then she immediately felt glad again, because she found a piece of bacon fat and a piece of bread in her pocket, and although they weren't as big as they had seemed in the darkness, even so she and Vasya had something to live on to start with.

"Vasya, get up," said Maria, "the guide who was told to get us home has run off, and we have to get there on our own. And he took all the provisions with him. There now, brother, see for yourself who you mistook for a good man and wouldn't listen to your sister, the only family you have now, since our mom isn't here with us, and our brother Kolya and sister Shura are far away."

Vasya didn't say anything, he was clearly feeling guilty.

They clambered out through the hole and looked round. An open field extending in both directions: which way should they go? And they set off at random, but they arrived precisely at the same railroad line and the same junction where the guide Grisha couldn't do to Maria what he had done to her in the isolated barn, since here a station attendant might show up, and there were even sleepy people walking to and fro on the platform. If not for Vasya, nothing out of the ordinary would have happened, but Maria didn't reproach Vasya, in fact she didn't tell him anything at all about what had happened in the barn, but told him:

"I don't know the way home to Shagaro-Petrovskoe village, but I do know that we have to leave this place and go to a big station, where it will be easier to beg some food if we need to . . . As soon as a train comes, you climb in after me."

"I will," said Vasya.

The guide Grisha had disappeared and Vasya had started obeying Maria again, and he wasn't afraid of trains anymore, as he had been at Dymytrov.

In the train Maria and Vasya ate some of the bacon fat and bread that the guide Grisha had given Maria for what he did to her in the barn. But they didn't eat all of it, Maria hid some from Vasya for the next time, because Vasya wanted to eat everything. Maria and Vasya arrived at a big station and disembarked with all the other passengers, since the train wasn't going any farther. The brother and sister looked round and gasped in delight.

"Why, this is Dymytrov town . . . from here the tamba goes straight to our farmstead."

But an old man who was there explained:

"This, children, is not Dymytrov town, but Izyum city. Have you ever eaten those deliciously sweet dried grapes, sultanas? Well, this city is famous for producing them." And he smiled.

And although Maria was disappointed that this wasn't Dymytrov, but Izyum, what she thought about the old man was this:

"Old men don't often smile, but this one does smile, which means he's kind, and a kind man will give us something, since we've only got a tiny little bit of the bread and bacon fat left."

"Grandad," she said, "my brother and I haven't eaten anything, sweet or dried, since we got parted from our mother . . . In Christ's name, help us with what you can . . ."

"We know your kind," said the old man, immediately turning angry, "you prowl through the trains, and if there's a briefcase lying unwatched, you try to make off with it . . . I'll show you . . ."

Maria grabbed hold of Vasya's hand and ran away from this old man along the platform, and from there into the station building.

The station building in Izyum wasn't like the one in Kharkiv, it didn't have a glass ceiling, or a white, gleaming stairway, but it, too, was beautiful and warm, there were lots of benches, and even an odd-looking tree, like the ones in Kharkiv, standing in a tub, although there was only one.

"Never mind, Vasya," said Maria, "we'll live here well enough for a while. I know how to beg, I have a plaintive voice, if one person doesn't give, another will. Just look how many people there are all around. I'll go and ask, and maybe they'll give me something. Just let anyone try to lay a hand on us here. It's light here even at night and there are lots of people. Only God forbid, Vasya, that you should start stealing in order to live . . . Did you see how angry that old man got? He wasn't angry at us, he was angry at thieves . . . Never do people wrong, Vasya, and people will stand up for you at any moment, but if you do people wrong, they'll leave you to sink or swim . . . How good did it feel for us to be in that dark barn at night, in the middle of a field, with that bad man there, the one that you took a liking to, Vasya, in your foolishness . . ."

Maria said this to teach Vasya a lesson, and Vasya listened, because he was dependent on Maria to gather alms. And here at the Izyum station, Maria gathered them quite successfully.

"In the name of the Lord," she said, "Jesus Christ . . . the Son of God . . ."

In response to this entreaty, people both old and young, both men and women, gave her alms. And even some Party members couldn't refuse a request from a child, even if she did ask in obsolete, old-regime church terms. One passenger was definitely a Party member, because he was wearing a leather coat and he had a saber scar like Pyotr Semyonovich, the tractor-drivers' foreman, and this Party-member passenger handed Maria a paper bag, in which there were five split-pea pies. Sometimes people even gave her herrings, and sausage, not to mention the bread, so here at the Izyum station, for the first time Maria and Vasya ate bread, if not to their absolute heart's content, then at least not in desperate hunger. At night the children slept on benches in a warm corner and they were satisfied with their life.

But every fortuitous stroke of luck that fate has not included in its plans is precarious and temporary. One day Maria came back after gathering alms and saw an angry woman standing beside Vasya, like the woman who had come to collect Zhorik in Dymytrov town.

"There she is, my sister," Vasya said, and pointed at Maria.

"Very good," said the woman, "but where's your mother?"

"We got separated from our mother," Maria said.

"Then let's go."

She led Maria and Vasya out of the station building into a windy square, where there were other children standing, but thankfully not ragged urchins, like the ones in the railroad-car reception center in Kharkiv: Maria had already learned to spot mischievous ruffians. They were all lined up in pairs and led away. Maria, of course, walked with Vasya and held his hand. If it had been earlier, when Maria still lived at the farmstead, she would have strained her eyes, gazing around at the buildings and the people. But now she didn't really pay much attention to Izyum, she was thinking more about where they would be taken and what they would be fed. They were led to a stable yard, where there were several stables, and standing in the middle of the hard-tamped surface of the yard were tethering posts with chains, surrounded by numerous heaps of dung. The woman with short-cropped hair told them she was a teacher, but she didn't give them her name, only said she was a teacher. She opened the large doors of one of the stables and there was musty straw on the floor, but only a few horses, and at the far end of the stable was an empty space.

"Make yourselves comfortable," the teacher said, "wait here until I come to take you to have lunch. But don't go anywhere on your own, a horse could kick you and kill you."

After saying that she left. Maria and Vasya sat down apart from the other children behind a heap of straw and ate the alms that Maria had gathered at the station. Suddenly Maria noticed a boy slightly younger than her, but a little older than Vasya, coming toward them.

"My name's Vanya," he said.

"So what?" Maria asked.

"Well, give me something to scoff."

"Get lost!" said Maria, "there's barely enough for me and my brother . . . You can scoff what they give us all for lunch . . ."

And he went away, without saying anything.

The communal lunch didn't come soon. A few hours later the teacher came back, lined everyone up in pairs, and led them to a canteen beside the stable yard. Perhaps if she was still on her starvation diet at the farmstead Maria would have eaten this lunch with pleasure, but after she had been given such generous charity at the Izyum station and had tasted herrings, and sausage, and split-pea pies, Maria only ate this lunch with difficulty and out of necessity. And she noticed that Vasya was finding it hard to eat too. "Aha," Maria thought, "Vasya and I probably won't survive if we don't go begging for alms." And Vasya needed to be taught to beg too: as things were, he was growing up an idle lazybones and any time now he might take to stealing.

And that was how things turned out. At the same time every day, in the afternoon, the teacher came and led them to the canteen, where they were always given vegetable and noodle soup, hot water with flour, wheat porridge without any fat and a piece of bread. For the rest of the time, they all went off to look for something to subsist on, some by begging and some actually by stealing. However Maria never let Vasya away from her side, although she could see that he didn't like begging. And since he didn't like begging, he wasn't often given anything, because every kind of work requires effort and skill. But if he didn't actually beg, at least he could stay close by, he could stand around the corner or sit on a bench for a while. In order to make Vasya do as she said and stay interested, as soon as Maria begged a piece of something good, she gave it to him. Maria begged in the beer parlors and near the slightly more prosperous houses, but she only rarely went to the station and she never visited the market, and that was all because of Vasya. She knew there were lots of thieves there and they could have a bad influence on Vasya. The days passed like that, and they spent the nights in the stable.

There was an old man at the stable yard, a night watchman who was nicknamed "Rooskie." He was kind and affectionate, he liked the children, and they liked him. He would gather all the children round him in the stable before they fell asleep and tell them stories. When he started, some of them fell asleep straightaway, but others kept listening until late. Maria listened until late, and so did Vasya. The old man had various different stories: about the Tsarevich Ivan, and the orphan Marfushka, and Ilya of Murom, the conqueror of the Muslim infidels. And there was another one, the most interesting story of all, about God's little child, Jesus Christ. The old man would prop his wrinkled, white-bearded face on the palm of his hand, ponder a bit, turn a bit sad, and then begin.

"In a faraway kingdom, in a place far, far away, great sin lay across the land. And the Lord decided to save the people from sin, and he sent his own beloved child, his little son Jesus, down to the world. As soon as Jesus appeared among the people, their life became good. He took some bread, and fed everyone until they had eaten their fill, and sprinkled them with water from the Jordan river, and said: 'Now you shall be a baptized people, an Orthodox people, and the Jews, because they don't want to work, but only keep their shops in the sacred temples, shall not know the Kingdom of God.'

And the Jew-Yids plotted to kill God's beloved child, Jesus Christ. And chief among the Jews was Judas-Antichrist." And the old man would raise his finger in the air, as if to threaten someone in the darkness, and listen to the horses stepping from one foot to another and snorting at the far end of the stable. "Judas-Antichrist gathered together the entire Jewish *kahal* (that means his gang of brigands) from all round the world, and told them: 'As long as Jesus Christ is alive, we can never overcome the Orthodox people, never make the Orthodox men and women work for us, and we shall never be able to take the Orthodox children's blood to cook our matzah,' (that's their unclean, unleavened bread.)' One day Jesus Christ went into a garden, and Judas and the other Jews were lying in wait for him in the bushes. They seized Jesus Christ, dragged him up onto a hill and nailed his hands and feet to a cross, thinking that he would die. But he didn't die, instead he rose up to heaven by the power of God, and appeared to the Orthodox people again from heaven and said: 'Here I am. Don't believe the Jews when they say I'm dead, and pay them back for all my godly suffering . . .'"

It was an interesting story, but a long one, so that by the end most of the children were already asleep. However Maria didn't fall asleep, neither did Vasya, and that boy, Vanya, who had come on the first day and asked for something to scoff, didn't fall asleep either, he listened right to the end. The old man always told the end differently. Sometimes Ilya of Murom and Alyosha Popovich answered Jesus Christ's call, sometimes it was Stepan Razin and Emelyan Pugachev, and sometimes it was Yermak Timofeevich, the conqueror of Siberia. And so it was every night. The horses snorted, and the moon peeked in through the window of the stable from below the roof . . . Eventually Vasya couldn't hold out any longer, his head would droop onto his chest and he would start gently snoring.

"Vasya's gone to sleep," Maria would say then, and gently guide him into the corner, where she had spread out some straw in advance, lay him down on it, and lie down beside him herself. Maria liked these late-night stories, but later she regretted allowing Vasya to listen to them, since at the same time Vasya made friends with Vanya, the boy who had asked for something to scoff.

One day Vasya said to Maria, who was getting ready to go into the town to beg for alms:

"I won't go with you, I'll go with Vanya."

"Little brother," Maria said to him, "Vasya, have I ever done you wrong? Whatever I beg—you get the very best bit of it . . . But Vanya will teach you to steal, I know he goes to the market."

"So what if he does go to the market?" Vasya replied. "They give more at the market, and better things too."

"I know how they give at the market," Maria answered. "The people there are greedy, the ones who buy want things to be cheaper, the ones who sell want things to cost more. There's no place better than a beer parlor or a prosperous house. People at the station are good givers, but at the market they're suspicious, they're afraid of thieves. If you get on the right side of someone, they'll give you something, but if you don't they might beat you. Come with me, little brother, you won't go hungry."

Vasya didn't listen to Maria, and he went with Vanya. That evening he came back and said:

"Maria, give me some bread, I didn't beg anything." And Maria answered him reproachfully:

"Instead of going running to the market, you should beg for alms, do some work . . ." But she gave him some bread anyway.

The next day he didn't bother to say anything to her and didn't even show up for lunch. He came back late with Vanya, both sucking on sugar candies and looking pleased with themselves. Maria understood everything straightaway and she didn't ask Vasya about anything, but she took Vanya off to one side and asked:

"Are you two stealing at the market?"

"Yes," Vanya answered.

"Vanya," Maria said then, "you're responsible for yourself, but I'm responsible for Vasya to our mother, who we got separated from on our journey . . . And to our sister, Shura, and to our brother Kolya . . . Don't lure Vasya into stealing, Vanya."

"We don't steal, we beg," Vanya replied with an insolent laugh. "I fooled you."

"You lie like a yapping dog," Maria said angrily and walked away from Vanya, thinking: "The only hope now is for them to transfer us to somewhere else soon, and assign us to different orphanages, so that Vanya and Vasya will be separated."

Rumors about a transfer had been in the air for a long time and then one morning the teacher gathered all the children together and said:

"Children, a truck is coming today, and you'll all go away, but I don't know where to. This truck won't take all of you at once, you'll be transferred in groups and so if any of you have brothers and sisters, stay together to get into the same group."

As soon as the teacher told them this, Maria went dashing off to warn Vasya, but there was no trace of him. The vehicle arrived, an open truck. It took one group and Maria waited. The truck came back and collected a second group, and Maria started worrying: Vasya still wasn't there. What should she do? If she went to the market to look for him, they could miss each other. If he came back to the stable yard, they'd put him in the truck and take him away without his sister. What anguish Maria suffered, how fiercely she cursed Vanya for inciting Vasya to go stealing, and on a day like this! How fiercely she cursed herself for allowing Vasya to listen to the old watchman's late-night stories, which had led to Vasya and Vanya becoming friends! The truck came for a third time and collected another group, and now there were only a few children left, just enough for one more trip. Maria's nerve failed and she ran to the market, searched for Vasya, and called his name, but she didn't find him anywhere. And she ran through the areas of the town near the beerhalls, where she and Vasya used to beg, thinking maybe he really had come to his senses, given up stealing, and started gathering alms, and she even ran to the railroad station. She ran back to the stable yard, soaking wet and exhausted: Vasya wasn't there, but the truck had already arrived and they were seating the last children in it. Maria started asking them to leave her there and not take her away until she found her brother, but the teacher said:

"Your brother steals, we know that, so you want to stay here and steal with him, do you? We'll find him and bring him to where you are . . ."

Maria wept and tried to explain that she was responsible to her mother for Vasya, but the teacher and a man with gray hair grabbed her firmly under the arms, like Grisha had done in the barn, put her in the truck, and ordered the other children to hold her. Although she had surrendered to Grisha, since he had twisted her arm, here she fought to the bitter end for her brother Vasya, struggling frantically, even though the hands holding her were hurting her, and she shouted probably as loudly as she had only ever done before at the main railroad station in Kharkiv, when she and Vasya got separated from their mother. And eventually she managed to break free and jump off the truck, but the teacher and the man with gray hair caught her, grabbed her under the arms and put her back on the truck. The truck set off to the sounds of Maria's wailing and cursing, and Maria's mouth remained open, cursing these people, until they had driven out of Izyum and across a bridge, and set off through the fields. When they were already a long way from Izyum

Maria ran out of energy and surrendered, and they stopped holding her. And once again, as she had done after what Grisha did to her in the barn, she fell, not into a sleep, but a stupor. It was as if she could see everything, but didn't understand anything. She remembered that only two children out of the entire group were left at some village or other: herself and a girl slightly older. They led the girl away somewhere and told Maria:

"Stay here and wait."

But now there was no one guarding her and as soon as she was left alone she ran off.

She ran out of the village and set off along the road, and no sooner did she find herself out in the fields and all on her own for the very first time, for although the other members of her family might not have been with her often, in her travels Vasya had always been there beside her, and no sooner did she find herself out in the fields than she sensed a change in the world, and when she looked, she saw it was snowing . . . "Oh, Lord," she thought, "how will I ever find Izyum, where Vasya was left behind, in cold weather like this, and when I'm famished too?" She wrapped herself more tightly in the old jacket she was wearing, buried her face in the collar to warm her chest with her breath, and set off.

Walking on and on, she saw the fields turning white as the snow fell thick and fast, and the more thickly the snow fell, the more bitterly the cold sapped her strength. The ground under her feet was white and pure, and the sky was slightly darker, but also white, and Maria was a dirty-black blemish moving through all this whiteness. Had she been capable of understanding herself, this was the very moment when she would have sensed how superfluous her life was to the world and how badly it spoiled this beauty. But fortunately for her, Maria could neither see herself from the outside against the backdrop of this first snow, nor understand herself from the outside in the way that individuals inclined to philosophizing can. But had she been capable of philosophizing, she would have been horrified to discover that so far, no one had ever really needed her, not even her brother Vasya, and the only person who had ever derived any pleasure from her existence was a bad man: to be specific, Grisha, who had raped her in a barn. Despairing human thoughts such as these, not drawn from learned treatises, are an expression of that rare, fruitful atheism, which is more acceptable to the Creator than the tepid singing of psalms or the widespread practice of idolatry. Although Maria's own soul and her reason were separated from her by an infinite distance, her mute heart, devoid of the divine gift of utterance, was always with her, and she started crying, since she had neither words, nor concepts, but only these meaningless sounds.

This lamentation was not ordinary, common, weeping, in the way she had wept only recently, as they drove her away from Vasya, not clamorous weeping with curses, futile and fruitless lamenting. This was the divine lamentation, from the heart, with which the Lord sometimes rewards those devoid of reason, substituting this lamentation for the great truths accessible only to the prophets. And the little beggar girl Maria, who had been abandoned by her mother and her older brother and sister, who had lost her younger brother Vasya, and whose absence from God's world could have deprived no one of any pleasure, save for a rapist, who had abused her body in a barn, was exalted through this divine lamentation amidst a white sky and a white earth, and through this lamentation, devoid of reason, but genuinely heartfelt, she attained unto the consolation of the Lord, which he pronounced through the prophet Isaiah:

"As one whom his mother comforts, so I will comfort you . . . And you shall see, and your heart shall rejoice; your bones shall flourish like the grass . . ."

She read this admonition of the Lord without words and understood it without reason. Consoled by this precious gift of divine lamentation that had been granted to her, reassured and with her heart unburdened, Maria walked across a snowy field and arrived at some snowbound railroad buildings. But it wasn't Izyum, it was Andreevka Junction.

"Never mind," thought Maria, calm at heart, "here I shall always be able to feed myself on charity, and perhaps I'll think of something . . . Do I really need to get to Izyum? Perhaps my brother Vasya isn't there anymore, perhaps he had already left in the morning, when I was running around like a madwoman, first to the market, then round the town? Perhaps he set out with his friend Vanya to steal in another town? And although it's painful to think that I didn't take good care of him, perhaps when she turns up our mother, and our brother Kolya and our sister Shura will understand that I couldn't even take care of myself, and not judge my failure too harshly."

After she thought that Maria felt completely at peace with herself and decided to make a start on gathering alms from the local passengers at Andreevka Junction, since she was desperately hungry. But just as Maria did not beg at every house, neither did she beg from every train. If she saw a train arrive crammed full of people and the people were dressed in rags and tatters like herself, and their belongings were packed in sacks and baskets, Maria didn't approach them: it was better just to sit on a bench in the warmth for a while. But when she saw that a train was wealthy, with not too many people, and they had suitcases, she approached them to beg.

And then a wealthy train like that arrived, and Maria went to that train to beg. She saw a young man get out of the train, holding a shiny suitcase, and a young woman without a suitcase got out with him. Maria was about to ask them for alms, but her courage suddenly failed her. She had never seen such beautiful people before, and they smelled beautiful, it was as if they smelled of honey. And without even knowing why, Maria followed them. And as she walked along, she heard the young man say to the young woman:

"I won't take this train to Kharkiv, I'll travel to Lgov via Kursk."

When she heard that, Maria clutched her head in her hands: "Oh, dear God in heaven . . . Our oldest sister Ksenia works in a rest home in Lgov." It felt to Maria as if she remembered that and somehow didn't remember it at the same time. But the young man had mentioned Lgov, she definitely remembered that.

Meanwhile the young woman walked away and the young man was left alone. And Maria started crying. Of course, she didn't cry in the same way that she had in the middle of the snowy field, not simply on her own account, but intentionally, in order to attract attention. The young man looked at her and asked:

"Why are you crying, little girl?"

"I got separated from my mother," Maria said, "and my oldest sister Ksenia lives in Lgov town, she works in a rest home, but I don't have any money to get there."

"So you're hungry, then?" the young man asked.

"Yes, I am," Maria answered.

"The let's go to the buffet first, and I'll buy you something to eat," the young man said.

The buffet at Andreevka Junction was small, not like in Izyum city, but the young man said something to the waiter, and he immediately brought a roasted chicken and a bottle of delicious, sweet water. Maria ate all of it, while also looking at the young man, and she was so distracted by how handsome he was that she didn't even notice the taste of the chicken.

It should be noted that after what Grisha did to Maria in the barn, some kind of change had taken place in her. Maria seemed to carry on living, eating, drinking and sleeping, and didn't feel any change, then suddenly she would feel that there was a change, and she liked this change. She liked it so much that at times she felt she wanted to find herself in a dark, isolated barn standing in the middle of an open field, but not with Grisha, with someone else, only she didn't know who . . . But now she had seen this young man, she realized who she would like to find herself in the barn with, and even if it hurt she wouldn't try to defend herself or cry out. And the idea came to her that instead of going to Lgov to see Ksenia she could attach herself to this young man. But she didn't know how to tell him about this. Meanwhile the young man said:

"Eat quickly, little girl, we don't have much time. In a moment you'll come along with me."

Maria was delighted at that, she finished gnawing the bones, drank the entire bottle of sweet water and only afterward realized what she'd done and felt ashamed.

"I'm sorry," she said, "I ate it all, there's nothing left for you."

The young man simply laughed: he had regular, gleaming-white teeth.

"Never mind," he said, "I'll grin and bear it."

Maria set off after the young man and as she walked for the first time in many days she felt a desire to sing. It should be noted that in previous times Maria used to sing with her mother and her sister Shura. They sang the Ukrainian songs "This Moonlit Night," or "Pour me a mug of tea, goodbye, I'm on my way." Singing this song about tea had obviously been a bad omen, but it was pleasant to remember about the other songs. And Maria walked along after the young man like that, abandoning herself to her pleasant memories. They walked up to the railroad car again and when the young woman saw him through the window, she ran out onto the platform, embraced him and cried, as if they hadn't seen each other for ages. And the young man said to the young woman:

"Valya, take this little girl to Kharkiv, and there she'll beg a ride to Kursk, and from there to Lgov, where her sister is."

"You're going to Kursk yourself, and then to Lgov."

"I won't be setting out for a while," the young man replied, "and this girl needs to go soon . . . My place is free now, after all . . . Here's some money for you." And he took out the money.

"I don't need any money," the young woman replied, "let her come."

And Maria stepped into a railroad car of indescribable beauty, upholstered all over in silk, with a mirror and soft seats. She sat down at the window beside the small cream-colored curtain and glanced out at the young man.

And the young woman sat down at the other side of the window and didn't seem to be looking out the window, but Maria could see that from time to time she did glance out, and then again only a little bit later. "Aha," Maria thought spitefully, "maybe I'm going away from the young man, but you're going away from him too . . . So you won't have him and I won't have him."

At that point the train set off: it felt as if someone picked Maria up in their hands and started carrying her, it was so gentle, without any sound at all.

"What's your name?" the young woman asked.

"Maria."

"And how old are you?"

"I don't know."

"Are you from the country?"

"Yes," Maria replied, "the Meadow Farmstead at Shagaro-Petrovskoe village."

"You're probably not even fourteen yet," said the young woman, "you're twelve . . . A happy age, without any men and misery."

And after that she didn't talk to Maria about anything, she sat in the corner without speaking and sometimes she pressed a little, lacy handkerchief to her eyes with red-nailed fingers as sharp as needles. It was only when they arrived in Kharkiv that the young woman spoke to Maria again:

"Here's some money for you," she said, "go and buy yourself a ticket to Kursk, and there you can buy yourself a ticket to Lgov."

"God save you," Maria replied, as her mother had taught her to thank people, "only please give me some bread, in Christ's name . . . It's a long journey, and who knows if I'll beg anything, or what kind of people I'll meet."

"There's more money here than you need for the ticket," the young woman replied, "you can buy yourself some bread and sausage . . . And I don't have any bread, I'm hungry myself . . ."

Maria thanked her once again and left, and she didn't see that young woman again. She went to the station building and it didn't seem so big to her anymore, although it was still as beautiful as ever. She spotted the bench her mother had sat on beside her sack and she recognized the white, gleaming stairway that she and Vasya had run about on . . . And there were the odd-looking trees in tubs . . . A lump rose in her throat and she started crying, and she cried bitterly, but she couldn't cry like she had in the snowy field on the way to Andreevka Junction, so after her crying she still had a heavy, sad feeling in her chest. No one had ever given her paper money before, but they had given her copper coins for alms, and she knew where to go to ask for bread and sausage, only she didn't know where to go to buy a ticket. But a young man, who she chose to ask out of the many people there, showed her where people bought tickets and she bought a piece of stiff, green cardboard.

This young man wasn't as handsome as the one at Andreevka Junction, but Maria liked the way he looked too, and perhaps if she was left in a dark barn with him she wouldn't cry out either . . .

The sausage Maria bought was hard and black and after the roasted chicken in the buffet at Andreevka Junction Maria didn't like it, since she had been spoilt by wealthy charity, not because there was such a great amount of rich charity about, but because Maria had learned to beg from a certain kind of people in a certain kind of place.

"What, you don't like the sausage?" asked a man dressed in a greatcoat and footwraps. He had a red face too, as if he had been standing out in a hard frost. "I used to ride on that sausage . . . As the song goes: 'But Budyonny's cavalry went for sausage.'" He laughed. "If you don't like horse sausage, give it to me."

Maria broke off a piece and for the first time in her life, instead of accepting charity she gave it, and as she gave it she realized how enjoyable it was and what pleasure people who gave charity were giving themselves . . . Beggars shouldn't thank the people who gave them alms, it was the ones who gave who should thank the beggars for bringing them pleasure by their very existence.

Although the man was dirty he had a pleasant smell of cologne, like the smell of the young man at Andreevka Junction. He took the horse sausage that Maria had given him with his trembling hands and immediately started gnawing on it. Maria only found him pleasant while she was giving him charity, but when he started gnawing on the sausage he became unpleasant and she walked away, thinking bitterly: "Vasya doesn't even have sausage like that. How can you possibly collect a lot by stealing, you'll just get beaten, and I didn't teach him how to beg for alms." However she had the bitterness of their separation under better control now, and if Maria had studied philosophy she would have realized that her bitterness had now become optimistic, for all optimism, even the universal kind, exists for the sake of one's own interests. "It's all right," thought Maria, "I'll track down Ksenia, she'll find Vasya more quickly than me, because she isn't a country girl any longer, she lives in a city." Maria had bread, and sausage too, even if it was horse sausage, and she set out, as it said on her ticket, to Kursk. All night long she rode in her own place, sitting there like a lady and pushing away anyone who encroached on her place with her elbows.

In Kursk, too, there were lots of people and trees in tubs, but Maria was already accustomed to that and took less interest in strangers, she only thought about how she could get to Lgov town and how she could gather alms, since her Kharkiv bread and sausage had run out. However, now spoilt by the easy charity in Izyum town, the fortunate meeting with the young man at Andreevka Junction and the journey in a luxurious railroad car, Maria had clearly grown lazy and she started begging the way Vasya begged, not putting any heart into it. Nobody in Kursk gave her anything, and one woman that Maria approached in the name of Christ suddenly slapped her face. Maria ran away and hid behind some crates at the end of the platform. But she wasn't crying, she was thinking about how she could get to Ksenia in Lgov, since she didn't have money for a ticket anymore. She shouldn't have bought that sausage, and she could have bought less bread, or not bought any at all, but begged it. And as for the woman who had slapped her face, Maria settled her nerves by thinking: "Never mind, she mistook me for a thief. . ." But then she immediately thought sadly: "That's probably what every day is like for Vasya. I have to get to Ksenia quickly, so she can find Vasya."

Suddenly Maria saw two dirty-looking boys about her own age, who had a girl with them.

"Was it you," asked the taller of the two boys, "who stole the woman's suitcase?"

"No, it wasn't," Maria replied.

"What are you doing sitting here then?" the girl asked.

"Where should I sit?" Maria replied. "If I need to get to Lgov town and I don't have any money for a ticket?"

At that both boys and the girl burst into laughter and said:

"Come to Lgov with us . . . The train's there, already waiting," and they pointed to some platform cars with piles of sand.

"They're ragamuffins, of course," thought Maria, "but I need to go . . . If they pester me, I'll start shouting."

They clambered up onto a platform car and set off.

"Come on," said the taller of the two boys, "cuddle up with us, or you'll croak."

Maria sat separately at first, but the wind on the open platform was chilling her to the bone, so she crept into the general heap. As soon as she sat down, the boy who was taller started pinching her: the other boy had already been pinching the girl in their group and sticking his hand up under her skirt for a long time. Maria thought: "Let him pinch me, I can't stop him anyway, but I won't let him get under my skirt," and she squeezed her knees together. Maria could see that he didn't have a man's strength, like Grisha, he couldn't part her knees. The boy realized that himself, and he said:

"Let's you and me fool around a bit. What do you want with a sister in Lgov? I've got a father back in Kharkiv and I've run away from him. We'll ride around on the trains and have a good life." Of course Maria understood what he was inciting her to do, but she pretended to be a little fool.

"No," she said, "I need to find my sister in Lgov, so she can help me find my brother Vasya." And while they were still talking like this, there was Lgov already.

"Sorry," said Maria, "thanks for the company." And she jumped down off the platform car.

"Why, you bitch," the boy said and made as if to chase after her.

But Maria warned him.

"I'll shout and scream!" And he didn't chase after her.

In Izyum city sometimes there had been a fine rain, and sometimes the sun had been baking hot, but Maria realized that she couldn't spend the night on the street here in Lgov town: there was snow, and it was cold in the station building, which was small, even worse than at Andreevka Junction. "If I don't find my sister Ksenia," Maria thought, "then I'm done for . . . Who's going to let me into their house to get warm? . . . Or I'll have to ask to be put in an orphanage myself, and that's what I'm most afraid of."

She asked a man walking by how to get to the rest home.

"Which rest home do you need, little girl?" he asked.

"Which one? . . . The one where my sister Ksenia works."

"But which one does she work in? There's the 'Steep Slope' rest home, and there's the 'Tenth Party Congress' rest home."

"I'm not local," said Maria, "I don't know."

"Then go to the 'Steep Slope,' you'll find out what you need to know there." And he showed her the way.

Maria set off surrounded by snowdrifts, for in Lgov town the streets were narrow and the buildings were low, and there had obviously been a blizzard during the night. Maria walked along, shivering from the cold, a cold so intense that it was impossible to stop, look round and understand where in Lgov she could gather alms most successfully. The final remnants of wealthy charity had already passed through and out of her, the final drops of the vital juices from her previous strokes of luck had been expended, and Maria had once again become the starving little girl she had been back home at the farmstead . . . At this point she would have been glad even to have bulrush leaves, if it was the season for them . . . But at the same time Maria didn't lose hope that she was already close to her rich sister . . . Maria had got it into her head that Ksenia was rich. "Since she doesn't acknowledge our poor country family and she doesn't tell us anything about herself," Maria thought, "she has to be rich."

Maria arrived at the very edge of the town, where there was a river that was already frozen over, so that only the steep bank made it possible to distinguish the river from the white fields that began beyond it. She saw a fence like the one beside their house, at the sanatorium . . . But when she tried to walk in through the gates an old man stopped her:

"Now then, you get away from here."

"Grandpa," said Maria, "I haven't come to beg for alms . . . My sister works here, I've come to see her from a long way away."

"What sister?"

"Ksenia."

"And what's her surname?"

"I don't know her surname."

"Now then, you get away from here."

"Grandpa," said Maria, "I've come from a long way away, from the Meadow Farmstead . . . Our father died last year, because it was a hungry year. Our mother was left with five of us children. And our house collapsed, and the collective farm administration gave us another house, near the tamba, and our mother stayed in that house, because we'd all got swollen up, we didn't have a single rag left, only what was on our backs, and what we slept on, and apart from that, nothing but tatters."

"All right, then," the old man said, "go to the office and ask about your sister." And he let Maria through.

Maria walked in through the gates and looked: there was a beautiful, old, white building with a garden all around it, completely covered in snow, and old men and women were walking about in this garden. Maria was afraid to ask them anything. She thought: "That old man believed me, but these people might not believe me and chase me out. Then what would I do?" And she set off at random or, more precisely, toward the smell of millet porridge and fried onions. As she was approaching the porch, a fat woman came toward her, carrying out a bucket of kitchen slops, and steam was rising from the bucket. Maria had more trust in fat people than thin ones, a fat person always had something to spare, but a thin person wouldn't often share, a thin person wanted a handout for himself.

"Please, Aunty," Maria asked, "where's my sister Ksenia here?"

"Korobko?" the woman asked.

"Yes," Maria replied delightedly, and to herself she thought: "If she's Ksenia, she has to be my sister, even if she is Korobko."

"She doesn't work here any longer," the fat woman replied, "she quit on May Day and left town."

At that Maria started crying so bitterly and uncontrollably that the fat woman immediately started crying with her right there, still holding the bucket. And then she said:

"Don't cry, little girl, I was Ksenia's friend, so I know her address . . . She moved to Voronezh city, she married one of our clients."

"But how will I get to Voronezh city?" Maria asked and carried on crying.

"Come on," the fat woman replied, "I'll give you some soup, and then we'll see what can be done."

She led Maria, thoroughly chilled and shuddering, into the dishwashing room, sat her down on a stool and gave her a metal bowl of hot soup. Maria remembered for a long time the plump, waterlogged hands with short fingers that handed her a bowl of hot soup on a stool in a warm corner: for Maria there was something of God in those hands. She didn't remember them forever, there's no need to remember things forever, the Lord Himself is all you need to remember forever, not His manifestations, but she did remember them for a long time . . . There are good deeds done by people, which are not sanctified from on high. At the Andreevka Junction, Maria had eaten the roasted chicken and accepted money from the beautiful woman in the train without feeling anything at all, in the same way that she accepted the usually paltry alms she was given, such as a crust of bread or a five-kopeck coin . . . But she accepted this bowl of the previous day's soup in the corner of the dishwashing room with exultation, just as there had been exultation in her lamentation in the middle of the snowbound field on her way to Andreevka Junction, so also there was exultation in her gratitude for the previous day's reheated soup, given to her in Lgov town. This was not human goodness, but God's own goodness.

And again, for the second time, Maria read the precepts of the Lord without words and accepted without reason that which is constantly revealed to the prophets through their righteousness and reason. And she heard without words and understood without reason that which was spoken through the prophet Isaiah: "O afflicted one, storm-tossed and not comforted, behold, I will set your stones in antimony, and lay your foundations with sapphires. I will make your pinnacles of agate, your gates of crystal, and all your wall of precious stones."

And for the fat woman by the name of Sophia, an illiterate washer of dishes, who was good, not with human goodness, but with the goodness of God, this was not the first time she had heard the Lord without words and understood Him without reason. And now, not with her own reason, which was tongue-tied within her, but with a silent heart, through the prophet Isaiah she understood this: "Is not this the fast that I choose . . . is it not to share your bread with the hungry and bring the homeless poor into your house; when you see the naked, to cover them, and not to hide yourself from your own flesh?"

And Sophia took down a wadded jacket that was hanging in the corner, handed it to Maria and said:

"Put it on or you'll freeze." And she also said: "When I come off my shift I'll go to the station with you and I'll persuade the conductor to take you to Voronezh city, since I don't have any money for a ticket."

Sophia finished her shift at midday and before that she fed Maria again twice, once with millet porridge and once with fried onions and macaroni, and she gave Maria a piece of bread and a herring.

Maria and Aunty Sophia reached the station and as soon as the train arrived the woman Sophia told Maria to look dejected and perhaps even cry a bit. But hard as Maria tried to cry, this time she couldn't do it.

"All right," said Aunty Sophia, "perhaps we'll persuade the conductor without any crying."

They chose a conductor who seemed to look right: not the quiet one who blandly refused everyone, because his car was jam-packed, but the one who swore at everyone and shoved them in. Aunty Sophia walked up to him and started talking without any preamble, telling him about Maria's misfortunes.

"What do you want?" asked the angry conductor, interrupting Aunty Sophia. "Why are you telling me stories? I could tell you stories of my own."

"Take the girl to her sister in Voronezh," said Aunty Sophia.

"And who might you be to her?"

"Nobody," said Aunty Sophia, "but now the two of us will be her parents."

The conductor didn't say anything, but Aunty Sophia stayed there beside him: she didn't go away, and she told Maria to stand there too. When boarding was over, the conductor said:

"Let her squeeze in where she can find space."

Sophia hugged Maria, they exchanged kisses, Sophia made the sign of the cross over her and spoke empty words, accessible to everyone and pronounced by many, not God's words, but human words:

"May our Lord Jesus Christ keep you and save you." She said it to the conductor too. But he replied:

"Drop that, lady. Your Christ was annulled by decree ages ago, you'd do better to pray the little girl doesn't run into a ticket inspector . . ."

And after all, he was right, that conductor of car number seven. A simple person is not strong in God's word, but in God's work. Only the prophets are strong in God's word.

And so, through God's work as realized by the dishwasher and the conductor of railroad car number seven, Maria was delivered to Voronezh city, where the train arrived after dark, when the night was at its very blackest. At first Maria thought she would wait at the station until morning, but then she changed her mind: "After all," she thought, "she is my sister." Maria asked a militiaman on duty at the station where the street was, and the street turned out to be really near the station. "I'll go," Maria decided.

The streets in Voronezh were wider than in Lgov and in general she took a liking to Voronezh at first sight. "It's a bit like Izyum," Maria thought, "they're poor almsgivers in Kursk, but in Izyum they gave well. If I don't find my sister, I'll spend the winter here, in Voronezh. And if I do find my sister, all the more reason for staying over the winter with her help." Maria walked along the street, pondering like this until she turned, according to the address (for she knew how to read and write, she'd learned that before the famine), into a courtyard, where everything was quiet and dark, since it was nighttime and the people were sleeping. She walked up to a doorway, once again according to the address, and started knocking on the double door. She knocked and she knocked, but no one opened up. "Could my sister really have gone away?" Maria thought despondently. "Or perhaps she can't hear me, and I ought to knock at the window round the corner." Suddenly that very same little window swung open of its own accord and out jumped a man wearing white trousers tucked into his felt boots. It was only when he tore straight past her, running at full tilt as if dogs were chasing him, that Maria realized it wasn't trousers, but long drawers that he had tucked into his felt boots. She was bewildered and then she heard someone unlocking the door. She dashed to the door and saw her mother standing there, only looking much younger and very beautiful: she looked a bit like the young woman who had taken Maria on the train from Andreevka Junction. Her mother was wearing lipstick but her face was pale, in one hand she was holding a lighted candle and with her other hand she was holding the collar of her blue, gold-trimmed dressing-gown closed.

"Who's there?" she asked.

And the moment she spoke, Maria immediately realized that it wasn't her mother, but her rich, beautiful sister Ksenia.

"Ksenia," Maria said, "it's me, your sister Maria."

At that Ksenia gave a startled cry, dropped the candle, embraced Maria, burst into tears and led her into the building. And it was all true, all just as Maria had expected. It was a wealthy apartment with a chest of drawers and a sofa in one room: Maria was familiar with all this from houses where the people were good almsgivers. And in the other room there was a wide bed, with the bedding lying open and two huge pillows.

"I wondered who it was knocking at night," said Ksenia, crying, "but how did you find me, little sister?"

Maria started telling her about their father, who had died the previous year, and about the house that collapsed, and about Vasya. Ksenia asked:

"Which Vasya is that?"

"He's our little brother," Maria replied.

"Do we really have a little brother like that?" Ksenia asked. "I know Kolya, and our sister Shura, and you, but when I went away, you were still a little baby crawling about on the floor."

"We have another little brother too, Zhorik," said Maria, "only he's not at home now." And she told Ksenia about Zhorik too.

Whatever Maria said, Ksenia cried. Maria told her everything, but she didn't tell Ksenia what Grisha did to her at night in the barn, she kept that secret. And she didn't say she'd seen the man who jumped out the little window in his long drawers, she kept that secret too.

"All right," said Ksenia, "all right, little sister. In the morning my husband Alexei Alexandrovich will arrive. He's a railroad engineer and a good, kind man, we'll win him over, we'll persuade him, and then we'll keep you here with us for the winter, and after that we'll see . . ."

And so it was, in the morning the railroad engineer Alexei Alexandrovich did arrive. Maria saw that this man was warmly dressed in a sheepskin coat, padded trousers and felt boots, but when he pulled off his three-flapped fur hat, his head was bald. Ksenia started hugging and kissing him, she hugged him so tight that Alexei Alexandrovich said:

"Let me get a wash first, sweetheart, I stink of fuel oil."

"And this," said Ksenia, "is my sister Maria, who's come to stay with us for a while."

"Let her stay," Alexei Alexandrovich replied. "It's a roomy apartment, there's plenty of space."

Maria started living there. She rose at the crack of dawn when it was still dark night outside and in the warm kitchen, where Maria slept, she had to light a candle, in order to start doing the cleaning. Alexei Alexandrovich got whole crates of candles for a cheap price from somewhere, so he could economize on electricity. First of all Maria cleared away her bedding of old, warm shawls and jackets from off the kitchen floor, in order to start washing it, and as soon as it got light, she went into the rooms, sat down with Alexei Alexandrovich and Ksenia, drank some sweet tea, ate a piece of bread with pork dripping or jam and went back to her cleaning, this time in the rooms . . . Imperceptibly the time for dinner came round, when Alexei Alexandrovich came home. Dinner was always hearty and delicious. Ksenia was a good cook, she had been a cook at the rest home, after all. Sometimes there was borshch, probably the kind of borshch that the old beggar woman from their farmstead used to dream about being given in a wealthy home, sometimes there was macaroni with a meat sauce, or meat patties with boiled millet. Or pancakes. Maria ate and thought: "Ah, if only I could bring Vasya here . . . And Shura and Kolya . . ."

After dinner Maria set about washing the dishes, and for a long time she washed them under Ksenia's supervision. First she boiled up a tub of water, so that there was something to wash the grease off the plates and the knives and forks, and then she rinsed off each plate, knife and fork with cold water.

And Maria felt contented, she was enjoying spending the winter there. As soon as there was a free minute, she either went to the market with Ksenia, or simply went to look at Voronezh. "Voronezh city is a good place," she thought, "not like Kursk. It's not just that I'm with my sister here, you could live by gathering alms here and not lose any weight." So Maria was passing the winter like this, and then one day Ksenia said to her:

"You have to clean Alexei Alexandrovich's work boots, because he's going on a work assignment."

Maria started cleaning the boots, and they were heavy, with thick, double leather plus a flannelette lining and iron plates nailed onto the heels and soles. Maria really wore herself out, she used up lots of old rags and lots of boot polish, until the boots gleamed and the leather turned soft. Alexei Alexandrovich put the boots on, stamped his feet on the floor and said:

"Well, now I won't get my feet wet. You know sometimes, darn it, a pipe bursts and in felt boots your feet get soaked." Alexei Alexandrovich left and Ksenia said:

"Maria, don't sweep the floor any more today, that's a bad sign. Go for a walk if you like, and then go to bed."

Maria went out and strolled around Voronezh for a while, until it started getting dark and when she came back she saw Ksenia sitting in front of the mirror, and Ksenia's face was so beautiful, it was probably just as lovely as the face of the young woman who had travelled with Maria in the train from Andreevka Junction. "If only," Maria thought, "our mother could see Ksenia now, how happy she would be!"

"Maria," said Ksenia, who was in a jolly mood, humming a tune. "Maria, eat a meat patty and some bread, and go to bed. Don't do any cleaning today."

Maria ate a hearty supper in the kitchen, then lay down on the soft old shawls, and fell asleep quickly. She was woken up in the middle of the night by quiet conversation and quiet laughter. "Alexei Alexandrovich has come back," she thought.

Meanwhile the conversation died down, and suddenly Maria heard Ksenia moan. "She's fallen ill," Maria thought, "Ksenia's fallen ill." She went over to the door, but the door was locked and she couldn't get out of the kitchen. Maria stood by the kitchen door and listened. Ksenia carried on moaning, and she was moaning so melodically, it sounded as if an intense pain was making her sing a song of joy. And Maria suddenly remembered how Grisha had moaned in the dark barn when he violently forced himself on her. "Will I really never experience anything like that?" thought Maria. "Food can be begged, and a clever person can get a place to stay for the night, but how can you beg that kind of pleasure?" And Maria was suddenly seized by a fit of chilly shivering, as if she was out in the freezing cold in the middle of an open field, although she was in a warm kitchen in a building. And she wanted to be back in the dark barn, on the straw, if not with the handsome young man from the Andreevka Junction then even, if needs must, with that same Grisha. "The second time," Maria thought feverishly, "perhaps I'd learn to moan like that too."

However Ksenia's quiet moaning suddenly broke off abruptly, and an indescribable racket started up, as if someone was trying to carry the chest of drawers out of the apartment and it had got stuck in the doorway. Maria heard several voices shouting at the same time, including Ksenia's. Moreover, if Maria had been versed in music, she would have realized that these voices all kept shouting on a single note, without moving on to articulate speech. Suddenly the kitchen door swung open and a man burst into the kitchen, who was already familiar to Maria because on that first night, when she had just arrived in Voronezh, she had seen him jump out of the little window in Ksenia's apartment, and Maria had kept that a secret from Ksenia. And once again he was wearing long, white drawers tucked into his felt boots. He burst in and dashed straight to the window. And Alexei Alexandrovich burst in after him, warmly dressed with his cotton-wadded trousers tucked into the boots that Maria had cleaned. And close behind him Ksenia ran in, completely naked. Although Maria was frightened by all this, she was so dazzled by the sight of Ksenia naked that she gaped at her wide-eyed, instinctively comparing Ksenia with herself. Ksenia's milky-white breasts were full and erect, and at the end of each breast there was a long, red nipple, like baby Zhorik's little finger. Instead of breasts, Maria had little bumps that had to be located by groping, with nipples like pimples. Ksenia's body was milky-white too, without any bones, her belly and legs were firmly articulated with each other, and since she had currently abandoned all shame as a consequence of the fierce fight between the two clothed men, it was not her immodest private parts that were exposed, but her beauty. Every so often, one or other of the brawlers would glance at her, and then they started fighting less fiercely. Ksenia ran in naked, but it was as if she were dressed, whereas if Maria had run in naked, she would have remained naked, and where Ksenia had beauty, Maria would have had immodest private parts. Maria hadn't thought about that before, but since Grisha had violently forced himself on her in the barn, she had started thinking about it, and now, looking at Ksenia, Maria realized that if she let anyone be intimate with her in the future, it would only be in the dark. But Ksenia could do it in the light . . .

And so, through Grisha and through subsequent events, Maria was initiated into the third plague that the Lord visits on people, and of which the prophet Ezekiel spoke. The third plague is the beast, also known as lust. This third plague of the Lord is special, since the prophets have no fear of the sword, and famine, and pestilence, but they fear the beast. King Solomon, a righteous man, was chastised with this third grievous punishment. And Dan, the Viper, the Antichrist knew that, while treading an earthly path, he need not fear the first plague, the sword, for he was immortal; he need not fear the second plague, famine, for his shepherd's bag was full of the impure bread of exile; and he need not fear the fourth punishment, earthly sickness, for he was subject only to the chastisements of the Lord; but the third plague of the Lord, earthly fornication, was one of which he should be fearful.

And Moses, who led his people out of subjection in Egypt, said that the third plague would come, and Jeremiah, who many centuries later guided his people out of subjection in Babylon, said that the third plague had come already. For although Moses did not yet know the fate of King Solomon, a righteous man, for Nehemiah, who did know it, it was already a parable:

"Did not Solomon the king of Israel sin on account of such women? Among the many nations there was no king like him, and he was beloved by his God, and God made him king over all Israel. Nevertheless, foreign women made even him to sin . . ."

Wherein, however, lies the secret of the third plague of the Lord? Why are not only sinners, but also the righteous, susceptible to it? Because the sword, and famine, and sickness merely torment, but the beast, in tormenting, also bears fruit. Because in the third plague there are not only tares, but also wheat.

This is why neither reason nor righteousness can save anyone from it. Ascetics, those abusers of the body, do not save anyone from it: they only lead people to the monstrous disfigurement so clearly apparent in the example of the Alexandrian monk with whom medieval Christians replaced the image of Jesus from the tribe of Judah.

In His outrage at woman for the apple from the Garden of Eden, the Lord gave the third plague into the charge of a powerful evildoer, and therefore it can only be resisted by means of nonresistance to evil by force, as the prophet Jeremiah taught, and as Jesus from the tribe of Judah reinforced this teaching seven centuries later. But it is only possible to save yourself on the terms of the prophet Jeremiah's proviso: let the evildoer take everything, but you in turn must take your own soul as your spoils from the evildoer. Love was actually invented in order to take spoils from the evildoer, fornication, to take back your own soul. In order to separate the wheat from the tares and, after having paid tribute to the beast of carnal lust, preserve your fruitfulness. But to attain such love, it is necessary to fulfil God's curse and master your reason, which has been seduced by the serpent. And if this seduced reason is great, then even a righteous man may be overpowered, as King Solomon was overpowered, when a woman defeated God within him. And yet, feeble reason is an even greater hindrance to spiritual effort, since the diminution of reason leads to a diminished desire to master it, and the propensity for sloth increases. And the highest manifestation of spiritual sloth is the beast of carnal lust. So was it also in ancient times.

"Lift up your eyes to the bare heights," the martyr-prophet Jeremiah said sorrowfully, "and see. Where have you not been ravished? By the waysides you have sat awaiting lovers, you have polluted the land with your vile whoredom. Therefore the showers have been withheld, and the spring rain has not come; yet you have the forehead of a whore; you refuse to be ashamed."

"At the head of every street you built your lofty place," said the prophet of exile Ezekiel, "and made your beauty an abomination, offering yourself to any passerby and multiplying your whoring."

The railroad engineer Alexei Alexandrovich was thinking the same thing, but in his own Voronezh manner. He took a swing and punched the man in long drawers in the teeth.

"What are you hitting me for?" the man in long drawers asked, wiping away the blood.

"For your villainy," Alexei Alexandrovich clarified.

"Hit her," said the man in long drawers, "I only did what she asked me to."

At that Alexei Alexandrovich kicked him with one of the boots that Maria had cleaned, a boot with iron toe and heel plates, and as heavy as a cobblestone. This blow set the man with long drawers tucked into his felt boots staggering backward, with short, ceremonial steps, as if he were on parade. He crashed into the window, smashing out the pane of glass, and dove out through the aperture with his felt boots uppermost, instantly disappearing from the kitchen, and leaving behind in the kitchen only Alexei Alexandrovich, warmly dressed and still in his boots, and Ksenia, naked and barefoot, since Maria, on the floor in a corner, had been forgotten by everyone and didn't really count. Husband and wife were left virtually eye-to-eye. For a moment or two he looked at Ksenia with bloodshot eyes, without even taking off his three-flapped cap. Then he reached out his hands in order to grab her for retribution. Ksenia didn't try to resist, she merely dodged the grab for her throat with a turn of her full hips and instead of her throat,

Alexei Alexandrovich, clearly in a trance, started choking Ksenia's full, milky-white breast, which made the nipple, as long as the little finger of a babe in arms, go stiff, and with his other hand Alexei Alexandrovich embraced Ksenia's voluptuous beauty, whooped, lifted her off the floor like a heavy chest of railroad tools, pressing his palm against a spot below Ksenia's rounded belly, and carried her out of the kitchen, and as she was being carried, Ksenia swung her plump arm with a dimple at the elbow, firmly locking the kitchen door.

For a while loud noises could be heard coming from behind that door, and Maria burst into tears, but not for long. After a little while it went quiet, and then Ksenia suddenly started moaning melodically again. And so, having lost her lover, Ksenia seduced her husband . . . And Maria was overcome by another fit of chilly shivering, but this shivering was far more intense than previously, this shivering was a response to everything that had happened as well as the draft from the broken window. Maria didn't sleep all night long, but spent the whole night trying to get warm: she took all the old shawls she had spread out on the floor to sleep on, wrapped them round herself and walked to and fro, from corner to corner. In the morning, when it was already late, Ksenia finally came into the kitchen, with her face looking crumpled, drowsy and plain, although every day before then it had always been beautiful.

"I tell you what," said Ksenia, and her plain face grimaced. "Alexei Alexandrovich and I have decided to send you back home to the country. We'll put you on a train, and give you some money and provisions . . . do you agree?"

"Yes," Maria replied.

No sooner had she said "yes" than she really did start longing to see her own house and her own farmstead, and the garden plot opposite their house for gathering berries, wild strawberries and mushrooms. And farther on the church, and the club beside it, and the little river flowing at the bottom of the knoll, with the watermill on it. The little river flowing on to a different village, and the tamba leading to Dymytrov town, and the reserve on the other side of the tamba.

"I really tried to get home before," said Maria, "only Vasya and I simply couldn't find our own village. We went to lots of villages, but we didn't find ours. And we had a special guide assigned to us." But Maria didn't go into any more detail about Grisha.

"But why not?" asked Ksenia. "Surely you know our village is in the Dymytrov district?

"I know you can get to Dymytrov town by following the tamba, but I didn't know what the district's called," Maria replied. "Our parents never taught us anything, they didn't have any time for us."

From Ksenia Maria learned that their mother was also called Maria, and their father was called Nikolai, like their brother.

"But I'm afraid my brother Kolya and sister Shura will blame me because I left Vasya in a strange place and didn't take good enough care of him."

"It's not your fault," Ksenia replied, "it's not your fault that all of us and our lives have been scattered about like this."

After saying that, she glanced round at the firmly closed kitchen door and spoke in a whisper:

"Take this and don't let anyone know, hide it as safely as you can and take good care of it, because there's money in it. I'll give you some money and food separately, by agreement with Alexei Alexandrovich, but this is money from me personally for our mother. And if our mother's not at home, then give it to Kolya and Shura," she said, holding out a package to Maria, then she added:

"Hide it in your knickers, only don't lose it when you go to relieve yourself."

Maria did that and Ksenia took her to the station straight from the kitchen, so Maria was never in the rooms again and she didn't say goodbye to Alexei Alexandrovich. But she and Ksenia said an emotional goodbye: Ksenia hugged her and kissed her, and cried, and then Maria waved to her until she disappeared from sight. And beautiful Voronezh city disappeared with her.

Maria set out in her own seat as an independent traveler and in addition, between her legs, held in place by the elastic, she had the package with money for their mother from Ksenia. Maria rode along without talking to anyone, in order to keep the money safe, and also without sharing her bread and sausage. If someone had asked, she would have shared, but she was reluctant to take the initiative. "It would be better to take what's left to Kolya and Shura," she thought. "The farmstead is a hungry place." But no one asked Maria for bread, and no one guessed about the money.

Maria reached Dymytrov town, and the joy of arriving in familiar places actually brought tears to her eyes. "Everywhere's different," she thought. "Kursk is a bad city, Lgov's a bit better, Izyum and Voronezh are really good, but nowhere's as good as being at home." Maria set out through Dymytrov town and recognized the building where their mother, also called Maria, had spread out straw for them to sit on and left them, while she went to the fair to get dried plums, and that was when the strange woman had taken her brother Zhorik. Maria walked out of the town and set off along the tamba: she recognized the place where the stranger gave them bread and for some reason their mother took fright and threw it into the field. And the farther she walked, the more familiar, dear things she noticed. There it was, the reserve, completely white, glittering in the sun, with its branches weighed down by snow. There was the little river, and the wheels of the watermill frozen to the ice. And then she could see the church on the knoll. Maria didn't see anything strange to her, as she did when she and Vasya were searching for their village with their guide Grisha, who raped her in the barn. Everything she saw then was unfamiliar, but now everything was her very own. There it was, Shagaro-Petrovskoe village, in its winter image, snowbound and beautiful, with smoke rising up from the houses. And on the street there were masses of people with flags, all walking along in a crowd. And Maria heard this conversation between a man, whom she vaguely recognized, but not completely, and a local peasant, whom she knew to look at.

"What's the celebration about?" the man asked.

"This, comrade, isn't a celebration, it's a Party funeral," the peasant replied.

"Who's being buried?"

"They're burying the foreman Petro Semyonovich, after he was murdered," the peasant replied.

"Who killed him, then?"

"The miller killed him, it couldn't be anyone else," said the peasant. "The miller and his younger son, Lyoskhka, for the older son, Mitka, who Petro Semyonovich strangled . . . And the way they killed Petro Semyonovich left him lying there, not like a dead man, but like beef or pork on a meat stall in Dymytrov town in prosperous times. Now they'll sentence the miller and his son to be shot, they've been taken to Kharkiv."

Maria heard all this, only she didn't recognize the man who was asking the questions. However she did remember Petro Semyonovich. But although she felt sorry for him, she didn't cry. And she noticed that everyone around her was feeling sorry for Petro Semyonovich, but they weren't crying, and they were carrying him in a closed coffin, without speaking. Maria walked past them, and there was the Meadow Farmstead already, the fence of the sanatorium, the garden plot covered in snow, and her very own house opposite it. Oh, how her heart started pounding, how badly she wanted her mother Maria to open the door, hug her and shed a few tears, like Ksenia had, when she was seeing Maria on her way, and she wanted her brother Vasya to be there too, because he had abandoned his stealing and come back home before her . . .

But the door was opened by her sister Shura.

"Where have you come from?" she asked.

"I was in Voronezh city," Maria replied, "at our sister Ksenia's place."

"And where's Vasya?"

"Vasya," said Maria, "got lost in Izyum city."

And what Maria was most afraid of happened: her sister Shura blamed her.

"But how could you abandon Vasya in a strange place?" she asked.

And Maria didn't answer, there was nothing she could say. Her brother Kolya started speaking from inside the house.

"Who is it?"

"It's Maria, she's come back," said Shura, "but Vasya got left behind on the way."

And Kolya blamed Maria too:

"Why didn't you take proper care of Vasya? What answer will we give mother in our letter, when she asks about you and Vasya?"

As soon as Maria heard about a letter to their mother, she forgot her hurt feelings.

"Where's our mother?" she asked.

"Our mother," Nikolai replied, "is in Kerch city . . . But why didn't you stay with Ksenia, is she badly off, can't she feed you?"

"No," Maria replied, "Ksenia's well-off, she even sent some money, but I came back because I miss my own home." And after saying that, she took the package of money out of her knickers and handed it to Shura.

Shura took the package, and she and Kolya started counting the money. Shura said:

"Ksenia will always land on her feet, with a full stomach, and money too, and we can just rot here . . . In 1923, at the age of fourteen, she ran off with a traveling photographer, and she hasn't been home since then . . . So is she still living with the photographer now?"

"No," Maria replied, "she lives with the railroad engineer Alexei Alexandrovich, and before that she worked in a rest home in Lgov town . . . Mother told me that."

"Mother always spoiled her more than the rest of us," Shura said, "and when father was still alive, he loved her too, I remember . . . Since you're here, sit down, I'll pour you some borshch."

And she poured Maria some cold borshch, thinking that Maria would be grateful even for that, because before she left they didn't even have borshch like that to eat, but since Shura and Kolya had started working in the collective farm field at least some kind of food had appeared in the house, only of course, there wasn't anything to spare.

Maria was convinced of that very soon, as she started living on starvation rations again, and there was no one to beg from: this wasn't Voronezh or Izyum, here at home people were even worse givers than in Kursk. Her home district was beautiful in summer and beautiful in winter, it was only bad here in the fall and in spring, when it rained, but it was as good here in winter as it was in summer.

Maria walked across the snow-covered tamba, with wheel tracks from motor vehicles and carts on it, then set off along the path to the reserve. The felt boots and shawl that Ksenia had given her kept her warm, it was pleasant to walk in the wadded jacket that Aunty Sophia, the dishwasher, had given her in Lgov, and her breath came smoothly and easily. In the reserve, when a bird was startled up and snow sprinkled down from the fir trees' branches, that was pleasant, it gave her such a good feeling. Only she felt hungry, and it was dreary on her own. In earlier times, too, neither her mother, nor her father, while he was alive, had spent much time with her, and neither had Shura or Nikolai, but she and Vasya had always been together: you could say that she had raised Vasya in her mother's place, and while he was still little, he had brought her joy. And in her own thoughts Maria started reproaching herself for not taking better care of Vasya. Perhaps at Andreevka she shouldn't have attached herself to the young man, but tried to make her way back to Izyum, to look for Vasya . . .

In this state of anguish Maria walked out of the reserve, and saw the crimson sun glowing above the snowy field. And she went down on her knees, which no one had ever taught her to do, turned her face to the crimson sun, held out her hand as she did when she begged for bread, and said:

"In the name of the Lord! Jesus Christ! The Son of God!"

And Maria remembered the story told by the kind old night watchman of the stable in Izyum city, about how the Jew-Yids killed the Son of God, and

Maria wept uncontrollably, since she did not know who would help her to save Vasya, for although the Son of God was alive, he was in heaven now, and Vasya was here on earth, in Izyum city . . .

Meanwhile, a man came walking by across the snowy field and asked Maria the same question that the young man at Andreevka Junction had asked her:

"Little girl," he said, "why are you crying?" Maria replied:

"I'm crying because the Jew-Yids killed the Son of God, and now he's in heaven, and my brother Vasya is here on earth, in Izyum city, but there's no one to help him."

And Dan from the tribe of Dan, the Viper, the Antichrist spoke in the words of the Lord, uttered through the prophet Isaiah, heavenly words containing the meaning of everything, which he had been saving for the very end, but as he was walking past, he had suddenly realized that the time had come to use these words, and afterward simply repeat them numerous times:

"I have revealed myself to those who did not ask for me," said Dan, speaking the words of the Lord, revealed through Isaiah, "I was found by those who did not seek me . . . Those who seek," Dan added after a pause, "shall not find . . . I have revealed myself to those whom I myself have chosen, and not to those who have chosen me . . . Let those who have chosen remember the words of my brother Jesus from the tribe of Judah, concerning his own bad children and the good-hearted dogs of strangers . . . The dogs shall not take away the portion of the children, even from the bad children . . . to the children a portion is given even unsought . . . So says Christ . . . Since either you have a strong flock, which takes away, or you have God, who provides . . ."

And having spoken, he set off across the field in the direction of the reserve, and was lost to sight. And it was only when he was lost to sight that Maria recognized from memory the stranger who had given her bread twice, and regretted that she hadn't asked him for bread, since the foreman Petro Semyonovich was dead, and her mother was in Kerch city, and there was no one to take the bread away, and she could have eaten her fill. After all, she didn't know if Shura would give her even bitter, cold borshch or boiled grain without fat to eat. And memories of her well-fed life in distant places intensified her hunger here at home even more. A beggar who does not merely walk round his own farmstead, but wanders round the whole world, cannot be amazed by any kind of food. He tastes a bit of everything, from the poor man and from the rich man. "It's a pity I didn't ask him for bread," Maria thought again, "I didn't understand what this man told me, he's obviously from very far away, but I would have eaten some of his bread."

It got dark quickly. In the Kharkiv region the nights are frosty in winter, and when the stars come out and the moon starts sparkling, it turns even colder.

Maria hurried home and her sister Shura met her and said:

"Go to bed, Maria, sleep, since you need to get up early in the morning. Nikolai and I have decided to send you to mother in Kerch. Do you agree?"

"Yes," Maria replied, and thought to herself: "I do miss our mother very badly, and perhaps I won't be as hungry there as here."

In the dark morning, when the cold moon was still shining, Maria got ready, kissed Kolya and Shura and walked out of the house. She had a sad kind of feeling, but not a very strong one. She had sought to find her own place, the home where she belonged, and now she was abandoning it without any regret, and going away to a distant, unfamiliar place, to Kerch city to see her mother. But it was good to go to her mother, her mother would take pity on her, and her mother would feed her with what she could. Farewell, reserve, farewell, church on the knoll, farewell watermill . . . She couldn't see Shagaro-Petrovskoe village any longer, just as she couldn't see it in Izyum city, where life had been good, and in Kursk city, where life had been bad, and in Voronezh city, where life had been good again with Ksenia. Maria set off along the tamba in the opposite direction now, toward Dymytrov town, to the station. Kolya and Shura had given her money for a ticket, but they hadn't given her any bread, and she couldn't beg any on the tamba, she would have to go hungry until she reached Dymytrov town. The beggar's law is: if you're hungry, summon up your patience. And indeed, in Dymytrov town she begged some rusks beside a wealthy house. Maria ate the rusks at the station and bought a ticket to Kharkiv, since they didn't sell tickets to Kerch. A train was a familiar thing for Maria now, and Kharkiv was nothing remarkable, like the first time. In Kharkiv she begged more bread from wealthy passengers, bought a ticket and set out to Kerch city, which she thought would be like Izyum or Voronezh, since her mother Maria wouldn't choose a bad city, like Kursk, to live in. She spent the day traveling to Kerch city, then spent the night still traveling to Kerch city and in the morning she woke up, looked out the window, and there was no snow, the sun was shining, and just beyond the railroad tracks was an immense, boundless blue field.

"That's the sea," they explained to her, "the water in it goes all the way to Turkey, a foreign state."

And Maria saw the land jutting up into the sky.

"That's Mount Mithridat," they explained to her . . .

Kerch city was nothing at all like Izyum, where people were good givers, or like Kursk, where people were bad givers, or like Voronezh, where life had been good with Ksenia . . . "And what will it be like here?" thought Maria, alighting from the railcar door's step onto the warm ground. Maria walked along, astonished by everything she saw, almost like the first time in Kharkiv, when she and Vasya ran around between the odd-looking trees in tubs. The streets were different from everywhere else, stony and steep, and seen from a distance, from the railcar, the sea was clear and big like a wide-open field, but from close up it was noisy and hazy and not even big, just a little bit bigger than a river: she could see the far bank, with lots of little houses that weren't standing on the ground, but standing on top of each other. "How can that be?" thought Maria, "what kind of marvel is this?" And she asked.

"That's not the sea," they told her, "it's the bay and the port. But the sea is round that corner there."

Maria walked along a stony street, and it was true: there was the boundless sea. "Although it's a strange city," Maria thought, "it's a good city, mom took a job in a good place."

Even so, Kerch remained a foreign city until Maria reached the outskirts and found the address where her mother lived. The houses in Kerch city were cheerful, built of white stone, but on the outskirts, where her mother lived, the houses were surly and smoke-blackened and built of red brick, like the buildings beside the railroad tracks in Voronezh. She walked into one of the blocks and asked where Maria Korobko lived, and they explained to her: not because everyone knew her mother, but because a woman who did know her happened to be there. Maria walked up to the door and knocked, and her mother's voice answered. When she heard her mother's voice, her arms and legs started trembling, tears gushed from her eyes of their own accord, and she ran in with a shout of "Momma!" And at that moment her mother was sitting on her bed, sewing a patch on a man's army tunic.

When she saw her daughter Maria she went pale and said to three other women, who were also sitting on their beds, doing work of their own:

"This is my daughter, Maria . . ."

And Maria's mother started crying even more loudly than Maria, and they cried so uncontrollably that the three women, who were also shedding tears, couldn't calm them down. But when they eventually did calm them down, Maria's mother said:

"You'll live here with me . . . There's yesterday's porridge in the cooking pot over there, have some . . ."

One of the women was called Olga, another was called Klavdia, and the third one was called Matveevna. And each of them gave Maria something . . . One gave her some bread, another gave her a sugar candy, and Matveevna gave her two apples.

"Take them," she said, "this is Crimea, fruit is the main food here." Then all three women went somewhere.

"Come on," said Matveevna, "let's take a stroll, girls . . . Let the mother and daughter have a talk."

Maria started telling her mother about her life, she told her about everything, but she kept secret the violent rape that Grisha had perpetrated on her in the barn, and she also kept secret how Ksenia's husband Alexei Alexandrovich had caught the man in long drawers with Ksenia in the middle of the night. And Maria's mother reproached her:

"How could you abandon Vasya like that so far away from home?"

"I know I'm to blame," Maria replied sadly. "I didn't take proper care of him."

"But at least my oldest daughter Ksenia has achieved what she wanted," Maria's mother said, "that's something I can be glad about . . . I had Ksenia when there was still plenty of bread and plenty of bacon fat, at dinner we ate a whole pound of bacon fat at a sitting . . . I was young and well-fed and your father Nikolai was still young and handsome, but though I had Shura and Kolya when life was still bountiful, I raised them when life was already hungry . . . And I had you, and Vasya, and especially Zhorik, when we were really starving . . ."

Just then there was a knock at the door, and an elderly man walked in.

"Have you patched my tunic?" he asked.

"I have," Maria's mother replied, "and look what a joyful surprise I have here, Savelii . . . My daughter Maria's come . . ."

"And that's a good thing," said Savelii. "Children should be with their mother while they're little . . ."

Maria started living with her mother and she become accustomed to that life, and accustomed to Kerch. Oh, how beautiful Kerch city was, she would probably never want to live anywhere else after here. You could live in a city like this until the day you died and never get miserable. Maria was surrounded by good people, who felt sorry for her. Uncle Savelii was good, and Matveevna was good, and Aunty Klavdia was kind, only Aunty Olga was a little bit unpleasant. Once Maria heard her mother say to Matveevna:

"Olga's annoyed because my daughter came to stay with me. She says she has three sons in the country, so now she has to bring them here . . . It's too crowded here . . ."

"Never mind," replied Matveevna, "Olga isn't in charge here, society is . . . Let Maria live here for a while . . . Only starting next fall, she'll have to get herself a school education: as it is, it's like she's living under the old regime . . . Surely that isn't what the Bolshevik revolution and our dear departed Lenin fought for?"

"But she finished three grades in school," Maria's mother replied timidly.

"That's not enough," said Matveevna, "you and me, we're both semiliterate . . . What have we achieved? We just dig the ground . . . But our children must become doctors and engineers . . ."

"One of my daughters, Ksenia, has a good, wealthy life in Voronezh," Maria's mother boasted. "She's a beauty, like me in my young days . . . Her husband is a railroad engineer. Maria stayed with her, and Ksenia fed her well, and gave her a shawl, and felt boots, and a wadded jacket."

"It wasn't Ksenia who gave me the wadded jacket, Aunty Sophia gave me the wadded jacket in Lgov town," said Maria.

"Don't you interrupt when your elders are talking," her mother said angrily, "you know, Matveevna, she's very spoilt . . . She went off with her brother Vasya, my youngest son, and she didn't take proper care of him, and he got lost along the way."

"The youngest isn't Vasya, it's Zhorik," said Maria. "The one the strange woman took away in Dymytrov town when you left us there to go to the fair, to sell your shawl and buy dried plums."

"I'll send you back to the village tomorrow," her mother said angrily, "I see you've got really spoilt with all your traveling about . . ."

And Matveevna supported Maria's mother:

"Don't you annoy the mother who gave you birth, she works hard for you."

Then Maria started apologizing to her mother for being rude, and her mother forgave her, and Matveevna forgave her.

This conversation happened some time during Maria's third month of living with her mother and it was the first time her mother got angry with her. As for reproaching her about Vasya, her mother had done that before, but this was the first time she'd got angry about it. The morning after Maria's mother got angry and then forgave her, Maria set out for Enikale town, which was as close to Kerch as Dymytrov was to Shagaro-Petrovskoe village. And we should note that Maria had already taken to walking to Enikale town quite often to beg, for although she lived with her mother, she was still hungry. Maria was afraid to beg in Kerch, in case Matveevna saw her, but in Enikale no one knew Maria. She chose the wealthiest houses she could, where Jews, Greeks or Tatars lived, and begged, and they gave to her. She walked along the seashore over the wet sand, breathed in the sea breeze, rejoicing, and she had strength in her, for even a person with typhoid fever has a healthy complexion at the seaside. By this time Maria had learned to swim in the sea as well as she did in a river. She had a spot on the road between Kerch and Enikale: where the sea didn't reach it, the sand there was soft and warm, and where the sea did reach the sand, it was firm and cool. The water was clear and you could see every stone on the bottom, a little farther on two big rocks jutted up, and farther away Mount Mithridat could be seen. Maria decided to take a dip on that day, since it was already spring, and the sun was as hot as it was in summer in the Kharkiv Region. Maria glanced round and there was no one nearby, so she took off her dress, and she wasn't wearing any panties, since it was so warm, then ran into the water, and suddenly noticed that her breasts, although they weren't like Ksenia's, were no longer just little bumps, and her nipples protruded instead of lying flat, like pimples. And her legs had become more firmly articulated with her belly: it was all beautiful, she even felt like stroking it herself, and she didn't feel ashamed to look at it in the daylight . . . But Maria didn't see the Greek, the former owner of a coffee house in Enikale town and now a public catering functionary, who was actually watching her. After breakfast this Greek liked to stroll along the seashore with his naval binoculars, in case he might get a free glimpse of a naked woman. This Greek saw Maria and he wanted her. As soon as Maria had finished bathing and put on her dress, and she was standing there, all fresh and clean, smelling of seawater, the Greek walked up to her and asked:

"Where are you going, little girl?"

"I'm going to Enikale," said Maria, "to beg for bread."

"That's a terrible shame," said the Greek, "and you such a beautiful little girl . . . Ah, that's not good . . . Come on, I'll give you some roasted meat, would you like some meat?"

Maria looked at the man: he wasn't Russian, he was handsome and rich, and she really liked the idea of eating some of his meat. She went to his house in Enikale town, with carpets everywhere and a sweet, pleasant kind of smell that wasn't Russian either. An old woman brought in a dish of hot roasted meat, sprinkled with a red powder. Maria took a bite and burned her throat, and the Greek laughed.

"That's Greek pepper . . . It's dry fire . . ."

Maria ate a lot of meat and it made her so tipsy that the Greek told the old woman to take away the bottle of sweet wine, which had proved unnecessary. And Maria lay down on a soft carpet, and the Greek lay down beside her. And Maria got what she wanted, she obtained what Ksenia had, she took from the Greek what Ksenia took from her lover and her husband, and what Grisha the guide had taken from her in the dark barn. And Maria heard her own voice singing, pouring forth in rapturous moaning, she clung on tight to the Greek, this well-fed, handsome, non-Russian man, and exploited his strength for her own satisfaction all day and all evening and all night.

"How sick your heart must be," the Lord declares through the prophet Ezekiel, "if you have done all these things, the deeds of a brazen prostitute."

From her infancy Maria had suffered the torment of the second plague of the Lord, famine, but deliciously sated hunger intoxicates, it arouses and inflames the body, and the place of the second plague of the Lord is then taken by the third, the wild beast of lust and fornication.

Maria kept the Greek there beside her until the morning, and she could have kept him there longer, but the Greek said:

"With us it is the man who should ravage the woman, not the woman who should ravage the man . . . You're a stupid little girl, you ate a lot of my meat and you want to ravage me, a Greek man . . ."

And the Greek threw Maria out, without even giving her something to eat in farewell. Maria went back to Kerch city, feeling desolate and hungry, since she had expended her satiety from the roasted meat on what she was doing with the Greek until the morning came. Maria reached the red-brick dormitory building that was the workers' barracks where she lived with her mother: she was dreading the meeting with her mother and thinking that she would keep what had happened secret, as she had kept secret from her mother her rape by Grisha in the barn, and the man in long drawers that Ksenia's husband had found with her. Those things had been easier to conceal, they had happened when Maria was on her own in faraway places, but now she was with her mother. Maria walked into the barracks with these thoughts in her mind and walked up the iron stairway, and Matveevna met her in the corridor with a tearstained face, and said:

"Where have you been? We've been searching for you, because your mother was hit by a train, and now you're an orphan."

At first Maria didn't understand what Matveevna was talking about. But when she did understand, Maria sat down on the floor of the corridor beside her door and stayed there. Meanwhile her mother was lying in a pine coffin, which had been set on a barracks dining table between four barracks beds. And a whole crowd of people were gathered round her, taking their leave, mostly women, but there were men too, friends of Savelii, who had cobbled together the pine coffin.

"Why are you sitting here?" Aunty Olga asked Maria angrily, and blew her nose into her handkerchief, then wiped her eyes. "Why don't you go to say goodbye to your mother?"

But Maria sat there beside the door on the floor of the corridor, without saying anything, and she didn't have an answer for anyone. By opening the door from the corridor slightly, a mere crack, she could just see the very top of her mother's motionless head, covered in Matveevna's white shawl. She looked for a minute or two and closed the door. A long time, perhaps an hour, went by before she opened the door a little bit further, making the crack a little bit wider, and saw her mother's white forehead below Matveevna's shawl. Maria closed the door again and carried on sitting there, without an answer for anyone, for a long time, then she opened the door wider, and saw her mother had a lighted candle in her hands, which were clasped together on her breast. Maria closed the door again, and no matter how insistently Aunty Matveevna and Uncle Savelii tried to persuade her to go in and say goodbye to her mother, she didn't go, she stayed in the corridor. And Maria opened the door another three or four times, wider every time, until she saw all of her mother, lying in the coffin in Matveevna's white shawl, with a candle in her hands, dressed in her black woolen dress, the one she used to wear on holidays back at home in the Meadow Farmstead... Maria remembered that when they walked through the reserve to see Maria's grandma and grandpa in Popovka village at Easter, and Maria's father was still alive, and Vasya was at home, only little, like Zhorik, and Zhorik wasn't even born yet, her mother was wearing this black woolen dress. Once Maria had seen all of her mother and become accustomed to the sight, she swung the door wide open, and walked into the room to say goodbye. In the coffin her mother's bare feet were as white as her face and her hands. And a lot of children, who lived in the hostel with their parents, even some from the other blocks, had come, and Aunty Matveevna was giving them all apples, spice cookies and small Crimean hazelnuts.

And so Maria lost her mother, and no one knew what to do with Maria after that. Although there were good people around her, they weren't kin to her, and Maria wasn't kin to them.

"We ought to send her to her sisters and brothers," said Uncle Savelii. "Do you want to go to your sisters and brothers?" he asked Maria.

"No," said Maria, "Shura and Kolya, who live on the farmstead, are hungry themselves, and Ksenia's husband in Voronezh, the railroad engineer Alexei Alexandrovich, has taken against me."

"Then it's the orphanage," said Matveevna, "there's a good orphanage here in Kerch." Maria started crying.

"The orphanage," she said, "is what I'm afraid of most of all."

"Then what do you want?" asked Matveevna. "At your age, there's no way you can be left unsupervised, or else you'll stray onto the wrong path and turn to either stealing or prostitution, or perhaps even both of them at once."

Maria replied:

"I've never stolen from people in my life, only begged from them. I didn't keep my brother, Vasya, away from stealing, and it's true I'm to blame for that. But I don't even know what prostitution is." Uncle Savelii laughed and said:

"That's when a loose woman takes money for doing what a respectable woman does for free."

"Ugh! You shameless man," said Matveevna, "saying such a thing in front of a little girl!"

However, Maria understood what they meant, she understood more about these things now, and she thought: "So what Ksenia did with Alexei Alexandrovich is one thing, and what I did with the Greek is something different . . . That thing is allowed, but this different thing is considered the same as stealing, and it has to be kept especially secret."

And she walked out of the room, terrified that they would guess about the Greek man from Enikale: she walked out in despair, wondering how she could avoid the orphanage in Kerch city. But she decided to live in Kerch, since Kerch was a good city, warm and by the sea, which Maria didn't have any idea about at all before she arrived here. Before she traveled from Dymytrov town for the first time, with her mother and Vasya, she didn't even know what a train was, although she did know what a steam engine was. And now she knew what a steamship was, and what a barge was, and lots of other things too, because she went to the port to beg. Several times she did the thing that had to be kept especially secret and was considered equivalent to stealing with sailors, but then a woman hit her much harder than that time in Kursk, and Maria stopped going to the port. And anyway, the sailors did everything in a rush, on hard benches or on the floor, and Maria wasn't able even once to exploit their male strength for her own satisfaction, the way she had exploited the Greek's strength. They didn't pay her with roasted meat, but with bread or dried fish, which she could beg without doing things that were considered to be the same as stealing. And when the woman hit Maria in the port she stopped wanting to do those things altogether, but the desire was still there to have that experience one more time and moan melodiously at what she experienced, the way her sister Ksenia had moaned with her husband and her lover, and the way Maria had moaned with the Greek, who had got angry in the morning for some reason and been annoyed with her.

Maria didn't go to the hostel where her mother had lived until she died, she was afraid that Matveevna would catch her and take her to the orphanage. Maria spent the night in all sorts of places, since the spring was warm in Kerch city, and when it rained she could always find an awning somewhere.

One warm night she decided to spend the night under an awning by the sea, since sometimes rain sprinkled down briefly from the starry sky and whispered something above the awning for a minute or two and stopped, then whispered again for another five or ten minutes. The moon hanging over the sea didn't even remotely resemble the Kharkiv moon, so gaunt, hungry, and listless, which, if it ever did glimmer, glimmered as if it had typhoid fever and it was only possible to like it because of this other moon's absence, and which, if it sparkled, then it was only in comparison with the Kursk moon, which was altogether gaunt and severe. The sea moon was a match for the richness of the Poltava moon, but it was also several times larger. And as well as that the Poltava moon, like the Kharkiv moon and the Kursk moon, hung firmly fixed, either above an open field or above a reserve-forest, but the sea moon always seemed to be in the process of falling. As if at any moment you might hear the splash as it fell into the sea. It didn't fall, and yet your heart was still agitated by this expectation that it would fall at any moment.

Perhaps on that night Maria was in a state of such heartfelt agitation because on the preceding evening people had given stintingly and she was hungry, and perhaps because today the whispering of the rain was somehow special, it seemed to say something to the awning for a while, then fall silent and think for a while, and then start speaking again. And the sky was covered in big, southern stars, but the moon hung in the sky as precariously as ever, and it was so big that it seemed to have moved right up close, and if you shut your eyes you would hear a splash, and if you opened them again, there wouldn't be a moon in the sky any longer. This was the state Maria was in, and she didn't even feel like sleeping. Suddenly she heard someone walking along the very edge of the sea, setting the wet sea pebbles swishing under his feet. She looked and saw it was a man. "I'll go," thought Maria, "and ask him for bread, and if he doesn't give me any for nothing, then I'll lie down with him under the awning, and he'll give me some bread or dried fish for that." Maria walked up to the man and recognized him as the stranger from her native Kharkiv region, but here, in Kerch city, where she had been completely alone since her mother's death, he didn't seem like a stranger to her. And holding out her hand for alms, Maria said:

"In the name of the Lord! Jesus Christ! The Son of God!"

And Dan from the tribe of Dan, the Viper, the Antichrist answered her:

"You are not appealing to me, but to my brother from the tribe of Judah. I am Dan from the tribe of Dan, the Antichrist, the Son of God for the curse that was first pronounced on Mount Ebal. It is not yet time for the blessing first pronounced on Mount Gerizim, and therefore my brother Jesus from the tribe of Judah will not answer you . . ."

Maria didn't understand anything he had said, since she had no reason, and there was nothing in these words spoken by Dan, the Son of God sent for malediction, that could be understood without reason. And Maria started crying. Then Dan, the Antichrist, the Viper asked:

"Why are you crying?"

"My father died a long time ago," said Maria, "and my mother just recently. And my older brother and sisters have turned their backs on me, I lost my younger brother, Vasya, in Izyum city, and now there is no one to look after me, and no one for me to look after . . . I'm all alone . . ."

Dan replied:

"Sorrow for your mother, weep for her, but your weeping will bring you no consolation She did not die from human causes, for the Lord also judges the poor man and does not favor a poor man in a lawsuit . . . Even jackals offer the breast and nurse their young; but the daughter of my people has become cruel, like the ostriches in the wilderness. The tongue of the nursing infant sticks to the roof of its mouth for thirst; the children beg for bread, but no one gives to them."

So said Dan, the Viper, the Antichrist, speaking through the prophet Jeremiah, and he took out of his shepherd's bag the impure bread of exile, bequeathed by the prophet Ezekiel, and held it out to Maria. And at last no one took away from Maria this bread, of which the Lord said:

"And you shall eat it as a barley cake, baking it in their sight on human dung . . . Thus shall the people of Israel eat their bread unclean, among the nations where I will drive them."

But the prophet Ezekiel besought from the Lord the right to bake the impure bread of exile, not on human excrement, but on cow dung.

And through this piece of impure bread Maria the little beggar girl was initiated into the divine providence, and all who had known and debauched her, even at the Lord's behest, became loathsome to the Lord, and all who had helped her, not even from God, but on their own behalf, became pleasing to the Lord. Through the impure bread of exile Maria was initiated into a foreign people, as Tamar was initiated by Judah and Ruth the Moabite woman was initiated through Boaz of Bethlehem, a city of Judea. And Maria did not choose, but was chosen. And Dan, the Viper, the Antichrist became intimate with Maria through the third plague of the Lord, the only one of the four plagues from which he was not protected on his earthly travels.

And they lay under the awning as the sea murmured in the darkness, and sometimes the rain whispered something for a minute or two, then fell silent, and Maria's only reaction to all the sounds reaching her from various directions was a joyful, melodious moan. But suddenly she heard a splash, as if something immensely heavy had plummeted down into the sea. Maria looked up from behind the bony shoulder of Dan, the Antichrist, and as she looked she saw that there was no moon in the sky. Everything immediately went quiet, the sea fell silent and the rain was hushed, as if both had started pondering, and Maria, curled up into a tight ball, in the way that all the homeless sleep in the chilly air of morning, fell asleep, tenderly warming in her Slavic womb the foreign seed, still fresh, of the sixth son of Jacob. And, getting up from off the sleeping girl, Dan, the Antichrist walked on along the shoreline.

From here it was not far to his native parts, and Dan could sense this, and his heart was pounding like the prodigal son's at the threshold of his father's house. He walked on over the Hellenic ground, where the Hellenes built their settlements beside Mount Mithridat before his brother, Jesus, was born. And where there was a Hellenic presence, Dan sensed his own kin, for the Hellenes were hostile, but not alien neighbors of Dan's people, whereas there are peoples who are alien, but not hostile, and there are peoples who are both alien and hostile . . . For just as there are no equal individuals, and yet all seem good to themselves, so there are no equal peoples, and peoples are subject to their own fates, just as individuals are. And there are peoples who feel comfortable with each other, and there are peoples who do not feel comfortable with each other, even though they are bound together by fate, as also happens with individuals . . . Morning had not yet arrived, but the forces of morning were already fully active when Dan from the tribe of Dan, the Viper, the Antichrist stopped to take a short rest not far from Enikale town. This was the same spot where Maria had bathed, admiring her own body, brimming over with vital, womanly energy, for the first time. It was a truly excellent spot, the transparent morning sea lent a precious, jewel-like sheen to the submerged rocks that could be seen in the shallows, but the frozen strength of the rocky crags jutting up out of the water was a reminder to those who were duped into gazing in admiration at the delicate splashing of the calm morning water that in the beauty of the sea, as in all boundless beauty, it is cruelty that predominates, and it is only possible to admire cruelty at moments when your heart is blighted and desolate. The beauty of the sea is antihuman, as the beauty of the cosmos is antihuman. For the human being spiritual grandeur lies, not in the sea and rocky crags, not in the world of the universe, but in a field, grass, a little river, the earthly sky . . . The Bible originated beside the sea, but almost all of its action takes place away from the sea, among valleys and rivers, in pastures, not in coastal cities, but in cities far inland. And is it by chance that the domains of the major tribes of Jacob's sons, who enacted among themselves the fundamental passions of the Bible, were far distant from the seashore? . . . The Lord appeared to Abraham on a hill, and to Moses in a thorn-bush, and Moses spoke with the Lord on Mount Sinai in the desert, and the Angel appeared to Jacob in a thorn-bush . . . Man lives beside the sea, and makes his living from the sea, he delights in the sea, however the sea can only teach that which is strong, but cruel; beautiful but vindictive; majestic, but heartless. It is no accident that, of all the tribes of Israel, only the domain of the tribe of Dan, which was fated to beget the Antichrist, lay by the sea. From Khatlon, leading on to Hamath, and Hazar Enan, from the east to the sea, lay the territory of Dan, who was created for cursing the affairs of man. And five domains farther on lies the territory of Judah, from out of which emerged the Christ, sent for blessing. Jesus from the tribe of Judah was only drawn to the sea out of dire need, he came for miracles, for walking on the water as if it were dry land, but his soul was in the desert, his soul was beside the river Jordan, his soul was in the Holy City . . .

And His brother Dan, whose domain lay by the sea, was not calmed by the sea. For without reason it is possible simply to rejoice by the sea, but the only conclusion reason can draw from the sea is calamity.

Dan the Antichrist looked at Mount Mithridat and saw a narrow beam of light from the rising sun emerge from behind the ruins of the medieval Genoese fortress, and this beam cleaved the dark clouds like a sword, so that the clouds were soaked in blood and if you squeezed them, the bloody rain would pour down into the sea until they were exhausted, becoming weightless . . . And even a faint wind would carry those clouds away. Dan saw the remnants of blood dripping down from off the sword and the bloody streaks on the waves. And Dan, the Viper, the Antichrist said to himself through the prophet Jeremiah:

"My anguish, my anguish! I writhe in pain! Oh the walls of my heart! My heart is beating wildly; I cannot keep silent, for you, my soul, hear the sound of the trumpet, the alarm of war . . ."

And again he spoke through the prophet Jeremiah:

"They have spoken falsely of the Lord and have said: He will do nothing; no disaster will come upon us, nor shall we see sword or famine."

And Dan, the Antichrist, the Jewish child who was maturing in his earthly travels and had grown into a youth, said:

"For several years already they have been punished by the second plague of the Lord, famine; they are always defenseless in the face of the third plague, the beast of fornication; they are tormented by the first plague of the Lord, the sword, and that brings in its wake all of the plagues together . . . For the Lord has said: 'The whole land shall be a desolation, yet I will not make a full end.'"

And so saying, Dan, the Antichrist, set out on his way again to consummate the curse foreordained by the Lord. His designated route lay to the town of Rzhev, to a completely different domain, to other human destinies. And although it was preordained that he should only appear in the town of

Rzhev six years later, in the year 1940 after the birth of his brother Jesus from the tribe of Judah, he quickly disappeared from those parts, and no matter how hard Maria searched, she could not find him.

Already convicted of prostitution and vagrancy, Maria gave birth to the son of Dan, the Antichrist, in the prison hospital. It was expected that by the logic of medicine the boy would not live, since his mother was still a juvenile and emaciated, but he did live and Maria named him Vasya after her lost brother. The infant Vasya had exceedingly black eyes, and his little anti-Slavonic nose almost touched his little upper lip when the boy smiled at his mother. And when Maria placed the nipple of her breast in his hungry little mouth, she yielded up all the vital energies of her body, derived with such great effort from the scanty prison gruel, but she moaned joyfully, melodiously, and the prison doctor said:

"There's something morbid about this . . . Perhaps she has latent syphilis?"

"And she got that kid of hers from a Yid, or from some Georgian or Armenian," said the prison hospital nurse, who had taken a dislike to Maria for her Jewish baby Vasya.

They took black-eyed Vasya from Maria and sent him to an orphanage. After that Maria stopped wanting to live, and she died in the prison hospital at the age of fifteen on February the 23rd, 1936, and was buried without a coffin. On the same day her prison rations were canceled, and her file was closed and consigned to the archives.

A Parable of the Torments of Evildoers

Life repeats life, fate imitates fate, as day repeats day and night imitates night... What is existence, but repetition and imitation... Day follows night, and night follows day. Spring imitates spring, fall imitates fall, and the basis of all imitation, and therefore of existence, is rational order. This is God's classicism. Isaac's fate imitates Abraham's fate, and Jacob's fate imitates Isaac's fate. All things that are most exalted, living by divine reason, and all things that are most earthly, living by divine instinct, repeat each other and live through imitation. Classicism is the imitation of the Lord through reason, or of the Lord's world through instinct. The prophet imitates the Lord, the people imitate the Lord's world. But the further civilization develops, the more innovation there is, and the less classicism. Initially, dogma appears. Classicism dies, tortured to death by its degenerate votaries. The innovator, who lacks the strength to do battle with living classicism, throws himself on the corpse and glories in his victory . . . And that is when, as Jeremiah prophesied, a wooden yoke is smashed and is replaced by a yoke of iron. Then the innovator-prophet appears, wishing to live by instinct, and the innovator-people, wishing to live by reason.

The innovator-prophet, wishing to live by instinct, spawns idealist materialism, eclectic social utopia and materialist idealism, that is, mysticism; the innovator-people, wishing to live by reason, spawns the human deity and idolatry, so that in his finest moments man becomes an atheist, and in his worst an idolator . . . Each individual strives to create something of his own and say something unique. However the patriarchs did not found what was pleasing to themselves, but what was pleasing to God, and the prophets did not speak their own words, but the words of God... This small, sheepherding people was just as depraved as all the other large and small peoples close to it in space and time or distant from it in space and time. It was differentiated from all the others only by its patriarchs and its prophets, and the Lord chose it for its patriarchs and prophets. And the prophet Jeremiah said:

"Your ways and your deeds have brought this upon you. This is your doom, and it is bitter; it has reached your very heart."

And the prophet Isaiah said:

". . . and our iniquities, like the wind, bear us away."

However people place too much trust in innovation and hope that their fates will be different. And then the repetition, from which they shrink in their happiness, over which they have control, comes to them in a catastrophe, over which they have none.

***

In 1940, in Rzhev town in the Kalinin Region, there lived a little girl by the name of Annushka. And her mother was also called Annushka. And this little girl knew her surname, Emelyanova. She had a brother who was called Ivan, whom for some reason everyone called Mitya, but no one knew why. And she had another little brother, Vova, who was two years old. But Annushka didn't have a father, he had been killed in the Soviet-Finnish War, since Rzhev was a northern town, and many men were taken from the north for that war. Annushka was born in that same region, only not in the Rzhev district, but in the Zubtsov district, in Nefedovo village. Annushka remembered living in Nefedovo village, and how in summer, early in the morning, when the sun shone with a caressing warmth, she liked to crawl out of bed while still sleepy, go outside in just her night shirt, sit down on the ground by the wall of the little wooden house, and finish her sleep like that. But now Annushka's address was Room 9, Barracks Building 3, Sector 3, Rzhev town. At this address she couldn't sit by the wall of a little wooden house for a while in the morning sunshine. The barracks building was nothing at all like the little wooden house. It had a bad smell, and it was not built of sound timber, but stucco and crumbling planks, and the ground in front of the barracks building was not soft, but dry and spiky, the puddles lying on it took forever to dry up, and there were scraps of newspapers soaking in them, along with broken bricks and oily rags. And there was also a constant droning, whirring noise, like lots of tractors all moving about at once, from the airdrome where Annushka's mother, also called Annushka, worked on a construction site. Annushka had known for a long time now that it was the airplanes droning, only sometimes she imagined it was the way she used to think about it during her first days there, when she thought it was tractors. Her mother used to take Annushka's brother Ivan-Mitya to a nursery school, and leave her brother Vova in Annushka's care, so Annushka had already taken a dislike to Vova.

The little wooden house in Nefedovo village was nicer than the barracks building in Rzhev town, but Rzhev town was a jollier place than Nefedovo village. In summer a circus came to the market square and it was jolly simply to be near it, even without a ticket: and in winter Annushka usually wore red felt boots, bought in a shop in the town. However the event following which Annushka was marked by fate did not occur in winter, when Annushka was wearing her beloved red felt boots, but in summer, when the circus came to the market square. That summer was sweltering hot, so that even the never-drying puddles in front of the barracks building had dried up, leaving behind only small patches of sticky mud here and there. The barracks building had lots of holes, through which cold drafts blew in during winter, when they were plugged with rags, but now, even though Annushka's mother had pulled the rags out, it was still stifling hot in the barracks building and Vova cried all the time, biting Annushka and refusing to eat his semolina pudding, which he spat out onto his little feet. Annushka, who knew that the circus had come to the market square and music was playing there, was furious with Vova, since because of him she was obliged to stay there in the stifling hot barracks building, and when Vova bit Annushka especially hard, she pinched him. Then he started crying even more loudly, so that Aunty Shura from room 12 glanced in through the door of their room number 9. She brought a bowl of warm water, washed Vova's little face, little hands and little feet that were smeared with semolina pudding, and he stopped crying and fell asleep. Then Aunty Shura went away, and Annushka was left alone with her sleeping brother Vova in the stifling hot barracks building. And then she decided that while Vova was asleep she would run to the market square, where the circus was. Everything was beautiful and jolly there, Annushka walked everywhere, looked at everything and laughed, even though there was no one making her laugh, until eventually a woman in a white bucket hat said to her:

"Little girl, what are you laughing at? Laughing without any reason is an indication of a feeble mind."

Annushka was laughing because it was better here in the festive crowd in front of the circus, listening to the music, than sitting beside Vova in the stifling hot barracks building. However she didn't try to explain the reason for her laughter to the woman, but simply walked away and carried on laughing. Suddenly the daylight dimmed and it started spitting with rain. Everybody started bustling, saying: "A storm, a storm, look at that dark cloud . . ." And indeed, from here on the market square she saw a dark cloud creeping toward her, and the motionless trees started shaking, the canvas dome of the circus big-top started flapping alarmingly and the music stopped playing. Then Annushka went running home, but before she had run through even a few streets, heavy rain started falling, bolts of lightning flashed down from the sky to the earth and thunder rumbled across the sky once . . . twice . . . three times . . .—but it was impossible to get used to it, and each time Annushka was terrified all over again. In the first minute Anuushka got so soaked that her dress clung to her body and she was winded too, but she couldn't run into the entrance of a building, or stand under a balcony with a jolly, jostling crowd of wet people, she had to run back home to the barracks building, back to the edge of town, where Vova was alone, and since he was even frightened by a door slamming (their mother had forbidden Annushka and Mitya to slam the doors because of that), he must be really terrified by now.

At the barracks building, where only recently all the puddles had dried up in the heat, rainwater was not merely standing in pools, but flowing like a swift river: it was above Annushka's ankle, even reaching her knees in places. The waterlogged door of Annushka's room had distorted and jammed, and when she finally managed to open it with the key she had pulled out from under a floorboard, water came pouring out into the corridor . . . Annushka was frightened and she shouted:

"Vova . . ."

But Vova wasn't in the bed. Annushka ran round the room, slopping through the water, crying and calling out to Vova. Then she saw the open window and decided that Vova must have climbed outside, and she shouted through the window:

"Vova, Vova . . ." She was afraid her mother would punish her because Vova had climbed outside.

Then she glanced under the bed and Vova was lying there face down. Annushka realized that Vova had fallen off the bed and rolled under it. Vova was wet and cold and his face looked as if he was crying, but without making any sound, and no matter how Annushka put him down, he just lay there in the same position. Then Annushka realized that little Vova was dead. When she realized that, she was very frightened. Annushka didn't feel sorry for Vova, since she didn't like him, but she was afraid that her mother would come back from work and punish her very severely because of Vova. Thinking about this, Annushka simply fell into despair, and she wished that she was dead too, like Vova, so that her mother wouldn't punish her and shout at her. But Annushka didn't know how to die, so she simply sat there with her arms wrapped round her head and cried quietly so that none of the neighbors would come into the room and find out that Vova was dead because of her.

When evening arrived and her mother came back from work, bringing Mitya with her from the nursery school, the first thing she saw was Annushka sitting on the floor with her eyes closed and her hands pressed tight over ears, in order not to see or hear anything.

"What's wrong, little daughter?" her mother cried in alarm, and the next moment she saw little Vova lying dead on the bed.

She screamed louder than she had ever screamed before, and her voice and her face changed, becoming quite unrecognizable. All the neighbors immediately came running, someone went dashing to the buildings superintendent's office to call for an ambulance, someone tried to give Vova artificial respiration by working his little arms and little legs, and someone said:

"It's no use, he's already dead."

Mitya, Annushka's brother, watched all this this with a sullen expression and didn't cry, since he was a calm and level-headed boy . . . But with her face and voice changed beyond recognition Annushka's mother, of whom Annushka was afraid even in her ordinary anger, had now become more terrifying than any wild beast of the forest to Annushka. She dashed at her daughter with a terrifying scream and struck her, not with her open palm, but with her fist, in a way she had never struck her before . . . Even when a mother or father strikes in rage, they are mindful of how much it hurts the child, and although their blow is painful, it makes allowances for the child's body. But this time Annushka's mother struck her without making any allowances for Annushka's body, in the way that people strike an enemy, and for Annushka the world suddenly went dark . . . People only strike their children like that out of bitter grief or terrible wickedness, for grief and wickedness are different shoots growing from a single root. She was about to strike Annushka again, but they restrained her.

Aunty Shura took Annushka and Mitya to her room, gave them each a toffee candy and applied a compress to Annushka's forehead. Annushka spent the night with Aunty Shura. The next day they buried Vova. A little child's coffin was brought from somewhere and they put five-kopeck pieces on Vova's eyes. Annushka wanted to go to the cemetery, but Aunty Shura wouldn't let her, and she saw her mother through the window, not crying any more, but walking along behind Vova's little coffin in a black shawl with Mitya walking beside her.

Annushka spent the next day at Aunty Shura's place too, and had dinner with her: she ate delicious mushroom soup and potatoes with baked milk. In the early evening Annushka's mother called in to see her and she wasn't crying angrily now, but affectionately, and she was like herself again. She kissed Annushka hard and took her away with her, stroking her and hugging her to her bosom so tightly that level-headed Mitya said:

"Careful, Mom, you'll crush Anka like that."

From that time on, Annushka's mother started treating her differently, scolding her less often and not beating her at all. And in her heart of hearts Annushka was glad that Vova had died. Now in her free time she strolled around in the street or went to see her mother at work, and they let her in. In general, she preferred being with grown-ups and didn't like children. Annushka liked it when people felt sorry for her, but children never feel sorry for anyone, for they are pitiless creatures. The neighbors' children teased her, and she was teased in school too. Her mother tried transferring her to a different school, but they teased her there. She tried sending Annushka to a different Young Pioneers' summer camp that didn't belong to the enterprise her mother worked for, but to a milk-processing plant. But Annushka ran away from the camp because she couldn't wake up when she needed to go for a pee while she was asleep. She got on well with her brother Mitya and he consoled her when she was harassed by the other children, but he never stood up for her. He just walked up to her quietly and said:

"Let's go home, Annushka," and held out his hand to her.

So brother and sister would walk home like that, holding hands. From September Mitya also started going to school, but they didn't tease him, even though they knew he was Anka-wee-wee's brother. Only instead of calling him Ivan, as he was listed in the class register, according to his official documents, all the children called him Mitya, and this went so far that even the teacher would occasionally call him Mitya instead of Ivan . . .

In any event, although Annushka didn't actually get used to the teasing, she came to terms with it and managed to live with it, especially since Rzhev was a large town, with enough space for her to give her vicious mockers a wide berth. And they gradually stopped teasing her quite so much, because a boy with a lisp joined their class, and everyone started teasing him. Even Annushka teased him. So after Vova died, Annushka's life was going quite well, until another disaster occurred. This disaster didn't occur in summer, when the circus came to the market square, but in winter, when Annushka wore her favorite red felt boots.

One afternoon, while Annushka was heating up some meat patties for herself on the primus stove, because she attended the second shift at school, but at that time Mitka was already at school and their mother was at work, the door opened without anyone knocking and two men she didn't know walked in.

"Are you alone, little girl?" asked the one wearing white felt boots trimmed with fur.

"Yes," said Annushka.

"Well then, sit on that chair over there and keep quiet," said the other man, who was wearing a black sheepskin coat.

Annushka sat down on the chair, and the men started rapidly dragging everything out of the wardrobe and packing it all into suitcases. They pulled out the drawers of the dresser and glanced into the bedside cabinet, walking past Annushka as if she wasn't even there. Then they left, taking the sewing machine with them as well as the suitcases.

When Annushka's mother got the chance of a ride going her way, she used to come home for lunch. She arrived and saw everything was gaping wide open, the wardrobe was empty, the sewing machine was missing, and Annushka was sitting on a chair. Annushka's mother started shouting, and all the neighbors came running in again, like the time when Vova died.

"We've been robbed!" Annushka's mother shouted. "They've taken everything . . . Even Kolya's suit, the one I was keeping to remember him by . . . Kolya's woolen cloth suit that he only wore twice." And she burst into tears.

Their neighbor from room 11 said:

"I heard someone walk past, but I could hear Annushka was home, she was fiddling with the primus stove, and I thought some relatives had come to visit."

"But why didn't you shout out?" Aunty Shura asked Annushka.

"I was afraid they'd start beating me," Annushka said.

"But why didn't you cry out when they left with the suitcases?" asked their neighbor from room 11.

"I was afraid they were hiding behind the door," said Annushka, "and they'd start beating me as soon as I shouted . . ."

At that point Annushka's mother hit her again for the first time in a long time, only not with her fist, like when Vova died. She slapped Annushka with maternal restraint, but even so it still hurt. And at that moment the buildings superintendent arrived and said:

"Blows won't improve the situation, but tell me, little girl, would you recognize these thieves if you saw them?"

"Yes," said Annushka, "one has a black sheepskin coat, and the other has white boots."

"Right," said the buildings superintendent, "line up all the men from the barracks buildings . . . They could be some of the newly hired men who've only just been set on . . . there's no end of dekulakized elements among them."

They lined up all the men from the barracks buildings on a snow-covered vacant lot, then Annushka walked out and she felt scared. Her mother, the buildings superintendent and two militiamen were there beside her. She set off along the line and all the men gazed at Annushka in fright, and she gazed at all of them in fright. They walked right along the line once and Annushka didn't recognize anyone. There were familiar faces and unfamiliar faces, but the men who had carried out the robbery weren't there.

"Never mind," said the superintendent, "you can never spot them the first time round."

They set off a second time. Again all the men gazed at Annushka in fright and Annushka looked at all of them in even greater fright, and because of her fright she couldn't make out anything at all: the faces all looked the same, and even the familiar faces looked strange.

"Never mind," said the superintendent, "let's give it a third try . . . Maybe he's frightening you with his stare."

Annushka really was shivering as if she had a fever and she didn't know who to point at. And her knickers had been wet for ages because she was frightened and it was hard for her being out in the cold, and again she didn't know who to point at . . . So she pointed at the third man from the end on the left.

"That one," she said.

"Little girl," the man she had pointed at shouted, "I'm from Zubtsov . . . Pochivalin's my name . . . I've got seven children . . ."

"Well, so what?" said the superintendent. "You might be from Zubtsov, but you can still steal the property of a Finnish War widow." And he punched the man in the teeth.

The blood immediately started flowing and at the sight of blood Annushka started crying.

"All right," said the superintendent, "take the little girl away. He'll squeal on his accomplice anyway."

Annushka's mother led her into the barracks building and didn't scold her or hit her anymore, she was affectionate with her, just like after Vova's funeral. A few days later the buildings superintendent walked into room 9 and said:

"Your things haven't been found yet, Anna Alexeevna, but I have some news to cheer you up . . . They'll figure out if that rat stole them or not, but they've already figured out for certain that in '34 he set fire to a collective farm grain store. And taking into consideration your help in unmasking him, and the fact that you are the widow of a Finnish War hero and you have two children, and also your grief at the death of your youngest son and your losses from the robbery, it has been decided to offer you living accommodation with a job nearby. You can go to warehouse number 40 to register."

Warehouse number 40 was located in the town and the job there was in a warm place. Annushka's mother was delighted.

"Our thanks," she said, "to Comrade Stalin for his concern . . . Since I have children . . . the youngest died . . . and then we were robbed . . ."

First her joy turned to tears and then she started laughing again through her tears, since she had lived to see the back of the barracks building.

They gave her an apartment on the far side of Rzhev town, on the outskirts, not close to an airdrome, but beside a cemetery. The building used to be the cemetery church, but the church had been shut down not long before Annushka moved into it, and now her address was 61 Labor Street. The refurbishment work had been carried out hastily, in order to make the apartments available for people who needed them as soon as possible, so there were saints' faces peering out from the poorly whitewashed walls, and a poorly daubed Crucifixion of Christ showing through where the bedside locker stood and the radio loudspeaker hung. Annushka's mother papered over it with newspapers and on the newspapers she hung a portrait of Stalin. But the thick church walls were damp, the newspapers came unstuck and wrinkled up, and a half-length portrait of Christ appeared beside the half-length portrait of Stalin, so that they could have been taken for comrades-in-arms.

This church had been closed and the priest had been arrested because it had been determined that on the first Sunday of Lent an anti-Soviet meeting had been organized under the guise of the Orthodox feast and the veneration of icons. Supposedly the miraculous icon of the Rzhev Mother of God, an image not made by human hands, had appeared here and the municipal department of health had asserted that people had not only kissed it, but also scraped paint off it onto their food and clothing, which encouraged the spread of infection. The refurbishment office, which was experiencing difficulties in getting accommodation approved for occupation, immediately drew up an estimate for the cost of refurbishment work at the church and this estimate proved to be rather low, just for removing the icon screen, demolishing the altar and various minor construction jobs . . . Only a few months later, the first Stakhanovites moved into the former church, now a new apartment building at 61 Labor Street, beside the cemetery. Even though the walls here were rather damp, and even though they turned moldy in summer, and were covered with hoarfrost in winter, and even though the chimneys, constructed in careless haste, smoked badly and made the walls sweat, nonetheless those walls did protect people from the bitter cold and the wind better than the stuccoed planking of the barracks buildings.

Annushka's mother, Annushka, liked it here, and Annushka herself liked it here, but Ivan-Mitya didn't reveal how he felt about the former church as compared with the barracks building, since he was taciturn by nature.

Their stolen property was never found and returned to them, but they managed to muddle through without it and acquired a few new things, since Annushka's mother was now an individual with responsibility for material assets, and she earned more at warehouse number 40 than on the building site at the airdrome.

And then, when they had more or less started feeling at home and had even bought Annushka a winter coat with a quilted lining, a man showed up and announced that he wanted to examine the murals on the walls and the place where the altar and the icon screen used to stand. Once again Annushka was alone and once again she was frightened of being beaten, so she sat down on a chair with a sinking feeling and kept her mouth shut, although the man didn't make her do anything of the kind.

This man was Dan, the Viper, the Antichrist. The earthly years had aged him and he had learned to talk to people without feeling any inward repugnance, which is beyond the ability of the heavenly angels, only the prophets are capable of it, and even so not all of them, and not always. Dan knew that to love a human being meant overcoming his repugnance for them. However in their moments of weakness, not even the great prophets had been able to conceal their repugnance for people. This was the case with Moses in the period between the first and second sets of the tablets of the law, after he smashed the first set of tablets in his anguish at having to devote his sublimely exalted heart to such ignoble beings, who preferred the fleshpots of Egyptian slavery to manna from heaven in free Sinai, and this also happened to Dan's brother Jesus from the tribe of Judah, who constantly felt repugnance for his own apostles, that spiritual rabble he had chosen, not out of his own desire, but out of necessity, and who were incapable of spiritual insight into this usurper's audacious plan to save his own people, which was just as perverse as all other peoples, and by saving it realize God's Great Design . . . It also happened to Elisha, who, piqued by the offences that people committed against him, decided that he must become a prophet and impudently requested of the prophet Elijah:

"Let there be a double portion of your spirit on me." And Elijah replied to him:

"You have asked a hard thing; yet if you see me as I am being taken from you, it shall be so for you, but if you do not see me, it shall not be so . . ."

What happened thereafter inspired a Russian poet of Pushkin's time, Yazykov, and the grandeur of this passage in the Bible and the grandeur of Yazykov's youthful inspiration were celebrated by Gogol in "Selected Passages from Correspondence with Friends." Gogol wrote that in the following poem Yazykov had excelled himself in conveying the sublimity of his theme. And indeed, here Yazykov's hand acquires a robust, entirely Pushkinesque vigor:

When, in blazing flame and sounding thunder,
The prophet made his swift ascent on high,
A powerful, invigorating fire
Into Elisha's soul did enter.
Thus fervent genius doth rejoice,
Perceiving its own potent grandeur
In the flight of another genius,
Flaming and thundering in splendor.

As Elijah "ascended on high in blazing flame and sounding thunder," his spirit entered into Elisha, who set out from Jericho to Bethel, no longer a baldheaded man, whom people scorned and spurned, but a prophet. Adults were now afraid to mock and laugh at him, but children, who lack the necessary reason to conceal their cruelty, also lack the necessary reason to fear their own evil-doing. And this is why, in human rebellion, in human anarchy, in human totalitarianism, there is always puerile play, and a puerile society is always a totalitarian society. The Lord does not show partiality for either the great or the lowly, in the sight of the Lord all are equal, and the Lord punishes childish cruelty and childish malice. However, he punishes it at a mature age, when the punishment is especially severe. As he walked to Bethel, Elisha was not yet fully cognizant of the prophetic genius within him, he had not yet surmounted his repugnance for cruel people still in their early childhood. "And while he was going up on the way, some small boys came out of the city and jeered at him, saying, 'Go up, you baldhead! Go up, you baldhead!' And he turned around, and when he saw them, he cursed them in the name of the Lord. And two she-bears came out of the woods and tore forty-two of the boys."

The prophet Isaiah said:

"If a wicked man does not incur punishment, he will not learn righteousness."

The wise King Solomon replied:

"The righteousness that dies punishes the evildoers who live on."

The Lord only rarely kills an evildoer in the presence of the truth, more often he kills the truth in the presence of the evildoer, and then one evildoer sinks his teeth into another's throat. In killing the cruel children, Elisha punished the evildoers wrongly, for they should have been punished at a mature age, when their appetite for life had also matured. Such occurrences result from those moments of weakness of the soul, when even a prophet finds it impossible to conceal his repugnance for a human being and postpone the punishment for his sins.

And this same thing occurred with Dan, the Viper, the Antichrist here on the streets of Rzhev. On many occasions during his earthly life in the Kharkiv region and in Kerch and in Rzhev Dan the Antichrist had overheard malicious words spoken behind his back, sometimes in a whisper, but sometimes more loudly, when a man's tongue had been loosened by drink. At first he thought these people had guessed that he was the Antichrist, sent for malediction. And then he had supposed that they hated the tribe of Dan, having learned of the prophesies of Jeremiah concerning the Antichrist, who was destined to emerge from this tribe. But eventually he realized that they hated all the Twelve Tribes of Israel equally: Reuben, the first son of Jacob, and Simeon, and Levi, from whose tribe the great prophet Moses emerged, together with all the Levite priests, and Judah, the begetter of the psalmist David, and the wise Solomon, and Jesus from the tribe of Judah, whom they depicted in pagan images in their churches, and then prayed to those images, and Ephraim and Manasseh, the sons of Joseph the Fair, and the tribe of Benjamin, from which the martyr prophet Jeremiah emerged, and Zebulun, and Issachar, and Gad, and Asher, and Naphtali . . . All Twelve Tribes were hated equally. And then Dan, the Antichrist realized that evildoers would only receive their punishment at a mature age, when they had perceived the value of God's world, and if they completely failed to comprehend it before the grave, then God's punishment awaited them after the grave . . . However in moments of weakness both Christ and the Antichrist sometimes act in a manner contrary to the intention of the Lord who sent them and implement God's will prematurely . . .

One day, as he walked along a street in Rzhev, Dan overtook a certain individual wearing a baggy, drooping, unbuttoned, rust-colored coat . . . Everything he was wearing that had buttons was unbuttoned: the jacket, some kind of knitted waistcoat and the shirt, but there weren't any buttons on the blue undershirt, so it could not possibly be unbuttoned, and therefore it had been torn open. This individual had an unexceptional kind of face, but each of its commonplace features was rendered distinctive by virtue of being exaggerated to such an extent that it became a symbol. His hair was light brown, tinged with gray, but it stuck out in straggly clumps, the hollowness of his cheeks was emphasized by two longitudinal furrows and gray stubble, the northern eyes had faded to a faint, watery blue, the standard Slavic nose was adorned with a multitude of red, threadlike veins, and the lips, entirely unexceptional in their form, were so thickly caked with dried spittle and mucus, that you could not help but shudder at the thought of any woman happening to kiss them. As Dan was overtaking this individual he suddenly glanced at Dan's face and seemed to recognize him. An agonized spasm of hatred contorted that foul face to its utmost extreme, parting the bloodless lips glued together by mucus and spittle so that the man's speech mingled with the fetid stench of his decrepit innards as he gasped out words at Dan's back, straining them through the putrescent colander of his yellow teeth:

"Ugh, a Yid, I hate 'em . . . Yid . . ."

The simple Russian man does not always pronounce this word in this way, but only when he is at absolute rock bottom. The simple Russian man more often pronounces the word "Yid" as if he is biting into a succulent apple, he pronounces it with relish, with a crunch. The word "Jew" is also rather good for gargling with, if your throat is either hoarse with fury or clogged with rejoicing. And yet the word "Jew" can by no means be compared with the word "Yid" . . . The word "Jew" lacks the concise, artistic acuity that distinguishes a glass of vodka from a mug of kvass. A gulp of kvass is good on a hot day, but only as incidental support and not for the basic foundation . . . The cultured Russian thinker will most often transform the word

"Yid" into an adjective, into a characterization of phenomena and events. In the cultured Russian individual's tradition "Yiddishesque" is more frequent than "Yid," and moreover it is a sonorous word, with three melodious notes.

He articulates the phrase "a Yiddishesque idea," and it is as if he has followed a shot of vodka with a bite of hazel grouse and wiped his full, luscious lips with a crisply starched napkin.

But it was a long time since the certain individual who encountered Dan had wiped his fossilized lips, reeking of fusel oil, on his greasy sleeve, for he was truly at rock bottom. And he uttered those words in a state of desperate unreason:

"Ugh, a Yid, I hate 'em . . . Yid . . ."

And then Dan's heart yielded to provocation, just as the prophet Elisha's heart yielded to provocation and he punished the cruel, wicked children on the road from Jericho to Bethel prematurely, contrary to God's plan, and therefore inadequately. As Jeremiah foretold, Dan set a stumbling block in that certain individual's way. The wretched state of the sidewalks in Rzhev and good 1941-batch grain vodka helped with this. The individual did not fall forward, face-down, smashing and bloodying his forehead and his nose, or on his side, breaking his arm, but backward, striking the back of his skull against a cobblestone and dying, thereby reducing by the very merest of trifles the magnitude of the multitudinous and far-flung Slavic tribe. The certain individual did not utter another word, his final word was "Yid," and instantly, with this word still on his lips, he appeared before the Lord, who asked no questions before dispatching him directly to a cauldron of boiling oil, where he was treated disrespectfully and cruelly flogged on his ribs, already so gaunt and emaciated after the Revolution and Five-Year Plans. Here below on earth, the poor fellow's fellow-tribesmen gathered round him, attempting to wash the back of the injured man's head with a little water brought in the empty milk can of a peasant woman who happened to be walking by on her way from the market, until the arrival of free, socialist medical assistance. Perhaps one of his fellow-tribesmen might have heard this drunken man shout out "Yid" to some Jew or other passing by, but so what? And how do you tell the difference between Rabinovich from the haberdashery kiosk and the Antichrist, sent by the Lord for malediction? They are all children of the same father, although with different mothers, which is why every one of them shares a common beginning, but they have no common ending.

The certain individual was buried two days later and the Antichrist came to watch the funeral. And Annushka also came to watch, since she lived beside the cemetery and every day she waited for the music to begin. In this world the certain individual was called Pavlik, that is Paul, like the Apostle Paul from the tribe of Benjamin, the first Jewish convert to Christianity on earth. Of course, when Paul was still a persecutor of Christians, he was called Saul, and it was only later that he started being called Paul, of which he was extremely proud, as he was proud of his Roman citizenship, and he was an extremely fervent Christian, even though he had never seen Christ alive. Our certain individual, however, had been called Pavlik from birth. There had been a moment when, at the insistence of his godfather, he had almost been named Vasya (that is, Vasilii,) but in the end he had been named Pavlik after all.

The might-have-been Vasya and actual Pavlik was seen off on his way to the accompaniment of the railroad workers' club brass band, since he used to work in the Rzhev railroad workshops, possessing as he did the proud status of a hereditary proletarian and, in later times, of an incurable alcoholic. And no sooner had he acquired the status of an incurable alcoholic than he started singing in public the renowned Russian ditty "Beat the Yids and Save Russia," which is best performed in the tenor range, and Pavlik had a genuine tenor voice.

Although even to this day this little ditty is regarded as a ballad of the people, nonetheless, like many popular folk songs, it did have an author once. And that author was Markov the Second, the State Duma deputy for Kursk city. But like many popular songs that the people had taken up, it had shed its specific authorial attribution long ago and stood the test of time. And so Pavlik used to croon this little ditty in his tenor voice.

Pavlik used to be summoned to the workshops' union committee and reprimanded for his residual vestiges of the old regime. Especially after he started skipping work. His wife used to weep:

"You'll die at the bottom of a fence, no one will come to help you."

"Ah," Pavlik exclaimed, gesturing with one hand, "if I die, at least they can make me into sausage . . ."

But when Pavlik died in an accident, people did come, in fact there was quite a numerous crowd. With wreaths. They carried the coffin to the far end of the cemetery, where there were fewer crosses, and more graves with little stars. And they set a little star, not a cross, on Pavlik's grave, so that even in the next world he would remain under the aegis of the Soviet regime.

The proletarian folk from the railroad workshops did not know what Dan, the Viper, the Antichrist knew. In the next world Pavlik had ended up in an apolitical cauldron of tar, and his last word, "Yid," had stuck to his lips in the form of hot tar, and was chafing his mouth with its sharp edges. The other sinners in this cauldron, who were also suffering eternal torment, already hated Pavlik for his excruciating, piglet-like, tenor squeal of "Yid." That pain never abates even for a second, and Pavlik's agonized shriek never falls silent even for a second. But here, down below, where the sky is like the eyes of northern Slavs, Pavlik's body lay quietly in a red coffin.

It was early spring in the year 1941 after the birth of Dan's brother Jesus from the tribe of Judah. In the Kharkiv region and even in Kursk, the snow was already melting in the afternoon sunshine, but in Rzhev the winter had not even begun to falter. The snow lay steadfast and motionless on the graves, the branches of the cemetery trees were devoid of life and the mourners breathed out swirling eddies of steam. Dan the Antichrist glanced round, looking at the face of the dead man and the faces of the living, and recalled one of Moses' early commandments:

"If a thief is found breaking in and is struck so that he dies, there shall be no bloodguilt for him, but if the sun has risen on him, there shall be bloodguilt for him . . ."

This was one of the numerous Biblical commandments composed in a manner that is not entirely clear. The Biblical style avoids excessive clarity, for what is unduly clear is a slogan. There are commandments that require a significant effort and there are commandments that require only a minor effort, like this one. However, there is not a single commandment that can be gulped down without any effort at all. Here is the exposition: a thief surprised in the daytime, it says in the commandment, is entitled to lenience, but the alliance of a thief and the night excludes any right to compassion.

Dan looked and he thought: "The sun is shining, but the people around me have night-time faces." And he understood this to mean: "They shall bear bloodguilt for their own selves . . ."

And at that very moment the Antichrist saw in the crowd a sharp-eyed girl, completely unlike Maria, whom he had met in the Kharkiv region, and with whom near Kerch he had been stricken with the third of the Lord's plagues, the beast of fornication . . . Although she did not resemble Maria, she reminded him of Maria, and the Antichrist started watching her. He followed Annushka into the cemetery church, and saw that the church had been transformed into living accommodation. Then he asked if he could take a look at the places where the altar and the murals had been . . .

These murals nauseated him, for they violated a sacred principle, the second commandment of the Law of the Prophet Moses. As a Jew, he knew that denial of God is inherent in any symbol of God. And also that this denial had already begun during the persecution of the Christians, in the catacombs, where they had depicted an emaciated Alexandrian monk on the walls, under the name of Jesus Christ from the tribe of Judah, foretold by the prophet Isaiah. Moreover, for them the very name "Judas" (from "Judah," meaning "praised") was a curse, for they were not merely hostile, but also alien, and that which is not comprehended always has a categorical meaning, mechanically learned by rote and pronounced by the lips, but not by the reason, in the way that speaking birds pronounce human words . . . Judas was cursed, but Jesus Christ was also considered dubious if they could not constantly see his image, which they themselves had created.

"Seek the image of Christ in His words, recorded in the Gospels," the most rational fathers of the church advised those who doubted. But with their alien national worldview, in their hearts the founders of the religion could only believe in something that was alien to them if their eyes saw something that was their own. Dan, the Viper, the Antichrist knew where such believing with the eyes led.

In the same way as here in the Rzhev cemetery church, it was possible everywhere to paper over old icons and idols with newspapers and put up new icons and new idols. For what people saw before their eyes was what they believed in, and what they did not see, they did not believe in, as the old folk saying has it: "What the eye sees not, the heart craves not." And the longer people see the same thing in front of them, the more they believe in it. It was no accident that images of the fat, mustachioed Assyrian bathhouse attendant, who had taken the place of the emaciated Alexandrian monk, were hanging everywhere before the eyes of these people. Here too, hanging beside the papered-over image of the Alexandrian Greek, was an image of the mustachioed Assyrian . . . But spiritual faith in the Self-Existent cannot be papered over with newspapers and attempts to replace Him with an Assyrian bathhouse attendant would fail, just as the attempt made in the desert of Sinai to replace Him with a golden calf had failed.

While Dan, the Viper, the Antichrist was thinking this, Annushka sat there terrified, waiting for him to open the wardrobe, pull out all the drawers and start taking all their newly acquired belongings, including Annushka's brand new coat with a quilted lining. However despite the strange feeling she had, Annushka kept furtively glancing at this man, thinking that when they lined everybody up after the robbery, and led her along the line, she would be able to recognize the thief without making a mistake. Annushka watched and watched and then suddenly, through the window, she saw her mother walking toward the building along the path past the cemetery, leading Annushka's brother Mitya by the hand. Her mother's face had a mournful expression, so she had probably been to visit Vova's little grave, since now they lived with that little mound of earth close by and she could visit Vova's grave every day. Annushka was delighted when she saw her mother and she mastered her fear, jumped up off the chair and ran out to meet her mother, shouting:

"A thief, there's a thief in our home . . ."

Her mother started shouting too, prompted by the bitter experience of the previous robbery. Fortunately, the people living in the church building were far more civic-minded than the people in the workers' barracks building, since only the best had been given accommodation here, in accordance with their hard-earned labor entitlements. They promptly gathered round to help another person in distress. There wasn't an armed militiaman nearby, but one of these Stakhanovites had been awarded a hunting rifle as a special bonus and he brought it with him. Before Dan even realized what was happening, a dense crowd had blocked his way out of the section of the church building that was divided off by wooden partitions to form a room. The people gazed at Dan with gleeful hatred, in the way that people usually gaze at weak enemies. This gaze of gleeful hatred is precisely the gaze of an antisemite in his finest moments, when he pronounces the word "Yid" as if he is eating a ripe apple.

"We were robbed only recently, and now again," Annushka's mother lamented, "thank you, daughter, for staying calm and keeping your wits about you."

"And they say they only steal in trade, but otherwise they're honest," someone said.

"We should stuff him in an envelope with stamps stuck on his backside," said the Stakhanovite who had been awarded a hunting rifle as a bonus and was holding it at the ready.

They people tried to close in around Dan the Antichrist as they had once closed in around his brother Jesus from the tribe of Judah. For they were the very same people, and Dan the Antichrist knew this about them, although they did not know this about themselves. However Dan had not been sent for blessing, but for cursing, not for their sake, but against them, and therefore they could not lay a hand on him. The crowd abruptly parted into two, neighbors standing together were parted, husbands and wives standing together were parted, Annushka and her mother were parted . . . And when they came together again, the Antichrist was no longer in the room, he was already far away from Labor Street, although still within the bounds of Rzhev town. Afterward the people said many things. Some said that the bandit had been holding a knife, others said it was a Mauser pistol, and yet others actually said it was a kulak's sawn-off shotgun. But since no belongings had been stolen the incident was somehow quickly forgotten, especially since they all felt embarrassed in front of each other about what had happened during the attempted arrest. And after leaving the church that was defiled by both old and new pagan images, Dan, the Viper, the Antichrist found himself on the far side of Rzhev, on the outskirts of the town in the vicinity of the airdrome, near the workers' barracks building that Annushka had lived in until recently.

Evening was falling, but here there was no evening hush, as there is in the fields when the sun sets during winter. The falling of evening was accompanied by the roaring and growling of aeroengines and the quivering of the frosty air. And once again Dan saw the sword that he had first seen near Kerch, when it clove the bloody clouds above an ensanguined sea. This time the sword's hilt was set against the evening sun, while its sharp edge ran off and away to disappear beyond the snowy roofs of the western outskirts of Rzhev town, and the snow on the roofs was the color of arterial blood. And Dan, the Viper, the Antichrist heard the words spoken by the Lord through the prophet Ezekiel:

"Woe to the bloody city, to the pot whose corrosion is in it, and whose corrosion has not gone out of it! Take out of it piece after piece, without making any choice. For the blood she has shed is in her midst; she put it on the bare rock; she did not pour it out on the ground to cover it with dust. To rouse my wrath, to take vengeance, I have set on the bare rock the blood she has shed, that it may not be covered. Therefore thus says the Lord God: Woe to the bloody city! I also will build a great fire."

Following these words the sun sank and the vision of the sword and the blood disappeared. Dan, the Viper, the Antichrist walked along a street lit by sparsely sited streetlamps on the outskirts of Rzhev town, past the calm evening light in the windows of houses, with the dry, frosty snow crunching under his feet, and he disappeared from sight at the spot where the wall of the recently built milk processing plant began. Passersby are rare in the outskirts of Rzhev town at that hour, and it was a long time before a new passerby appeared, wearing a quilted jacket and quilted felt boots with high galoshes pulled on over them.

However Dan's vision did not come to pass immediately, only when Annushka had long ago taken off her favorite red felt boots and was expecting the circus to arrive soon. Suddenly Annushka heard all the grown-ups saying:

"War, war . . . The Germans, the Germans . . ." But at first nothing changed for Annushka because of this, and her mother also told one of their neighbors:

"There can't be any great changes for me, my Kolya was killed in the Finnish War."

Throughout June there were no changes, except that the circus didn't come. But in July the changes began. One day Annushka's mother came home from warehouse number 40 very preoccupied about something and said:

"Come on, children, let's pack up our things. We're leaving here and being evacuated to Kleshnevo village, seven kilometers away."

They hurriedly gathered their things together, packing the red felt boots and the coat with a quilted lining in case they had to spend the winter in Kleshnevo. And then they locked their room. They walked all day in the heat to get to Kleshnevo, only sitting down a couple of times to have a rest and a bite to eat.

"We have to hurry, children," their mother said, "to get a good place to stay, before all the others arrive."

They reached Kleshnevo early in the evening, and they were put in the school, but Annushka saw that there were lots of other people there and no one was glad to see their mother, or Annushka, or Mitya . . .

They lived in Kleshnevo as if they were in a train, always watching their bundles, and when their reserves of food ran out, they immediately started feeling hungry. So Annushka was glad and Mitya was glad when their mother said:

"Let's go back home to Rzhev town. It's almost September, time for you to go to school."

The walk back to Rzhev took less time than the walk when they left it and they felt less tired. They were delighted when they found everything at home safe and sound and decided that things would be easier now.

And it was certainly better at home than in Kleshnevo village, despite the war. Their mother went back to work at warehouse number 40, and they were better fed. Not as well as before the war, of course, but still better.

In the evening of the last day of August their mother told them:

"You're going to school tomorrow, children, let's put your books in your briefcases, so you won't have to look for them in the morning and won't be late for the first lesson."

No sooner did they start gathering the books together than they heard a rumbling sound from somewhere. The last time there had been a rumbling like that was during the powerful thunderstorm in which little Vova had died. Annushka was frightened and her mother grabbed hold of Mitka's hand in alarm.

"Let's run to the vegetable garden," she said, "we'll lie down between the ridges."

Since there was a vacant lot beside the cemetery, the authorities had allowed the Stakhanovites living in the former cemetery church to cultivate private vegetable plots there. Annushka saw that some of the Stakhanovites, who hadn't been evacuated in time, were also lying in the vegetable garden, huddling down between the ridges of earth. Just at that moment there was a really loud crash close by in the cemetery. And then another one. White smoke started creeping around and there was a sudden smell of burned fried eggs. Annushka started crying, but the Stakahnovite who had been given a hunting rifle as a special bonus comforted her:

"Never mind, little girl," he said, "don't be afraid. Soviet power isn't done for yet."

After the shelling Annushka went back home with her mother and Mitka and none of them slept all night long. There were trucks and carts moving about, they could hear people talking and Soviet power carried on existing until morning came. But with the morning German power arrived.

"Children," their mother said, "stay at home, don't go outside."

But German power didn't wait for Annushka and Mitka to go outside: it came into their house, tramping along the corridor in a way that wasn't Russian, and immediately set to work behind a wooden partition, immediately set about overcoming someone's resistance, and easily overcame it, since might was on its side. Annushka was afraid, so afraid that she actually felt curious and glanced out into the corridor. Annushka hadn't lived very long, but she had seen people being beaten many times, since she lived in a country where people were often beaten. Of course, on most of these occasions she hadn't seen someone beaten bloody, but she had even seen that a couple of times . . . The superintendent of the workers' barracks houses had struck the man she pointed out as a thief so hard that he bled, and she had seen little brats fight so fiercely in front of her that they drew blood. Annushka also knew how much it hurt to be slapped hard, and she still remembered how hard her mother had punched her when Annushka failed to keep an eye on Vova and he died . . . But Annushka had never even suspected it was possible to beat a man as hard as the Germans were beating the Stakhanovite whose heroic labor achievements had been rewarded by the Soviet authorities with a hunting rifle. There was absolutely no question here of bloodshed being avoided, it was as if someone had been carrying a basin full of blood along the corridor in the way that housewives carry a basin of soapy water after doing the laundry, then stumbled in the darkness and spilled the blood across the floor. The Germans struck each new blow with increasing revulsion, and therefore with reduced vehemence, since their boots were getting soiled with blood. And they walked round the body spreadeagled in the corridor in the way that people walk across a muddy field in the fall or spring, skipping from tussock to tussock. And then a German dressed in non-Russian style said something to a man dressed in a short cotton jacket from the Rzhev department store. And without even knocking, that man jerked open the door that Annushka was standing behind and shouted to her mother:

"Hey you, you Stalinist whore, get out here . . ."

Annushka immediately started crying and clung on tight to her mother, and Mitka clung onto her too, and then, in a revelatory flash of archetypal Slavic kindheartedness, the Polizei told their mother:

"Don't be afraid, they won't touch you. The commissar here has to be carried and the German gentlemen are too fastidious, since he's all bloody."

Annushka's mother and another woman who lived there lifted up the Stakhanovite and carried him away. His wife and children had been evacuated, but he had stayed behind, shipping out factory equipment . . . At first the Germans ordered the women to carry him to a cart, but halfway there they changed their minds and told them to carry him to the cemetery. The carrying of the Stakhanovite mutilated by the Germans' boots was supervised by the Polizei in the cheap, mass-produced cotton jacket.

"Carry him as far as you can, ladies," said the Polizei, "that will be best for you . . . So he won't be stinking right in front of the building."

Annushka's mother and the neighbor carried the Stakhanovite past the pre-revolutionary railings and past the beggarly crosses, and they also walked past the little grave in which Vova was buried, which had a headstone. They carried the Stakhanovite to the Soviet graves with stars and halted not far from a grave with a star that was still fresh, in which lay Pavlik, who had been killed by the Antichrist and died with the word "Yid" on his lips.

"Dump him," said the Polizei dressed in a jacket from the Rzhev department store and armed with a Russian "three-line" Mosin rifle that had a Russian three-edged rod bayonet, of the kind widely celebrated in song, attached to it.

However Annushka's mother and the neighbor didn't simply drop the Stakhanovite, but set him down gently on the cemetery grass, with his head resting on Pavlik's grave, as if on a pillow.

"And now go," said the Polizai.

No sooner did Annushka's mother and the neighbor woman turn to walk away, than they heard behind their backs a short, sharp "thwack," like the sound usually made by peasants chopping firewood, followed by a short sobbing sound. Annushka's mother and the neighbor-woman started walking faster, but even so the Polizei very soon overtook them, wiping down his bloody bayonet with a handful of grass.

"The don't give us enough cartridges," he complained guilelessly, "it's a captured Russian gun and the cartridges are captured too, they're hard to come by." And then, seeing that the women didn't answer him, he added angrily: "Make sure everything's washed and swept clean today. The Germans will be billeted here with you, understand?"

And their life under German rule began. New Germans replaced preceding Germans endlessly. Some were cruel, others were more humane. The Germans usually arrived early in the evening, to stay for the night. The cruel ones drove Annushka's mother and Annushka and Mitya outside with kicks. The humane ones drove them out without kicks. In the beginning Annushka's mother and Annushka and Mitya spent the night in the street, although in Rzhev the September nights were cold. Luckily for them, there wasn't any rain, but what would happen when the rainy weather started? Annushka's mother tried knocking on the doors of nearby buildings and asking to be let in, but everybody was afraid because they thought they were Jews, and the Germans were looking for Jews. And when Annushka's mother lifted Mitya up to the window to show that they were Russians, the people still wouldn't let them in anyway, because they might be a communist's family, or a partisan's . . . However they managed to find a kindhearted old woman who did let them in, and after that, every time the Germans came to their overnight billet and drove them out, they went to the old woman's home for the night, and even moved their bedding and pillows there. In the morning the Germans went away, and Annushka's mother, Annushka and Mitya went back to their home and didn't recognize it . . . And there was that German stink, the inimitable stink of peas . . . Even when the cold, frosty weather set in, they had to open the windows as wide as possible . . . All day Annushka's mother washed and cleaned, and Annushka helped her, and Mitya brought water, then the Germans arrived at their night billet again . . . It should be noted that, apart from everything else, Annushka's mother was afraid the Germans might find out about the portrait of Stalin that she had carefully wrapped in one of her deceased husband Kolya's old shirts, and concealed among the Soviet graves at the far end of the cemetery. But no one knew, no one made any inquiries and Annushka's mother stopped worrying. She tore the newspapers off the walls and exposed the old church murals, because she had heard that the Germans respected God. However, one day in the course of an especially frenzied rampage fueled by schnapps, the Germans scribbled all over the saints' faces with charcoal, drew a six-pointed star on the crucified Christ's forehead and wrote the words "Judische Schwein" (Jewish pig) on his face . . . Annushka's mother was afraid to clean this off and she told Annushka and Mitya not to touch it . . .

They were very hungry, barely even surviving. Sometimes Annushka's mother would bring some beets, or carrots, or potatoes from somewhere or other. One day Mitya made friends with a boy in the street and the boy said to him:

"You know where the army barracks used to be? There are lots of our men there now, behind the barbed wire. Let's go and ask them for bread."

Annushka said:

"Don't go, Mitya, it's dangerous, the Germans will beat you and they could kill you."

Mitya did go and he came back alive, but without any bread.

"We ask them for bread," he said, "and they ask us for bread."

And that very day Annushka's mother didn't bring anything.

"What are we going to eat?" Annushka thought.

Then one day, in the evening, the Germans showed up as usual for their overnight billeting. Annushka's mother dressed Mitya in his coat, and put on her own coat, and Annushka started buttoning up her coat with a quilted lining, but one German said:

"Nein, nein . . . No, no," as if he was telling them to stay. Annushka's mother was bewildered, but the German smiled and took out a photograph.

"Kinder," he said, "my little child . . . Zwei . . . Also two . . . I speak a little Russian."

And after that he took out two dry rusks and gave one to Annushka, and the other to Mitya. And he took out a third rusk and gave it to Annushka's mother. This German took a particular liking to Annushka.

"Gut, gut," he said, "you should learn German . . . I am a teacher . . ."

This German didn't leave the next morning and Annushka's mother was glad he stayed. He lived with Annushka's mother and Annushka and Mitya for almost a week, and Annushka's mother grew attached to him, and Annushka also grew attached to him, only Mitya acted warily with him. This German was called Hans and he was the first German in many months who would pass on to them a piece of bread, or a piece of pork fat, or a small amount of pea concentrate. This German never spat, he didn't blow his nose onto the floor, and he ate tidily. After eating, he would take a spool of thread out of his pocket, break off a piece and start using it to clean the remnants of meat and peas off his teeth. After the cleaning he burped once, then once more, and called Annushka, to teach her German. Annushka quickly picked up a lot of words and learned to count: ein, zwei, drei . . .

"Brot," said the German, "bread . . . Anna mit Grossvater gehen schpazieren . . . Anna goes for a stroll with her grandfather . . ." He noticed the six-pointed star drawn on Christ's forehead, and the inscription in charcoal, written across Christ's face "Judische Schwein." "Judische Schwein," he said, and laughed, "Jewish pig."

"Judische Schwein," Annushka repeated jauntily. "Anna mit Grossvater gehen schpazieren . . . Ein, zwei, drei . . ."

However toward the end of the week Hans turned sad, and one morning he buttoned on his greatcoat, picked up his machine gun, put on his helmet and became an ordinary German, so that Annushka even felt frightened of him.

"War, war," he said sadly to Annushka's mother. "Rzhev bad, Cologne good." And he sighed. At that point he noticed Annushka looking at him in fright, as if he wasn't kind, jolly Uncle Hans, who fed her pork fat and taught her to speak German, but an ordinary German, who drove her outside with kicks. Then Hans smiled, winked at her, pointed at the six-pointed star crudely drawn in the middle of Christ's forehead and the inscription written across Christ's face. "Judische Schwein," he said.

"Judische Schwein," Annushka repeated, "Anna mit Grossvater gehen schpazieren . . . Haus—house, Vogel—bird, Katze—cat, Hund—dog."

"Gut, gut," Hans laughed, patted Annushka on her head once again, bowed to Annushka's mother and left, because they were calling to him from outside and making fun of him.

Early that evening new Germans arrived and one of them looked like Hans. Annushka's mother whispered to her that she should talk to the German in their language, which Hans had taught her, since while Hans had lived there for the last week, they had felt protected and a little bit of German food had come their way.

"Judische Schwein," said Annushka. "Anna mit Grossvater gehen schpazieren . . . Haus—house, Vogel—bird . . ."

The German laughed and just like Hans he said:

"Gut, gut . . ."

And straightaway, to make him feel even better disposed to them, Annushka's mother brought a basin of warm water for him to wash in and a clean towel to dry himself with. The German had a wash, then dried his hands and face, then looked at Annushka's mother and grabbed hold of her skirt below the waist. Annushka's mother squealed in fright, and then squealed again, because Mitya butted the German with his head so hard that he swayed on his feet. However before the German could hit Mitya, Annushka's mother hit Mitya herself, only not on his head, which the German was aiming at, but on his backside. And as she hit Mitya, she shielded him from the infuriated German with her back. And so the German didn't hit Mitya, he just drove them all outside, as the other Germans before Uncle Hans used to do.

In the morning, Annushka's mother said:

"Children, you stay here, and I'll go home and wait until the Germans leave, and take what I can of our things . . . We'll go to Agarkovo village, I have a cousin there, perhaps we can find a place with her."

Their mother set off to go back home, praying for the Germans to leave, since now that there were no more Soviet authorities, there was no one left that she could appeal to except God. And her request was granted: the Germans came out, got into a truck, and drove away. Annushka's mother immediately went to their room. Of course, everything there was smashed, covered in trash and soaked with urine. But the clean towel that Annushka's mother had given to the German was still lying in the middle of the bed. Annushka's mother grabbed hold of this clean towel, and it was heavy. Inside it was a heap of the firm, healthy Aryan shit that can serve, in combination with cranial measurements, to characterize the Aryan race. It cannot possibly be confused with Slavic shit, and especially not with the Jewish variety. On this occasion, however, the German had not wrapped his German shit in a Russian towel so that its racial purity could be analyzed, but for the purposes of German pig-meat humor, a full-blooded humor which, in his opinion, contrasted quite distinctly with chicken-livered, tubercular Jewish irony. Only the most gifted of Slavs were capable of appreciating the German spirit: however Annushka's mother, who was also Annushka, did not belong to the finest elements of her race, she did not feel that she was an Aryan and, unlike a certain well-known 19th-century Russian literary figure, was not bent on achieving Aryan unity from the Urals to the Rhine. Her life reflected only her own vulgar interests, and now she quickly grabbed those of her belongings that came to hand.

Soon afterwards Annushka's mother, Annushka and Mitya were trudging across a snow-covered field to Agarkovo village. Not walking, but trudging, since they were carrying things. However the first place they arrived at was not Agarkovo village, but Kleshnevo village again, and again no one there was glad to see them. They were let in to spend the night, but not given anything to eat, since the people there didn't have anything for themselves. In the morning the family walked on to Grigorievna village. Here Annushka's mother managed to beg a small amount of frozen boiled potatoes. They weren't allowed into the house, since the people were afraid of typhoid-carriers, but the potatoes were brought out into the yard in a newspaper. It was only as the evening of the next day was drawing in that they arrived at Agarkovo village. Agarkovo village was small, with only about ten houses, no more than that, but it was quiet here, the Germans had only been here once, and had only passed through.

Although Annushka's mother's cousin was not very glad to see them, she let them in and fed them. Annushka, her mother and Mitya started living in Agarkovo village. They lived there through the winter, and through the spring, and in the summer, when it was already August, Agarkovo village was liberated by Soviet troops. Oh, the joy of it! Agarkovo village was small, and every small house was crammed to bursting with Soviet soldiers quartered or spending the night there.

Your own soldier stinks too, but the stench he gives off is familiar, not hostile. And it should also not be forgotten that Russians and the other inhabitants of Russia eat only a small amount of meat, with rather more grains and fermented foods. And therefore, although the stench is intense, it is not acrid. But a German's basic foods are dried peas and pork fat, and a German's stench is highly calorific and persistent . . .

And then disaster struck. As soon as the Soviet troops liberated Agarkovo village, Mitka came down with some kind of illness. His mother put him on a passing wagon, took him to the army doctors at the infirmary and told them she was the widow of a soldier who was killed in the Finnish War, and they took pity on her and kept Mitka in for treatment. After a few days Mitka started recovering, he even came out onto the porch to see his mother and Annushka, and he brought some of the bread they gave him so that he could eat as much as he wanted.

"Eat it," he said, "or else you'll croak . . ."

"But this new joy was once again negated by a new disaster. A large number of German planes suddenly swooped down on Agarkovo village in the night, and by morning there was nothing left of Agarkovo. The people who managed to escape took what they could with them into the forest. This forest was three kilometers away, and now there were Soviet troops positioned there. But in the forest the villagers lived separately from the soldiers, in their own village community, and Annushka, her mother and Mitka lived separately from the villagers, since they were regarded as outsiders.

Annushka and her mother lived in a dugout on a hillock, beside a little stream. In this dugout Mitya had a soft bed to lie on: to help him get well his mother had spread out all the clothes she had with her. And there was a cage hanging in this dugout, with a little bird in it that Annushka had found in the street when Agarkovo was bombed. No matter how loud the gunfire, screaming and children's crying was on all sides, the little bird started singing as soon as the sun appeared. Annushka came to love this little bird, and Mitya came to love this little bird too, in fact he absolutely doted on it. He took great pains to give it grass to lie on, sunflower seeds and fresh water . . . One day Annushka and her mother were mowing rye close by, and Mitya was lying in the dugout, listening to the little bird singing. Suddenly an artillery shell came flying in, followed immediately by another one that landed right beside the dugout. A cloud of smoke swirled up, but Annushka's mother didn't wait for the wind to blow the smoke away, she ran into the smoke to get to the dugout where Mitya was lying. And Annushka ran after her. Peering though the smoke they saw Mitya crawling out unharmed. But the dugout looked as if a plow had driven straight through it and the trees around it were scorched

When they looked again, they saw the cage lying on the ground, with the little bird lying dead in it . . . They felt sorry for the bird, remembering how it used to sing, but what could be done? Mitya said:

"I could tell it was coming my way and I climbed into the dugout and huddled up in a corner, thinking this was the end and everything was going to collapse . . ."

Quite soon afterward an army wagon arrived and took Annushka, her mother and Mitya deeper into the forest. Here in the forest Mitya recovered completely. But Annushka and her mother immediately fell ill . . . They lived in a shelter of fir-tree branches, but it was a poor shelter, since there was no one to build it properly. Annushka's mother became ill on the first day, and while she was still on her feet, she and Mitya tried to drag over a lot more branches, so that the shelter would be dry when the rainy weather set in. But Annushka wasn't able to help them at all, her head felt hot and too heavy to lift, and her arms and legs felt hot and heavy. Annushka and her mother spent several days lying there like that. Mitya supported them as well as he could: he brought them water and also rubbed ears of rye and hulled sunflower seeds, which he gave them to eat.

One morning they heard a red cross wagon from the infirmary driving around. Two female soldiers started walking round among the civilians, giving them vaccinations, and orderlies carried away the sick on stretchers and laid them on the wagon. They took Annushka's mother and Annushka, but they didn't take her brother.

"He's not ill," they said.

When the orderlies picked up Annushka's mother to carry her away, she told Mitya:

"Son, don't go anywhere, stay with the people. I'll come home soon, back to the shelter . . ."

Annushka heard her mother speak these words, but she didn't hear or remember anything after that. When Annushka next came round, she saw she was lying on a stretcher in a ward in a large tent. The moment she came round, she started shouting and calling for her mother and someone said to her:

"Don't shout, your mother's lying there beside you."

"Turn me on my side, I want to see my mother."

Annushka heard these words too, but she didn't hear anything else until she saw that she was lying on a floor covered in straw, with men and women she didn't know lying close together beside her, and a blue-faced man with his mouth open was jammed hard up against her . . . Annushka cried out, but without any words: it was just a shout. Someone said:

"Orderly, take out the ones who have died, how many times must we ask? . . ."

And then Annushka blacked out again. When she started recovering consciousness, she was lying in the same room with other people, only not on the floor, but on beds . . . Annushka immediately started crying and carried on crying until she saw her mother lying beside the opposite wall . . . And so it went on, every time Annushka came round, she cried until she saw her mother and calmed down when she saw her. But when Annushka saw her mother being put on a stretcher and taken away she started crying again, and they explained to her:

"Your mother's being transferred to the next ward . . . This one's only for typhus cases, but patients with dysentery aren't supposed to be here . . ."

"Where am I?" asked Annushka.

"This is a hospital," they explained.

"And what village is this?"

"It's not a village, it's a town," they explained. "It's called Pogoreloe Gorodishche."

Annushka heard this name and then she either fell asleep or blacked out, she couldn't tell which. She came round because she was being placed on a stretcher.

"Where are you taking me?" Annushka asked.

"We're transferring you to a different hospital," said an orderly. "It's not far away, only eighteen kilometers."

They carried Annushka through the ward where her mother was lying. Annushka saw her mother, burst into tears and started pleading:

"Put me with my mom . . ." And her mother told her:

"Don't be afraid, little daughter, I'll come for you soon."

And they carried Annushka away.

Annushka was in the other hospital for a long time, and she couldn't recall her illness very distinctly. She could only recall being discharged. It was fall already, with hoarfrost in the shade. Annushka was dressed in her winter coat with a quilted lining, but barefoot. To warm up her bare feet, she needed to walk fast, but she wasn't strong enough to walk fast. Annushka set off along the street and started pestering a boy who was there.

"Where are you going?"

"To Pogoreloe Gorodishche," he answered. "That's where I'm from."

Annushka was pleased to hear that.

"I want to go with you, I need to get there . . ."

"Come on then," said the boy. "I know the way . . . It's six kilometers to the forest, and another twelve kilometers after the forest."

They walked all day to reach the forest that was six kilometers away. A road had been cleared through the forest and this road was covered with small tree trunks, and over the tree trunks there was a layer of cold, muddy slush. Annushka stepped into this slush with her bare feet and thought: "I won't make it." But she walked on anyway. "I'll walk as far as that broken tree, but I won't be able to go any farther," Annushka thought. She reached the broken tree and carried on walking. But as she walked along she was still thinking: "I'll walk a little bit farther, and my body will turn completely numb, even though I'm wearing my winter coat. My feet don't belong to me anymore anyway. It's a mystery how they can carry me along." And then Annushka heard a cart approaching. The man on the cart saw that Annushka was barefoot, stopped his horses, climbed down, and put Annushka on the seat. And although he didn't let Annushka's companion, the boy, sit on the cart, because the whole cart was full of crates, he did help him to walk. And in that way they reached Pogoreloe Gorodishche town by nightfall.

In Pogoreloe Gorodishche Annushka walked up to some soldiers on patrol and they pointed out to her the way to the hospital. Annushka walked to the hospital and said to the people there:

"I'm looking for Emelyanova . . . I'm her daughter . . ."

One woman said to another:

"Emelyanova's in a very bad way . . ."

However for some reason Annushka didn't really grasp that her mother was in a bad way, she only understood that her mother was alive. Annushka walked into the ward and saw her mother still lying there in her coat and shawl. Annushka walked closer, and she didn't recognize her mother. She recognized her from a distance, but not from up close. As if it was her and not her at the same time. But Annushka's mother recognized her immediately and said:

"I couldn't come to you as I promised, little daughter, but I'll come soon . . ." And the nurse said:

"Go to the Farmworkers' House until morning, little girl, you can spend the night there."

The soldiers on patrol pointed out to Annushka the way to the Farmworkers' House and when she reached it she was let in for the night. Annushka was so tired that she fell asleep immediately on the floor beside the stove. When she woke up it was already morning. A soldier was standing over her, and he asked:

"Where are you from, little girl?"

"From Agarkovo village," Annushka replied.

"Then go to the commandant," said the soldier, "and he'll give you a travel document for any vehicle going your way."

The soldier gave Annushka some bread. Annushka ate the bread and went to a place pointed out to her by soldiers on patrol. She walked into the building, where there more soldiers. Annushka wasn't afraid of soldiers because, living in Rzhev, close to the airfield, she was used to having military men nearby all the time. Annushka went in to the soldiers, and some commanding officer there gave her a travel document for any vehicle going her way. When Annushka arrived back at the hospital the people told her:

"Emelyanova's a bit better."

Annushka showed her mother the document, and she said:

"Clever girl, my little daughter . . . Go home to the forest, Mitya's all alone there, you know . . . I'll get well soon, then I'll go to the commandant for a document too and I'll come . . ."

Annushka went to the road, but no one took her into their vehicle for a long time until she found some traffic controllers, showed them her document, and they put her in one. When Annushka arrived, she found the place in the forest where the village people lived . . . She saw that the fir-branch shelter had completely collapsed, their soaked belongings were just lying there and nobody was going near them.

"Your things are infected with typhus," people explained to her, "they don't need to be guarded, the lice are guarding them."

"And where's my brother?" Annushka asked.

"Your brother," they said, "cried for three days, then he went off to find the soldiers."

So Annushka didn't find her brother.

In the meantime the people moved back to their dugouts near devastated Agarkovo village for the winter. And Annushka went to live in the dugout of her mother's female cousin, who took her in rather grudgingly.

Annushka thought: "My mother will come and she'll soon find me here." However one day the cousin said to Annushka:

"Your mother has died . . ."

"Why is she saying that?" Annushka thought. "There's no mail and no telephone here, is there?" But all the same Annushka set out to find the road and went to Pogoreloe Gorodishche.

They wouldn't let her into the hospital, it was too early. So Annushka sat down on the porch, curled up into a tight ball to stay warm in the cold of morning and waited. The nurse raised her hopes:

"Emelyanova . . ." she said, "she ought to be in here." And she rummaged in a drawer containing documents. Then the nurse found a document and said: "Your mother died on October 7th, 1942."

And it was already October 13th . . . Annushka arrived back home in the forest with nothing . . . In the forest heavy snow had already fallen and none of the civilians were there. In her grief Annushka had forgotten that the villagers had moved to their dugouts for the winter. She wandered through the forest for a long time, but she didn't shout out or call for help, she walked quietly without saying a word. A soldier found her and took her to the dugouts. It was hard for Annushka to find a place in a dugout because they were all crowded, with two or three families in each one, and when she found a place she fell asleep, exhausted in her grief. In the morning she was woken by the sound of voices and she walked out of the dugout. Cold air, snow, wind. But now Annushka was wearing the ankle boots left by her mother. They were too big, but they kept her warm if she wrapped rags round her feet. Annushka saw an army wagon standing nearby, and all the villagers were being collected in it. Someone said:

"It's taking them to the train in Podgoreloe Gorodishche, for evacuation, because the Germans are advancing again."

They collected Annushka too, took her to Pogoreloe Gorodishche and put her on a train. Annushka didn't know if she traveled very far or for very long, she was feeling so wretched because her mother had died that she was in a daze. Suddenly, as if she was dreaming it, a bombardment began. Everything was burning and there were bullets flying everywhere. People were running. And Annushka ran too . . . The fires lit up the night as brightly as day and it was easy to find your way if this was your home territory. But this was foreign territory to Annushka and everything she came across was strange and unfamiliar. She ran into a house that was completely intact, but there was no ceiling. There was an undamaged stove standing in the house, with an icon in it. Then Annushka ran out and walked along the road, and she reached a big room, where there were a lot of women. It's good to walk on your own on your home territory, but in unfamiliar territory it's better when someone else leads you. A woman led Annushka away and brought her to another place. It was already morning, and quiet, with snow falling. A man came out of a house and Annushka was frightened because his right hand was clenched in a fist all the time. She only found out later that he was Kuzmin, the director of the orphanage and a war invalid: the fingers of his right hand had been twisted up into a fist forever by the blast of an explosion. Kuzmin took hold of Annushka's hand with his left hand, and led her into a room that was warm, with a jostling crowd of boys and girls in it, all dressed in the same orphanage style. And in addition many of the boys, especially the smaller ones, were dressed like girls, in dresses, because there weren't enough suits. The moment Annushka saw them, she knew she would be teased here, because all the children smiled at her with cheerful expressions, the way they used to do in Rzhev before the war.

Just like every family, every orphanage has its own customs. Here it was a time-honored custom to tease people and try to have fun. They were quick to think up a mocking nickname for Annushka, "crybaby," because Annushka sometimes huddled in a corner and wept for her mother and her brother Mitya . . .

It was actually a dark-complexioned little girl called Sulamith who had spied on Annushka and thought up the mocking nickname "crybaby," after which Annushka's life became unbearable.

This little girl had made such an effort to think up a mocking nickname for Annushka because before Annushka came the grownups and the children all used to tease her with the nickname "Jew girl." At first they had teased her as "Moscow smarty-pants," because she was from Moscow, and then they had started calling her "Jew girl," because she burred her r's. When this girl Mitha, (that is, Sulamith,) was first separated from her parents, she had been put in a different orphanage and no one there had teased her as "Jew girl," but here they had started teasing her like that almost straightaway. Of course, Kuzmin didn't tease her, but Kuzmin hadn't been there very long, he was considered an outsider and the children didn't respect him, but they loved their former director Aunty Katechka, who was now the housemistress, because she was cheerful, even though she was an invalid, a hunchback. When Sulamith cried at being teased and shouted that she would run away and find her mother, Aunty Katechka answered her:

"Where will you run to? If your parents were alive, they would have found you. Jews don't abandon their children . . ."

And Sulamith realized that she couldn't change anything. The children also didn't like Sulamith because she was always walking around looking for something on the ground, and she often found something. She found an apple, or some money, and in the kitchen they would give her something to eat for the money, or she found a little tin soldier.

"That Jew girl's lucky," they used to say about her, "she's lucky all the time, always finding something."

True, there was one pale-skinned girl called Glashenka, who wanted to be friends with Sulamith. This little girl, Glashenka, had been brought to the orphanage by her own mother. Glashenka didn't want to stay, even though they gave her a big apple. She cried and tore her mother's dress. Then they called her into the hall and started playing the piano, Glashenka started listening, and in the meantime her mother left.

Well, this little girl, Glashenka, wanted to be friends with Sulamith, but Sulamith didn't want to be friends with her. Glashenka hugged Sulamith, kissed her and said:

"I want to be your sister . . . Why don't you want to play with me, we're both orphans, after all . . ." Sulamith answered:

"My mother would never have abandoned me. She's very kind, with curly hair, and she used to wear straw hats, and other hats too. In Moscow she used to give out the same number of candies to all the children. And I loved her very much, even though they used to tease her and call her 'madam,' because she had curly hair, wore lipstick and wore hats . . ."

"My mother's nasty," Glashenka agreed and started crying.

Glashenka and Kuzmin were the only ones who didn't tease Sulamith by calling her "Jew girl." But Sulamith didn't like Glashenka, and she was afraid of Kuzmin and disliked him, just as everyone else did. And so Sulamith was delighted when they brought Annushka to the orphanage. Sulamith started stalking Annushka, and nicknamed her "crybaby." From then on they started teasing Sulamith as "Jew girl" less often, and mostly made fun of Annushka. But one day, following their usual habit, the most influential, jolly, and spiteful children went to make fun of their neighbor Fyokla.

This Fyokla, a wrinkled, bad-tempered old woman, lived alone in a little house close to the orphanage, and for as long as anyone could remember, perhaps even from before the war, the most influential children had gone there to make fun of her, calling her "Beetroot."

"Beetroot!" they shouted. "Granny Beetroot . . ."

In reply, Granny Beetroot's little ginger lapdog barked angrily, and Fyokla herself came darting out, screeching abuse and threats, which they found especially funny.

This time Sulamith also wanted to go and tease Fyokla in order to ingratiate herself with the influential children.

"Don't go," Glashenka begged her.

But Sulamith did go, and Annushka went, also to ingratiate herself with the influential children. Sulamith ran right up to the fence, where the little ginger dog was barking so maliciously, it was practically shuddering. She ran up and shouted:

"Granny Beetroot . . ."

The old woman came darting out, saw Sulamith standing there right in front of her nose and said:

"Why, you little Jewish Yid-girl . . ."

And then all the influential children stopped laughing at Fyokla and started laughing at Sulamith again. And Annushka, whom Sulamith had stalked, said:

"Judische Schwein," which means "Jewish pig" in German.

"So you can speak German then?" asked Kostya, a boy to whom everyone used to give some of their bread ration, so that he wouldn't beat them.

"Yes, I can," said Annushka, hoping to impress him, "Anna mit Grossvater gehen sparzieren . . . Anna and her granddad go for a walk."

"Fascist, Fascist!" shouted Kostya. "German, German . . ."

And all the influential children started shouting:

"German, German . . . Fascist, Fascist . . ."

After that they started teasing Sulamith by calling her "Jew girl" and teasing Annushka especially fervently by calling her "German" and "Fascist," and because they were both being teased, they started hating each other very much.

Then one day Kuzmin went away somewhere and came back looking concerned.

"The Germans are close," he said, "I've arranged for transport, it's time to prepare for evacuation."

However, a day went by, and then another, and no vehicle arrived, and meanwhile the bombardment became clearly audible. So far they were only bombing the railroad station, but it was still calm here near the orphanage. Kuzmin summoned Aunty Katechka and said:

"We can't stay here any longer . . . Bring me the lists of children so that I can destroy them, because the Germans are looking for Jewish children . . ."

Aunty Katechka said:

"You mean everyone's going to suffer because of one Jewish girl . . . If you destroy the lists, you won't be able to find the children . . ."

Kuzmin said:

"I'm ordering you."

Aunty Katechka said:

"This isn't the army or the front line, you can't give me orders."

Then Kuzmin smashed his fist that never opened down on the desk, and Aunty Katechka brought him the lists.

Kuzmin ordered the children to be lined up in pairs, holding hands. Annushka found herself paired with Sulamith: it just worked out like that, and they were both afraid to disobey Kuzmin. The children set off toward the station. But suddenly they saw trucks in the distance, coming toward them from the direction of the station.

"Those are German trucks," said Kuzmin, "I remember them from the front. Let's change our route, we'll go to the outlying villages instead."

They walked for a long time. Kuzmin and Aunty Katechka carried the smaller children in their arms. First they carried one, and then another, and in this way they reached Brusyany village.

People from the surrounding villages usually gathered in Brusyany village for the market, and today happened to be market day. Kuzmin was delighted, he made certain that there were no Germans there, lined the children up in a single row between the carts on the market square, and said:

"Peasant comrades . . . Here in front of you you see your brothers and sisters from the orphanage. I request you to take these children, choose one that catches your eye, or else they'll die."

And the peasants walked up and started examining the children and taking them. At first the strongest and most spirited ones, because they could help around the house and they could be used for work. And then, when only the small or sickly children were left, they just took ones they liked. When Glashenka was chosen, she begged the peasant woman to take Sulamith too. But the woman saw that Sulamith was Jewish and didn't take her. Glashenka started crying, hugged Sulamith, and said she would never forget her. But Sulamith wasn't thinking about Glashenka just then, she was worried whether anyone would take her. Almost all the children had been taken already. Only Sulamith was left, and Annushka as well, together with a weak little boy, and only Kuzmin was left there with them, since Aunty Katechka felt satisfied that she had given away all her favorite, popular children into good hands, so she had taken a job as a housekeeper for an old peasant. And there were fewer and fewer good hands left to take children, only ragged riffraff were left hovering around, probably homeless themselves, and they were only staying out of curiosity. Suddenly Annushka saw walking toward her the kind of stepmother that any orphan could only dream of. Cleanly dressed, with kind eyes and a neatly tied peasant headscarf. Any natural mother could only be worse. Annushka thought: "She's coming for me. They won't take the boy, he's sickly and shabby looking, and Sulamith's a Jew . . ." The stepmother walked right up close, looked at the children, then took off her crucifix necklace and and fastened it round Sulamith's neck. Sulamith hugged her kind new mother, who had chosen her.

"Momma," she said, "thank you for taking me as your child . . ."

And Annushka's heart was wrung with envy and despair. The maternal love of Annushka's natural mother had been taken from her by illness, and the maternal love of a stepmother had been taken from her by a Jewish girl, who had stalked Annushka in the orphanage while she was weeping for her dead mother and invented an offensive nickname to taunt her with. Annushka's heart was grievously wrung, and those who retain the practical reason of childhood in their tribulation are capable of committing great evils. Annushka wished for Sulamith's death, so that she, Annushka, would get the kind stepmother.

And was what she wished for so very difficult? How difficult was it to bring about the death of a Jewish girl in 1942 under German rule? No sooner had Annushka wished with all her heart than German rule instantly appeared on the market square of Brusyany village. And Annushka recognized one of these bearers of power as Uncle Hans, who used to give her bread and pea concentrate, because the Slavs were not yet liable to total extermination.

"Uncle Hans," she shouted joyfully. "Anna mit Grossvater gehen schpazieren . . . Vogel—bird, Hund—dog . . ."

Uncle Hans recognized Annushka as the little girl in whose home he had lived in Rzhev, and he recognized Sulamith as a Jewish girl who, according to the latest German rules of life on this particular planet, should not be living anywhere. The German national machine worked with precise differentiation: Kuzmin was led away to a camp for prisoners of war, the peasant woman was struck with a rifle butt, smashing and bloodying her face, Sulamith was removed from the zone allocated to the Slavic population of Brusyany village, her life was taken and her body was thrown into a ditch, and Annushka was loaded into a railroad freight car so that she could learn about German culture and German labor in Germany.

All this was seen by Dan, the Viper, the Antichrist, who walked far and wide through these fields of blood in this trampled land. Dan the Antichrist had seen both fresh blood and last year's dry bones. And in two years the Antichrist, the youth from the tribe of Dan, had turned gray. He had not been sent as an agent, but only as the Lord's witness . . .

He walked among the submissive and among the outraged, among those pining in advance for the life out of which they were being hounded, and those who were fortunate enough to have forgotten life even before their death. One day near Minsk he walked beside a certain individual from the tribe of Ephraim (for he knew who came from which tribe, even though they themselves did not know this). And this individual, a learned man and a philosopher, said as he walked to his grave in shameful haste:

"Our people should have departed long ago, for we are like an impertinent guest, who has overstayed his welcome in the home of the other races, a guest who is now being shown the door by force and in ignominy . . . We are a vile race, the Jews, and I am odious to myself . . ."

Dan, the Viper, the Antichrist looked around and, indeed, he did not see many righteous faces among his own people, walking from out of this place to the grave . . . This woman had fornicated, and that man had offended an orphan, this man had been miserly and made his family's life a misery, this man had philosophized squalidly, this man had prayed falsely, this woman had betrayed, this man had forsworn his faith. And Dan, the Viper, the Antichrist said:

"Who is banishing us, and from where are they banishing us? Perhaps the Lord is banishing us from Eden? Perhaps the holy angels are banishing us from heaven? No, sinful as we are, we are being banished from a fallen world by fallen sinners . . . Look around. Is fornication a sin in this fallen world? Is betrayal a sin? Or squalid philosophy? Or false prayer? In internecine violence we killed our own prophets from Jeremiah to Jesus, but is this a rare thing for a fallen world? How many bloody calumnies, how many malicious legends could be composed about other nations who have killed their own righteous people in internecine violence? What special guilt is imputed to us? Why is our entire people being driven out of this fallen, but familiar and lived-in world, why are they stripping away all the best that we possess, everything that is best about us, and keeping it for themselves? Go and make a home in a different world, acquire a historical destiny and other such possessions all over again!"

The Lord replied to his envoy, the Antichrist, on a fall day close to the city of Minsk, on the edge of an anti-tank trench inundated with the blood of all the Twelve Tribes of Israel:

"Yes, you do have a special guilt that is imputed to you, and this is the only possible guilt in a fallen but familiar and lived-in world, and it is only by this guilt that you are distinguished from other peoples and it is for this guilt that you suffer punishment, and you do not bear any other guilt distinguishing you from other peoples . . . There is only one true guilt . . . The name of this guilt is . . . Defenselessness . . . In this alone lies your guilt before other peoples, and in this alone lies your sin against Me. While you bear this special guilt before the world and this sin against Me, I forgive you all your sins. But when you redeem this terrible guilt, then I shall hold you accountable for your other sins also, for the Lord's retribution is never accomplished through the righteous, but always through terrible evildoers."

And Dan, the Viper, the Antichrist spoke to his people through the prophet Jeremiah:

"Fear not, O Jacob my servant," says the Lord, "I will not make a full end of you . . . But I will discipline you . . . I will by no means leave you unpunished."

After this the Antichrist returned once again to Rzhev town, where he had earlier been sent to the unrighteous martyr Annushka from the juvenile, kind-hearted fornicatress Maria, who had lost her brother and given birth in a prison hospital to an Antichrist named in honor of this brother, the Antichrist's firstborn, Vasya . . . Failing to find Annushka in Rzhev town, the Antichrist set out for Brusyany village, where Annushka had destroyed the life of Sulamith from the tribe of Manasseh, Sulamith, who was not destined to remain among the survivors and put forth a shoot . . .

The prophet Isaiah said: "For though your people, Israel, be as the sand of the sea, only a remnant of them will return. Destruction is decreed, abounding with righteousness."

There was an abundance of righteousness in this destruction, and it was accomplished for the people's terrible guilt before the world: Defenselessness.

But the destroyers, in a seven-fold repetition of Assyrian arrogance, said: "By the strength of my hand I have done it, and by my wisdom, for I have understanding; I remove the boundaries of peoples, and plunder their treasures."

The Antichrist inwardly replied through the prophet Isaiah:

"Shall the ax boast over him who hews with it, or the saw magnify itself against him who wields it?" And Dan the Antichrist said: "For your terrible wickedness the Lord has chosen you as an instrument of chastisement of the people for its guilt." There are wicked peoples, and there is unclean land. Wicked peoples, departing, carry away with them their wickedness and the land is cleansed. But unclean land is fixed, and all that issues from it is cursed for eternity. From the people of accursed land, neither remnant nor shoot shall remain, as no remnant has remained from Babylon, which was in all respects less sinful. In the Book of the Prophet Jeremiah it is said: "Jeremiah wrote in a book all the disaster that should come upon Babylon, all these words are written concerning Babylon."

The Lord sends Christ among the sinful peoples for blessing and the Antichrist for cursing, and the great prophets for exposition of the Lord's works, but it is not given either to Jesus, or to the Antichrist, or to the chosen among the prophets to set foot on unclean land. Therefore Jeremiah did not carry the book of his curse to Babylon himself, but sent it with those who were being driven into slavery: "And Jeremiah said to Seraiah: 'When you come to Babylon, see that you read all these words, and say, "O Lord, you have said concerning this place that you will cut it off, so that nothing shall dwell in it, neither man nor beast, and it shall be desolate forever." When you finish reading this book, tie a stone to it and cast it into the midst of the Euphrates and say, "Thus shall Babylon sink, to rise no more, because of the disaster that I am bringing upon her, and they shall become exhausted."'"

Dan, the Viper, the Antichrist knew that he was required to curse, but how and when the curse would be accomplished, only the Lord knew. However in order to perform the rite of the curse, the Antichrist needed a sinner, who was being driven in torment into slavery, for it was not given to the Antichrist, just as it was not given to Christ, to set foot on unclean land. Dan, the Viper, the Antichrist knew that among his people there were many evildoers and sinners, however the rulers from the unclean land, who had undertaken to distribute the comforts of the world in place of the Lord, considered slavery too tasty a morsel for a Jew, for in slavery you can sleep in a barn and eat leftover scraps, thereby maintaining your life. And this contradicted the guidance of the darling of the Aryan race, Martin Bormann, one of the supreme deities of Germano-Nazi paganism: "The Slavs will be the Aryans' slaves in this world, but the Jews are animals that have no right to exist." And so the Antichrist had to seek suffering evildoers among the other nations, to whom the comforts of German slavery were available.

Dan, the Viper, the Antichrist walked out of Brusyany village and set out for the railroad station, where Slavs were being dispatched to Germany in freight cars in order to become acquainted with German culture and German labor.

It was a genuinely northern day: Pushkin's "frost and sunshine," a sumptuous, glittering day. On that day anyone who still had any doubts concerning nature's complete lack of spirituality could see for himself that nature is a beautiful, but faithless wife for man. In times of joy and good fortune she is willing to lavish her charms and caresses on him, but in times of trouble she instantly abandons him and cozies up to the murderers by the bloody graves, indifferently eyeing the stiffening corpses of those, whom only recently she was gratifying with the greenness of her grass, the piquant aroma of fall leaves, and the pine-scented, snowy, swirling air . . . The murderers take over from their victims possession of the beauty, bounty, tenderness, and delights of nature, but the murderers cannot take possession of the Lord. This is why Abraham the Founder worshipped only the Lord and not the stars, which lead into the quagmire of fatalism, nor the sun, which evokes material beauty, nor the moon, which evokes mystical beauty, nor the transient youth of plants, nor the eternal age of rocks, nor the boundless sky, nor the indifferent water. One night in a vision the Lord said to Abraham:

"Fear not, Abraham, I am your shield, your reward shall be very great."

From that time onward, Abraham believed in the Lord, but he did not believe in the Lord's nature in the way that pagans believed in it, for it is common knowledge that the Lord is in nature, but the Lord is not nature. Like man, nature becomes consumed by arrogance, like man, at times it clamors against its Father and is blasphemous in either its ugliness or its beauty . . .

And at this moment in the vicinity of Brusyany village nature was blasphemous in this way over the trampled corpse of the Jewish girl Sulamith, who was not destined to receive the seed into her still-warm womb, and remain among the survivors to put forth a shoot. In the distance, above a glittering, snow-covered forest, the pure, frosty sun reposed on the fresh northern sky in inexpressible splendor, and whereas the rays of the summer sun, especially those of the summer sun in the south, acquire corporeal substance from the heat they contain and are therefore not entirely pure, the northern sun's rays are exceptionally insubstantial and limpidly transparent. Is this frosty limpidity not the origin of the icily calm, nightmarish quality of Nordic passions? And there, amidst this icy shining, amidst this glittering, sunny insubstantiality, Sulamith from the tribe of Manasseh lay in a ditch, frozen in her own blood, in the blood transmitted to her veins via many generations from Abraham himself, who concluded an alliance with the Lord. The Antichrist did not linger for long over the trampled corpse of Sulamith from the tribe of Manasseh, for Sulamith was not yet cold, the memory of her was still fresh, the kind peasant woman still remembered Sulamith clearly as she lay on her stove with her face smashed by a German rifle butt, she wept and lamented, and Annushka, who in the perversity of her infantile feelings had wished for Sulamith's death, also remembered her in the freight car, only not with grief, like the beaten peasant woman, but fearfully, as she had also initially remembered her brother Vova, who died in Rzhev town as a result of the thunderstorm.

Dan the Antichrist knew the great Biblical phrase: "Leave the dead to bury their own dead." While the memory of the dead is still fresh and has not yet cooled, remaining corporeal, until other dead people give this memory a decent burial, you can only remember a person who has died, but you cannot speak about them, for they are still human, and not God's.

The Antichrist walked past murdered Sulamith with a calm sadness, as people walk past the grave of a stranger, who is not related or dear to them. He walked on a long way beyond Brusyany village, where this sunny, frosty day of the Russian north was so blasphemous and rebellious against the Lord's feelings. The Antichrist saw many human bones. These were people who had been killed the previous year in the granite quarries, whom other dead people had already managed to bury. But there were also large numbers of bones lying in the open field, for people had been gathered together here from many places: from Rzhev town, and from Podgoreloe Gorodishche, and from Zubtsov, and they had been brought on platform cars along a narrow-gauge railroad track that was laid before the war, from the station to the granite quarries. In order to execute so many of them here, small, scattered groups had been gathered from all around, but even so, these were not the abundant executions of the south . . . And yet this northern execution, where people were gathered together in dribs and drabs, did possess its own scrupulous inexorability. By that time the secret German memorandum about the unsatisfactory work of the Einsatzgruppen (Mobile Killing Squads) had already been issued: "The numerous executions of Jews would not in themselves have provoked any objections, if technical errors had not been committed in the course of their preparation and implementation. Certain individuals, for instance, leave unburied bodies at the actual site of execution." This memorandum bore the number twenty-five and the date July 25, 1942. It was now the winter of 1942, and the technical shortcomings in implementation had still not been eradicated. In fact it was a German technical error of precisely this kind that presented itself to the gaze of Dan the Antichrist in the field near Brusyany village.

Looking around, the Antichrist suddenly felt the hand of the Lord on his shoulder and the same thing happened to him as had happened to the prophet of exile, Ezekiel, and as Ezekiel had done, he conversed with the Lord.

"The hand of the Lord was upon me, and he brought me out in the Spirit of the Lord and set me down in the middle of the field, and it was full of bones. And he led me around among them, and behold, there were very many on the surface of the field, and behold, they were very dry. And He said to me, 'Son of man, can these bones live?' And I answered, 'O Lord God, you know.' Then He said to me, 'Prophesy over these bones, and say to them: 'O dry bones, hear the word of the Lord. Thus says the Lord God to these bones: Behold, I will cause breath to enter you, and you shall live. And I will lay sinews upon you, and will cause flesh to come upon you, and cover you with skin, and put breath in you, and you shall live, and you shall know that I am the Lord.'"

The Antichrist saw bones start moving together in the snowy field, and each bone, although it had been flung a long distance, found its fellow bone, and there was a rattling sound, and then, behold, there were sinews on them, and flesh grew on them, and skin covered them, and all of this assumed the appearance of a crowd of recently buried corpses, standing under the cheerful northern sun like mournful dummies. It is well known that when a malicious dead person appears to a living person and wishes to mock the living person, he first of all breaks into a dance, since the dancing of the dead is especially terrifying for the living. But this was a different case, these dead martyrs were sad, and they stood motionless, as the Jewish girl Sulamith had lain motionless nearby in the ditch, frozen in her own blood, a trampled corpse left unburied in a violation of German sanitary regulations.

Then through the prophet Ezekiel the Lord said to Dan, the Antichrist:

"Prophesy to the breath; prophesy, son of man, and say to the breath: 'Thus says the Lord God: Come from the four winds, O breath, and breathe on these slain, that they may live.'"

And Dan, the Viper, the Antichrist, prophesied like the prophet Ezekiel, and the dead people came alive, an exceedingly great army of them. And through the prophet Ezekiel the Lord said to Dan, the Antichrist:

"These bones are the whole house of Israel. Behold, they say, 'Our bones are dried up, and our hope is lost; we are indeed cut off.' Therefore prophesy, and say to them: 'Thus says the Lord God: Behold, I will open your graves and raise you from your graves, O my people. And I will bring you into the land of Israel. And you shall know that I am the Lord, when I open your graves, and raise you from them . . .'"

After this, the Lord took took his hand from off the shoulder of Dan, the Viper, the Antichrist, and the reanimated dead once again disintegrated into bones scattered across the snowy field, the evening started drawing in, the forest turned gloomy, and the snowy radiance of the day dimmed. The Antichrist realized that this was a sign. He had to hurry to the station, before the unrighteous martyr Annushka was dispatched into slavery in an unclean land. It was for this that the Antichrist had been sent by the Lord to Rzhev town after Kerch city, to the unrighteous little martyr-girl Annushka after the kind-hearted little fornicatress Maria . . .

When the Antichrist arrived at the station, the evening was already dark and the streetlamps were glowing feebly, as wartime conditions required. Among the numerous trains, the Antichrist located the slave train from the sound of weeping, although this lamentation was muffled, since the doors of the freight cars were already locked and the train was about to set off at any moment . . . The Antichrist started walking soundlessly along the train, where the Germans who were dispatching Slavs into slavery stood in front of the freight cars. He did not walk soundlessly because he was afraid of being killed by the Germans, for that is an impossibility with the Antichrist. He walked soundlessly because for quite some time now he had been been feeling a keen desire to kill a German. He would have liked to kill all of them for the pleasure of it, but that would have brought him too much satisfaction, and he knew that in this world you must not have too much satisfaction. And therefore he was dreaming of the small satisfaction of killing at least one of them. But the Lord's emissary cannot ascertain for himself the thoughts of the Lord. The Antichrist knew that the Lord had not approved of the prophet Elisha's punishing the impious, wicked children with death. The Lord's emissary should only carry out his own task. And therefore the Antichrist walked soundlessly past those whom he yearned to kill.

The Antichrist saw the Germans open the doors of one of the freight cars for some purpose of their own, and he saw that it was packed to overflowing with people, mostly women, but there were also adolescents and young adults . . . When the Germans opened the doors, everybody inside crowded forward to get closer to the air, and Annushka was standing there, wedged between other people's bodies from all sides. The Antichrist took out of his shepherd's bag the impure bread of exile, devised by the prophet Ezekiel, and started handing it out to the enslaved Slavs. He gave Annushka some bread wrapped in paper, and told her:

"Eat this bread, and hide the paper in your clothing. And when you arrive in the unclean land, read out what is written on the paper, then tie a stone to the paper and throw it into the river of that unclean land."

Annushka glanced at the person who had handed her the bread and suddenly recognized him as the man who had come to their home in the former church in Rzhev town before the war, in order to rob them. Annushka was frightened and wanted to call the German, who had left his post to deal with some need of his own, for there was no other authority here apart from the German. However before she could call out, a woman standing beside her with a child in her arms suddenly said to the Antichrist:

"Good man, take my child, for I am starving to death and your bread will not last for long . . . My little girl will die in front of my eyes . . ."

The woman held out the child, wrapped in a red quilted blanket, and on finding itself in a stranger's arms, the child started crying loudly and hysterically. At this point the irregularity that had so far gone unnoticed became obvious. Indeed, it was no mere irregularity: what the Germans saw was incomprehensible to the Nordic mind. Standing there at the very center of the German military position, illuminated by the flashlights of German patrols as he breathed the frosty air, was a Jew who had not been killed, holding in his arms a child, which, if it were to grow up and hide away in a chink somewhere, would take cover under the identity of a different nation: then just try to find it, in order to eliminate it . . . For out of doctrinal inclination, the well-ordered German mind always believes in idealistic materialism, and in accordance with the doctrine of the separation of the races, Germans were incapable of supposing that a Jew was holding a Slavic child in his arms. In the Germans the fervor of hunters mingled with the outrage of tidy-minded proprietors, arousing a collective feeling of joy. The Germans joyfully came running to kill the Jew, they came running from all sides: from the water pumping station, and from the railroad station building, and from the nearby trains. And Dan, the Viper, the Antichrist joyfully accepted the situation that had arisen. He thought: "I am holding in my arms a child who is mortal and whom the Lord did not prevent me from taking. Therefore the Lord will forgive me if I anticipate his intentions to some degree, as the Lord forgave me when I set a stumbling block in the path of Pavlik the proletarian in Rzhev."

And the Germans started falling, clutching at their bellies, pressing hands that were turning cold and numb to lips bitten bloody in abrupt agony and spewing out bloody excrement from both of their ends. As if they had been machine-gunned, the entire squad of guards slumped down into their own bloody diarrhea on the snow-covered railroad platform. And after having seen the resolution of the Jewish problem in the anti-tank ditches of Minsk, after having seen the dry, snow-covered bones near Brusyany village, Dan, the Viper, the Antichrist observed the genuinely national features of those faces, livid and contorted in suffocation, and understood what earthly happiness was . . .

Subsequently the German authorities determined that the squad had been poisoned by spoiled canned rations and a German, an army lieutenant, was executed, thereby reducing the overall number of the dolichocephalic population still further.

As is well known, according to German doctrine dolichocephaly, or an elongated form of the skull, is a typical attribute of the German individual. But Annushka was a typical brachycephalic, with a round, Slavic skull, and therefore she worked as a swineherd, looking after pigs in the region of the Rhenish-Westphalian schistose massif . . . Her master was a typical dolichocephalic with a German skull, which he considered a rather rare thing, even among Germans, and an especial privilege of rural areas, since in the cities there was a substantial admixture of dark-haired individuals: Western Slavic and Romance nationalities and also, if truth be told, even Jewish elements, which posed a rather ticklish problem, since the Führer himself . . . shhhhh! . . . had black hair.

Much later, during the post-war period, Annushka's dolichocephalic master claimed that he had always been anti-Nazi and anti-Hitler, since the upper circles of the Nazi Party were dominated by round-headed brachycephalics and Hitler did not have a purely Germanic skull, in addition to his black hair. However in the days when Annushka worked for this master, he kept his inner mutiny well concealed from the Gestapo and strove to supply the German national table with various succulent dishes, including pigs' trotters with sauerkraut. Raising pigs and growing cabbage are laborious activities and Annushka, who was not accustomed to the German labor that kind Uncle Hans had told her about, grew extremely tired, especially so since, while cabbage did at least occasionally find its way onto her dinner-plate, pork never did. The other brachycephalics also found German labor tiring, but had no opportunity to restore their strength with a good German dinner.

Even so, the place where they labored as slaves was beautiful. Rolling hills alternated with valleys in which rivers meandered through a sequence of graceful curves. In many places the surface of the land that was to be cursed was almost completely covered with deciduous forests in which birds sang, and orchards in which ruddy-cheeked apples, pears and plums hung, or with vineyards and fields of wheat and barley. All of this required tending, but there were not enough of the intelligent dolichocephalics: at the behest of their dark-haired Führer they had set about imposing German order in the Lord's earth. And so, for the season of ripening fruit lazy, terrified brachycephalics were sent here. For the most part these were young people, who had entered their prime in slavery, and even with their frugal diet, they were prey to overwhelming desires, especially among the fragrant fruit-bearing trees.

One day Annushka was lugging along a heavy wicker basket, together with a brachycephalic from Kursk. Annushka liked this young man. He was snub-nosed and gray-eyed, and he whistled jolly little German tunes. Annushka intimated that she liked him by laughing at his little tunes. As they were taking the empty basket from the storehouse, where they had unloaded the apples, back to the orchard, the gray-eyed Kursk brachycephalic called Annushka into the bushes, where he suddenly grabbed tight hold of her, breathing heavily, as if he was carrying a full basket of apples again, flung her down on the grass, forced Annushka's knees apart with his own knees and stopped her mouth with his lips. Up to this point Annushka repeated the fate of Maria, who was raped not far from Izyum city in the Kharkiv region in 1933. Afterward, however, everything went differently for Annushka and for her rapist. Annushka was raped in the afternoon and in the early evening she complained about this to her master, the dolichocephalic. Her master, the dolichocephalic, who happened to read a bit of Goethe from time to time, disapproved of what he referred to as "horseplay on the part of young people," especially since he himself was half-paralyzed and abhorred activities of this kind. And therefore he gave instructions for the Kursk brachycephalic to be punished and he was beaten in the police station. However, since the pigskin boots on one policeman's feet were inordinately heavy, with iron heel and toe plates, the Kursk brachycephalic was beaten rather more severely than was required for justice, and he died. Then the dolichocephalic master, who, as we already know, read a bit of Goethe every now and then, was besieged by doubts, especially since it was hard to find workers and 1944 was a difficult year for German agriculture in general. The master started to regret the loss of a such a good worker as the Kursk brachycephalic and became furious with Annushka, who had led him, the master, to commit an injustice against a good worker, and he started punishing Annushka. He sent her to do all the most difficult tasks, he had her beaten for all sorts of offences, he fed her badly even in comparison with the starvation rations of the other brachycephalics, and he accused her of debauchery. And since Annushka was completely in his power, by the fall of 1944 her appearance resembled that of the Russian prisoners of war on the peat cuttings, where they were buried in the boggy soil, and where, as it happened, all the brachycephalics who died or were killed were also taken to be buried.

Annushka knew that the snub-nosed, gray-eyed young man who raped her in the bushes had also been taken there.

One day Annushka was lying on her heap of rags after a day that had been especially hard, since she had a fever and with a fever it is difficult to carry a heavy tub full of pig feed, clutching it against your belly, and she had ruptured herself. The pigs had already fallen asleep, only grunting occasionally behind their partition, but Annushka still couldn't get warm enough to fall asleep. She wrapped her arms round her bony knees, pressed them against her aching belly to make herself feel warmer, and suddenly in this position she became aware of the womb within her and remembered the young man from Kursk who had raped her.

And so, after the first plague of the Lord, the sword, and the second plague, famine, and the fourth plague, sickness, she was visited by the third plague, the beast of lust. And this came at an unexpected and inappropriate moment. Annushka recalled the young man from Kursk, or rather she dreamed about him, but she dreamed about him in a different guise and a different context, while her mother was alive and Mitka-Ivan was still there. It was as if this gray-eyed young man from Kursk had been with her everywhere. He had even sat with her on the grass in the warm, caressing morning sunshine in Nefedovo village . . . When Annushka was drowsing in nothing but her nightshirt, and that felt pleasant . . . And he was also there as a boy at Room 9, Barracks Building 3, Sector 3, Rzhev town, playing knucklebones with Annushka's brother Ivan, who was nicknamed Mitya . . . And this young boy also lived at 61 Labor Street, in the former church that was appropriated as living space for Stakhanovite workers, and went for walks with Annuska in the graveyard where her little brother Vovik was buried. Only the trees were a bit bigger and better tended, they were tended like the trees in a German orchard. There were a lot of fragrant trees and grapevines too, but there were also the berries that grew in the forest near Nefedovo village . . . Annushka and the young man from Kursk went to gather berries, they went into the bushes, and suddenly he grabbed hold of Annushka and tumbled her to the ground very easily, because Annushka deliberately yielded . . . Annushka clasped her knees tightly in her arms and pressed them against her belly, and that gave her a warm feeling that was very pleasant . . . But suddenly she was told: "Your mother Emelyanova died on the 7th of October, 1942 . . ." It immediately started raining with loud peals of thunder. Annushka forgot about the happiness she had experienced with the young man from Kursk and started running as hard as she possibly could, so that they wouldn't bury her mother without her. She ran up to the workers' barracks building, and there was water everywhere with no way to get through it, and the coffin with her mother's body in it was lying in the yard in the pouring rain. Annushka saw all the neighbors she remembered from the barracks building walk up to the coffin in order to lift it up and carry it to the cemetery. Annushka shouted:

"It's me . . . I'm Emelyanova . . . Her daughter . . ."

But they were too far away to hear Annushka's voice and she couldn't get across the water. Her neighbors leaned down to the coffin in order to carry it away and suddenly Annushka's mother sat up and said:

"Wait, there's something I want to say . . ."

Annushka clearly heard these words spoken by her mother, but she couldn't hear the most important thing, what her mother said afterward, because the water prevented her from getting close, and the water was rushing loudly and turbulently. Then Annushka started running straight through the water, the water was up to her waist, then it was almost up to her throat and there was no one helping her . . . Even so Annushka managed to struggle through it and run up to the coffin, but her mother had already finished speaking and lain back down, stiff and dead, the way she was lying before. The neighbors lifted up the coffin and carried it away . . . Annushka burst into tears, and she woke up crying beside the partition of a German pigsty, where the pigs grunted every now and then . . .

Rain was pattering loudly on the tiled roof, but there were no cold drafts anywhere, since a German pigsty is distinguished from a Russian pigsty by its immaculate cleanliness and efficient insulation. Annushka was not shivering from external cold, but from an internal chill, not from the wind, but from her fever. In her dream Annushka had wept loudly, since in her dream she was at home and there was no one who could forbid her to cry, but now she was awake Annushka wept quietly, since in waking life she was in German slavery. This was the same divine lamentation, from the heart, with which the Lord occasionally rewards those who lack reason, the lamentation with which Maria, the juvenile fornicatress, had wept in the field near Andreevka junction in 1933. At that time Maria had been exalted through this lamentation, she had read the Lord's admonition without words and understood without reason that which was pronounced through the prophet Isaiah:

"As one whom his mother comforts, so I will comfort you . . . And you shall see, and your heart shall rejoice; your bones shall flourish like the grass . . ."

When Annushka heard this admonition of the Lord without words and understood it without reason, she walked out of the warmly insulated German pigsty into the rain and set off along a track across the unclean land, which she was required to curse. As Annushka walked along the rain stopped, and the unclean land, convinced that it was eternal, delighted in the German moon, at the sight of which German hearts have shed so many sentimental tears . . .

Low, uniform German mountains rose up here and there, with dried-out volcanic magma adhering to them, and among these mountains there were cold, damp pastures . . . A continuous stretch of forest extended to the northeast of the river . . . The river itself flowed along a picturesque valley between rocky banks and clean, tile-roofed German villages slumbered along the banks . . . And all this was to be cursed by the Lord through his emissary Dan, the Viper, the Antichrist, and the curse was to be enacted by Annushka Emelyanova from Rzhev town, an unrighteous girl-martyr, who had been driven into slavery. Annushka walked up to the very edge of the rocky bank, sat down on a moss-covered boulder and took out of the lining of her coat the sheets of paper given to her by the Antichrist, for she had not forgotten about them. The sheets of paper were covered in writing in two languages: one that was unfamiliar and incomprehensible, like the tracks of birds' feet in snow or sand, and another, familiar one that she had studied in school. Hard as the German moon strove to take refuge in the clouds, the heavenly powers nonetheless obliged it to shine for Annushka and by its high-quality German light Annushka read out the curse syllable by syllable to the best of her ability. Although in slavery Annushka had begun to forget how to read, she managed to read out the curse of the Biblical prophets, now directed against an unclean land and an unclean people. With these curses the prophets had warned their people against sin. But sevenfold accursed is the one through whose rancor this sin is punished. For the Lord always chooses incorrigible evildoers for the execution of his wrath:

"I will set my face against you, and you shall be struck down before your enemies and you shall flee when none pursues you . . . and I will make your heavens like iron and your earth like bronze. And your strength shall be spent in vain, for your land shall not yield its increase, and the trees of the land shall not yield their fruit. I shall break your supply of the bread that fortifies a man, and ten women shall bake your bread in a single oven and you shall eat and not be satisfied. And as for those of you who are left, I will send faintness into their hearts in the lands of their enemies. The sound of a driven leaf shall put them to flight." Here is the curse from the prophet of exile Ezekiel: "I am the Lord. I have spoken; it shall come to pass; I will do it. I will not go back; I will not spare; I will not relent; according to your ways and your deeds I will judge you, but I will never find you again." And here is the curse from the prophet Isaiah, later repeated in the Apocalypse of John: "Your sky shall be rolled up like a scroll above your head." And looking upon the unrighteous earth the first biblical prophet, the Tekoa shepherd Amos, proclaimed curses and wrote them down in the manuscript bequeathed by the prophet Jeremiah: "I hate, I despise your feast days . . . Take away from me the noise of your songs . . ." And at the very end the prophet Amos added: "But let justice roll down like waters, and righteousness like an ever-flowing stream . . ."

At this point Annushka Emelyanova's proclamation of the manuscript of the curse concluded. The royal quartermaster Seraiah finished his reading of the manuscript of the curse on Babylon before dawn and Annushka also finished her reading of the manuscript of her curse before dawn, when it was time for her to go back to the German pigsty and lug heavy tubs of pig feed around, in order to avoid being beaten for lateness and indolence. And so Annushka hurriedly found a stone on the riverbank, tore a strip of cloth off her dress, attached this stone to the manuscript of the curse and threw the manuscript into the waters of the German national river.

A constant feeling of hatred is too desiccating for the soul, but a constant hatred of the German character and things German was now destined to become a national feature of the Lord's people, as a precaution against other, less capable historical enemies. And if, when they depart, the present generations and those immediately succeeding them take this hostility to the grave with them, then even so the distrust must remain forever: that rational, national distrust which, insofar as this is possible, renders a constant feeling of hatred an unnecessary, cumbersome and coarse form of national self defense. The national-mystical humanism of the Nazis deified Nordic man and set him up him as the measure of all things. They traced the rankings on the racial hierarchy downward from Nordic man, and standing on the lowest step was the dehumanized Jew, excommunicated from all the categories of humanism. And this is only natural. As people, Jews are just as bad as all the rest of humanity. But as a specific historical formation, as a Biblical phenomenon, they are a people close to God, and man intrinsically hates God, therefore he also hates Jews, and therefore many Jews, as people, hate themselves and their own Biblical destiny. This is so important that I feel the need to repeat it in rather different words. Of course, as a human being a Jew is just as bad as all people are, but according to the Bible, as he is a part of God's people, and since man is the enemy of God, in order to believe in God he has to overcome his own human nature, which has been cursed by God, and only a few individuals succeed in doing this, so a hatred for the Jew is perfectly natural. And the farther from God any given people is at its present level of development, the stronger is the hatred, and the more natural antisemitism is as a characteristic national attribute. And indeed, the actual history and fortunes of the Jews over the centuries demonstrate to man that he is not in control of the situation on Earth, but merely God's laborer and a vagrant. And as a result of this peoples, especially large and powerful peoples, who imagine God's vineyard to be their own property and repudiate the Biblical parable of the vineyard, hate the Jewish people, which by its own very history constantly, although frequently unintentionally, derides pretentious human claims to be the masters of God's vineyard. And just as the negligent workers in the Gospel parable repeatedly killed the messengers of the Lord, who reminded them of their obligations to the true Master of the vineyard, over the centuries frequent attempts have been made to solve the Jewish question. But the German nation made this undertaking the fundamental idea of its state at a critical juncture in its historical destiny, and under the guise of fulfilling its own historical duty to humankind. For, as already mentioned, the majority of people hate God, whether secretly or openly. They hate Him because He is strong and man is weak, because He is immortal and man is short-lived. And in their prayers they do more begging than glorifying, and in their myths they celebrate Titans such as Prometheus, the enemy of God and a martyr of humanity, who suffered for people's sake. Only a few people love God, and therefore, in its conclusive scientific solution of the Jewish question the German nation acted on behalf of the majority, who, according to the Gospel parable, aspire to become the masters of God's vineyard, and not His laborers . . .

As soon as the Lord learned that Annushka Emelyanova from Rzhev had proclaimed the curse three days before her death from a fever, He summoned God's emissary, the Antichrist, and said to him:

"Go to Bor town on the Volga and live there until you are needed . . ."

"Lord," the Antichrist replied, "I am not alone now . . . I have a Slavic child with me, a little girl, whose mother asked me to save her . . . The mother is no longer alive, she died in a railroad freight car on her way into German slavery . . ."

"Take the child with you," said the Lord.

So Dan, the Viper, the Antichrist set out for Bor town on the Volga with a little Slavic girl. The Antichrist had given this little girl the name Ruth, after the Moabite woman who became a member of the Antichrist's people at Bethlehem, unaware that the girl's village name was different, that in the village she had been given a Greek name, Pelagia . . . For even to the Antichrist it is not given to know everything. The Antichrist did not even know what lay in store for him this time. The Lord concealed this from him . . . All he knew was that a certain Vera Koposova lived in Bor town on the Volga with her two daughters, the elder called Tasya and the younger called Ustya. Vera's husband Andrei was currently at the frontline, although he was due to return to his family soon, since the first plague of the Lord, the sword, had already ended. Although the fallen world was deserving of punishment, the Lord understood that man could not endure the first plague for very long . . . Man could endure the second plague, famine, for longer, and adapt even more skillfully to the fourth plague, sickness: and as for the third plague, the beast of fornication, man had become completely reconciled to it . . .

Knowing this, the Lord sent a reward to Annushka the unrighteous martyr before she died, a special treat for the curse that she had pronounced: a happy dream. And Annushka never returned from her happy dream to her vicious, ungodly existence. In this dream the young man from Kursk grabbed hold of Annushka again and tumbled her onto the warm earth beside the little house in Nefedovo village, where once upon a time Annushka was born, and he did to Annushka with kindness what he had done to her with violence out of his fear while in German slavery.

When the other brachycephalic workers heard Annushka's dying moans at dawn and drew closer, they saw on Annushka's face an expression of that happy, mindless passion that is only possible at the very climax of the wedding night. Such cases are known and have been described in the medical literature: this is how people sometimes die in their youth, when at its end the exhausted body releases the unspent passions.

A Parable of Fornication

In order to compel man to undertake what is necessary, extreme measures are required. In order for the ordinary to exist, an aspiration for the great is necessary. But for man to understand the great, the great must needs be debased . . . The following chastisement by God through the third plague, the wild beast of fornication, occurred in Bor town in the Gorky Region, the former Nizhny Novgorod Province. The Koposov family lived in Bor town: Andrei Koposov, his wife Vera Koposova and their daughters Tasya and Ustya . . . And this is the parable into which their lives were molded.

***

It was 1948, a time when everything was fading into the past. The horrific suffering of the war was fading away and so were the bright postwar joys. This perception of everything already being over and done with lent a sedate, elderly aspect to people's feelings and their appearance. Even their hopes for the future were somehow elderly. At that time everyone's aspiration was to recover the prewar level of life, for the devastation of the war made them dream of the poor, prewar past as a rich, postwar future. Although this was openly stated in the state's plans, of course in people's souls this aspiration to achieve the past in the future was not a clear plan, but it did exist and it had an oppressive effect, since the human soul is neither a destroyed factory, nor a decline in the number of tractors produced from the prewar level.

During the war Bor, although not so very far behind the front line, was nonetheless on the home front and had not suffered any destruction or civilian casualties, although in other respects it had borne the full brunt of all four of the Lord's plagues. Notifications of death were common, famine was common, disease was common, fornication by women left behind and young people who had grown up was common. Slavic bravado also played its part in this. A woman might dismissively wave aside other people's reproaches or her own conscience like some annoying little puppy:

"Ah, the war will cancel everything out . . ."

However Vera Koposova waited for her husband to come home and remained faithful to him. She worked at a garment factory, sewing soldiers' quilted jackets and soldiers' quilted trousers, and raised her daughters, Tasya and Ustya, on her earnings and her husband's military allotment note . . . There were occasions when Vera was pestered by men. She was actually pestered by Pavlov himself, a man at whom even wives who were faithful to their husbands couldn't help glancing from time to time, not to mention those women who chose to sample the delights on offer, not wishing to deny themselves any longer. "Just the once or ten times, what's the difference . . . The war will cancel everything out . . . They're not losing out on anything over there . . ."

This Pavlov was a war invalid, but without any visible disfigurements, with two arms and two legs and his wounds concealed under his clothing. He was fair of face, with spellbinding blue eyes and a titillating little mustache . . . Vera saw that women always walked hastily along the street with him, eager to get him back to their place as quickly as possible . . . And as a sailor it was not Pavlov's habit to disdain anyone, neither an empty-headed girl, whom he seduced, nor a forty-year-old widow, who seduced him . . . However Pavlov did not make advances to Vera simply because she was beautiful and even the war had failed to age her significantly . . . Pavlov did not simply pester Vera just as he was, in the way he usually pestered women, but with gifts: a silk scarf and two whole cans of stewed meat, which, by the way, he had been given by a forty-year-old widow who worked in the food trade department.

"Here," he said, "this is for you . . . Remember a friend in your hours of leisure . . ."

This happened one evening on Derzhavin Street, not far from house number 2, where Vera lived. Even before the war the streetlamps here had not shone with a bright, intense light, but during the war it was completely dark. It is a well-known fact that darkness arouses a man, and Pavlov wished to exploit this darkness to the full, especially since it was summer and the grass had grown tall on a nearby vacant lot, where suburban goats grazed during the day.

At that time, during the war, it was not fashionable to give an importunate sexual pest a slap to the face and therefore Vera punched Pavlov on the nose, which was not a very feminine response and perhaps it was this lack of femininity that quashed his desire to repeat the attempt. He just swore obscenely at Vera, calling her a lousy bitch, pressed his handkerchief to his nose and left, having squandered his accumulated reserves of male dynamism, to go and see the forty-year-old widow, which he actually found more interesting at his age of twenty-three. And Vera went home to house number 2, where a joyful Tasya handed her a long-awaited "soldier's triangle," a folded letter from Andrei . . . And so the incident was forgotten in their joy . . . At that time Tasya was growing up, becoming more and more like her mother, and Vera had even begun plaiting her daughter's hair like her own, in one big braid. Ustya was still little. But in the fall of 1945, when Andrei came home from the war covered in medals, she met him on her own two feet, not in her mother's or her sister's arms.

Andrei found everything intact: an intact wife without any changes and intact daughters with pleasant changes. He even found the wooden workbench in the corner of the large room intact, with the prewar wood shavings still lying under it: Vera had deliberately left them there, as a reminder of her husband and the father of her daughters. Andrei remembered that Tasya used to like playing with those wood shavings and now he saw that Ustya, the daughter he didn't yet know, also played with them. And Andrei shed tears of joy. What other delights could a soldier who had been at war for four years wish for? And so the remainder of 1945 passed filled with joy, and the joy continued in 1946, although they had already begun to notice the hunger. In 1947 the joy intensified and they began dreaming about the well-fed pre-war period that had followed the hungry years of collectivization . . . The more time that slipped by, the more they dreamed about the pre-war past . . . In 1948 the hunger passed off to some degree, but the final postwar joys passed off simultaneously with it and the staid, elderly aspect that we have already mentioned became an established element of people's feelings and appearance . . . Life became calmer and duller. At the dance floor in the public municipal gardens they started playing lyrical, patriotic Russian waltzes and the captured German accordions no longer strained and strove in obsequious groveling to the foxtrots of the West. Young people played forfeits as they used to do in prewar days, but without any kisses. And even heavy drinking, which since time immemorial in the Slavic tradition had been pursued freely out in the street, now became a largely apartment-bound pursuit.

By this time Tasya Koposova had almost reached marriageable age: she had acquired every aspect of her mother's prewar beauty and the weight of her light brown braid was a match for the weight of her mother's, while her mother's woven braid of fragrant, gold-tinged hair also remained a match for hers. Both mother and daughter were in their prime: the mother in the prime of her womanhood and the daughter in the prime of her maidenhood. Looking at his wife, Andrei Koposov loved his daughter all the more, and looking at his daughter, he felt even more attracted to the body that his wife had saved for him during the war.

However this point marked the beginning of the parable for which, at the bidding of the Lord, the Antichrist had arrived in Bor town in the Gorky region. The Lord's third plague is ever-present on all sides, for even the Lord Himself is not at liberty to revoke it, as he can revoke His most terrible plague, the sword, or the second, famine, or the fourth, sickness. The third plague of the Lord, fornication, follows man around like his shadow, and you can only remove a shadow by removing the object casting it . . . But while the third plague of the Lord remains present everywhere, in this parable it is located center stage, at the focal point of everything.

Vera saved herself for her husband right through the war, but having lived with him for a year after the war, she stopped loving him. Perhaps this was a consequence of the general staid, elderly mood, the unspoken feeling that everything was over and done with, both the bad and the good. Even a great man is a slave of his time, so what could be said of Vera Kopova, a simple woman who used to be beautiful and was still beautiful now, although a chance passerby might not necessarily turn his head to glance back at her like before. The only man who would definitely glance back at her if he were the chance passerby was Andrei Koposov. But Vera had stopped loving him. What was more, Vera now felt a purely womanly contempt for her husband Andrei, contempt of a kind that couldn't possibly be shared: a decent woman would be ashamed to confide in anyone about it . . .

Andrei worked as a carpenter for the Communist Party's Municipal Committee, as he had before the war. In the evenings and on his day off he made little wooden troughs for kneading dough, storage tubs for vegetable oil, butter churns, spoons and salt boxes . . . The house always had a pleasant smell of wood shavings. And both daughters, the younger Ustya and the older Tasya, played with the shavings beside their father, although Tasya was already old enough to be a bride. The daughters loved their father, and they called him "tyatya," as he had taught them . . . For he came from one of those places where fathers were called tyatya . . . When Andrei had made a large number of wooden articles he would take them to the local market to sell, or even make the journey to Gorky . . . From there he would bring back flour and other foodstuffs. Vera always saw him off and when he came back she met him and fed him a delicious meal, and tidied up the apartment, and did his laundry . . . But when she went to bed with him in the evening, for the very life of her, she felt she simply couldn't do anything . . . When the usual nocturnal goings-on of a husband and wife started up between them, it felt as if she was being raped . . . She couldn't give a damn about her own female pleasure, but if only it wasn't all so disgusting . . . The best she could manage was just to lie there indifferently until Andrei achieved his male satisfaction and fell asleep . . . And when Andrei fell asleep Vera always tried to move to the couch and join her daughters there. Her daughters' couch was wide, big enough for three . . . And Andrei sensed her womanly aversion for him, although she never even hinted at it to him with so much as a single word. But in such matters words are superfluous . . . Andrei first started being offensive with his wife and then started beating her. The first time he beat her was when he came back from Gorky without any flour or other foodstuffs, but rip-roaring drunk.

"Good people told me, you slut . . ." he shouted. "About you and Pavlov here, during the war . . ."

And in front of his daughters he described with obscene frankness what she and Pavlov did there during the war . . . And after that he rampaged in the way that men originally from rural areas rampage in a town or an industrial suburb.

In the country, especially in former times, peasants used to rampage differently, they thrashed their wives within an inch of their lives, but they spared property, since living matter can regenerate itself, while property can't give birth to anything . . . However Andrei rampaged in the suburban settlement style. He dragged Vera around by her braid, and trampled crockery underfoot, and struck the sleeping couch with his carpenter's hammer. On one occasion he frightened Ustya to death by chasing after her.

"She's Pavlov's," he shouted, "I'll kill her . . ."

After that, as soon as Andrei went on the rampage, Vera immediately grabbed her daughters and left to spend the night with neighbors. There was a family of Ukrainians called Morozenko at number 8 Derzhavin Street and more often than not Vera and her daughters went there. Andrei didn't hit his workbench though, he earned money for bread and vodka with that. He didn't lay a hand on it, in fact the sight of the workbench actually muted his rage. And the sight of his older daughter Tasya also muted his rage. That was why Tasya stopped leaving with her mother when her father was rampaging and instead stayed with him and calmed him down.

"Lie down for a while," she would tell him. "Tyatya, drink some pickle soup, then you'll feel better."

The Russian rampager is always a great weeper when he carries things to the extreme and cripples somebody or kills them. Then his heart is immediately relieved of its stress and he becomes a little child: "Pity me, good people . . ." And people do pity him. One famous Russian writer saw this as an extremely valuable national characteristic. However in the presence of his older daughter Andrei could fall into this emotional, tearful state even without carrying things to the extreme.

"You're my own blood," he would say, "It was for your sake I came back from the war, not for that lousy mother of yours. It was for your sake I was only slightly injured by that mine in Poland." And he would start unweaving Tasya's braid and weaving it back together again. He would weep and kiss her braid. "Your mother's braid was just like this," he would say, "when we got married . . ."

But in Vera's presence Tasya was never able to calm her father down. When he saw Vera, he went berserk. And he didn't love little Ustya.

"She's not my blood," he would shout. "You picked her up on the side . . ."

"Oh Lord," thought Vera, "if only he would pick up a woman on the side . . . I'd struggle on beside him somehow for the children's sake, just as long as he didn't touch me." Vera listened hopefully to what the neighbors were saying. But although they spoke disapprovingly about Andrei, not once did Vera hear anyone mention adultery, even though it was a long time since he had lived with Vera as husband and wife. There was gossip about Vera's adultery, supposedly with Pavlov, but all they said about Andrei was that he drank and beat his wife, and he bullied the children . . .

Time went by and everyone became accustomed to this situation. Andrei became accustomed to the idea of his wife being dissolute, she became accustomed to her husband being a drunkard and a raging bully, and the neighbors became accustomed to the Koposov family being an unhappy, wretched mess. They became so accustomed to everything that Vera even knew the signs of when Andrei would start rampaging and when he would calm down. He would rampage wildly shortly before the new moon and at the new moon there was a respite. So she prayed to God (for after her life was transformed into hell, she had started remembering God, although she didn't go to church) that the days before the new moon would be those non-working days when Andrei carted his wooden products to Gorky and stayed on there for a day or two, spending his earnings on drinking with friends. He came back from there morose and quiet, and if he started rampaging after a while, he didn't rampage with unbridled tempestuosity. He tried to beat Vera, but didn't frighten Ustya and didn't touch their property. Vera had only one pleasure in life now, apart from her daughters, of course. She lived in a lovely area and loved her native place, Bor town . . . The local district was abundant in fish, mushrooms and berries . . . Even in her womanly distress she could find a reason for joy here . . . She noticed that recently Tasya had been looking at her reproachfully and was growing more attached to her father, while Ustya, whom her father didn't love and wouldn't allow to play with the wood shavings beside the work bench any longer, had started clinging more tightly to her mother. Vera was still working at the garment factory, not sewing soldiers' quilted jackets, but drab, double-breasted, blue or gray cotton jackets for general wear. And on every non-working day Vera and little Ustya would go into the forest . . . There were so many different pleasures to enjoy there: you could choose from among the pleasures of listening and the pleasures of looking . . . Vera had been raised on the forest air and she was intending to raise little Ustya, her favorite, on the forest air too. It was no accident that their town was called Bor, which is a Slavic word for "forest" . . . "Tasya blames me," Vera thought, "she's her father's daughter, and Ustya is the only family I have now . . ." But she was afraid that in his violent drunkenness Andrei might do what he had threatened to do to Ustya . . .

One Sunday at the beginning of winter, when the forest was especially fragrant, Vera decided to take Ustya out for the forest air, but she wasn't there . . . Vera called and called, but Ustya wasn't anywhere . . . Vera dashed into the house and Andrei was there, morosely working at his bench, but not drunk. Tasya was sitting beside him, cleaning up the wood shavings.

"Have you seen Ustya?" Vera asked anxiously.

"I haven't seen your Ustya," Andrei replied morosely, "I didn't sign on to chase around after your sins and watch over them." And Tasya said:

"She went to see old Chesnokova."

"What Chesnokova is that?" asked Vera, still anxious.

"The woman the Jews live with," Andrei said, smiling unpleasantly "So maybe it wasn't Pavlov you got her from, but a Jew . . ."

Then Vera recalled that there really was an old woman called Chesnokova living in house number 30, and people said that she had a Jewish man and his daughter living there with her . . .

Along Derzhavin Street in Bor town, which was part of the Gorky region, and also along the streets of other towns in other regions that were formerly provinces, the sentries of the nation, the gnarled roots of the people, used to sit and still did sit on the wall-benches of little houses and small wooden benches beside the entrances of multistory buildings: broad-shouldered old women, their heads and foreheads roofed over with fluffy shawls, who had previously given birth to broad-shouldered sons. Their asiatic cheekbones were set firm, the nostrils of their short noses were upturned and all maternal tenderness had long ago faded from their colorless eyes, for what point is there to sentimentality when standing sentry duty? . . . "We . . ." they said without using any words, but simply with their high-cheekboned, short-nosed appearance, "We are Russians . . . And where would you be from?"

And therefore it had become known to the whole of the street named after the great Russian poet Derezhavin, who had once blessed Pushkin, that the old woman Chesnokova, an Old Believer, had two Jews living with her: a father of about thirty and his daughter of about eight. Moreover you couldn't tell about the girl straightaway, you had to look closely, but it was obvious from the very first glance that her father was a Jew . . . Vera had heard about this too, but she hadn't attached any importance to it and had forgotten about it in her trials and tribulations. And now, with Ustya in mind, she thought: "I'll teach her to go wandering about anywhere at all without even asking, who knows what might happen, people already speak badly about our family as it is."

Old Chesnokova had lived alone in her little house since her two sons were killed on the front and her old husband died. She was said to be either an Old Believer or a member of some other sect. Vera saw her occasionally, but they didn't greet each other. When Vera reached house number 30 on Derzhavin Street she knocked. The old woman opened the wicket door.

"Is my Ustya with you?" Vera asked angrily, as if the old woman in front of her had done something wrong.

But old Chesnokova replied in a different tone of voice.

"Yes, my dear, she's here . . . She's listening to the gramophone. Come in, do . . ."

"What would I come in for?" said Vera, "call Ustya, it's time she came home." And she blurted out impulsively: "A fine friend she's found for herself. As if there weren't enough Russians for her to be friends with . . ."

"What's wrong with her?" Chesnokova asked. "Ruth's a well-brought-up little girl, she respects her elders and her father doesn't drink . . ."

And suddenly, without knowing why, Vera felt that she wanted to take a look at the Jews that her little Ustya had taken to visiting. She brushed the snow off her short fur coat.

"All right," she said as she took the coat off in the hallway.

Vera walked into the room where the gramophone was playing and saw her Ustya sitting at a table beside a pale, light-haired girl who you could never suppose was Jewish. But the little girl's father was definitely a Jew, although there was something unusual about him . . . You didn't often see Jews in Bor town, although there were plenty of them in Gorky city. Ustya spotted her mother, jumped up and said:

"This is my mother . . . And this is Rufina, my friend . . . And this is her tyatya . . ."

Vera took another glance at "Rufina's tyatya" and again she couldn't understand what was unusual about this Jew . . . The more Vera looked, the more frightened she became, and the more frightened she was, the sweeter the feeling in her heart became . . .

And indeed, by this time Dan, the Viper, the Antichrist had matured in appearance and his Biblical facial features had become finally and completely defined. Although his hair was prematurely tinged with gray after all that he had seen and and the tasks he had performed, in the course of his earthly travels he had attained the peak condition of masculinity. Perish the thought, however, that any woman might truly understand in what the male vitality of the Antichrist consisted. No it wasn't a secret depravity, it was a state of reclusiveness, of wounded vulnerability. It wasn't the devil in him that was seductive. What Vera saw and felt, but could not understand, was the power of God manifested in masculinity as it is in the phenomena of nature . . . Power that is not comprehended by reason is always especially frightening and Vera's womanly fear made her feel unpleasantly agitated.

"What kind of music is that you're listening to?" she said, "I don't understand it."

"It's a Jewish record," replied Dan, the Viper, the Antichrist.

"So that's it," Vera said, and laughed in a hasty kind of way, like a drunken peasant woman at a market. "Could you put on a Russian record, since I never learned any Jewish."

"We can put on a Russian one," replied Dan, the Viper, the Antichrist, and turning toward his daughter Ruth he said: "Bring the rhyming ditties from the dresser."

Suddenly Rufina, who was also named Pelagia, although neither she nor the Antichrist knew that, assumed a different expression and the good-natured, rustic features of a girl born in Brusyany village near Rzhev altered to express the genuinely southern, dry passion that is only possible in girls who have matured early.

"Tell your Ustya to leave," Rufina said, "I won't have anything more to do with her."

Old Chesnokova was startled by this and started scolding Rufina:

"Impudent hussy, don't go shaming your father in front of other people."

And her father the Antichrist also asked her quietly, without raising his voice as he looked into his daughter's eyes:

"What's wrong with you, Ruth?" He knew her as an affectionate, gentle, kind girl, but her place seemed to have been taken by someone else.

Instead of replying Ruth turned away and walked through into the next room.

"All right then, that's fine," said Ustya, "I won't play with the sourpuss anymore either. Let's go, Momma . . ."

Completely bewildered, Vera took her daughter and left Old Chesnokova's house . . . She had a strange feeling that her previous misfortune had not been enough and now she had picked up a new misfortune along her way.

A lot also changed in the Antichrist's family after the unexpected guest's visit. It should be noted here that the Antichrist loved his adopted daughter as only those who have been schooled in eternal love for their Creator, the Lord, can love children. That is why Jews love their children so much, although they often don't understand the reason for this, since for the people of Abraham love for the Creator is not so much a religion, as first and foremost a national instinct. Man's relations with his own instincts are not simple, they are often based on a misunderstanding, which may be scientific or philosophical in nature, or on denial, which is, of course, quite powerless. And therefore, among the numerous deniers of the Lord Jews appear especially spurious, and among talented atheists there are few Jews and much witty, frivolous French satire. As a general rule the atheistic Jew is either talentless or inconsistent. However even those Jews who deny the Lord follow the Lord's precepts in their daily life, and the great national instinct of love, in which they have been trained through the Lord, is manifested in Jewish mothers and fathers through their religious love for their children. What then could be expected of the Lord's emissary, the Antichrist, who was also a solitary man? He would have loved any child, totally expending the little love that remained to him after his love for the Lord. And in fact he loved his daughter rather more than that, having devoted to her even a smidgen of his love for the Lord, since a rational father always loves a daughter just a little bit more than a son. Of course Ruth-Pelagia also loved a father like this, and her daughterly love was not diminished in the slightest after the uninvited woman's visit, although she did become more nervous and thoughtful. And Ruth's moods also started changing rapidly.

One day Ruth came home from school cheerful and excited.

"Father," she said to the Antichrist, "it's really nice outside today, such lovely snow."

And indeed, large flakes were falling slowly and gently through the windless air. Ruth grabbed a soup plate and darted out into the yard to catch snowflakes. Then she came back, put the wet plate on the table and suddenly asked:

"Father, where did do you get me from?"

In all their life together Ruth had never asked this question before, but now she had. Well, any parent can hear this question from his child, although it is no longer a question for every child at that age, especially for a girl.

"One day," Dan, the Viper, the Antichrist replied to his daughter, "it was really, really cold and frosty outside, and there was a strong wind blowing. And I heard someone crying. I walked outside and there was no one there. And then there was more crying. I looked up, and you were sitting in a tree . . ."

Ruth smiled, but rather sadly, sat a bit closer to her father, nestled against him and said in a whisper:

"That woman who came, she was my mother . . ."

"Don't be silly, Ruth," said the Antichrist, "your mother died on a German train . . . And that was Ustya's mother."

"No," Ruth replied, "I took a close look at her. She has eyes like mine, and hair . . . But don't you worry. Father . . . You're the only one I love, and I hate her . . ."

"That's not good either," said the Antichrist. "What do you hate her for?"

"She looked at you in a bad way," said Ruth, "but before she was kind . . . I remember her churning butter by banging a bottle of milk against a pillow . . ."

After that the Antichrist started casting anxious glances at his daughter and keeping her close to him. And she tried to stay close to him too . . . Now the Antichrist walked his daughter to school and collected her from school, and they walked everywhere together, which brought them both great joy.

But from that day on, Vera knew no joy, not even the very slightest. Previously all her thoughts and strength had been devoted to avoiding her husband at night, for she had learned how to avoid him during the day. But now all her passion had been instantly and totally directed to the goal of giving herself to the Jew and unleashing all her pent-up female vigor with him, for she knew that she was still strong in womanly matters and even after two births her belly was still as firm as a young virgin's. The essential quality in her that her husband Andrei Koposov pined for, that drove him wild, was still sweet. Andrei beat Vera less often now, he was obviously tired of it, and the more estranged he became from his wife, the more attached he became to his older daughter, Tasya. He brought her presents from the market and when he wasn't working in the evening he liked to unweave and re-weave her braid in his corner by the workbench. The Koposovs' life had become less tempestuous, but no less bitter and harsh . . . When Vera wasn't working, she walked without knowing where she was going, for it had become hard for her to remain still and the thing she feared most of all was physical repose, since her greatest torment arose in the resting state. She made up a bed for herself on the floor beside the stove and waited forlornly, languishing until three or four in the morning, when she fell into a brief, pre-dawn sleep.

On one especially agonizing night in early spring just before the new moon, Vera decided to go to see old Chesnokova herself, but she couldn't go without a good reason. In the morning as she was getting Ustya ready for school Vera said:

"Daughter, go to see Rufina after your classes today and I'll come to pick you up from there."

"Oh no," Ustya replied, "I'm not friends with Rufina anymore. Sergeevna says they're Jews and they have lots of money."

Sergeevna was an old woman with high cheekbones and a short nose, who kept watch in the vicinity of house number 17 on Derzhavin Street, where her very appearance warned anyone and everyone: "We're Russians . . . And where would you be from?"

"Why listen to Sergeevna?" Vera exclaimed angrily, "Sergeevna's old. You should listen to what they teach you in school."

"They say the same about Rufina in school," Ustya replied, "they say she's got lots of money and her father's a cosmopolitan."

At this point Tasya put in a word too:

"Tyatya says we mustn't go there."

"Oh, you so-and-sos," said Vera, infuriated, "it's always tyatya this and tyatya that . . . your mother means nothing to you . . . Who raised you and fed you during the war? . . ."

"And papa defended us," said Tasya. "He was wounded three times and he's got state decorations."

"Even if he was wounded ten times," Vera said rancorously, "who gave him the right to treat me so badly, and beat me, and drink so hard? . . ."

"He drinks out of his misery," said Tasya, "because he loves you. Anyway, that's not something to talk about in front of Ustya . . . Off you go to school, Ustya . . . And it's time for you and me to be going, Momma."

Vera had got Tasya a place at the factory too, as an apprentice in the sewing shop. As soon as Ustya had gone to school, Vera said to Tasya:

"Why do you embarrass me in front of the child? Your father's taken you away from me, and now you want to take Ustya too. Ustya's fine now, but before she was alien blood, an outsider . . . picked up by chance . . . from Pavlov . . ."

"I already told you," replied Tasya, "tyatya says that out of his misery . . . He loves you, momma."

"Is that so?" said Vera, "you're still too wet behind the ears to have an opinion on this, you're still my daughter and you have to do as I tell you . . . Is that a decent way to think about your neighbors? Are you Stepanova, an old woman? . . . What have they taught you in school? They've taught you the friendship of nations. Are our neighbors really to blame for being Jews? Did they really choose of their own freewill to be Jews? . . . You should be ashamed of yourself. If you and your father won't let Ustya go there, then you 'll go there yourself to pay a visit . . . And ask Chesnokova for her embroidery pattern . . . Chesnokova has a good pattern for sofa cushions, I spotted it . . ."

"All right," said Tasya, "if that's what you want, Momma, I'll pay her a visit. But don't send Ustya there. Ustya's still a child."

After work mother and daughter arrived at house number 13 on Derzhavin Street, where Chesnokova lived. Vera knocked at the wicket door and her daughter Tasya stood to one side. And Tasya stayed there all the time, her expression and manner emphasizing her position off to the side of things. Her mother Vera, in her frantic passion at the thought that she would see the one person she yearned for by day and by night, became loud and fidgety. But Tasya stayed off at one side without saying anything. When Vera saw Chesnokova's lodger, the Jew, her mind clouded over almost completely and she could barely manage to stay on her feet, but she forced herself to remain standing and instead of asking Chesnokova for her pattern for embroidering cushions, she spoke saucily, as if she was a street trollop, as if she had never saved herself during the war when she was young, and hadn't lived exclusively for the sake of news of her husband from the front and her daughters, disavowing all other pleasures, and she said:

"Hello there . . . My daughter and I have come to listen to the gramophone, you won't turn us away, will you?"

"Have a seat," said the Antichrist, "Ruth will bring you the rhyming ditties from the cabinet right away."

Ruth went to the cabinet and brought the Russian rhyming ditties, but she had suddenly turned pale. And old Chesnokova, who was spying from her room through the chink beside the door, heaved a deep sigh:

"Oh, something bad is going to happen, Lord save us and spare us." And she crossed herself, not with the tips of her thumb and two fingers, a gesture only good for taking salt out of a salt box, but with two fingers, the correct way of doing it.

Meanwhile Vera took a fine, white cotton handkerchief out of her pocket, dusted off a chair and told Tasya, who was standing off to one side:

"Sit down, Tasya, I've dusted off the chair, since you're wearing a new dress," and once again she found her own words amusing and laughed.

Afraid of further awkward gaffes from her mother, Tasya avoided doing anything at all to contradict her and sat down on the chair, merely blushing at her mother's stupid behavior. And when she blushed her beauty, which was still delicate and not yet harassed by life like her mother's, was revealed to its full extent. Dan the Viper, the Antichrist noticed this beauty and his heart began beating in a strange manner, so that he was actually surprised by his own condition. For as an emissary of the Lord, he knew only divine love, he loved his daughter Ruth with divine love, as a father loves his daughter or a brother loves his sister. But Dan the Viper, the Antichrist did not know what human love was, he had never experienced its effect, although he had, of course, been taught the truth that everything good that people have is something divine, debased for human comprehension . . . Since only man's sins are made to his own measure. Thus human love is also a debased version of divine love. And moreover, whereas divine love partakes of eternity and is vast, calm, steadfast and unchanging, human love partakes of the moment and is hasty, inconstant, bewildering and garish.

Looking at Dan the Viper, the Antichrist, Tasya beheld his biblical visage and also felt her own heart beating, but was not surprised by this, although this was also the first time that such a thing had happened to her . . . In the state of virginal naivety, clarity is an inherent characteristic of love. They carried on sitting there, the Antichrist alarmed and astonished by his own condition, Tasya alarmed but not astonished by hers, Ruth pale with an unchildlike pallor, old Chesnokova gasping in her room as she sat on a stool beside the chink of the door, crossing herself in Old Believer style, and the gramophone laughing and squealing its Voronezh rhyming ditties, with Vera laughing and squealing in time with it and also clapping her hands. Suddenly Vera jumped up off her chair with her face as scarlet as Tasya's, only not from embarrassment, but from womanly exhilaration, and clattered her heels across the floor in Russian style, wedding style, like scattering peas out of a sack, flinging her arms out wide as if to say: "Look how vast our sweeping expanses are . . . The steppes, and the forests, and the rivers . . . Haven't you been to Siberia yet? The expanses out there are boundless, endless . . . And the Russian woman has populated all of that. In order to populate such vast expanses with people, you need a thorough understanding of what you're about. There are two cases when a woman needs to have a thorough grasp of her job: when the people are constantly being exterminated and need to be be replenished, and when the people live in spaces that are too large and need to be populated . . . In such cases a woman is required to have great skill . . . Skill as sweet as sweet berries, as sweet as honey, for the salvation of the people lies in its women's success . . ."

Of course none of this was spoken out loud, or even explicitly thought, but it was all there in that jaunty, female dance of which the Russian woman is capable. With a passionate, shameless shriek reminiscent of a woman's moans at the climactic moment of ultimate physical pleasure, flinging out her arms, as if dispelling the excessive heat on a Russian stove-top bed, Vera dashed about to the boisterous strains of the Voronezh ditties and then suddenly nestled close against Dan the Viper, the Antichrist, grabbing him and thrusting against his body her breasts that were still plump and firm, although they had fed two daughters, and were now aching and tantalizing her own flesh.

"Join me in a dance, Dan Yakovlevich."

Suddenly the very final drop of blood drained out of the face of Ruth, who was also named Pelagia, the little girl who was the Antichrist's adopted daughter, and she cried out in a hysterical, country-village fashion as she fell to the floor in a dead faint. Old Chesnokova immediately ran out of her room, stopped the gramophone and handed a mug of water to the Antichrist, who was leaning down over his daughter in fright.

"Let's go home, Momma," Tasya said in a quiet voice.

Confused by what had happened and heated after her dance, Vera stood there breathing heavily, and through this heavy breathing she asked in true Russian style:

"Perhaps I did something wrong? Perhaps I should apologize?"

"There's no need to do anything," said Tasya. "They have enough to deal with already, let's go Momma."

Without taking their leave, Vera and Tasya walked out of the house that they had thrown into disarray, each mulling over her own thoughts. Especially wide-ranging, expansive thoughts arise and the breath flows especially freely on the evening before a new moon in early spring. The air smells of melting snow, and the trees all around are like women in labor . . . Derzhavin Street is green when the trees' branches come into leaf, for the forest is close by, and then the old watchwomen station themselves in the shade of the trees wearing a different uniform: white headscarfs and flannel robes. But at present, in early spring, they had not yet changed out of their winter uniform, the poorer among them in quilted jackets, the wealthier wearing loose coats with fox-fur collars. The moment these sentries of the nation hear footsteps, they peer hard into the gloom, murmuring, their very appearance articulating the password: "We are Russians . . . And where would you be from?" . . . Could that be the Koposovs coming? A good-for-nothing family . . . He drinks and rampages, she's a harlot, and what can the children learn from that? Here comes Vera with her daughter at this late hour. Where from? Could it be from number 30, where the Jews live with Chesnokova?

Challenged as they walked along by the mute old women on sentry duty, the mother and daughter reached their own house, number 2 at the very end of the street. Andrei wasn't drunk, but he was tipsy and he would have liked to hit Vera once or twice for coming home late, but when he saw her with Tasya, he didn't try to hit her and just gave her a menacing glare.

Vera got dinner ready. She didn't have any dinner herself, but immediately lay down to sleep beside the stove, so Tasya put Ustya to bed, which was unusual, because Vera always put her favorite to bed. Vera was so tired and felt so indifferent to the life around her that she fell asleep instantly, although she had been certain that she would suffer agonizing insomnia.

From that time on she noticed a change in her daughter Tasya, a change that was not difficult for a woman and a mother to understand. At first this realization was like a sharp knife driven straight into her heart, but later, after thinking things over, Vera actually found this change very welcome. For a woman is always cunning and calculating in her boundless female insanity. Ever since the time of Adam woman has been irrepressible in her madness, and the Lord had good cause to tell her:

"I will surely multiply your pain in childbearing; in pain you shall bring forth children. Your desire shall be to your husband, and he shall rule over you."

But to Adam He said:

"Because you have listened to the voice of your wife and have eaten of the tree of which I commanded you, 'You shall not eat of it,' cursed is the ground because of you, in pain you shall eat of it all the days of your life . . . By the sweat of your face you shall eat bread, till you return to the ground, for out of it you were taken; for you are dust and to dust you shall return . . ."

And so woman's madness and woman's intractability laid the very foundations of human life itself, when sinful man was banished from paradise and cursed to labor in the sweat of his face . . . And when man made the transition from being fed by God to feeding himself, he had with him his wife Eve, a name that in translation from Biblical language, signifies "life." Thus, if at the very basis of the human life that began with banishment from the Garden of Eden both female madness and the very word "life" are combined in the name of a woman, can anything at all check woman in her impetuous desiring? This is also the reason why the third plague of the Lord, fornication, is so powerful and irrepressible . . . In this chastisement woman is the executioner, even if she herself perishes in this life . . .

Vera Koposova realized that she could only achieve her goal through her daughter's love, in the face of which the Jew was helpless, since he loved Tasya too . . . And having realized this, she concealed this cunning, irrepressible female madness of hers for the time being.

Meanwhile the fragrant Volga region spring ended and the young summer started, the forest came into bloom and the berrying season began. The cunning woman noticed that just recently, while her daughter Tasya still allowed her morose father to pamper her, unweaving and reweaving her braid as he used to unweave and reweave her mother Vera's braid in their young days, Tasya's response to his endearments had become more reserved. "Now is the right time," she thought.

"Tasya," she said, "go up to the crest on Sunday . . ." The "crest" was what local people called the high edge of a gully that was overgrown with forest, "Go up to the crest, Tasya, the raspberries are ready and your father needs fresh raspberry tea for his injured chest. I'd go myself, only I'm busy in the workshop, making up for my time off in spring, when Ustya was ill. Go, you won't be able to find another free day, they'll pick all the fresh raspberries and there'll be none left for you."

"All right," said Tasya, "I'll go." Despite her marriageable age, she was still obedient in ordinary matters, although in extreme cases she could contradict her father and mother if she felt that they were being unfair. But what was unfair about this, her mother sending her to the forest to pick raspberries for her father who had been wounded at the front? On the contrary, Tasya was actually glad to go: perhaps her momma's and tyatya's love might yet be mended?

"All right," she said, "I'll go."

"Now I just have to do everything else right," Tasya's cunning mother thought in her madness. And she set off, abandoning all shame, to house number 30 on Derzhavin Street, where she had previously acted in such a flagrantly disgraceful manner... This time old Chesnokova received her coolly.

"What do you want?" she asked, stopping Vera at the wicket door and not letting her inside.

However Vera noticed that the object of her passion, the Jew, was quite close by on the porch, sorting berries with his daughter.

"Granny Chesnokova," said Vera, "I see you've already gone berrying in the forest... Did you go to the crest? I need berries really badly, because my husband was wounded and he has to have an infusion of fresh berries."

"Well then, go," Chesnokova replied, "the crest's awash with berries. It's a bumper crop this year."

"The problem is," Vera said, "that I'm busy working on Sunday, so I have to send my daughter Tasya to the crest on her own. It's a remote spot, and she's a young girl. She's afraid to go alone, and I'm afraid for her. Are any of you going up to the crest?"

"No," Chesnokova replied. "We've already been, look, we're sorting the berries. But what is there to be afraid of? The last bear was seen three years ago. They shot a lot of the bears, and they moved farther away from people, deeper into the forest."

"They shot a lot of bears," said Vera, "but that wicked man is still in one piece. That wicked man is a greater menace to girls than a bear. Whoever might pester them, God forbid that it should be Pavlov."

Pavlov was still as well-known as ever in Bor town: mothers used him as a satanic figure to frighten young girls who were impatient to stray too far on walks:

"Go on then, and Pavlov will catch you!"

Pavlov had changed in one way: whereas during the war any woman at all would do for him, nowadays he only had eyes for fresh young girls and even, or so it was said, for little girls of only nine or ten, who were large, voluptuous and striking for their age. Pavlov himself was almost thirty . . . However he got away with everything, since his front-line friends who held responsible positions in the town covered for him. At least, that was what people said. But there were dark mutterings about the villain too. On one occasion a rumor spread that Pavlov had been caught red-handed committing rape and he was in jail . . . And then two or three days later Pavlov was seen, back again strolling drunk along the main street near the movie theater and in the park near the dance floor, a fine handsome figure in his navy peacoat, although a little on the flabby side, pestering the girls and starting fights . . . Aggrieved and resentful fathers and mothers of young girls wrote to the local newspaper, the Bor Pravda. At the newspaper office, they started pondering. On the one hand, they needed to respond to the workers' wishes, but on the other hand, they had to avoid offending Pavlov's protectors. And so the Bor Pravda newspaper resorted to a tried and tested gambit, having recalled the existence of so-called imaginative literature, which could not be held accountable for anything, since it did not deal in concrete facts, but in general, USSR-wide or even worldwide phenomena. The very best form of such generalizations is poetry. And by fortunate happenstance a versifier turned up, in accordance with Marx's assertion that "the demand produces the Raphaels." Of course, this versifier was no Raphael, but at least he was local, born and raised in the family of a simple worker at the gas-fired boiler house of the Bor Central Hospital. And his mother was a bookkeeper. This versifier of Russian nationality, whose family name was Somov, dreamed of studying at the Literary Institute in Moscow, but as yet he was pursuing two lines of self-development independently, lyric poetry and satire, although he was actually keener on satire.

And so he mocked his own surname, Somov, for being reminiscent of "som," the Russian word for "catfish," and also other similarly fishy names, such as Yorshov (reminiscent of "yorsh," meaning "ruff"), Karpov (for obvious reasons), Shchukin (reminiscent of "shchuka," meaning "pike") and others, but there he could not find any surnames like Sterlyadev (reminiscent of "sterlyad," meaning "sterlet") or Sevryugov (reminiscent of "sevryuga," meaning "sturgeon"): such surnames were too expensive . . . With a track record like this and abilities along these lines, Somov was a perfect match for the Bor Pravda's requirements. And so he satisfied its demand. Firstly he changed the location of the action from Bor town to Moscow city, where he himself had been yearning to go for a long time. Secondly, he changed Pavlov's surname to Prokhorov and his first name from Stepan to Ivan. Following the path blazed by the Greek writer of fables Aesop, Somov wrote a sort of satirical fable, which began like this:

On Moscow's honor roll of frontline vets
A certain Ivan Prokhorov could be found,
Yet this Ivan, a shabby character,
Was quite unfit to bear his scars from wounds
Earned in fierce battle for our Soviet power.
But of such matters we shall speak anon,
Meanwhile, for now, listen . . .

There followed a verse-form listing of all the hideous outrages committed by Pavlov. The first blow struck against Somov in response came from Pavlov himself, who was not deceived by Somov's Aesopian language. Somov fled from the second blow by vaulting over the fence of the park beside the dance floor. However the third blow, which came from the local Department of Agitation and Propaganda ("Agitprop"), was absolutely crushing, especially since Somov had been counting on asking the department for a character reference in order to overcome the competition for places at the Moscow Literary Institute . . . Somov had heard that the competition to get into the institute came mostly from Jews, and if you were Russian and you had a character reference, then you were automatically entitled to a place . . .

Agitprop declared him guilty of nothing less than sycophancy and the attempted slander of the heroic defenders of the Homeland, who had shed their blood . . . At the Bor Pravda offices, doors were anxiously slammed shut, creating drafts. Some there escaped with a slight fright and a note in their personnel file, while others were completely deprived of the opportunity to participate in subsequent cultural construction. The Bor Pravda published a letter from a group of frontline veterans entitled "Against the scurrilous verse slander of a certain Somov," which was written by the Agitprop functionary Vladimir (Vilner.) After he had been granted this rock-solid defense Pavlov's brazen behavior knew absolutely no bounds and people in Bor town were afraid to let a pretty young daughter out of the house.

But people wanted to go for walks, especially since the summer evenings in Bor town are so fine that a young heart frets and pines when deprived of them. The streets are green, the forest air mingles with air from the river to create an absolutely unique potion, waltzes in the renditions of the local fish processing plant's brass band waft on the breeze, and glowing above everything is a godless, astronomical sky, beneath which people actually feel calmer, since it delights everyone but imposes no obligations on them at all. Simply drink in the air with your seventeen-year-old lungs, dream about love, glancing from time to time at the moon and the stars . . . If only it weren't for Pavlov . . . It was terrifying for a girl to think she might run into Pavlov late in the evening . . .

Tasya ran into him once not far from the place where Pavlov had tried to rape Tasya's young mother Vera during the war. And even at about the same time in the evening, but of course that was all coincidence. Pavlov grabbed hold of her without saying a word, but by some miracle Tasya managed to break free and get away from him. In her torn blouse, shuddering bodily, she flung herself on her mother's breast. Andrei was away at the time, he had taken his wooden wares to sell in Gorky. He came back a couple of days later, fortunately in a relatively calm state, at the new moon. Vera said to him:

"You drink with Pavlov, he's a frontline veteran and he's supposed to be your friend, but the day before yesterday Pavlov tried to rape your daughter."

Andrei's face darkened and he said:

"He probably thought the daughter took after the mother and was an easy lay," then he went out somewhere, although it was already night. He came back half an hour later and said to Tasya: "Don't be afraid, daughter, walk wherever you want, he won't touch you again. I may not know how to write poems, but I'll gouge his eyes out."

And after that Pavlov actually never did go near Tasya again, he only looked at her from a distance every now and then. But even so Vera had no certain guarantee that her daughter was safe, for she knew what Pavlov was like when he drank and his male urges surged up . . . They said he took a little old rifle with him on strolls in the forest, as if he was going hunting . . . And was Pavlov the only one a young woman needed to be on her guard against? . . . Vera had loved and protected her daughter for as long as she could remember. How great therefore must have been the female madness that had taken possession of her, in order for her to exploit her own daughter for her own purposes. This woman had a cunning purpose in mind when she went to Chesnokova's house to announce that her daughter was going up alone to collect raspberries on the crest where the stream ran out of the gully, and also going as early as possible, about seven, so that there would be fewer pickers and more raspberries.

When Vera's daughter rose at the crack of dawn, ate a hurried meal, took a basket and set off into the forest, her mother followed her. She had made up the story about being busy in the factory workshop. Vera cautiously sneaked through the bushes, wondering apprehensively: "Will Dan Yakovlevich come or won't he?" She had found out a lot about him. She had found out that he had come here from somewhere near Rzhev city, that he was a widow, his wife had been killed in the war and here he worked as a night watchman at the fish processing plant, an unusual profession for a Jew, so he was probably relatively stupid for one of them: they always managed to find a cushy job. Vera did not know that since the Antichrist had acquired an adopted daughter, he could no longer live on nothing but the bread of exile bequeathed by the prophet Ezekiel, and that among modern professions that provided a living, the profession of night watchman was the most suitable for Dan, the Viper, the Antichrist, for it was pursued well away from people, and that being under the night sky vaguely reminded him of his native occupation as a shepherd. Vera had found out many things about the Jew living with Chesnokova, but there was very much that she did not know. Above all, of course, she did not know that Dan Yakovlevich was the Antichrist, the Lord's emissary . . . One thing she did know for certain, as a suffering woman and a loving mother, was that Dan Yakovlevich and her daughter Tasya had fallen in love, but they did not know how they could meet and did not dare to arrange a meeting . . . A woman who feels passion for a man who loves her daughter finds herself in a strange condition. Either she feels her daughter's flesh as a part of her own and rejoices, or she senses her own sickness in this flesh and suffers, even starting to hate it, as a person starts to hate their own hand, foot or head and curses them when they hurt badly . . . And so, sometimes delighting through her daughter in her own womanly happiness, sometimes seeing her daughter's happiness as another's good fortune that plundered and stole from her, Vera could have lapsed, not only into madness of the flesh, but also insanity of the mind if the instinctive cunning for which Eve was cursed by the Lord had not suggested to Vera that in her torment she must not trust in feeling, but in reason. To revel in feelings is only rational in times of happiness. And no sooner had she realized this than she became an ordinary adulteress, consumed only by an inordinate passion that had to be satisfied by exploiting every possible means . . . And so she devised a plan to arrange a meeting between the man she craved, but had no access to, and her own daughter, whom she loved.

The cunning woman stole on, following her daughter, and before she knew it, there was the crest, a wild, remote place. The gully was overgrown with trees and bushes, the stream babbled quietly and the spot was simply teeming with raspberries. But the Jew wasn't there, he hadn't come, although he had definitely heard what Vera said. Vera sat down some distance away, so that her daughter wouldn't see her, and moped, feeling sick at heart. But Tasya, all unsuspecting, started plucking raspberries. She carried on collecting them until she had almost half a basketful, when suddenly she heard branches crunching and the Jew walked out into the clearing, also carrying a small basket. Tasya looked up, dropping her basket, and the berries scattered across the ground. And a force that appeared strange and comical to the heavens flung the lovers into each other's arms: Dan, the Viper, the Antichrist, whose earthly domain lay from Khatlon, leading on to Hamath, and Tasya Koposova from Bor town in the Gorky Region. They embraced without words, without tears, without sighs and stood there, each holding on tight to their own: the Antichrist holding Tasya, Tasya holding the Antichrist. They stood there in each other's arms, while Vera lay in the bushes, with every last fiber of her being aching. However once again the crazed woman outwitted the torment of her lascivious passion and maintained her female reason intact . . . Meanwhile the Antichrist and Tasya carried on standing there in each other's arms without moving until Tasya, a delicate young woman, felt her arms and legs starting to turn numb from this passionate immobility. Then the Antichrist, who could now sense in himself every sensation of his beloved, asked:

"Will you come tomorrow?"

"Yes," Tasya replied, "after work, at six o'clock. Our sewing shop closes at five, but I have to get changed." And they parted without a kiss. The Antichrist left quickly, for the Antichrist knows how to disappear instantly, but Tasya stayed to gather raspberries, so that her mother would not be suspicious. And her mother, having overcome her weakness, felt glad about what had happened, which had come about as she had planned.

And between the Antichrist and Tasya there sprang up a constant love. Of course this was not the divine love with which a brother loves his sister or a father loves his daughter, but neither was it the human love with which a man loves a woman. However since the Antichrist could not love otherwise, and this was the first time that Tasya had ever loved at all, they did not find such a love surprising. They always met at the same spot, beside the stream at the beginning of the gully overgrown with forest . . . When Tasya caught sight of Dan, she would take a few steps toward him, like a sleepwalker at the full moon, and at the final step her strength would desert her and her knees would start to buckle, so that she would have fallen in a faint, but the Antichrist never allowed her to take that final step, which might perhaps have been into her salvation: when Tasya grew weak she always fell, not onto the ground, but onto his breast, and they stood there without any kisses or any words. Their meeting was the same every time, for only shallow love requires variety. Tasya received everything in full measure from the Antichrist's embrace, and her virginal purity and delicacy allowed the Antichrist to avoid that plague of the Lord, lust, to which he was as susceptible as all earthly beings. And so in the forest near Bor town in the Gorky region, the age-old dream of a third possibility, neither carnal nor ascetic, was realized.

In attempting to rape angels the inhabitants of the city of Sodom, those pioneers of the modern sexual revolution, were seeking a third possibility. Tamar's first husbands, the brothers Ir and Onan, sought a third possibility.

But Ir died and when Onan went intoin unto his brother's wife, he spilled his seed on the ground, immortalizing his name as a term for human sickness or caprice. Other perversions also arise from searches for a third possibility, neither male not female, however no third organ can be found and no sexual "perpetuum mobile" can be created. As yet only one case of a third possibility has been known: neither carnal nor ascetic and not, of course, the Greek substitute of Platonism, although in the area of substitutes sin is talented, of which Greek Christianity is an example . . . But here there was no substitution. In the summer of 1949 Tasya Koposova of Bor town experienced a third possibility . . . She found it because she did not seek it . . . There also exists, however, the law of dialectical materialism, which does not necessarily have to be studied from Feuerbach, since it is expounded clearly enough in the Soviet song: "A cheerful man is a man who laughs, a man who wants is a man who achieves, a man who seeks will always find."

Stepan Pavlov, whose entire life had been a rejection of the opium of the Bible, wished to obtain Tasya, and therefore he sought her everywhere and found her on the crest, beside the gully, in the arms of a Jew. He was walking through the forest with his gun, whistling a little song about a jolly breeze, in which the fundamentals of dialectics were articulated. But what was this he suddenly spied from afar, what was going on here, my lads? The Jews had grabbed everything for themselves, and the girls too . . . He broke off his whistling and shouldered his rifle, and who knows what he was planning to do in that first instant . . . Then he gathered his wits and in an intense fit of bitter resentment thought of a more artful plan. "Nobody in this town dared to beat me, but her father, Andrei Koposov, struck me. All right then, if a Russian lad and a frontline veteran isn't to your liking, you can have a home-front Jewish rat for a son-in-law." Pavlov crawled forward in frontline style and when he got close he overheard the time of Tasya's meeting with the Antichrist the next day. Pavlov knew where to look for Andrei, so he found him easily and without any dialectics. In the center of Bor town, opposite the movie theater, there was a small plywood pavilion known as "The Blue Danube," although the sign said "Beer, mineral water, cold snacks." Nobody knew how a foreign river came to feature in this way in a town on the Volga. Perhaps the pavilion had been given its name by one of its local patrons, who had taken part in the storming of Budapest and the taking of Bucharest or Vienna. The only actual fact was that the plywood pavilion really was painted light blue. The saleswoman in this pavilion was Nyura, with whom Pavlov had lived at one time. Before Pavlov started on his drink, he was in the habit of engaging Nyura in contentious squabbling about having received short measure or having been shortchanged. But she always gave him as good as she got, she was a woman who had achieved complete equality.

"You," Pavlov told her cheerfully, "are a bitch."

"And you are a scumbag," Nyura cheerfully replied.

"You're a thief . . ."

"And you're a useless prick . . ."

"Fuck your mother . . ."

"Fuck yours, it'll be cheaper . . ."

At this point, under the influence of what he had just seen and experienced, Pavlov told Nyura:

"You're a Jew, a Yid . . ."

Nyura burst into tears.

"What kind of Jew am I, why is he insulting me like that, guys?"

The regular patrons intervened.

"Stop getting peeved at Pavlov, Nyura . . . He isn't worth it . . . And you, Styopa, come over here, we'll have a drink . . ."

Andrei Koposov was also in the pavilion, but with a different group. They started drinking separately and ended up all together. When the groups merged like this, Pavlov said to Andrei Koposov:

"Let's step outside, I've got something to tell you . . ."

"Let's go," said Andrei.

Their drinking companions, aware of their falling-out, started trying to calm them both down:

"Drop it, guys, you're both frontline veterans, what scores can there be between brother Slavs?"

At that time "brother Slavs" was a fashionable turn of phrase, brought back from the front. Pavlov replied:

"I'm not going to hit Andrei, because I know he'd break my ribs, but I need to talk to him, heart to heart."

They went out and stood by the pavilion wall, smoked "Labor" postwar papirosas and sprayed their pee on the pavilion's foundation. In addition Pavlov twice relieved the pressure in his bowels at full volume. Just as Pavlov was about to start speaking a stray dog ran up and started demonstrating its devotion, which distracted him from his thoughts.

"Ah, you bastard," Pavlov shouted, throwing a stone and hitting the target. The dog yelped and disappeared, squealing.

"Well, what did you want?" Andrei began, seeing that Pavlov was hesitating, and moved back a few steps so that if Pavlov came at him to take revenge for the last blow, he could kick him in the bread basket again.

Pavlov spotted this gesture and said:

"You've got it in for the wrong guy, Andriusha . . . I'm a frontline veteran, and you're a frontline veteran . . . Tasya's the daughter of a frontline veteran, and my intentions concerning her are serious . . . But there's this Jew, who sat out the entire war in the rear, and he's seducing her."

"What are you talking about, what Jew?" Koposov shouted.

"Don't you go grabbing me by the shirt like that," Pavlov replied. "That Jew who lives with Chesnokova at 30 Derzhavin Street."

And he told Andrei what he'd seen . . . Andrei went red in the face, then turned pale and shouted out three words:

"I'll kill him!"

"Hold your horses," Pavlov replied, delighted that his blow had landed harder than a fist in the teeth. "You're always giving me dark looks, Andriusha, even if we're drinking together. You believe the rumors that I was mixed up with your wife. I admit she did try to get it together with me, but I gave her the brush-off, because I respect frontline comradeship."

Andrei grated his teeth.

"Leave my wife out of this, we're not talking about her. We're talking about my daughter."

"And I've got a plan concerning your daughter," said Pavlov. "When they meet at the crest tomorrow, we'll catch them red-handed . . . Agreed?"

"Agreed," Koposov replied, "come on, let's have another drink . . ."

They had another drink and Andrei relapsed into a dull, somber silence, the kind when you can't tell what to expect from a man when the silence ends, whether he'll fall into a deep, heavy sleep or kill someone. But Pavlov became expansive, positively gushing with the kind of merriment that simply demands a rousing performance of some well-known Russian rhyming ditty inherited from your grandfathers and great-grandfathers. True, he was hoarse and his voice was no longer one that made it a pleasure to perform, not a tenor, but he bellowed out the words with gusto.

"Beat the Yids and save Russia . . . Chaim has shut his shop . . . That funny couple, Abram and Sara . . . Gallant Yankel in the war . . . We defended them and saved them, and they crucified Christ, they sold out Soviet Power . . . We're in the trenches and they're in their shops . . . During the war I never saw a Jew on the front line . . . A certain Jew went to the front, but then shot himself out of fright . . ."

He started bawling so loudly that the militia recognized his familiar voice and thought Pavlov had started another fight at the Blue Danube. However when they arrived there was a noisy racket, but no fight.

"Why are you making that din, Pavlov?"

"Well, why do the Jews drink our blood?"

"Don't cause a disturbance now, Pavlov," said the sergeant.

"But they're allowed, are they? Robbing a father, a frontline veteran, of his own daughter . . ."

"Who's robbing which father of who? If you've got proof, write a formal statement . . . Which father's being robbed of his daughter, what are you talking about?"

"Why, my friend here . . . During the war he . . . He spilled his own blood . . ." Pavlov was too drunk to talk sense.

At this point Andrei slammed his fist down on the table, thereby costing Nyura the saleswoman a certain sum of money in crockery and glassware breakages.

"Shut up, you bastard . . ."

"Not another word," Pavlov replied. "Everything's in order, Sergeant, everything's in order . . ."

"To hell with you," said the sergeant. "Sort this out between yourselves, but no disturbing the peace . . ."

He went away. After that Pavlov had another drink without saying a word, then another one, and then he dozed off with his forehead planted on the table, but he was woken up by a gentle night breeze, with his back propped against a wall.

Everything was quiet, the town's peaceful slumber was at its very deepest point. Bor town on the Volga knew how to sleep sweetly. There was not a single lighted window to be seen, whichever way he looked, not a single sound except for leaves rustling, not a single movement except for the twinkling of the stars and the moon disappearing and then reappearing in the gaps between the dark clouds.

As Pavlov was in the process of awakening in the midst of this tranquility, something unfamiliar was taking place within him, but what it was he couldn't understand. Perhaps it seemed to him that he was a little child again, looking out through a dark window from his cradle; or perhaps he fancied he heard a word that was spoken only to him, for there is a personal word for every individual, and if that person fails to hear it, it remains unused in the world; or perhaps he seemed to see that twinkling of the lofty stars for the first time, and at that he felt his thickset sailor's forehead tightly clenched in an unfamiliar agony, as if at any moment something might spurt out from under that forehead's immense block of gray stone, which served for the secure incarceration of any pure thought.

However no sooner did he stir, sigh and straighten his numbed limbs than he immediately returned to own current needs, that is, first of all he thrust his hands into his trousers. If his trousers were dry or only damp with pee, then he went to Valiushka, a young nurse, or to Tanechka, a technician with the municipal department of public services, or to Ninka, or to Alexandra Ivanovna, or somewhere else, there was a wide range to choose from. But if his trousers were wet and slimy through and through with excrement, that is, when he woke from a drunken sleep with a putrid backside, which happened especially often in the summer season, for in summer they ate fruit with their drink, apples or Volga plums if they were available, then he only went to one of these places, to see Alexandra Ivanovna, the same widow from the food trade department who had once seduced him, a young war invalid, and become the first in the long list of Pavlov's women in Bor town. This widow was now approaching fifty and she was always willing to receive Pavlov, wash him off, feed him and put him to bed . . . It was summer now and since on the previous evening Pavlov had drunk a lot and also eaten a lot of the unwashed, slightly rotten apples in which that bitch Nyurka traded, on awakening and feeling the full extent of his condition he set off to see Alexandra Ivanovna. At her place he slept out the remainder of the night and part of the day, since he had to be as fresh as a daisy for that evening's baiting of the Jew.

Koposov and Pavlov had planned this little job artfully: one was artful out of grief and the other was artful out of malice. Koposov left his work a little ahead of the set time, Pavlov left Alexandra Ivanovna a little ahead of the set time, and they met, not up at the very crest, but at the triangle, another place that existed in the forest, but how it had got that name had long ago been forgotten . . . Pavlov was tipsy, Koposov was sober, but with a well-honed carpenter's ax tucked into the belt under his jacket.

"They're there," Pavlov said in a quiet voice, "at the spot. I scouted the place out already, they're standing with their arms round each other, just like they always do . . ."

The Slav is taciturn in his excruciating fury, saving up his hatred for the decisive moment. Koposov set his hand on his ax and started off along the track in the direction indicated. He cautiously parted the wet bushes, since there had been a light sprinkling of rain early in the morning, and then indeed he saw his daughter in the distance, in the arms of a Jew . . . The Slav is silent in his fury, but at the decisive moment he can give vent to the ferocious shriek of his ancestors, which they uttered as they plundered the Carpathians during the great migration of the peoples, dreaming of settling not along the Dnepr, but along the Danube . . . Precisely such an inarticulate shriek was uttered by Koposov, the anguished father clutching a carpenter's ax in his hands . . . Pavlov, however, shrieked in a more contemporary and articulate fashion, thus: "Beat the Yids and save Russia."

Catching sight of them, Tasya started trembling bodily and crying in her beloved's arms for the first time out of fear.

"Who are they?" the Antichrist asked.

"It's my tyatya and his friend Pavlov," Tasya replied, weeping and trembling.

"What do they want?" the Antichrist asked, for it sometimes happened that at critical moments he ceased understanding the life around him and a celestial disgust for human beings welled up from deep inside him.

"Run," Tasya said to Dan through her tears, "my tyatya will only beat me, because he loves me, but he'll hack you to death, because he hates you. Run, my tyatya has an ax . . ."

"He won't touch us with his ax," said the Antichrist. "He won't touch us with anything except his hands."

"He hits very hard, he could cripple you," said Tasya, still trembling in fear, "and Pavlov likes to throttle people."

Meanwhile Koposov and Pavlov were already running down the slope, slipping on the wet grass, and getting closer. Their menacing features were quite clearly visible. Moreover, in Koposov's case the menace was mingled with suffering, which rendered his face hideous in the extreme. In Pavlov's case, however, the menace was mingled with merriment, which made him look like a charming, witty Slavophile satirist.

"Nestle close to me, my beloved," said the Antichrist. "Nestle close with all your might and do not be afraid of anything . . . They will not hit us too hard."

"Why won't they hit us too hard?" Tasya asked, half swooning. "Why won't they, if they hate us?"

"Because," the Antichrist replied, "they won't have time to hit harder . . . As soon as they touch us both of them will die . . ."

Tasya was already trembling, but what she now saw close beside her face threw her into a feverish delirium . . . Peering out from the mild Jewish features of her beloved, the Viper's flaming, death-dealing eyes blazed with the very hatred of Hell, of God's Universal Chastisement . . . Tasya turned cold and no longer felt afraid for her beloved, who seemed to have disappeared, but for her father.

"Don't hurt my tyatya," she said, although it was not clear with whom she was pleading, "don't hurt my tyatya . . ."

"That's a pity," said the Antichrist, "it means I shall have to spare the other one too. For they conceived the same intent, and at this moment there cannot be separate punishments for them . . . But later their punishments will differ . . ."

Koposov and Pavlov were unable to stop, just as a man running down a high mountain is unable to stop. Koposov and Pavlov went running by, hurtling past the embracing lovers as if they were borne along by some mysterious wind . . . They were carried through the bushes and into the gully, dragged down the clayey slopes made slippery by the rain and flung into the stream babbling peacefully between the rocks . . . This involuntary gallop left Koposov and Pavlov incapable of controlling their own bodies, arms and legs.

"Agh!" Yielding to blind impulse, Koposov struck his carpenter's ax hard against a wet boulder. It was a fine ax, but the handle cracked and shattered.

And tipsy Pavlov could feel the stones in the brook with his bones.

"Uh-oh . . . Oops . . . Sneaky snuffboxes . . . That slippery grass . . . The Jew was saved by the morning rain . . ."

When Koposov and Pavlov disappeared into the gully the blazing fire in the Antichrist's features was instantly extinguished and Tasya saw her beloved before her once again.

"I'll go," said Tasya, "I'll go home, and you go too . . . I'll let you know where and when we can meet next time, because we can't meet here any longer . . . Don't be afraid for me, goodbye for now." And they kissed for the first time, for from that day on, that which was most exalted in their love, that third possibility, was over and their love became human, with kisses and a craving for variety.

When Tasya got home and saw her mother Vera, she felt alarmed.

"Momma," said Tasya, hugging her mother and pressing up against her cheek-to-cheek, so that the two gold-tinged braids, the mother's and the daughter's, lay side by side, "Momma, I've fallen in love with someone . . ."

"Who is this man?" asked the solicitous mother and cunning woman.

"The night watchman at the fish processing plant," Tasya replied, "the one who rents lodgings with old Chesnokova."

"Why give me such a roundabout answer?" her dissembling mother asked. "Wasn't it me who first took you to see Dan Yakovlevich?"

"Ah Momma, he's so sweet," her daughter blurted out in spontaneous sincerity, which drove her mother, who was in love with the same man, into a jealous fury.

"But if your father finds out . . ." Vera said angrily, as if she hadn't arranged everything herself.

"Tyatya already knows," Tasya replied.

At that Vera jumped to her feet in genuine fright.

"Since when?"

"He just found out now."

"And what happened, did he beat you?"

"He wanted to."

"So he couldn't catch you?"

"Perhaps he couldn't," her daughter replied rather strangely.

However the prospect of further ambiguity in their conversation was peremptorily terminated when the door was kicked wide open and Andrei Koposov appeared in the doorway. At the sight of him little Ustya immediately burst intro tears . . . And he truly was a frightening sight: clothes lacerated by branches and smeared with clay, a mouth with badly bitten lips, twisted to one side, white-knuckled fingers already clenched into fists. Without saying a word Vera dashed in front of him to protect her daughter and without saying a word he swung his arm back and struck her in his habitual fashion, not really very hard. But from lack of practice he struck his daughter Tasya a terrible blow, bloodying her instantly . . . Seeing her daughter covered in blood the wretched woman realized what she had done and that she alone was to blame for everything. She instantly understood the terrible nature of the Lord's third plague, the wild beast of fornication . . . And perhaps she heard without reason, merely as a roaring noise in her temples, Moses' curse for fornication:

"The Lord make you a curse and an oath among your people, when the Lord makes your thigh fall away and your body swell . . ."

She dashed at her husband with her arms raised, either to defend her daughter even at the cost of her own life or to confess everything to her husband in front of the children. But there was no longer any need to defend anyone or anyone to confess to . . . No sooner did Andrei strike his daughter than he went limp and started weeping uncontrollably, but not in a manly way, as he had always done when he used to beat Vera in an unrepentant frenzy. Andrei lay facedown on the bed and Tasya sat down beside him, pressing a handkerchief to her battered and bloodied nose, and put her hand on his head. Vera realized that she was superfluous here and not only did her repentance evaporate, but her desire to go through with her plans for her own sake and her own satisfaction actually increased.

"Come on, daughter, let's take a walk," she said to Ustya, who was frightened, "let's go to the forest and get a breath of fresh air." When Tasya and her father were left alone, he said:

"Sweetheart, you're my only happiness, you know that. How could I wish you harm?" And Tasya answered:

"Tyatya, I know you didn't want to do it, it was Pavlov who put you up to it . . . He's a creep . . ."

"I know," Koposov replied. "Of course Pavlov's a creep, even if he is a frontline veteran, but surely there are other guys in town? Isn't this a Russian town?"

"Tyatya," Tasya replied girlishly, just like a seventeen-year-old, "without him I don't want to live, without him I might as well throw myself in the Volga . . . Believe me, tyatya, your daughter who loves you."

Andrei Koposov was silent for a moment and then he said:

"You get this from your trollopy mother, she's a total disaster . . . It's no accident you resemble her so much in looks."

And the conversation ended with that, although it had seemingly begun with frank speaking and ought to have resolved many issues. However it didn't resolve anything. Vera and little Ustya came back, Vera started cooking dinner and Andrei went to his workbench in the corner to start chiseling wooden jars for vegetable oil, troughs for kneading dough, butter churns and other wooden articles that he intended to take to Gorky for the next fair.

It was while her husband was away on this trip that Vera was intending to put her plan into effect. And her plan was so daring that even she couldn't believe it would work, but she didn't want to believe that it was impossible either.

A woman who scorns shame should not have a powerful passion, her salvation lies in philistine mundanity . . . Vera did not know this truth, and even if she had, she could not have complied with it . . . For many years she had lived alone with her female desire, which was initially unassuaged by virtue of the rational circumstances of war and later by virtue of her own madness. This desire had matured within her like a strong spirituous liquor, of which a single gulp is enough to cast you into oblivion . . . Behold, death: behold, birth: behold eternity . . .

A human being is only capable of understanding eternity by greatly debasing this divine feeling . . . Only through fornication, through lust, can a finite being touch the eternal, and mutual love ennobles the shameful nonentity of a human before the face of God. There may be an exalted idea higher than mutual love, but such cases are rare and not entirely human, although they do happen to human beings . . . After the destruction of Sodom the idea of saving the race prompted Lot's daughters to indulge in fornication with their father, whom they themselves had rendered intoxicated. The idea of the Messiah's Birth prompted Tamar to indulge in fornication with her husband's father, Judah, after first dressing up as a whore to deceive him. That which had prompted Vera to desire fornication with the Antichrist, her daughter's beloved, was concealed from the unfortunate madwoman. But as has already been noted, she was cunning and persevering in her madness. She knew that Dan Yakovlevich was always at home by midday, since he used to catch up on his sleep after the night shift, and this meant she had to find a moment when Old Chesnokova and Dan's daughter weren't there. Especially the daughter . . . For did not the daughter of a beloved father feel jealous of him even with her own mother, let alone with female interlopers? And Dan Yakovlevich was dealing with an entirely special case, since Rufina was a highly strung girl, who was quick to turn pale and could even faint away . . . And yet her appearance was at odds with such passions, in fact she had the appearance of a village girl. Vera herself had looked the same at her age and hadn't understood what was what until she was sixteen, until she got married . . . Of course, once she got married, she had very quickly learned all about everything . . . But judging by her pale complexion and her swooning, this girl Rufina had nothing left to learn, even at only ten years of age . . . And she was cunning, she seemed to possess the cunning of a woman. But as far as cunning was concerned it was easy enough to see who would prevail.

And in the matter of cunning Vera did prevail . . . She waited until old Chesnokova and Rufina set out to the market, watched them all the way to the market, and then knocked on the little wicket door. Dan opened it.

"Good morning," said Vera. "Is my daughter Tasya here?"

"No," the Antichrist replied in embarrassment, "she doesn't come here anymore."

"So she only goes up on the crest?" Vera asked and Dan latched the wicket door shut.

But a latched door hook or the mere sight of a door latched from the inside immediately throws an uncontrollably craving woman into a fit of passion. How could Dan, the Viper, the Antichrist, a native of a country in which whores had often threatened the plans of the prophets, possibly not understand this passion? Dan himself had fallen victim to the third plague of the Lord in the vicinity of Kerch city with the underage fornicatress Maria in 1935. And the Antichrist told Vera:

"I will give you what you want, only then go away . . ."

Weary at heart, Vera the unbridled harlot replied:

"There is nothing I want but you . . . if you will not be with me, I shall send my daughter Tasya, whom you have come to love, far away from here, and you will never see her again . . . She will not dare to disobey her mother and my husband, her father, will help me in this."

And the Antichrist said to her through the prophet Ezekiel:

"You are not like a prostitute, because you have scorned gifts, but like an adulterous wife, who receives strangers instead of her husband. So you are different from other women in your whorings. No one solicits you to play the whore, but you give gifts and uncover your nakedness to your lovers."

Vera answered him in kind, languishing in her lustful yearning.

"I have not uncovered my nakedness to anyone since long ago, not even to my husband. I wish to uncover it only to you. My gift to you is not adorned with gold and silver, it arose from my blood and is alive with my blood . . . It is my beloved daughter Tasya . . ."

The Antichrist said:

"Do you know, woman, that the Lord punishes an ordinary loose woman for an ordinary sin, of which people have many, but your fornication is punished with a special judgment that is shared by both adulteresses and those who spill blood . . ."

And Vera, the Russian woman who had populated an immense, formerly underpopulated continent with her skills, replied:

"I accept it all . . ."

For once skills of the highest order have been developed out of necessity, they can no longer be restricted only to what is necessary, but seek opportunities to manifest themselves as an independent inner impulse . . . Every skill that serves other purposes eventually aspires to serve itself, to be a skill for skill's sake and delight in itself. Such also is the skill of a woman. And where skills are of the highest order, this is already art, whether it is the art of poetry or the art of carpentry or a woman's art . . . Dan, the Viper, the Antichrist looked at Vera and asked:

"Do you know how the Lord's judgment punishes this? By condemnation to bloodthirsty fury and jealousy."

"I accept it all," Vera merely repeated in reply, leaning back against the wicket door that was latched from the inside, because her legs would no longer support her.

Dan, the Viper, the Antichrist looked at Vera again and saw before him the still-young mother of his beloved Tasya, from whom he could be parted if he did not satisfy the physical passion of the woman who had carried Tasya in her womb . . . This was something not entirely human, a combination of many things, although the Antichrist did not know if it included an idea like Tamar's idea . . . The Antichrist also recalled the words of the prophet Ezekiel: "Behold, everyone who uses proverbs will use this proverb about you: 'Like mother, like daughter.'" He recalled that his last tryst with Tasya had ended with a kiss, that is, with the debasement of that exalted and undifferentiated condition that had arisen between them. Perhaps at the next tryst he and Tasya would desire even greater variety and then the third plague of the Lord, to which the lascivious woman wished to subject him, might come crashing down on her delicate, pure daughter . . .

"All right," said the Antichrist, "but remember what the Lord says: 'I will bring your conduct down on your own head.'"

"I accept it all," she said in a whisper.

In old Chesnokova's yard there was a shed of the kind often to be found in such semi-urban, semi-rural yards. Old Chesnokova had once kept a cow and various other livestock there. Now she had been obliged to renounce the cow because of the high post-war tax, which was levied not only on a cow, but also on every little chick owned by private individuals, in order to eradicate private property-owning interests. There was still straw lying in this shed, left over from past livestock, together with various old clothes, the bicycle that belonged to Chesnokova's oldest son, who had been killed at the front, and utensils that were no longer required in the household . . .

When Ruth, also called Pelagia, the Antichrist's adopted daughter, told old Chesnokova, without even knowing why, that she had to go home to her father and, on arriving there, did not find him anywhere, at first it did not occur to her to look for him in the shed, since she assumed that he must be on the crest in the forest . . . Ruth had known for some time about his trysts with Tasya, Ustya Koposova's older sister, but she had said nothing, only crying quietly at night. Not having found her father, Ruth was about to go to her room, lie down and cry, since there was no one at home and no one would find out about her sorrow. However a rustling sound in the shed attracted her attention. Ruth cautiously walked closer and peeped through a crack, and the young girl caught a glimpse of hell such as is rarely given to anyone to experience even in adulthood. She saw her father as a terrifying monster, with a woman's naked legs rising up over him and seeming to devour him . . .

In the corner of the shed Vera flung herself onto her back on the straw to rest her loins comfortably, her loins that were satisfied for the first time in a long time, that were breathing greedily, as the chest breathes the pure mountain air. No, this was no ordinary breathing, not the mundane in-breaths and out-breaths of the loins from which Tasya and Ustya had been born . . . These were full-chested breaths at the very summit, where the air is so pure that only a little higher it would no longer support life, for life requires an admixture of that which is lower, of that which is simpler. Here every in-breath is unique, every in-breath is the first, and every out-breath is a sweet remembrance of what has just happened. But the deeper the in-breaths, the shorter each breath becomes, until there is no out-breath, but only an eternal, deep sigh, such as there is before death, for the last thing in living respiration is an in-breath. The out-breath is already exhaled by a corpse . . .

Ruth, a young, living girl who had found herself in hell, saw the woman's legs sink feebly, heavily, lifelessly down onto the fusty straw. And the sun's radiance was extinguished. The twilight of an overcast day descended and in the darkness of the shed Ruth could only vaguely make out the shadows of her father and the woman moving about and hear the woman's low, happy laughter . . . And the same thing happened to Ruth as had happened to Annushka Emelyanova, the unrighteous martyr, in the village of Brusyany, when someone else's happiness prompted her to commit evil. And in that place, close to the square of the occupied village of Brusyany we have already said: "Those who retain the practical reason of childhood in their tribulation are capable of committing great evils." Ruth instantly realized how to repay her father for what he had done to his beloved daughter and repay the woman for the acts she had committed with her father. She knew from Ustya where the Koposovs lived. It was nearby on Derzhavin Street, house number 2. She ran there and saw Ustya sitting in the yard sorting berries.

"Where's your sister Tasya?" asked Ruth, also called Pelagia.

"None of your business," replied Ustya, "I'm not friends with you anymore, you're a Jew and you've got a lot of money." At this point Tasya walked into the yard and said to her sister:

"Who taught you to say that? You should be ashamed of yourself."

"As if I cared," said Ustya, "she hasn't come to see me, you're the one she's looking for."

"What's wrong?" Tasya asked and immediately took fright at Ruth's appearance, for Ruth was very pale. "Has something happened to your tyatya?"

"Yes it has," Ruth replied. "let's go to our house . . ."

Beside herself, Tasya ran after Ruth: she ran into the yard and toward the house, because she and Dan had agreed to meet only in the forest or some other distant spot.

"Not this way," said Ruth and pointed to the shed. "Look through the crack and see what my father is doing with your mother . . ."

Completely bewildered now, Tasya looked through the crack and saw what Ruth had recently seen. For the Antichrist and Vera realized that this was their carnal celebration, which would never be repeated, and so they were striving hard to prolong it . . .

Instantly a change took place in Tasya. Where had her maidenly delicacy disappeared to? The original mother Eve, unbridled in her passion, who seduced Adam, gave birth to Cain and was cursed by God, was suddenly manifested in Tasya to punish the sin of fornication with the sin of jealousy . . .

She ran out of the yard of house number 30 on Derzhavin Street and ran to the river jetty to wait for her father, who was due to return today from the market in Gorky. And Ruth, also called Pelagia, ran off into the forest and walked for a long time, hoping to lose her way: she ran into the densest thickets, until she fell down, exhausted, in the bushes, to expend the remainder of her strength in weeping.

Tasya sat there at the jetty, turned to stone, thinking no thoughts, listening indifferently to people's conversations and the yelping of the small, greedy Volga gulls known as "terns." In the evening her father arrived. He had sold his wooden wares and although he had taken a drink, enough money had been left over for flour and pork fat . . . He was pleased to see Tasya . . .

"Hello, daughter . . . Are you waiting for your tyatya?"

"Yes," Tasya answered, "since now you are not only my tyatya, but my momma too . . . My momma has destroyed my love . . . I'm afraid even to say what I saw her doing in the Chesnokovs' shed, and who with . . ."

"Then don't say it," her father replied in a quiet voice, speaking unhurriedly, although he stooped lower under the weight of the foodstuffs he had brought from Gorky, as if the flour and pork fat had been transformed into cast iron, "Don't say anything, daughter . . . Let's go home . . ."

When they reached home, Vera met them in an unusually cheerful mood and she was even affectionate with husband, which had not happened for a long time.

"Look, I've lit the stove," she said, "I'm going to cook up some buckwheat pancakes . . ."

The Koposovs had a stove of the kind that is known in Russia as a "Russian stove," although similar stoves can be found in other places. But in Russia many things are called "Russian," including Russian birch trees, although many of them grow around the world, and the Russian sky, although it can also be found elsewhere. Well then, the Koposovs had a Russian stove, in which they baked bread, and on which cabbage soup cooked in a cast-iron pot turned out well and pancakes browned quite splendidly . . . Andrei liked buckwheat pancakes and as a matter of fact, Vera was a dab hand in this area, but it was a long time since she had cooked any.

"Good for you, wife," said Andrei, casting off the foodstuffs in the way that people cast off an intolerably heavy burden, "I just happen to have got hold of some wheat flour, and buckwheat flour too, and some good pork fat . . . Cook the pancakes with pork fat, in real Russian style . . . Pancakes come out just perfect with pork fat . . ."

"I can use pork fat," said Vera, trying her hardest to be agreeable, and when she walked past him she ran the palm of her hand over his hair, stroking his hair and actually caressing him.

"Have a wash after your journey, Andriusha . . ." she said.

"I already washed," Andrei answered, "but Tasya, why don't you take Ustya and go for a walk while the pancakes are cooking? It's nice weather out there."

"That's right," Vera said hastily, "you take Ustya for a walk, daughter."

Without saying anything, Tasya took Ustya and went out, and no sooner did the latch lock the door shut from the inside than Vera's desire for her husband awoke for the first time in a long time . . . She walked up, sat down beside him on the bench, started tenderly examining the buttons on his completely washed-out frontline tunic and thrust her hand into the collar, up close to the body from which she had long ago been separated by her female madness . . . And at that moment Andrei grabbed her by the throat with one hand and by the leg with the other, in the way that people grab a chicken before they kill it, and carried her towards the stove.

"What's this . . . what for? . ." Vera shouted in fright.

"What this is, is for me to know, and you ought to know what it's for . . ."

Then Andrei struck Vera's head against the corner of the stove, so that her light-brown braid was instantly soaked with blood, and then he started shoving Vera into the hot stove. He shoved her in with one hand, adding straw with the other. The straw flared up . . . But then someone knocked at the door . . . Their neighbor used to come to borrow bread, she would knock for a while and then go away . . . But this time she didn't go away and kept knocking as hard as she could . . . As if this time she hadn't come on her own account, but God had sent her . . . The latch was bouncing up and down . . . This knocking brought Andrei to his senses and he let go of Vera: she jumped up, bloody and scorched, jerked the latch open and ran outside . . . Tasya and little Ustya were there, running toward her, both crying. Suddenly, halfway there, Tasya remembered her father's quiet voice and turned to hurry back to the house . . . Then Andrei also appeared in the doorway, saw the indignant people all around, saw his wife Vera, bloodied by him and scorched by him, with their crying daughters hugging her, and said:

"Come into the house, don't let people see you like this."

"You're a monster," they shouted at him from all sides, "what do you mean by beating your wife? Is there no controlling you at all?"

"Come into the house," Andrei repeated, "I won't beat you anymore . . . I'm not feeling so good."

By this time someone had already brought Vera a wet towel and applied the damp fabric to her injured head, which had stopped hurting so badly and the blood wasn't flowing any more, it had clotted . . . Vera took both her daughters and went back into the house.

"Give me some bread and salt," Andrei said to Vera, "I'm hungry."

Vera gave him some bread and salt and he sat down on his bench and ate it all, a large hunk with the crust.

"Now give me some water," Andrei said, "I'm thirsty." Vera gave him a large wooden dipper of water and he drank it in a single gulp, without pausing.

"Give me some more," he said.

She gave him more . . . And again Andrei drank a full dipper in a single gulp.

"Now I'm going to sleep," he said and climbed up onto the Russian stove.

After a while Vera and her daughters heard him snoring.

"Now we'll go to bed too," Vera said, and she and her daughters lay down on the couch.

Little Ustya fell asleep, but Vera and Tasya didn't sleep, they just lay there without speaking . . . Suddenly they heard Andrei groan.

There are different kinds of groans. There's a living groan, when a person calls for someone to come to them, and there's a groan of indifference to everything living, when someone groans to tell themself what they can no longer say in any other way. If he could have said it differently, Andrei would have pronounced words that he didn't know and had never heard or read, the words of a psalm:

"I am grown faint from clamoring, my throat is parched, my eyes are weary from waiting for God."

There are moments and circumstance in which it is possible to say this with a groan. But even if Andrei Koposov had been holding a psalm book in his hands, he would not have said it more clearly than he did say it with a groan, since in a number of places the Russian Bible is clumsily translated. For instance Psalm 84, verse 4, the text needed by the dying man here, is translated as "For my soul is sated with misfortunes and my life has drawn near to hell," whereas in the original it is "For my soul is sated with abuses and my life has drawn near to the grave."

The life and death of Andrei Koposov from Bor town in the Gorky Region, the former Nizhny Novgorod Province, confirms the inaccuracy of this translation in the Russian Bible. There is a great difference between "a soul sated with misfortunes" and "a soul sated with abuses." It is unjust to be obliged to descend into hell as a result of misfortunes, but constant abuses will inevitably lead to the grave . . . This is one of the inaccuracies of the Russian text of the Bible. Fortunately, however, a deathbed groan does not require a translation.

"We ought to take a look to see what's wrong with your father," said Vera.

"I can't, I'm afraid," Tasya replied and she suddenly felt a sharp pain in her belly that set her body shivering all over.

Then Vera got up, moved the curtain aside and saw her husband lying on his side. His eyes were open and their gaze was unusually intense and remote.

"Are you uncomfortable lying like that, Andrei?" Vera asked.

Andrei didn't reply, continuing to gaze with a strange intensity into the corner of the room, where the pre-dawn gloom was swirling and eddying . . . Vera started turning her husband over to lay him in a more comfortable position on his back, and at that very moment, as she was turning him, he died. But Vera did not immediately realize this. When an immense tongue that looked as if it could not possibly have fitted into a human mouth was suddenly flung out of Andrei, as if by a wave, and then this immense tongue was immediately pulled back in, as if by a spring, and disappeared,

Vera still did not understand. But when Andrei's legs straightened out of their own accord and his eyes closed, Vera understood and started weeping over her dead husband, sitting at the head of his bed . . .

Little Ustya woke up and started crying, although she did not yet know that her father had died, but because her mother was crying . . . For every time when her tyatya beat her momma and her momma cried, Ustya immediately used to join in her crying . . . And Tasya was unable to approach her father for the first few minutes following his death because her belly pain had become diarrhea and she was shivering violently. And so she spent those minutes outside in the chilly night air.

It seemed as if that terrible night would never end, and yet it did. In the morning everything was just as it ought to be. Little Ustya was taken to neighbors and Vera and Tasya washed Andrei's body in a wooden trough. This was the first time Tasya had ever seen her father's naked body, and in addition to a daughter's grief she felt within her a distressing sense of shame. Vera had also not seen her husband's naked body for a long time and in addition to a wife's grief she felt within in her a sense of horror and a strange revulsion. When they started dressing Andrei they couldn't find a good pair of socks, because while spending all his money on drink he had worn out almost all of his clothes. Vera had to cut off the feet of her only pair of good silk stockings, so that they looked like socks, and stretch them onto her dead husband's feet. But once dressed up in his best suit and laid out in a coffin, for his wife and daughter Andrei Koposov immediately assumed the aspect of their very own dear departed, concerning whom, according to pagan superstitions, everything bad was to be forgotten and only the good was to be remembered . . . That dear departed by whom people make vows, by whose sacred shade they are comforted in their griefs and to whose disappearing, decaying body a woman is sometimes more faithful than she was to her husband when he was alive, full of vitality and male vigor. Vera knew that now she would be faithful to this decaying body until she died, and Tasya knew that she would be faithful to her dead father's wishes, whereas she had not been faithful to the wishes of her living father . . . The Koposov clan would not be continued through a Jew . . . It would be a Russian clan, a Volga Region clan . . . Continued through driver, second-class Vesyolov, the son of the old national sentry woman Sergeevna. And Tasya would give birth to two sons, Andrei Vesyolov and Varfolomei Vesyolov . . . Of course, she could not see this far ahead at that moment and she did not even know her own future surname, but she did know that this surname would be Russian . . .

When the people gathered to see off the late lamented, almost the whole of Derzhavin Street came for the event, apart from Old Chesnokova, the Old Believer from house number 30. Pavlov also showed up: he was tipsy, of course. He walked up to the coffin, sat down beside it, looked at the deceased and grabbed hold of his hand.

"Andriusha, what's up, my old frontline pal . . . Let's go and have a drink." The dead man lay there silently, like a stuffed dummy. Pavlov let go of the dead hand and it fell back onto the dead chest. "I'll be going now," said Pavlov, "or else I'll start crying." And he left.

Meanwhile the sentries of the nation, the old women on their benches, spread the word:

"At the Koposovs' in number 2, Koposov has died . . . His promiscuous wife drove him to his death. And at number 30, where the Jew is, his daughter has disappeared, this is the second day they've been searching for her. That Jew has gone absolutely crazy because that daughter of his has probably drowned in the Volga . . ."

And Sergeevna added on her own behalf:

"If only they would all go crazy and drown in the Volga . . ."

Sergeevna's son, Sergei Vesyolov, the future continuer of the Koposov clan, concerning which he was still unaware, laughed when he heard this observation of his mother's and said:

"Momma, if they all drown in the Volga, the fish will all die out because of their stink . . . But apparently that Jewess didn't drown in the Volga, she got lost in the forest . . . That's where she was last seen . . ."

"Never mind," replied Sergeevna, "the forest will do just as well . . . You can't find your way out of there if you simply don't have a clue, and in the thickets a bit farther off a bear could tear her to pieces or the merry man could have his way with her . . . That would do well enough . . ."

It really was the second day that the Antichrist, almost out of his mind, had been searching for his daughter, for it was not given to the Antichrist to know what the Lord would desire. He did not know where Ruth was, but he did know why she had disappeared and he was suffering with the boundlessly religious suffering of a Jewish father who absolutely dotes on his child. Kind old Chesnokova was suffering together with him, but she was suffering in the Russian manner, with a subconscious awareness of the boundless extent of space and her people. No matter how much you lost, there would always be more.

"What can you do, my darling?" she said, "God gave and God has taken away," she said.

But when every soul and every inch has been counted, the grief from a loss is boundless . . . And in his grief as a Jewish father the Antichrist, the emissary of God, did not wish to trust in God's providence. And speaking through the prophet Jeremiah, he expressed that to which the righteous man Job had devoted his entire life, and on the vulgarization of which atheism is based:

"Righteous are you, O Lord, when I complain to you, yet I would plead my case before you. Why does the way of the wicked prosper? Why do the treacherous thrive?"

The Lord replied to the Antichrist, who had lost his adopted daughter Ruth, as the Antichrist replied to Maria, who had lost her brother Vasya. He replied through the prophet Isaiah:

"I have revealed myself to those who did not ask after Me; I have been found by those who did not seek Me. 'Here I am! Here I am!' I said to a nation that was not called by My name . . ."

The Antichrist recalled what he already knew, but had forgotten in his misfortune. He who did not choose, but has been chosen, cannot ask the Lord questions. He must ask himself the questions and wait for answers from the Lord.

Once again he set out into the forest, into the thickets from which he had only recently returned, soaking wet from the forest dampness . . . And the farther away the Antichrist walked from places where people congregated, the tighter became the grip of his miserable anxiety of spirit and the more vehemently he craved solitude for his anguish, like a wild beast that hides away from everyone in order to die, for the accomplishment of this serious matter must not be marred by the trivialities on which mundane daily life is based . . . It is good to live among your own kind, and it is good to die far from your own kind . . . And the Antichrist realized that he had not been sent here by the Lord in order to curse, but in order to be cursed. Only the Lord can curse without himself being cursed.

Dan the Viper, the Antichrist sat down on a mossy, decaying tree stump and grasped his head in his hands. Meanwhile his daughter Ruth, also named Pelagia, was nearby, only a ten-minute walk away through the fallen trees and the prickly bushes entangled in spider webs. This was her third day of wandering about in the forest, feeding on berries and leaves, drinking from forest puddles and sleeping with her back propped against tree trunks. Her voice had almost disappeared from shouting and her dress was torn to tatters by the branches . . . So now, on emerging into a meadow warmed by the sun, she decided to take a short rest, lay down and fell asleep in her weariness. Her sleep was deep, it led her far away from this place, and she only realized where it had led her when she awoke. While sleeping like this she was discovered by Pavlov, the "merry man" himself, who was always ready to take advantage of a girl in the forest, and especially this Jewish girl, just as old Sergeevna had hoped he would.

Since Andrei Koposov's funeral he had drunk, reminisced and cried, but had not visited any women, and so he had accumulated a large reserve of male vigor . . . He had been carried away from the wake drunk and he had rushed off into the woods with his little rifle only slightly more sober. He wandered into a thicket where he had never been before. And there, like a mirage appearing to the gaze of a thirsty man in the desert, Pavlov beheld before him a sleeping girl, absolutely defenseless . . .

Pavlov saw that her bare legs were strong and well developed for her age, and that her incipient breasts were fresh and firm. The exhaustion and fear that Ruth had suffered during her days and nights in the forest had merged into the repose of a pure sleep, and the girl's face was rendered seductive by its expression of trust in both man and beast there among in the forest thickets . . . Growling inarticulately, Pavlov dashed toward her and when he leaned down, she opened her eyes. If only Pavlov had reflected on this situation, if only he had recalled those moments when he himself was awakening at the foot of a fence amidst solitude and tranquility, in anticipation of that unique word addressed only to him, which was searching for him in this world! But that word did not come to him and the rapist was actually delighted by the Jewish girl's awakening: a merry hatred came over him at the weakness of what he hated.

"Oh, how I'll break your little crock for you, little Sara," Pavlov cried out in exultation. "Oh, I'll make you really poorly. Oh, azoh'n'vei . . ." For, like any Slav in a state of unbridled passion, he knew two or three Jewish expressions that he had learned off, for the most part sad ones, which seemed to him especially funny and which his Slavic tongue genuinely did mangle in a most comedic fashion. "Oh, azoh'n'vei," Pavlov repeated, and suddenly he sensed someone's hot, damp breath behind him . . .

It was two she-bears, who had emerged from the forest thickets in the same way that the biblical she-bears emerged from the forest near Bethel to punish the wicked children at the summons of the prophet Elisha. Although Pavlov had a rifle hanging on his shoulder, it was a worthless little weapon, and the bears were already there beside him. It would be bad if they dented his ribs, but even worse if they tore him to pieces. Pavlov burst into tears. He just stood there crying, without stirring a hand or a foot, in a sulk.

"I want to live," he said, without even knowing who he was telling: the girl he had wanted to rape or the irrational wild creatures.

The two she-bears leaned toward Pavlov and sniffed at him . . . They didn't like him . . . They spat in his face, first one and then the other, slathering his belligerent sailor's features with slimy saliva. Then they sniffed at Ruth, licked her hands and went on their way through the forest thickets. When the she-bears left, the physical equilibrium Pavlov had derived from the imminent horror deserted him and he fell just as he was standing, tautly erect. The way that suddenly paralyzed people fall . . .

Half paralyzed and deprived of the power of speech, he crawled through the forest for a day and a night toward people, toward life. At nineteen hundred hours the following day he crawled out onto a road and since, fortunately for him, in that area it was not difficult to meet a Russian person, the paralytic was able to explain his situation and asked to be taken to Alexandra Ivanovna, the fifty-year-old widow. For the power of speech had gradually returned to him, although his male vigor had abandoned him forever.

However Alexandra Ivanovna, the food trade department employee, was willing to accept him in any condition, since she was the only one of all his women who loved him, and from that time onward she pushed him out in a wheelchair every day to take the air, telling her acquaintances:

"The old frontline wounds are taking their toll . . . Styopa's been laid low . . ."

And through the portent by which Pavlov, who had wished to rape her, was deprived of his male vigor, Ruth understood that she was the prophetess Pelagia, born in Bryusyany village near Rzhev town. She recalled what she had been told in her dream and that Pavlov had interrupted that dream. Just as Elisha received the spirit from the prophet Elijah, so Pelagia had received the spirit from her father, the Antichrist. And Pavlov had been instrumental in this. So the Lord had had a good reason for creating even Pavlov.

Pelagia started walking and soon found her father, sitting forlornly on a rotten tree stump. And she said:

"Here I am . . ."

The Antichrist dashed to his living, unharmed daughter and they joyfully embraced.

The prophet Jonah, who spent three days in the belly of a whale, purged the city of Nineveh of sin with his curse. And the Antichrist, who had sinned, was purged by a curse. Dan, the Viper, the Antichrist said:

"Forgive me, Lord."

And the father was answered by his daughter, the prophetess Pelagia:

"The Lord is my strength and my praise is the Lord."

She knew now who her father was, but her father did not know who his daughter was and he thought that Ruth had learned the words of the prophets from the old woman Chesnokova, the Old Believer. And Dan, the Viper, the Antichrist said to her:

"Ruth, my daughter, you grew up in these parts, but now we must leave them."

"That does not matter," the prophetess Pelagia told him, "for wherever you are, my home is there."

The Antichrist was glad to hear this, since the Lord was sending him to the following place: in Vitebsk on the 29th of September, 1949, Alexander Semyonovich Kuharenko, born in 1912, would be convicted of being a dangerous enemy of Soviet power and sent to the Burepolom correctional labor camps. And this is the beginning of the next parable.

A Parable of Pestilence of the Spirit

There is an eternal Russian question, one that could be called fundamental: Who is trying to destroy Russia? When a Russian individual asks this question he immediately looks around, unless of course this individual is a staunchly Russian writer. If he is doubly Russian, that is, both a Russian individual and a staunchly Russian writer, then he does not look around but, after asking: "Who is trying to destroy Russia?" he gazes intently at a wine-soaked tablecloth as if seeking the answer to this most important Russian question there.

Under Vladimir the Great, known in Russia as "the Baptizer," the Russian individual was a pagan on the threshold of the Islamic Faith. At that time Russian mosques of stone and wood stood in the land of Rus. If the epic hero Mikula Selyaninovich had worn a turban and Princess Yaroslavna had worn a yashmak, there would have been none of the fateful questions so characteristic of Christianity. But at the final moment, in defiance of the opinion of the majority of the nobility and the whole of the people, Vladimir recalled his delegation from Khorezm and sent it to Byzantium. And so, instead of Russian Islam it was Russian Christianity that appeared in the world, by pure happenstance. But how Christian in fact is the geography of Russia? In the East from the Urals to the Altai Mountains Russia extends into Asia, in the South, Russia is bordered directly by Asia in the form of Turkey and the Balkans, and that Russian treasure, the Volga, flows into Asia . . .

Behold the image of the young Russia, the icon-painting image of an unreflective northerner . . . Round-headed, with brown hair in the east and black hair in the south, with narrow eyes that are light-colored in the east and dark in the south, and prominent Asiatic cheekbones set directly beneath the eyes. For three or four hundred years this high-cheekboned Russia has cherished a national state idea. However if we trace things back to their origins, to the geography of the time when the Eastern Slavs, who had been driven away from the Don, settled on the Dnepr, at that time we find a traveling Arab merchant who looked into their restless, nomadic eyes and said: "If this people learns to ride horses, it will become a scourge of mankind." He spoke prophetically, clearly and quite unenigmatically. The most fathomless enigma is when there is no enigma. The most fathomless well is the one that has not been dug. Russia's culture is linked to Europe, but its civilization is linked to Asia. This is a problem, but not an enigma. A problem needs to be solved by means of intense intellectual effort, which deflects attention from the constantly shifting national idea. An enigma does not need to be solved. You can ponder on an enigma whilst in the condition, so sweet for the Russian individual, that is described in Gogol's "Dead Souls": "You do not think about anything, but the thoughts pop up in your head themselves." It was clearly in this condition that the fateful question: "Who is destroying Russia?" arose, and it has remained unanswered to this day. It was not thought up, it just popped up in someone's head . . .

However, an answer was supposedly found with the assistance of adroit thinkers from the masses of the people and the extreme nationalist intelligentsia. Who is destroying Russia, that seems quite clear . . . The answer simply popped effortlessly into their heads . . . But who is assisting them in this? Yet another question . . . Oh, how accustomed the Russian has become to these questions, that Russian Orthodox Christian who since time immemorial has been inured to questions by disasters and adversities.

"Save Russia," they call to him.

"But how?" he groans, weary and tormented.

"That's obvious, beat them!"

Although the Russian is weary, he can always find the strength for a beating.

"Who, these ones?"

"That goes without saying . . . And those ones too . . ."

"Well, God will forgive me for these, but those are our own kind. As the folk song says:

Go out now, go out, my lad,
Look at this wide, wide world,
So many people standing there,
You mother and father among them.
Tell me, tell me now, my lad,
How many souls have you killed?

Eighteen Orthodox folk,
Two hundred and seventy Yids.
For the Yids you'll be forgiven,
But for the Russians, never . . ."

"We'll forgive you for the Russians too . . . Look at Russia, it's full of Russians, countless numbers of them. No matter how many you scoop out, there won't be any fewer. The Russian woman set her mind to the job and populated Russia. And those who've been scooped out won't be missed in these wide expanses . . ."

Indeed, after reading the appalling memoirs of eyewitnesses, young Russians or generations as yet unborn may think: "Oh, how terrible Russian life was then . . . And how did people live with all that?" But there was nothing terrible about it, for the most part people lived normal lives. They even lived joyfully, with faith in justice, and the Russian climate facilitated that. The Russian climate did not presuppose extreme heat, and in the extreme cold people kept warm by clapping their hands in applause. In 1937, for instance, there was a good spring season, everything blossomed early and the people started gathering its wits again after the blazing passions of collectivization, and in 1949 the postwar hunger came to an end. Only a tiny minority was suffering: they could be counted on your fingers, if you took each finger as a million . . . But Russia is not narrow, cramped Europe. Here they are not used to counting people on their fingers. Since time immemorial people here have lived in communal concord, to the envy of others. However the Russian individual cannot be envied in every respect. And why is that? The destroyer tries hard. The destroyer strives constantly to harm Russia . . .

"And where is he?"

We have come back to the old question: Who is trying to destroy Russia? Look around you, or even gaze at a tablecloth soaked in wine, with your cheek propped on your hand . . . The punitive agencies try to solve this ancient national enigma in their own manner.

And in the summer of 1949 Alexander Semyonovich Kuharenko, the head of the Grain Procurement Agency for the Vitebsk Region, found himself numbered among the destroyers of Russia.

"This is not God's business," the Lord thought, "there does not seem to be anyone here to curse with a divine curse. They have cursed themselves, and it is not hard for even limited human reason to understand that."

But man has a certain sickness: what he cannot understand, he wishes to understand, and what he can understand, he does not wish to understand . . . A sinful man contracts this sickness of the spirit from another human, and it is the fourth plague of the Lord.

"In this matter I shall make sickness, a pestilence, my cornerstone," the Lord decided. "A pestilence can gnaw at the spirit just as well as at the soul and the body."

And so the Antichrist, the emissary of the Lord, became involved in a parable of pestilence of the spirit.

***

Alexander Semyonovich Kuharenko was Belarusian by nationality. A second-cousin comrade of the Russian. In any listing of the nationalities, the count from one to three, that is, the Slavic ranking, is clearly defined, but after that there is no clarity. Sometimes the Georgian is fourth, sometimes the Uzbek, the Moldavian or even the Kazakh: sometimes the Georgian is sixth, after the Estonian, and the Kazakh is seventh, ahead of the Moldavian. The fourth placing is variable, but the first three, Slavic places remain firmly fixed. The Belarusian is third after the Russian, following immediately after the Ukrainian . . . This is rather good, bearing in mind that since time immemorial the Belarusian has lived on infertile land . . . In the 19th century one well-known excoriator of autocracy wrote: "The Oryol Province peasant has sunk to a level at which he has become as poor as a Belarusian . . ." After all, the principle of equality was not brought from the West, it only appears to have been engendered by the slogans of the French Revolution. In the postwar period the administrative and managerial apparatus of Belarus consisted to a significant degree of former partisans. Influential partisans tried to appoint their own fighters who had survived to leading positions . . . Among others, the demolition expert Kolya Yarnutovsky found himself in a leading position. He married Svetlana, the secretary of the municipal public prosecutor's office. He married for love, but life didn't turn out well for them. Even so, they lived constantly busy working lives, without any kind of immoral behavior. And according to the registry office records, they had two children. So they might have remained completely unaware that they were bereft of happiness, if not for the happy Kuharenko family . . . In fact they could not understand what the Kuharenko family's happiness actually consisted of, but they knew that Sasha and Valyusha were happy . . . And indeed, what did this happiness consist of? The fact that large yellow flowers grew beside the Kuharenkos' house? The fact that on non-working days Sasha Kuharenko liked to ride his bicycle wearing an orange silk shirt, with his daughter Ninochka seated in front of him? The fact that in summer Valyusha wore a white blouse and a gray skirt, with a white headscarf, and in winter she wore boxcalf leather boots and a jacket with a fluffy, reddish-gray collar? The fact that the Kuharenkos ate dumplings with painted wooden spoons? Svetlana tried to imitate all of this and she even learned to cook Belarusian potato dumplings better than Valyusha. But there was no happiness of the kind that Sasha Kuharenko manifested to everyone around him. Even though both families lived in identical material circumstances that were rather good for devastated and immolated postwar Belarus and they both worked equally hard in order to move beyond this postwar state of ruin.

Since time immemorial the Belarusian has loved his poverty-stricken little mother Belarus, as the Ukrainian loves his rich peasant mother Ukraine, and the Russian loves his large, broad-shouldered Motherland. But he has always loved her with a less conspicuous love, in a cool, Polish-Lithuanian manner, although without any Polish flamboyance... Belarusian nationalism lacks the Ukrainian offended passion, the Russian pugnacious elan and the Polish Catholic theatricality. For the most part this land is a marshy plain covered with dense forests cut across by rivers that substantially overflow their banks in spring. The fertility of the soil is low: the swamps, bogs, spring flash flooding and impassable mud have rendered interaction within the population difficult, especially in former times . . . The single, unifying idea required for nationalism was expressed less brightly here and to a large extent it was borrowed by the small intelligentsia from pronouncements by Poles and Lithuanians: it did not mature and ripen in the viscera of the people, which in the most remote places, for instance the area around the Pinsk Marshes, retained a tribal, rather than national, consciousness for an extremely long time. Neither the haughty Greco-Roman educator nor the cruel Mongolian pillager showed any great interest in these beggarly marshes, but these marshes were subjected to invasion by the homeless Jewish masses displaced to this area by nations who had understood Darwin's law of survival long before it had even been formulated. This idiosyncratic Jewish expansion, with knapsacks and bundles instead of knives, when the homeless man came to join the poor man, facilitated the appearance of a genuinely unified national idea and under Polish and Lithuanian tutelage this idea rapidly became world standard. In other respects the nationalism of Belarus is little known and it is unlikely that it had ever developed to any serious degree in the prohibited anti-Russian direction. For this reason there were far fewer arrests on charges of nationalism in Belarus than in Ukraine. However there were some, and they devastated both the happy Kuharenko family and the unhappy Yarnutovsky family.

Kuharenko was the official head of the Grain Procurement Agency and it seemed only natural that if he were to end up in prison, it would be for agricultural crimes. However he was actually imprisoned on cultural charges. One day in a certain village he came across an old book by the writer Burachok-Bogushevich entitled "The Belarusian Pipe." It said in this book that ". . . the Belarusian language is as humane and genteel as French, German or any other language. Do we really have to read and write only a foreign tongue?" Kuharenko took this book to the local pedagogical institute, where he learned from a department head, Senior Lecturer Bogdanovich, that Burachok-Bogushevich was the founder of modern Belarusian poetry. The official head of the Grain Procurement Agency also learned that in addition to Burachok-Bogushevich, the revival of Belarusian culture had also been facilitated by Yanka Luchina, who had printed Belarusian poetry from 1889 onwards and published his own anthology "A Bundle." By coincidence Senior Lecturer Bogdanovich was a distant relative of the prerevolutionary writer Bogdanovich, and he joyfully seized on the interest expressed in the Belarusian national idea by this high-ranking official from the partisan nobility and asked him to organize an exhibition.

Alexander Semyonovich Kuharenko truly was a great lover of everything Belarusian, including eating Belarusian-style and singing Belarusian songs. And from national songs and national food it is not far to national culture. But in 1949 culture had become the most dangerous area of all, just as demolition work had been in 1942. Kuharenko forwarded the senior lecturer's suggestion to Yarnutovsky, who worked in this dangerous area of socialist construction, to be precise, in the Department for Agitation and Propaganda. Yarnutovsky, who continued to be amazed by the strange happiness of the Kuharenko family and because of this visited them less often now, asked his wife Svetlana, the secretary of the municipal public prosecutor's office, for advice and then decided to consult the relevant official instances. As a result of this consultation Senior Lecturer Bogdanovich was arrested. The senior lecturer had attempted to present a distorted, positive picture of the struggle waged against Russia by the Polish landowning class, which regarded Belarus as its own cultural conquest . . . Bogdanovich was arrested on the second of June and in the morning of the nineteenth of June, during breakfast, they came for Kuharenko . . .

On the previous day the Kuharenko family had been in the forest, all together, for a happy family derives a special joy from being at full strength not only at home, but also outside the home. They had all walked along the forest path together, Sasha leading his wife Valyushka by the hand and their daughter Ninochka leading Mishenka, her little brother.

The Belarusian forest is a different thing from the Volga Region or Ukrainian forest. For a Belarusian the forest is the same as the river for a native of the Volga Region and an open field for a Ukrainian. The forest fed and clothed the Belarusian for centuries. Here the forest vegetation, its berries and mushrooms, do not merely provide additional sustenance, for a Belarusian the harvest of mushrooms and berries is his very staff of life. Since time immemorial incomers may have eaten in their towns, choking on a meager bread roll with herring and rust-red, bitter onions . . . But it is the Belarusian villages that feed and sustain the Belarusian . . . Strong villages, as reliable as the walls of home . . . They will warm and preserve you . . . And there are the sunny forest glades, covered in berries . . .

"Stop, children," said the father, "look over there, a snake . . . Look children, Ninochka and Mishenka . . . A Belarusian is not a true Belarusian until he has killed a snake, that's what our people believes . . . Take a stone Ninochka, and go and kill the snake."

Valyusha became anxious.

"Where are you sending the child, what if it bites her?"

"What do you mean?" said Sasha. "Isn't she a Belarusian girl? She can't be afraid of snakes. And I'll be beside her . . ." At this point little Misha started crying and said:

"Don't kill the snake, he wants to live too, he's got little children too."

"Oh, sonny boy," said the father, "how can we feel sorry for a snake? Look at what he's doing right now. He's warming himself in the sun. And when a snake warms himself in the sun he sucks in the sunshine. And after that there's a lot less sunshine left for the summer. Now think, how many snakes are there on earth and how many times is it summer on earth? Every summer an entire multitude of snakes sucks in the sunshine, so if you're a man, then kill a snake. It's your duty. And if you're a Belarusian too, you have no right to walk past a living snake. That's our national belief."

He leaned down, picked up a stone with one hand, and cautiously led Nina after him with the other . . . In the meantime the snake had thoroughly warmed itself on the forest grass and in its rejoicing it had lost its cunning in the face of its eternal enemy and for a short while forgotten the Lord's warning curse from the time of Eden, when Eve was seduced:

"Because you have done this, cursed are you above all livestock and above all beasts of the field; on your belly you shall go, and dust you shall eat all the days of your life. I will put enmity between you and the woman, and between her offspring and your offspring; he shall bruise your head, and you shall bruise his heel . . ."

Nina threw the stone at the head of the snake that was dozing on the grass and had lost its cunning in its pleasure, and she hit it, pinning down its head. The snake started writhing about, for it did not believe that the Lord's curse deprived it of the right to live, since man was also cursed, and woman was cursed with a special curse. The snake started writhing about, the snake that had only recently been luxuriating in the warmth of God's one and only sun, from which all suck the warmth, all thereby reducing it. However the snake was hacked into small pieces with a partisan sapper's entrenching tool by the father and his daughter Ninochka, and Valya led Misha, who was crying, away from this sight. But they did not see that another two snakes, a large one and a small one, were observing the happy family from the bushes with cold eyes full of hatred.

"Congratulations," the father said and kissed his daughter. "You are now a true Belarusian girl, since you have followed our national belief and killed a snake with your own hands."

Ninochka remembered the non-working day of the eighteenth of June particularly for that . . .

On the nineteenth of June at about nine o'clock, while the Kuharenko family were eating dumplings for breakfast with painted wooden spoons, two men showed up, both wearing leather coats, although it was a sunny morning.

"You're under arrest . . ."

And all this took place, not exactly without any fear, but in a way that was somehow not serious.

"Show me the warrant," Kuharenko said.

The skinny man with a mustache, who was clearly the one in charge, groaned, reluctantly reached into his pocket and showed Kuharenko the warrant . . . Kuharenko saw that the legal requirements had been observed and the warrant had been signed by Vasilii Makarovich, the public prosecutor. And when he saw the signature of Vasilii Makarovich, beside whom he had sat at a meeting only two days earlier, his heart suddenly felt heavy. The hearts of happy families are united as one and there is an invisible connection between them. Sasha started feeling unwell and Valya, who had been sitting there turned to stone, started crying.

"Don't cry, Valya," said Sasha, kissing her mouth, still smeared with sour cream from the dumplings, "don't cry, you'll frighten the children."

But it was too late. Ninochka burst into tears, grabbed hold of her father and clung to him, while Mishenka, on the contrary, huddled up in a corner.

"Ninochka," their father said, "yesterday you killed a snake in the forest. Why should you be afraid? Your father will come back soon. I'll go now, buy you a doll and come back."

"Bring me back a knife," said Mishenka.

"No," said his father, "a knife is sharp, you'll cut your finger. I'll bring you something else, Mishenka, something good."

Although Mishenka was little, for some reason he had realized that his father was not just going for a walk, he was going to a quite different place. But their mother Valya, Sasha's loving wife, had understood less at the beginning than her own little children, for in acquiring experience of life, she had learned not to understand what was obvious. However she did everything a wife is supposed to do when her husband is arrested. She quickly gathered his things together and said goodbye without any commotion, in order not to frighten the children, and when she followed Sasha out to the car that he was getting into, she suddenly saw the vast world and herself, insignificantly small in this world . . . Ninochka also saw all this from the window: of course, she didn't notice the vast world through the window, but she saw the street and remembered her father walking away, she remembered his back . . .

The Yarnutovs had been arrested on the same day, an hour earlier . . . Kolya and Sveta were arrested and the little children were sent to the infant orphanage in Vitebsk city . . . And so Valya realized that even in this she and Sasha had been more fortunate. But she did not know for how much longer they would remain fortunate, so she decided to take advantage of her good fortune . . . She hastily dressed the children, sliced some bread, poured some warm semolina pudding into a half-liter jar, tipped some candies into a little child's pouch for hanging across the shoulder and said:

"Let's go to the railway station, children."

They reached the railway station.

"Ninochka," said her mother Valya, "now you'll go to your Aunty Klava in Moscow."

"What about you?" Nina asked.

"I'll stay here with your father," Valya replied. "Ninochka, you're a big girl already, on your journey don't tell anyone what happened to your father, just take care of Mishenka."

Valya suddenly felt dizzy and she remembered that under the Germans there had been a concentration camp on the outskirts of Vitebsk and from behind the barbed wire women had asked passers-by for bread or asked them to take their children. Valya and her friend Stasya, who was later killed in their partisan unit, tore the barbed wire open with their bare hands and took a boy about two years old from his mother and another two boys about six years old and a little girl about eight years old . . . The Germans on the guard towers started shooting at them, so they weren't able to take the other children, whose mothers were jostling each other out of the way as they attempted to hand them over . . . In moments of danger a mother usually clasps her child to herself, sometimes however she tries to save the child by giving it away or sending it away and trusting in precarious chance, for in inhuman situations the day is more terrifying than the night, a crowded street is more terrifying than a wolf-infested forest and what is close and familiar is more terrifying than what is strange . . . What did those loving mothers feel as they jostled with each other, trying to separate their own children from themselves? If they had been feeling grief and suffering, they would not have been able to do that . . . No, in an inhuman situation the impulses of the heart only doom a person and doom everything human. Only the cruel instinct of the female animal, and not maternal feelings, can save the child . . . And so Valya hastily kissed Mishenka and Ninochka and put them in a car of the Moscow train and when the train had set off without any problems and the children were no longer with her, instead of bitterness Valya felt joy . . . Valya walked along several streets in joy and only started moaning when she walked into a deserted, litter-strewn square. There was a "Beer and Beverages" pavilion nearby. Valya walked into it and drank some vodka.

The inhuman instinct that had helped her to send her beloved children away from herself also helped her to deal with the horror that was closing in around her. The vodka didn't get rid of her horror, but it made her soul smaller and weaker, and weak souls tolerate intense grief more easily. After her drink, Valya went to see Kuleshov in the local NKVD, since she knew him from the partisan movement. There she got into a squabble with someone in the reception office. After that she walked along the street and people gave her a wide berth. Three days later she was arrested. And that was how a happy family was destroyed.

In Vitebsk, Sasha Kuharenko was still on familiar terms with his interrogator, but in Minsk they started beating him and trampling on him, crushing his fingers under their heels, and with the help of these violations of socialist legality they ascertained all the details of his Belarusian nationalism and his collaboration with the Gestapo during the war. Then the investigation was closed and on September the 29th the trial took place . . . While Sasha was still trying to prove his innocence, while he was still striving to uphold the truth and demanding justice, it was very hard for him and he didn't often think about his children and his wife. But when he relaxed, forgot about his own positive achievements and his unjust treatment by others, things became easier, entirely effortless in fact, and he no longer thought about anything except his wife Valya and his children Ninochka and Mishenka.

This is what happened to the children . . . Nina and Misha reached Moscow safely, at first feeding themselves on bread, semolina pudding from the jar and candies, then buying tea and biscuits from the conductor. Their fellow passengers also treated them to sausage. The moment Ninochka was left to herself she became an independent woman, in many respects demonstrating the same tenacity as Maria from Shagaro-Petrovskoe village in the Kharkiv region, who travelled in exactly the same way without her mother and with only her little brother Vasya in 1933, although in different circumstances . . . Nina told the passengers that they hadn't had any parents for a long time, that they had been raised by a woman who wasn't related to them, but now their Aunty Klavdia had been found in Moscow . . . In general a child is more capable of lying and enjoys lying far more than a grown-up. After all, every lie is part of a game. Little Misha also joined in this game of his sister's and they completed their journey in that way. One kind fellow passenger, an old Muscovite, took the children to the address that Valya Kuharenko had written out in four copies, in case it got lost, and put in the children's pouch for hanging across the shoulder. There was a hare embroidered on this pouch and before they left the house Valya had hung the pouch across Ninochka's shoulder. She hadn't sent Klavdia a telegram: firstly so that the children's departure would be less conspicuous, and secondly because she knew that Klavdia would not be pleased that they had come, so it was better to do everything unexpectedly. She and her sister had not written to each other for a long time and she did not like her sister's husband, who was Jewish by nationality.

Klavdia was much older than Valya: she had once been very beautiful and before the war she had married an art critic from Moscow, whom she had met in Yalta. This art critic's full name was Alexei Iosifovich Ivolgin. Alexei Ivolgin and Klavdia had a son. Savelii, who was clearly the result of an unsuccessful mixing of bloods: he was sickly and broody, although he was more given to hallucinations than to thoughts. They all lived together in a large apartment in one of the best possible places in Moscow, on Tverskoi Boulevard. The apartment's drawback was that it was located on the first floor. But that was not so very serious, since in old buildings the windows were set up high, almost at the same level as the second floor of new buildings, and there was a basement floor, which was also occupied, below the apartment. The real problem was that the Ivolgin's apartment was communal, and the most annoying thing of all was that in addition to the Ivolgins, who occupied three rooms, the housing office maintained a janitor's lodge in a little room there. So although there was only one neighbor, they had to share the kitchen, and the bathroom, and the telephone with him and they felt very constrained in general. Ivolgin had written many times to many official offices and solicited petitions from the numerous cultural institutions with which he collaborated, but all in vain. The janitor's lodge in the Ivolgins' apartment existed, and a janitor lived in it: the Tatar Ahmed, a foul-mouthed individual "with a little knife," from which Alexei Ivolgin had once taken refuge in the toilet. If he had locked himself in the bathroom, things would have gone badly. The door there was rotten and weak, and the latch could barely hold it shut.

"Go to Fadeev," Klavdia told her husband angrily, "no one but Fadeev will help us to get rid of the janitor's lodge."

"How can I appeal to the General Secretary of the Union of Soviet Writers about such a trivial piece of nonsense?" Ivolgin replied, gesticulating. "People are already talking about me as it is . . ."

"Let them talk," Klavdia replied, also gesticulating, for the wives of Jews very often adopt similar gestures to those of their husbands if a couple lives separately and not as part of a large Slavic family, into which the Jewish husband has been adopted . . .

"But I'm not acquainted with him," said Ivolgin.

"What do you mean, not acquainted?" Klavdia responded. "At the civil requiem for Mikhoels he said hello to you."

"Fadeev said hello to everybody there, because he was very upset," Alexei Iosifovich replied.

"But he didn't say hello to me," said Klavdia, reducing the entire conversation to meaningless repetitions, in which she could get the upper hand.

"To you, no, but to me, yes," Ivolgin eventually shrieked in an agitated voice.

"Don't shout," Klavdia shouted back, also in an agitated voice. "You all love to shout all the time."

"Who are 'we'?" Ivolgin asked, turning scarlet, that is, he didn't so much turn scarlet in fury as blush in shamefaced indignation, as he did every time at the word "Jew" when he heard it anywhere for any reason at all, as if he had been caught out doing something secret, as Klavdia had recently caught out their son Savelii doing something secret in the toilet... On that occasion Savelii had blushed shamefacedly in the same manner...

Ivolgin's appearance was indeterminate. His surname was quite outstanding, and it was genuine, the name in his passport, for his father, a member of the prerevolutionary intelligentsia and a Russian patriot, had advantageously changed his name, as he put it: "from a cat in Hebrew to a bird in Russian . . ." Alexei Iosifovich had been lucky with the surname Ivolgin, only his patronymic rather let him down. Many people did not even know that Alexei Ivolgin was a Jew. At the civil requiem for Mikhoels, where Fadeev, Zubov and other eminent Soviet individuals spoke, Alexei Ivolgin had also said a few words. The word "Jew" was not mentioned at the requiem and Alexei Iosifovich's soul had only shuddered within him twice...

However Ahmed the janitor had somehow guessed that his hostile neighbor was a Jew.

"Yid," drunken Ahmed shouted, "I'll carve you up a little bit..."

"Go to Fadeev," said Klavdia, "that Tatar will maim you and Savelii, or don't you give a damn for your son? You still haven't made any inquiries about a good psychiatrist. "And in her exasperation, she said something that hurt her husband very badly: "It's bad enough that you endowed him with such a long nose... Children tease him in the street..."

"What has that got to do with me?" Ivolgin asked agitatedly, blushing. "Look, I've got a normal nose, and my father didn't have a Jewish nose."

"Then who does have a Jewish nose, is it me or my father, a village barrel maker?" Klavdia asked and, seeing her husband blushing in his usual manner, she added: "All that's needed now is for you to accuse me of antisemitism. when all the Jews in our institute know that I'm not an antisemite and my husband is a Jew."

"What has antisemitism got to do with it?" asked Alexei Ivolgin. "You know that I take a broadminded view in these matters."

Then he fell quiet for the rest of the evening and didn't say anything more to his wife, for this squabble had taken place in the evening, naturally in Savelii's absence. After taking up the book "Selected Works of Russian

Thinkers of the Late 19th Century," seating himself with it in his favorite rocking chair and reading the phrase: "Recall from what humble beginnings the primal Russian peoples arose and what greatness, glory and might they have now succeeded in attaining..." he started thinking bittersweet thoughts about how good it would be if he had been born to Slavs, the indigenous population, or at least to Tatars or Yakuts. What a fine, humane non-Jew he would have been, how much he would have done for those unfortunate enough to have been born to a Jewish father and mother, but the fact of the matter was that it was too late to change anything now. If you were born a Jew, then that was also for ever, just as if you had died a Russian. Perhaps it would be even worse for his son Savelii, even more hurtful. A half of him was missing, but only a half... Ah, what great riches it meant to be Russian, and how little store Russians set by it, how inadequately they loved Russia... He knew there were a lot of Russians whose love for Russia was inadequate... But if only he, Alexei Iosifovich, were allowed to be Russian, what a Russian patriot he would be... However he knew there were a lot of Russians who were displeased when a Jew loved Russia, who jealously resented a Jew's love of Russia and liked it better when a Jew was an enemy to Russia. And also that there were a lot of Jews who provided justification for such galling thoughts... Yes, yes he could point his finger at such people... They did not appreciate Russian bread, they did not appreciate Russian hospitality... Ungrateful people... Ah, how he hated them... Because of them, we all suffered... Take Klavdia, she was Russian... The Belorusssians were also practically a Russian tribe...

After this, as usually happened in such cases, his thoughts scattered in numerous different directions at once and became boring, just as since time immemorial all kinds of conversations and debates about Jewishness had always become boring after the initial, vital fervor. And in addition Savelii showed up in a darkly agitated state, looked at his parents and asked:

"Have you been arguing again?"

And so they sat down to have dinner. Alexei Iosifovich thought that, apart from boring, habitual thoughts about Jewishness, a boring, habitual argument with his wife and Savelii's dark agitation, this evening would be memorable only for its heavy rain and nothing more... But the evening proved to be memorable above all else for Ahmed's disappearance... He was gone for two days, and then they found out from their district militiaman Efrem Nikolaevich that Ahmed was in jail. He had stabbed someone with his little knife.

"Immediately," Klavdia declared joyfully, "go immediately and get a petition signed to request that nobody should be moved into the room."

In order to put together such a petition, three influential signatures were required: they all definitely had to be Slavic, but preferably Russian . . . Ending in "-ov" or "-in" or, at a pinch, in "-enko."

Ivolgin went running to one office: the influential Russian signature ending in "-ov" was away on official business. He went running to another office: the signature ending in "-in" was on vacation in Crimea. He went running to a third office and here, although he did not obtain a Russian signature, he did obtain a Slavic one ending in "-enko." He ran back home in a cheerful mood and Klavdia met him with irate bitterness.

"Too late . . . you can go pickle your Slavic signature. They've moved someone in . . . And with a daughter too . . . At least Ahmed was alone."

Ivolgin saw that the lock had been removed from the door of the small room and he could hear voices from inside it, a man's and a woman's.

"Who is it?" Ivolgin asked with his eyes.

"Come on, you fool," Klavdia replied with her eyes. They walked into the living room, sat down at the grand piano and sank into dejection.

"Who?" Alexei Iosifovich asked with his voice this time.

"A Jew, of course," Klavdia replied.

"What?" said Ivolgin. "A Jewish janitor? . . . What a joke," and he laughed.

"There's really nothing funny about it," said Klavdia, also smiling, "but everything will depend on the first conversation . . . We have to put them in their place straightaway . . . I think that will be easier here . . . If worst comes to worst, I'll split his head open with a cooking pot. That will teach him to crowd me out of my own home in my own country. He has to remember that he's living in the Soviet Union . . ."

Alexei Iosifovich knew that his wife, a bookkeeper at the Ministry of Road Construction, was quite capable of hitting someone with a cooking pot, if she was sure that that they wouldn't stab her with a little knife for it, in Tatar fashion, or take her to court for it, in Jewish fashion.

"Well, never mind," she said, "I'll show them who they are in court . . . They've overrun Moscow. Now they're even taking janitors' jobs."

"No need for that," said Ivolgin, "never mind the court, leave them to me, I understand them better than you do. Jewish impertinence is afraid of a harsh word. They always want to agree things in a whisper, a whisper. But you can't talk to me in a whisper. I'll show them that I'm not interested in their problems," and he walked out into the corridor.

That was where the first encounter with Dan, the Viper, the Antichrist, took place . . . In order to avoid greeting him and instead say something harsh the art critic first pondered, wrinkled up his forehead and came to a halt, from which the Lord's emissary, the Antichrist immediately realized exactly who he was. The individual standing before him in carpet slippers, a string vest and silk pajamas was from the tribe of Reuben, Jacob's firstborn, which had once once been strong, but had long ago fallen into decline: there were not many of its members who would be included among the remainder and yield fruit . . . This individual standing before the Antichrist was the ending, but the beginning had been in Egyptian slavery, when Pharaoh's ravages and cruel harassment did battle with the tenacity and desire to live of the sons of Jacob. The more Pharaoh ravaged them, the more they multiplied, until Moses was born in the tribe of Levi . . .

However when Moses was born a great many bad things had already multiplied, for in oppression, when man does not live but merely survives and God is not there beside him, there is nothing through which what is good can survive, but what is bad survives beside the fleshpots, living its habitual life.

The tribe of Reuben, one of Israel's strong, good-hearted firstborn, had brought forth the person who was standing before the Antichrist in carpet slippers and silk pajamas, peering through unclean eyes and fondling the putrid folds of his pudgy belly like a beloved child with hands unaccustomed to toil. That which stood before the Antichrist in the corridor was the quintessence of squalid abomination and evil. But squalid abomination is not capable of creating anything perfect, it is not even capable of creating perfect abomination or a perfect evildoer. Why then is there so much perfect, boundless evil? Who engenders it? It is engendered by the good . . . Only the good yields fruit, however it yields not only its own like, but also its own opposite . . . All that is evil grows out of the good, although that which is good also grows out of the good . . . Why has the Lord allowed this, why has evil multiplied even among His own people? There you have it, the ludicrous question of the atheists and the insane question of the mystics . . . Why does the Lord need Alexei Iosifovich Ivolgin, when there have been Moses, Jeremiah, Isaiah and Jesus of Nazareth?.. The answer is simple for a person who reads and rereads not only the late Christian appendix of the Gospels, in which there is not a single self-substantive word, but also God's poem about the creation of the world, the primary foundation of the Bible, without which it is impossible to understand anything that follows . . . Ivolgin exists because after Eden man is a cursed creature. He is cursed to labor and cursed to history, whereas in Eden there was neither labor nor history. By the grace of God prophets and righteous men live on earth, by His grace the good exists in itself, whereas evil is a derivative of existence. It is his understanding of this that distinguishes the prophet from the mealy-mouthed humanist . . . But when, after peering into the ominous smile of a downtrodden atheist peasant, Alexander Blok renounced humanism, his was a voice crying out in the wilderness, for evil had multiplied too greatly . . . Humanism had also multiplied, fruitless in the general masses and only fruitful in combination with individualism, with the individual personality. At first antibiblical, Christian humanism flourished and then on one sixth of the earth's land surface it was deposed by antibiblical Christianity's illegitimate son, materialist humanism, which the art critic Alexei Iosifovich Ivolgin served faithfully and loyally, being an internationalist Jew or, speaking in Christian terms, a convert, baptized not through pure water, but through pure, silver-tongued ideology, which in principle is the same thing, being derived from the good that engenders evil.

"Old tea," the Jewish art critic said to the Jewish janitor when an idea finally occurred to him, "is not to be poured into the bath." And Alexei Iosifovich continued in a loud voice, without any of that silly whispering: "We are not obliged to clear up after you and your daughter."

No sooner had Alexei from the tribe of Reuben pronounced his communal etiquette snub than Dan from the tribe of Dan remembered something about him that Alexei Iosifovich naturally did not know about himself. He was a distant descendant of a Jew who in the times of Egyptian slavery Moses had rescued from a beating by an Egyptian, actually coming to blows with the Egyptian and killing him. And the frightened Jew had shouted at Moses:

"Who appointed you as judge over us?"

This Jew knew that, after taunting him for a while, the Egyptian would have let him go and he could still have reached the fleshpots in time. But Moses, his uninvited defender, had spoiled everything . . . And speaking with the sarcasm that in later times became typical of modern art, that ancient Jew in Egyptian slavery exclaimed:

"And who appointed you as our leader? . . . So are you thinking of killing me too, as you have killed the Egyptian?"

That is what the imperfect Russian translation of the Bible says. In the original it says that this Jew "bared his teeth at Moses." This is a precise definition, a distinctive stigma. This present-day Jew was of the same kind as those who had bared their teeth at Moses. And in fact, looking at the Antichrist, who was extremely tired and whose hair had turned gray on this earthly journey of his, Alexei Iosifovich thought he saw something pitiful and provincial in the face of this Jewish janitor. A hilariously spiteful idea occurred to Ivolgin, for after all he was a Russian art critic and he could well be moved to laughter by the world-weariness in Jewish eyes, just as it had once amused Voltaire, that favorite and darling of Russian humanist freethinking.

Then Alexei Iosifovich opened his mouth, baring his teeth that had chewed a substantial amount of Russian bread and Ukrainian sausage: a combination of gold crowns at the front, chrome-plated dental bridges at the sides and light-coffee-colored bone in the gap between. As he believed, it was here in the mouth that a good Jew was rewarded for his faithful and loyal service with food and drink and air to breath . . . His most significant award had not been pinned to his chest, but placed here, between his teeth . . .

"Ha-ha-ha," said Ivolgin, pronouncing the sounds distinctly and discretely, without any of that Jewish whispering.

And the Antichrist inwardly said to him, without speaking, through the prophet Isaiah:

"Whom are you mocking? Against whom do you open your mouth wide and stick out your tongue? Are you not children of transgression, the offspring of deceit?"

However the Jewish world-weariness that had amused Voltaire and moved Ivolgin to laughter was not only in the Antichrist's eyes, it was also in Ivolgin's eyes, albeit in a more squalid and paltry form . . .

For after all, everything paltry is the great, infinitely debased . . . Debase great world-weariness to the extreme and it is transformed into ordinary, cowardly fear. No matter what Alexei Ivolgin did, his eyes constantly, involuntarily repeated one phrase over and over again: "I'm afraid, I'm afraid . . ."

"Fear not, Abram," the Lord told the Initiator.

This was one of the fundamental provisions of the Lord's covenant with Abram and of the transformation of Abram into Abraham, the transformation of a Babylonian wanderer into the Initiator of the Lord's People . . . But those who multiplied in Egypt beside the fleshpots of slavery began to forget the Lord, in the first instance setting aside precisely this covenant.

"Be afraid, you have to be afraid," they say to this very day, "the hare is afraid all its life, and it lives . . ."

This is what they teach their young relatives after a good glass of cherry liqueur. And so, from under the welter of brilliant ideas in a philosophical treatise we suddenly hear:

"I'm afraid, I'm afraid . . ."

And it is also there in the deliberations of a learned apostate: "I'm afraid, I'm afraid." And also in the skillful, talented, church-and-birch-tree lyrical work of a poet dreaming that the Russian reader, after all the "prayerful litanies" so dear to his heart, and the "leaf-strewing autumnal gardens" so caressing to his ears, and the picturesquely represented Christmas snow, the Russian reader will forget, or at least forgive, the poet's Jewish origin . . . In this way they have abrogated the covenant with the Lord . . .

And no sooner did one of them, Alexander Iosifovich Ivolgin, laugh, baring his teeth to the Antichrist, than the fear in his eyes increased. And speaking through the prophet Isaiah the Antichrist addressed all of them in the female person, for they had all been born to weak, fragile woman and they were all her flesh:

"Whom did you dread and fear, so that you became untrue and did not remember Me, did not keep Me in your heart? Is it because I held my peace, even for a long time, that you ceased to fear me?" And the Antichrist added from himself: "He who fears people too greatly does not fear God . . ."

Meanwhile, through the fear that was his strongest, most productive feeling, the art critic Alexei Iosifovich Ivolgin somehow became more intimately involved in what was taking place in the corridor of the communal apartment, although he did not understand this. However he stopped laughing and hastily withdrew to his own quarters without saying anything more.

"I will show you your truth," said the Antichrist, looking at the stooped, corpulent back of Alexei from the formerly glorious tribe of Reuben, "I will expose your truth and your deeds, and they will not be to your advantage . . ."

And so the neighbors parted, and the corridor was left empty.

"I showed him who's the master here," Alexei Iosifovich told Klavdia when he was feeling bolder in his own sitting room, "and he didn't dare to let out a squeak in reply. An ordinary small-town Yid . . . It's their fault that we are not liked."

But after walking into his own little room the Antichrist sat down with his adopted daughter Ruth to drink tea. After the incident in the forest near Bor town father and daughter had not spoken much to each other, but they looked at each other more often, and there was a shared light and a shared smile in their glances . . . And it was right that the life shared by the gray-haired emissary of the Lord and the young earthly prophetess should be like this . . . Sometimes father and daughter would exchange a word or two and then be silent again. For after all, people talk to each other a lot in order to free themselves of the oppressive feeling of the distance between their souls and their estrangement from each other. When her father fell silent for an especially long time, the prophetess Pelagia knew what he was keeping silent about. Then she would pick up a Bible that bore a faint fragrance of an old woman's life. The worn binding gave off an odor of sweetness, cinnamon and mildew, the well-thumbed pages smelled of decay and in well-loved places they bore underlinings or inscriptions that all seemed to be in the same blue pencil. The Book of Psalms and the Proverbs of King Solomon were especially copiously underlined and inscribed . . . This bible had been given to Rufina by the old woman Chesnokova, a member of the Old Believer sect . . .

For an individual who had absorbed much culture and amassed understanding as property, not as a gift from the Lord, these inscriptions and underlinings possessed no value. And for an individual who had acquired a sophisticated understanding, replete with Voltairean satire, these inscriptions could provoke laughter and reinforce a firm conviction of the pitiful nature of simple, popular faith . . . And this is indeed the case, if one is speaking only of the simple faith of the masses, which can comprehend only rites and superstitions. For authenticity is an even rarer thing in simplicity than it is in reason. But the entire Bible is contained in such rare, divine, extreme exceptions. Others can only place their hope in ritual and an honest, intelligent mentor: a priest among simple folk or an intelligent religious philosopher in a cultured milieu. However the history of religion has demonstrated how rarely such hopes are realized. Either the intellect or the honesty is inadequate to the task. The following was underlined in blue pencil in the Proverbs of Solomon by the uneducated Old Believer Chesnokova: "The fear of the Lord is a fountain of life, that one may turn away from the snares of death." It is possible to philosophize for a while on this, although a sophisticated intellect will not discover any serious sustenance even here. But further on there is this: "Better is a dinner of herbs where love is than a fattened ox and hatred with it . . . Better is a little with the fear of the Lord than great treasure and trouble with it." At this point the sophisticated intellect will positively laugh out loud at such childish obviousness from a wise man. It will laugh, failing to understand that the wise man is not speaking with reference to that morality in terms of which people have been taught to think by thoughtless priests and mealy-mouthed humanist philosophers, but with reference to the sense of egoistic self-interest, the very sense that they genuinely trust in their own actions.

"Egoist," King Solomon is saying, "if you love yourself, it is better to eat a dinner of herbs with love than beef with hatred."

The humanist philosopher strives to teach the good on the basis of a morality that is alien to human nature. The Bible teaches people the good on the basis of human egoistic self-interest, for in contrast with the humanists' approach, it does not ignore human nature, and in contrast with the fascist adepts, who base themselves on evil and teach evil, the teachings of the Bible are based on eternal, ignoble human nature.

"A man of violence entices his neighbor," the prophetess Pelagia saw, reading the next underlined proverb, "and leads him in a way that is not good. Whoever winks his eyes plans dishonest things, he who purses his lips brings evil to pass. He is a furnace of malice . . ."

At that moment someone rang the front doorbell, but neither the father nor the daughter stirred. For there was no one to come to see them when they were in the building.

"Gray hair is a crown of glory; it is gained in a righteous life," the prophetess Pelagia saw next as she continued reading the Proverbs.

The person who had rung the doorbell was the kind fellow-passenger who had travelled from Vitebsk with Ninochka and Mishenka. After ringing he did not leave, but withdrew round a corner and waited to see if the children would be admitted. If they had not been admitted for some reason, he would have taken them to the children's room at the militia station. However they were admitted with loud exclamations, apparently of exultation, uttered by a woman's voice: satisfied with that, this man, who wished to remain anonymous, departed with the pleasant feeling of having performed a kind act. The woman who had exclaimed was Klavdia: she had recognized her sister Valentina's children, who had arrived without any warning telegram, and immediately suspected that this meant trouble. Unfortunately the kind man had only imagined that the exclamations at the meeting were of exultation. After letting the children in, Klavdia began anxiously asking where their mother and father were and why they were alone . . . Ivolgin immediately started fussing, repeating again and again:

"Klavdia, don't fuss, we have to get to the bottom of this . . ."

However Savelii, the sickly, half-blood juvenile, who was lying on the sofa, examined with interest gray-eyed Ninochka, his cousin, whom he was seeing for the first time. Mishenka burst into tears at this reception and then Ninochka started blinking her beautiful, catlike little eyes, which she had inherited from her mother.

"There, you see," said Ivolgin, who still preserved within himself the instinctive responses to children's tears of a weak-willed Jewish man. "First of all we need to feed them."

"Yes, of course," Klavdia hastily agreed.

They gave each of the children some of the previous day's warmed-up soup and a meat patty with macaroni. While they were eating, Klavdia and Alexei Iosifovich closeted themselves in the bathroom and read the letter they had discovered in the children's pouch with a little hare embroidered on it. In actual fact Klavdia only read the letter as far as the lines about Sasha's arrest.

"Of course," she said, turning pale and dropping the sheet of paper, "She couldn't care a fig about me before, but now she's in trouble she wants to destroy me too. She refuses to understand that my husband is a Jew and we have to be entirely above suspicion."

"What has my nationality got to do with anything?" asked Ivolgin, shuddering inwardly as he always did at the mention of his terrible, shameful true nature.

"You know what," Klavdia shrieked spitefully, "and don't pretend that you don't. You sacrificial lamb . . . Do you want the same thing to happen to you as happened to Sherman?"

"What has Sherman got to do with this?" said Ivolgin, trying to restrain his racing heart. "Sherman was in contact with his relatives in America." And then he heard that familiar phrase "I'm afraid, I'm afraid," start off at a run and then accelerate into a gallop, and his very soul was dragged out of him. "I'm afraid, I'm terrified," cried the soul of this member of the formerly glorious tribe of Reuben, the soul of one of those of whom the Lord spoke through the prophet Ezekiel:

"But when they came to the nations, wherever they came, they profaned My holy name, in that people said of them, 'These are the people of the Lord, and yet they had to go out of His land.'"

"I'm afraid, I'm terrified," croaked Ivolgin's soul, already hoarse from shouting out as it was dragged out of his body in the way that a man being arrested is dragged out of bed in the night, and Ivolgin said in a husky whisper:

"I heard that there's a serious trial taking place in Belarus, they're trying the nationalists . . . Bogdanovich and the others . . ."

"Senya, we have to decide what to do about Valya's children," said Klavdia, speaking firmly now, without any agitation. "Valya might take offence, but I can't keep them here with me. I have a child too. And it would be difficult for us financially, but that's not the most important thing . . ."

"All right," Ivolgin said hastily, "only let's not talk about this now. Now we need to sleep . . . We'll deal with this in the morning . . ."

Alexei Iosifovich knew perfectly well in general terms what his wife had decided, although he didn't know all the details yet: however he was afraid to hear what she had decided spoken out loud and he was trying to postpone that moment . . . He was just as afraid of ignoble actions as he was of noble ones. He was afraid of everything and even when he dared to shout at those who were formally his subordinates, he still felt afraid of them.

Before Valya's children, Ninochka and Mishenka, went to bed, they gave each of them a glass of thin berry-juice jelly and a bread bun, just as they always did with their own child Savelii. They made up a bed for them on the sofa in the sitting room and the tired children quickly fell asleep. Savelii went to bed in his own room where the inside lock had been removed from the door: a locksmith had removed it on Klavdia's instructions after Savelii was caught out in the youthful sin that was also committed by Tamar's second husband Onan, so that Savelii would feel that his parents could walk in at any moment and catch him at his sinful business. However that night his parents had no time for all that and they rose early in the morning with equally puffy eyes and went off to work without eating any breakfast. But the children again ate meat patties with macaroni, washing it down with berry-juice jelly and then occupied themselves with games. Little Mishenka clambered into the big grandfather clock and started trying to catch the pendulum. And Savelii asked Ninochka:

"Can you do gymnastics?"

"What do you mean?" Ninochka asked in surprise.

"It's very simple," said Savelii, "I lift you up and you make all kinds of movements with your arms. Do you know what I mean?"

"Yes," said Ninochka, "I used to play like that with my father in Vitebsk . . . He used to lift me way up high in his arms . . . And he took me for rides on his bicycle . . . And he taught me to recite poems . . . Like this . . .

Beside the school is a new house
And we live there, it's very nice.
We go running up the stairs,

Counting every floor there is:
First floor, second floor, third floor, then
The fourth floor and we're home again."

Savelii remembered that as a little boy, before he started going to school, he liked looking at fashion magazines with pictures of beautiful women in them and running his finger along their smooth, glossy legs and this gave him a sweet, pleasant feeling, like sucking on a piece of candy. He did not know, of course, that the bad mixing of blood is often punished with the fourth plague of the Lord, sickness, and the third plague, the wild beast . . . Nonetheless, while still a child he realized that it was best to sit down with a fashion magazine and run his finger along the women's glossy, gleaming legs somewhere in a private little corner . . . And so from an early age he grew accustomed to associating his sweet feeling with seclusion. He observed the little girls in the yard from his seclusion, avoided the girls in the classroom and suffered, until one day in the school toilet a certain boy taught him a shameful pleasure . . . He also liked going to see the circus or gymnastics exhibitions and watching men lift women up by their legs and hips. And so, when he was left alone with his young female cousin, since the little boy didn't count, he decided to try it himself for the first time and his heart started pounding as it had never done before. And he understood, not with his mind, of course, for he was still too stupid, but he understood with his arms what a woman's body was and that any secondary pleasures that Tamar's second husband Onan might have indulged in were pitiful in comparison . . . Oh, the soft, moist weight of a woman, for the sake of that it was worth committing acts of reckless insanity . . . Did gymnasts and circus artists really experience the same thing every day? . . . He was not yet familiar with the tedium aroused in a sated individual by sumptuous dishes such as golden-brown roasted geese and carp baked in sour cream . . . He was a boy from a family in 1949 Moscow that was reasonably well-off, but nonetheless fed itself on large saveloys and meat patties.

Ninochka also liked it when Savelii lifted her up, she squealed and waved her arms about, and Mishenka clapped his hands. The children got so carried away that they didn't notice when the grown-ups came back. Klavdia walked in precisely at the moment when Savelii was trying to persuade Ninochka to perform a gymnastic balancing exercise with him, but she wouldn't because it felt too ticklish. Eventually Ninochka consented and although she squealed, she allowed Savelii to push his hand rather a long way up.

"What's going on here?" Klavdia shouted, turning as white as a sheet: it was a rhetorical shout, because she knew perfectly well what was going on. "Stop that immediately."

"We're playing," Nina said, laughing.

Klavdia grabbed Savelii and dragged him into his bedroom, where she smacked him hard on the cheek. Alexei Iosifovich followed them in and also struck the boy, but not so painfully, for after all he was a Jewish father.

"That's another reason why we have to send them away," Klavdia said in a whisper, "a strange girl in the house will debauch Savelii."

"Yes, yes, I agree," Ivolgin replied and his heart started fluttering in fright in its habitual fashion, "but they definitely have to be given lunch first . . . Before we . . ." And he stopped short.

After lunch Klavdia told cowed Savelii:

"You'll stay here . . . Your father and I and the children are going out to deal with some business. Is that clear?"

Guilty Savelii didn't dare disobey and he lay down on the sofa. The Ivolgins and the children of their repressed relatives the Kuharenkos got into a trolleybus and rode to the Belarusian Station. At the Belarusian Station they went to the mother-and-child room. Klavdia and Alexei Iosifovich sat the children down, walked away into a corner by a window and started talking in whispers. Then Klavdia went out and Alexei Iosifovich walked over to the children and sat beside them, pondering on something. After pondering for a while, he said something to Nina and led her over to the window where he and Klavdia had whispered earlier:

"You're a big girl already, you must understand that your parents have been arrested and it's impossible to hide that. While you're with us they'll always find you, because we're relatives. So take Misha, carry him into the general waiting room and start crying. If they ask why you're crying, tell them that your mother has abandoned you and she isn't coming back. And your surname is Ivanova."

Ninochka was a conscientious girl and she did as her elders told her. She took Misha, walked into the large waiting room and started crying. Only she wasn't crying for the mother who had supposedly abandoned her and gone away, but for her mother from Vitebsk, and she cried for her real father too. People started walking up and asking what was wrong. And a woman with a red arm band, a station duty manager, also walked up to her.

"What's wrong?" she asked. "Why are you crying, little girl?"

"Our mother left us," Ninochka answered as her Uncle Alexei had told her to do, "and she's not coming back for us."

And she suddenly felt a painful ache in her chest and got such a bitter feeling of pity for herself . . . and for Mishenka.

"That's right," said the station duty manager, "I saw their mother with them in the mother-and-child room," (she had obviously seen Aunty Klavdia with the children and taken her for their mother.) "Take your little brother and come with me," said the station duty manager.

Ninochka picked up Mishenka in her arms and set off after the station duty manager. As she was walking past the station telegraph office, Ninochka saw Uncle Alexei, who was peeping out from behind some other people's backs and looked at her anxiously. And then Uncle Alexei was gone. Ninochka followed the station duty manager through connecting tunnels between platforms, then along a platform, then along a street near the station. Mishenka was heavy, Ninochka was ready to drop and her hands were coming unclasped, but then they reached a building. The station duty manager went away and the two children sat on the floor in a little corner on their own for a long time. Eventually they were called into a different room with a militiaman sitting in it. The militiaman started asking who they were and where they were from. Remembering Uncle Alexei's instructions, Ninochka answered as he had told her to and Mishenka was frightened, so he said nothing. But when a severe-looking woman with a comb in her gray hair came in and also started asking questions, the children burst into tears and Ninochka told the woman everything that had happened, and that their surname wasn't Ivanov, but Kuharenko. Then they were given a good dinner and they lived in that building for three days, after which they were sent to Tobolsk town on a train.

At first they found themselves in the Makarenko orphanage, which was located seven kilometers from Tobolsk in an old nunnery in the middle of a forest. It was a nice place. In the summer they walked to the Irtysh and Tobol rivers to bathe in the water. And beside the orphanage there was a tree nursery, where little foxes lived, and the orphanage children used to go to look at them. But later there was a fire. People said that the nuns had set fire to the orphanage because the Soviet authorities had taken the buildings away from them and reassigned them for raising orphans. After the fire all the children were transferred to the Krupskaya orphanage in Tobolsk, but it wasn't as nice there. Then suddenly one morning Nina was summoned to the headmistress of the orphanage and told:

"Kuharenko, tomorrow we're sending you away."

"Where to?" Nina asked.

"You'll see when you get there."

"But what about my brother Misha?"

The headmistress didn't answer her. In the morning Nina said goodbye to Misha and she and some other children were taken very far away in railroad freight cars. They brought them to a place where everything was very bad. The food was barely enough to live on and the teachers were spiteful. There were huge, round-topped hills all around and the children were frightened with stories about bears so that they wouldn't abscond. One day Nina saw a column of either convicts or prisoners being led past. Nina remembered one woman, because an armed escort hit her and the blood ran down across her face . . . After that day Nina became very highly strung and talked back to her elders, so they locked her in the basement where the orphanage's sauerkraut was stored.

The educational regimen in this orphanage was strictly enforced and the punishment for any breach of discipline was implacable . . . Tears were not taken seriously here.

In general, since time immemorial Russians have loved to weep a bit and show pity, it's in the Russian character. But in 1952 Russian national life, which now expressed the life of the entire state system to a greater extent than ever before, became unified to an extreme degree, acquiring a harsh, monastic structure. Normally the salvation of a young, immature soul lies in not taking too serious an attitude to life. Since time immemorial this lack of seriousness had been the Russian soul's companion, saving it from ruination at difficult moments. But by the time the steely, militarily disciplined year of 1952 arrived this salvational lack of seriousness had been eradicated everywhere and the merriment had even been eliminated from antisemitism. People didn't joke about Jews any longer, they didn't make fun of them any longer and the number of funny Jewish jokes had dwindled drastically. But on the other hand a large number of harshly written articles appeared, published literally at the extreme limit of the ruling ideology. It seemed as if the spoken word was on the point of breaking through into print at any moment . . . From a rhyming couplet in the evening to a newspaper in the morning. The couplets of the famous rhyming ditty "Beat the Yids . . ." were not sung with any rakish jollity, but austerely, like a hymn . . . The burned-out, exhausted Russian soul had completely changed, and now the air was charged with expectation, not of a jolly Orthodox pogrom, but a medieval, Catholic pogrom . . . After being thoroughly sucked by a vitriolic Polish mouth, the Polish candy "Yid" had been accepted from that mouth by another mouth that was also Slavic, but wider and less bony, and it often tasted sweet rather than bitter . . . Oh, how pleasant it was to hold it in your mouth, it was as tasty for chasing vodka with as a fresh cucumber. And in a scholarly conversation it refreshed the mouth most pleasantly. It intimated to the staunchly Russian man of letters an answer to the eternal Russian questions . . . The Polish candy "Yid" was a fine, tasty thing, but by the steely, militarily disciplined year of 1952 it had become a bitter pill. It burned people's mouths, making them contort their faces.

Oh Lord, what terrifying faces Alexei Iosifovich Ivolgin saw, and so many of them! His soul no longer even shouted out "I'm afraid," but simply shuddered without any words.

"Call Fadeev," Klavdia whispered in bed.

"To remind him about my address at the civil requiem for the Jewish bourgeois nationalist Mikhoels?" Alexei Iosifovich retorted in a haunted voice.

"Why remind him?" said Klavdia. "Do you think he even remembers where you met him?"

"No, no," said Ivolgin. "Right now the most important thing is to be inconspicuous."

But it's not easy to be inconspicuous when the Russian question: "Who is destroying Russa?" looms so large, scorching and nagging at the Russian individual. It's easy enough to vanish at a wild, flamboyant Russian wedding by lying under the table and pretending to be drunk, but just try to disappear when Russian resentment is drawing up its balance sheet, when Russian speech is full of vicious hissing and buzzing sounds . . . You walk along the street and there's hissing and buzzing on all sides. It's happening in public spaces, enterprises, movie theaters and public transportation: they're buzzing everywhere . . . Streetcar-trolleybus antisemitism is not a new phenomenon, but these days municipal transportation has been transformed into protest meetings on wheels. The freedom of speech guaranteed by the Constitution has always been upheld in this area, but now there are more orators in the buses than in England's Hyde Park. Even in former, jollier times Alexei Iosifovich was afraid when loud gossiping started up among the passengers. On one occasion a jolly individual boarded a trolleybus (something that happened only rarely, but did happen) and this jolly individual sniffed at the air and said:

"Happy garlic day to you, comrades . . . It's not yet clear exactly who smells so fragrant, but then, isn't that fragrant odor our common, collective reality now?"

Some people remained silent, but some laughed, while Alexei Iosifovich lowered his eyes and pulled his head down into his shoulders. He hadn't eaten any garlic, but his heart still skipped a beat. Any moment now they would jab him under the ribs with that terrible word . . . They were about to say it . . . But they didn't say it . . . The danger passed . . . And it passed the next time too . . . And a third time . . . But Alexei Iosifovich carried on waiting. And a Russian individual in a number 20 trolleybus following its route from Marx Prospect to Silver Pines Forest (a quaint, whimsical Slavic place name), looked at Alexei Iosifovich point-blank and said:

"If our prescriptions didn't have to be written in Latin, we'd have strangled all you Yids ages ago."

And the spontaneously consolidated collective of the trolleybus remained approvingly silent in support of its orator. For in a Russian collective a Jew is an important, essential detail for the experiential perception of national unity.

Alexei Iosifovich did not step, but tumble out onto the square of that Russian genius, Pushkin, and he sat there for a long time, clutching at his heart.

Two days later he travelled to Leningrad on a business trip for the journal "Theater" and a Russian individual traveling in the same compartment spoke to him "heart-to-heart" all the way.

Generally speaking, the antisemitism of municipal public transportation is radically different from the antisemitism of railroad transportation. In municipal transportation the distances are short, the space is crowded and the cast of characters changes rapidly, all of which leads to dynamic action and loud shouting, with brief, clearly formulated slogans. The situation in railroad transportation is quite the opposite. Here there is more space and plenty of time, and you can get a feeling for people. Here there are thorough deliberations concerning "the truth of the matter," here there is analysis. And here, providing that he wishes to discuss and not shout, the antisemite's fundamental rule is observed. The antisemite's fundamental rule is to say that many of his friends are Jews, and then to discuss brotherhood. Dostoevsky's essay of March 1877, "The Jewish Question," was written entirely in the soothing-lullaby style of railroad transportation antisemitism.

"Yes, yes," said Alexei Iosifovich, nodding, "I agree with you . . . I have always been an internationalist, I abandoned the prejudices of my nation a very long time ago . . . Even my surname is international, Ivolgin, and I am married to a Belarusian woman. And I gratefully endorse Dostoevsky's clarion call: 'Long live brotherhood!' I agree with him that the Jew is more likely to be unable to understand the Russian than the Russian the Jew. Just between the two of us," he added with his eyes gleaming, pleased to have chanced upon a cultured individual and not a loud-mouthed bawler, "... just between the two of us: I have never liked Jewish women ... But Slavic women are an entirely different matter." And Alexei Iosifovich, the art critic, smacked his lips.

In actual fact, while wishing to make a smutty comment to his traveling companion, Alexei Iosifovich had spoken the truth. When a people becomes demoralized, it is the women who are affected in the first instance, since the women create the national image of a people. In those prosaic concentration-camp townlets, the *shtetls* of Eastern Europe, amidst the sour wedding nights of male cousins and female cousins, in rooms that are sweltering hot, so that consumptive lungs will not be chilled by any draft, from generation to generation the glorious image of the biblical beauties has sunk ever lower. And women with disproportionately large noses and bony hips or pendulous bellies have given birth to people who are narrow-boned, stoop-shouldered, feeble and chronically ill ... Because all those who have managed by some chance to retain the healthy heritage of their origins have tried to flee from their Jewishness, despite the severe prohibitions of the dogmatic Talmudist. To save their lives the healthy have fled from the prosaic concentration camps in which Jews were imprisoned and left to degenerate and become extinct ... The few beautiful women have also fled, following their biological instinct and seeking to continue, not their own, perishing posterity, but the sound posterity of others. The intelligent have fled. The tenacious have fled. The skilled and competent have fled ... Into any chink, into any interstice ... As Herzen wrote: "The Yids were cunning and disingenuous out of necessity." No one convened international forums concerning their situation, no one established international humanitarian funds to support them. Those who were perishing saved themselves. They fled from Jewish ways in order to preserve their own humanity. But the price that they paid for this was far greater than the price that Faust paid to Mephistopheles. They did not sell their soul, but their spirit. The soul preserves the basic humanity in a person, but the spirit preserves God in a person. Those who fled from their Jewishness saved their soul but doomed their spirit ...

That was how Alexei Iosifovich's grandfather, with his first name Chaim, which sounds so comical to the Slavic ear, and his surname Katz, fled from his *shtetl* ... The surname Katz is good for earning in Germany, but a different one was required for earning in Russia ... And Iosif Katz, Chaim's son, bought the surname Ivolgin from a district police superintendent. He paid a cheap price, only five silver rubles. And if he had traveled farther, into some remote country district, he could have bought the surname of His Imperial

Majesty, Romanov. However Iosif Katz, a dentist, bought his surname in St. Petersburg, where life was more expensive. And he took what he was given.

So Ivolgin it was. And subsequently how grateful his son, Alexei Iosifovich Ivolgin, was... For a Jew in Russia this inheritance was better than any amount of capital, better than a house with a plot of land. The freshly minted Iosif Ivolgin was one of those Jews who had a good life, since they were more capable than others in their own professions and Russia needed more and more skilled engineers, lawyers and other professionals in areas that were regarded with suspicion by Russian tillers and owners of the land. These Russian patriots of Jewish extraction grouped themselves around the St. Petersburg newspaper "Rech'" (meaning "Speech") which the Black Hundred newspaper "Russkoe znamya" (The Russian Banner) referred to with some justification as Jewish. The more denunciatory articles "Rech'" published about Zionism's attempts to corral Jews into the framework of a narrow nationalism, instead of promoting fraternal collaboration with the great Russian people, the more demoniacally "Russkoe znamya" fulminated, printing its own anti-Zionist articles, which had more boisterous intoxication and gusto, demanding action to prevent the global Jewish *kahal* from seizing power over all mankind... The Black Hundreds were rough carpenters, while the Jewish Russophiles were fine craftsmen... Doctor Dubrovin, the leader of the Union of the Russian People, turned green in the face when he read the newspaper "Rech'"... The educated Jews had taken into their own hands the noble cause of the genuinely Russian individual, antisemitic propaganda, and appropriated all the sweetest parts of it... Those despicable tricksters, they even managed to turn antisemitism to their own advantage...

Oh, that newspaper "Rech'"... Alexei Iosifovich had actually begun his own career in literary criticism in it as a very young journalist, when he published a brief article about how doctrinaire talmudists in a certain *shtetl* were persecuting a youth who had accepted Christianity. And he claimed that the district police superintendent was ignoring the priest's complaints, having been bribed by wealthy benefactors of the synagogue. Now, however, Alexei Iosifovich was permitted less and less often to speak out against cosmopolitans on the pages of the newspapers, and that was a very bad sign. And recently an altogether unpleasant incident had occurred. Alexei Iosifovich had written a large article, analyzing how Mikhoels' outwardly romantic devices were a transparent cover for petit bourgeois Jewish nationalism. It was an article for the current times, but it had not been accepted. And suddenly he had seen it in a slightly modified, more primitive form, published over a well-known signature ending in "-ov." Alexei Iosifovich was completely at a loss. Ultimately he couldn't give a damn for any "weighty monument of bronze." But in its original form the article would have been far more valuable to the cause of patriotic propaganda . . . Yes, what Doctor Dubrovin dreamed about in the turbulent Orthodox pogrom year of 1905 had been put into effect in the steely, militarily disciplined year of 1952. The Jew was being expunged to an ever greater extent from Russian patriotic propaganda. Even his professional competence was being sacrificed for the sake of principles. Parlous times had arrived for Alexei Iosifovich. The newspapers were unanimous in foregoing his services and there was no way of knowing if he might even be deprived of his income from the university.

"Call Fadeev," Klavdia whispered in bed, "he'll help. If not for what happened to my sister Valya, I'd go to him myself as your wife, a Belarusian."

At that time Alexei Iosifovich was developing a disease that afflicts those who expect nothing good from the outside world. They start fearing their own front door more than any wild beast . . . Any moment now they'll ring the doorbell, they'll yell terrible accusations, clamoring barbarously and stamping their feet . . .

Their neighbor the janitor rose early. As he listened to the footsteps in the corridor with his forehead aching, Alexei Iosifovich thought: "A janitor, now that's a safe profession for a Jew. Our neighbor is cunning, and I didn't realize it. Only if there's a genocide will the profession of janitor fail to provide any protection. But if the extermination is implemented in accordance with the class struggle, then being a janitor is absolutely safe."

"Call Fadeev," Klavdia kept repeating stubbornly, in a slinky voice, seeing her only salvation in psychological hanky-panky.

"All right," said Alexei Iosifovich. "I'll call him tomorrow."

He himself couldn't tell if he had said it to appease his wife or because he really had made up his mind . . . But what did "tomorrow" mean in 1952 for an individual working in that most dangerous area of socialist construction, culture? Every "tomorrow" required new sacrifices: this "tomorrow" was like some baleful pagan idol. And they didn't substitute sheep for human sacrifices, as Abraham had substituted a ram for Isaac as a burned offering at the prompting of an angel. And the sacrificial human herd was dwindling, shrinking so quickly that they had started taking victims from among the sleekest and best groomed. In every article concerning the ideological struggle, at every narrow party session and broad general meeting new sacrifices were demanded. And Volgin's "tomorrow" also arrived, he was dragged under the knife and subjected to dissection at a seminar on the representation of the class enemy in contemporary drama. And just what was it that they had recalled from the time when Ivolgin was young and striving to attract attention to himself? Where else could he have attracted attention to himself if not in polemics? More specifically, in polemics against those who believed that the class enemy could only be portrayed as comical and grotesque: "A Komsomol member supposedly cannot create an image of the class enemy with all the subtleties of his psychology. Of course, it is possible to portray a class enemy as both comical and grotesque. In this way the author can express his own attitude, his hatred for the class enemy. But this will be a satirical device, which should permeate the entire work."

"In other words, Ivolgin exhorts us to create, alongside the grotesque image of the class enemy, a grotesque atmosphere of Soviet reality, in order not to distort the overall artistic impression. He tells us that beside a modern-day Khlestakov a modern-day, positive, full-blooded Soviet character cannot exist, that what is required is a Soviet Gorodnichy and some kind of Soviet Skvoznik-Dumukhanovsky . . ."

"It's so stifling in here, as if someone has grabbed me by the throat . . . If only I could open all the windows . . . The windows are wide open . . . Have pity on me . . . Don't forgive me, I cannot hope for that, simply have pity on me."

"I quote: 'Portray the class enemy as he really is, depicting his philosophy and psychology in full, and the full extent of his activity . . .' In other words, under the guise of objectivity Ivolgin is exhorting us to drag antisemitic diatribes out onto the stage . . ."

Ivolgin . . . Ivolgin . . . Ivolgin . . . Ivolgin . . . And suddenly someone said: "Katz" . . .

"Ivolgin-Katz, like Meyerkhold, of whom he is so fond, belongs to the constellation, if I may use that term, which Lunacharsky called 'the jaundiced intelligentsia,' and despite Luncharsky's own subsequent errors, in this matter he was right . . ."

"Stanislavsky also paid homage to the alien influence of bourgeois realism . . . However he found the inner strength . . ."

Alexei Iosifovich found himself in a very strange state now, a kind of psychological mirage, an unexpected condition. He had never forgotten the words spoken by the Russian man on the number 20 trolleybus traveling on its route from Marx Prospect to Silver Pines Forest: "If our prescriptions didn't have to be written in Latin, we'd have strangled all you Yids ages ago."

They were strangling him now. Could they really have learned to write Latin themselves? No, my dear people, you still don't know what Latin is. Latin resides in the innermost recesses of our hearts. It is buried deep, like a dear departed friend, covered over with the people's robust black earth and the barren clay of the intelligentsia's contrition.

"There was a solemn service set for four o'clock. I was in heaven. The sonorous strains of the organ. The long vistas of white veils. The delicate tinkling of little silver bells, tinkling as they were shaken by the delicate hands of pale-faced boys. A choir of angels. Banners of delicate, perfumed lace. Candles. And daylight outside the windows. Incense. Billowing smoke from the censers. And a golden autumn outside the windows. Statues of the Holy Virgin and the gentle tapping on the stone floor of people at prayer, like the whispering of leaves outside the windows. I stood there for a long time, until fatigue obliged me to leave."

That is Meyerkhold from the time of his production of Maeterlinck's "Sister Beatrice." That's what Latin is, comrade . . .

When the seminar ended, on their way out everybody saw Alexei Iosifovich sitting in a deep, soft armchair in the lounge just outside the conference hall. Lit from the side, his face was the firm face of a white marble corpse. His torso was steeply reclined and the back of his head was resting against the upright back of the armchair, while at the same time his white marble hands were extended far in front of him and folded on the grip of a richly decorated, thick, knotty walking stick with a copper monogram, covered in yellow lacquer. He sat there like that and everyone walked past him as if they were stepping over a violated corpse. When the Lord looked at him, He took pity on His Own holy name, which had been dishonored and said:

"It is not for your sake that I am about to act, but for the sake of My holy name, which you have profaned among the nations to which you came. And I will vindicate the holiness of My great name, which has been profaned among the nations, and which you have profaned among them. And the nations will know that I am the Lord, when through you I vindicate my holiness before their eyes. I will take you from the nations and gather you from all the countries and bring you into your own land. I will sprinkle clean water on you, and you shall be clean from all your uncleannesses, and from all your idols I will cleanse you. And I will give you a new heart, and a new spirit I will put within you. And I will remove the heart of stone from your flesh and give you a heart of flesh. Then you will remember your evil ways, and your deeds that were not good, and you will loathe yourselves for your iniquities and your abominations. Then the nations that are left all around you shall know that I am the Lord; I have rebuilt the ruined places and replanted that which was desolate. I am the Lord; I have spoken, and I have done it."

So said the Lord, gazing on Alexei Iosifovich from the tribe of Reuben, trampled underfoot in his negligible nonentity, and as He spoke the prophetess Pelagia was reading at home, having opened the bible given to her by the old woman Chesnokova at the book of the prophet Ezekiel and seated herself on a stool by the windowsill. And at that time her father Dan, the Viper, the Antichrist was in the yard, sweeping up the fallen leaves that were stuck to the ground and waterlogged from the rain. This was a long, difficult job, it dragged out until the evening and his adopted daughter, the prophetess Pelagia, took a wooden spade and went out to help her father. They worked like that until the stream of other residents walking by carried past them their neighbor, Alexei Iosifovich: he was walking as if he were blind, feeling his way with a richly decorated stick bought in Sochi. Then they finished their job and in their mutual love they went to their room to drink their happy, inexpensive evening tea. But the Ivolgins sat down to their rich, bitter dinner, which followed a recipe from the parables of King Solomon: roasted fatty beef...

In his agonizing despair Ivolgin-Katz ate a lot of fatty beef and went to bed. The mood in the Ivolgin family was ghastly. Even Savelii the half-breed youth, who had not thought deeply for a long time about anything except the female body, having experienced it courtesy of his cousin Ninochka, felt afraid for his father today and said:

"Daddy and Mommy, I won't upset you any more..."

However Klavdia, absentminded in her despair, shouted at him:

"Go to your room!"

After that he went to his room and there, alone and with no one to supervise him, he indulged in his nasty practices. And Klavdia started up again with her usual pillow talk.

"Call Fadeev... Or it will be too late."

"All right," Ivolgin replied, "I'll call him tomorrow."

And he fell asleep or simply lapsed into unconsciousness in his fear. And then he had a dream, in which he really did call the General Secretary of the Union of Soviet Writers, member of the Central Committee of the Party and deputy of the Supreme Soviet. He spoke on the phone with Fadeev. But the phone was a cone of newspaper, like the ones that they roll up in kiosks or at the market for certain kinds of foodstuffs. Of course, it was not only through the paper cone that Alexei Iosifovich established contact with comrade Fadeev. There was something like a satchel hanging over his shoulder, and Alexei Iosifovich knew that this was part of the apparatus of direct communication. But he could only feel its weight, he couldn't see it at all and he couldn't touch it. So in reality there was only the newspaper cone, into which he spoke as if it were a megaphone.

"Good morning, Comrade Fadeev," Alexei Iosifovich said.

"Good morning, Comrade Ivolgin," the cone relayed back to him.

That was a relief: *He called me comrade. He didn't call me Katz.*

"Comrade Fadeev," Alexei Iosifovich said into the cone, "today at a seminar on the depiction of the image of the class enemy in drama a group of individuals underserving of political trust leveled absurd accusations against me . . . Yes, absurd, Comrade Fadeev . . ."

There was a long silence in the newspaper cone, but it was clear that the line was still open and Fadeev was simply pondering in order not to give just any old answer. And after the pause comrade Fadeev replied through the newspaper cone:

"Do they really pay me money for loving my grandfather?"

"Comrade Fadeev," Alexei Iosifovich shouted into the newspaper cone "comrade . . . please clarify . . ."

The contact was fading, Alexei Iosifovich couldn't squeeze anything more out of the newspaper cone. He woke up in a cold sweat.

It was far into the night, in fact almost dawn, which is the moment of least movement in a large, sleepless city. The night has already fallen silent and the day has not yet started dawning . . . His wife was sleeping and on the other side of the wall it was quiet in Savelii's room. Alexei Iosifovich quickly sat down at his desk and by the light of the electric plug-in lamp he wrote a brief, clear letter to Fadeev . . . "This happened . . ." he wrote, "and this . . ." Then he got dressed, tiptoed out into the corridor, trying to hold his breath, opened the door and went outside, walked for a short distance, shivering in the damp air of the fall dawn, as far as the first mail box, and after he had dropped the letter into it all his limbs suddenly started shuddering and he put his arms round the cold, official metal box and started weeping like a drunk for his ruined life. What had destroyed it? Why did he feel so bitter? Was this the first time a man had ever gone under on this planet? But he had not lived for the sake of his own nature and he was not going under for the sake of his own nature. It wasn't Ivan and Maria who had come together in order to conceive Alexei Iosifovich, that was what was destroying him . . . It was bitter, bitter . . . Ah, if only he could have been the fruit of an immaculate conception, and not of Iosif Chaimovich . . . Alexei Iosifovich leaned his forehead against the indifferent, cold metal of the mailbox, in which from that moment on his letter to comrade Fadeev, written under the influence of a terrifying dream, would lie, irretrievably separated from him. And through his wordless lamenting he repeated the prophet Jeremiah's curse on himself: "Cursed be the day on which I was born! The day when my mother bore me, let it not be blessed! Cursed be the man who brought the news to my father: 'A son is born to you,' making him very glad. Let that man be like the cities that the Lord overthrew without pity, let him hear a cry in the morning and an alarm at the noon, because he did not kill me in the womb, so that my mother would have been my grave, and her womb forever great."

And through his national lament Ivolgin-Katz felt his own genuine soul for the first time: previously he had only shamelessly trembled and panicked in a Jewish manner, but he had shamelessly laughed and wept in a Russian manner. Everybody has their own way of lamenting and their own way of feeling fear . . . In his fear the Russian is religious, the Jew in his fear is an atheist. The Russian individual laughs extravagantly, forgetting everything in his laughter, which is heady, juvenile and antireligious, and he weeps from his soul, without restraint . . . But genuinely Jewish national laughter and genuinely Jewish national weeping do not include the brazen Russian atheistic freedom. The Jew's laughter is for God, and his lament is also for God . . . There is no self-abandonment in either his lament or his laughter, in both he always observes himself from the outside . . . The laughter is ironic, the lament is rational . . . Only in fear does the Jew lapse into self-forgetfulness, into atheism, violating Abraham's promise to the Lord . . .

After that fall dawn when Alexei Iosifovich first wept in the Jewish manner, something happened to his soul: he took to his bed and started waiting to be arrested . . . However the steely, militarily disciplined year of 1952 ended and the year of 1953, a special, armor-plated year, began, and still his arrest had not come. "This is impossible," Alexei Iosifovich thought anxiously, "they'll arrest me in January, on some set date."

In the evenings the planet Venus shone brightly. Might it not be that star of Bethlehem? Was Christmas not perhaps connected with Venus?

There was Dan, the Viper, the Antichrist, clearing away the snow in the yard and on the sidewalk in front of the building, remembering how cold and starry the January evenings were in Bethlehem, where the Moabite Ruth was united with Boaz and continued the line of Judah. And voluptuous Venus was glittering in the constellation of Sagittarius . . . In the second half of January there was a lot of snow, the Antichrist could not cope with it on his own and his daughter, the prophetess Pelagia, helped him . . . By that time Venus had already moved into the constellation of Capricorn, and by the end of the month, the time of melting snow and black ice, Venus had moved into Aquarius.

"They'll arrest me in February," Alexei Iosifovich thought, "it was early in February that the killer doctors in white coats finally confirmed Dostoevsky's sober-minded railroad-travel deliberations . . . Not for, but against . . ."

Throughout February there was black ice and March began with winds and black ice. Venus, the Christmas star, was now shining in the constellation of Aries . . . On the second of March Alexei Iosifovich was finally arrested. They got him up out of his bed, where he was lying, completely covered in mustard plasters, and took him straight out into the cold, influenza-bearing wind.

The interrogator was a Ukrainian by the name of Serdyuk. A military, Cossack name. There could easily be a Sergeant Serdyuk, or a General Serdyuk or a retired army man of letters Serdyuk . . . In this particular case it was a Captain Serdyuk . . . A young man from Vinnitsa, a region where they knew all about Jews.

> There was once a certain Chaim,
> Adored by all who knew him . . .

Serdyuk drew up the minutes, trying to brush aside the intrusive little tune as if it were a fly.

"Right then, ugly puss, where do you hide the gold?"

And suddenly, in his fright Alexei Iosifovich snarled back:

"Dear Soviet investigator, why not just say 'ugly Yiddish puss' . . ."

Then, assuming a more formal tone, Serdyuk said:

"Please be so kind as to familiarize yourself with this material." And he held out a cardboard folder.

Delighted at his little victory, Alexei Iosifovich half-rose to his feet in order to take the folder, and at that moment Serdyuk smashed a Cossack fist like a sledgehammer into his teeth. Alexei Iosifovich set off, staggering backwards on half-bent legs . . . He staggered on and on . . . The office was not large, but neither was it small . . . On and on and on . . . He reached the limit and smashed the back of his head against the wall.

And so Captain Serdyuk, having conducted the interrogation incorrectly, was charged with that offence when legality was restored. He was dismissed from the state security service and he enrolled in a dental college, since he was still young and could choose a different, but related career. Previously he had smashed teeth out, but now he was learning to put them back in. That is, he was rectifying his mistakes. And Alexei Iosifovich Ivolgin from the tribe of Reuben, who was killed at the interrogation, finally became a member of his own people.

In that year the icicles hanging from the roofs were long, promising a long spring. And the migrating geese flew high, promising a lot of water, with rivers overflowing their banks. And a lot of sap accumulated in the birch trees, promising a rainy summer . . . Between the spring flashfloods and the summer rain, the special, armor-plated year of 1953 was eroded and washed away. Everything became limp and damp, losing its seriousness. And a fat, round-faced, prosperous-looking man with humorous folksy catchphrases suddenly set about explaining to Russia the country's eternal riddle. However that was just a little later. Before that extremely uninteresting times had set in and the people lived uninteresting lives for about two years, so that the Antichrist and the prophetess Pelagia had no tasks to perform and the Lord did not send them to a new one . . . The prophetess Pelgia only used her abilities once, to punish Savelii, who had been peeping into the toilet from the bathroom, tormented by the third plague of the Lord . . . Being so young, the prophetess punished Savelii too harshly and he was taken away to a psychiatric clinic. Then Klavdia, a lonely woman, inconsolable widow and suffering mother, started paying visits to the janitor . . . Like all people who are spiteful by nature and have suffered crushing grief, she had not grown kinder, but more foolish. But even her foolishness was different: spiteful people are fidgety even in their foolishness. Their tears flow easily for all kinds of reasons, they share their sorrows with anyone with garrulous ease. And somehow, from being a quarrelsome woman capable of standing up for herself, Klavdia became a helpless, foolish, bothersome old woman . . .

She was discovered in this condition by Ninochka Kuharenko when she arrived to visit her aunt. Despite all her trials and tribulations, Ninochka Kuharenko had grown up to be a beautiful, strong, not very intelligent young woman, following which she had recently married . . . When they met after such a long interval the niece and her aunt liked each other. Ninochka later told the Antichrist and the prophetess Pelagia about the meeting:

"We threw ourselves into each other's arms and wept, shouting loudly."

After that the aunt and niece often drank tea together with the janitor Dan Yakovlevich's family. Ninochka, a garrulous young woman, told them her story:

"My parents, my mother and father, were repressed in forty-nine, and so were the Yarnutovskys in the same case. Of course, I was still little then, but I remember a lot, even from the time when I was carried around in people's arms."

At this point Klavdia usually wept and said:

"You did well. You made your way in the world and didn't go down the wrong road. Ah, you're so like my sister Valya."

"I searched for my parents for two years," Ninochka told the Antichrist and the prophetess Pelagia. "First I found Yarnutovsky's old mother, Vasilina Matveevna. She had been stubbornly searching Belarus for a long time too, but she hadn't applied to the All-Union search network, because she was ill and illiterate. But she was very worried about her son Nikolai. We were helped in our search by the former minister of justice of the Belarusian Soviet Socialist Republic, Comrade Vetrov."

At this point Klavdia started crying again, recalling her husband Alexei Iosifovich and her son Savelii's unpleasant illness.

"Come on, Aunty," said Ninochka, "now you've got upset."

"No, go on, go on. Dan Yakovlevich is a kind man. Oh, how good it is to tell a kind person about your grief, I know from my own experience what a comfort that is."

Ninochka continued:

"I couldn't find my father, obviously he's not still alive, or the Yarnutkovskys either, but I did find my mother Valentina . . . Only after I had searched for my mother and met her, I was naturally disappointed in her when I saw she had totally ruined herself with drinking. I was very hurt to see that she hadn't managed to stand firm during that difficult time of her life and had given up. But after finding me, she couldn't stay that way and she ended her own life, she drowned herself in the Volga . . ."

Ninochka stopped talking and fell silent: Klavdia didn't cry in her usual manner, although this might have seemed like the most appropriate moment for weeping . . . The Antichrist and his daughter, the prophetess Pelagia, also said nothing. "So there it is, as clear as day," thought the Antichrist, "the suffering that is the measure of all things for the Christian philosophers. However only a good person is rendered more intelligent by suffering, while a bad, characterless individual is rendered more stupid. That is why suffering and stupidity are the most common things in the world."

"My father Alexander Semyonovich Kuharenko was imprisoned in the Burepolom camps, and no one knows where he got to after that, but my mother told me that he wrote letters to her until she dreamed that he had died."

"I had a beautiful sister," said Klavdia, pressing a handkerchief to her eyes.

"Yes," said Ninochka, "my momma had a well-built figure and a very attractive kind of beauty. In summer she wore a white blouse and a gray skirt, with a white headscarf, and in winter she wore boxcalf leather boots, a skirt with a fine-check pattern and a jacket with a reddish-gray collar . . . I remember that there were yellow flowers growing beside our house . . . Sometimes I feel bitter, especially in the evenings . . . But never mind . . . You know, I work on a truck, like my husband Fedya, a driver. I chose my line of work deliberately. If there's a war I'll be first to go to the front, I'll get into a tank and take revenge on all the imperialists for all of us. I understand that everything would be different if not for the imperialist encirclement."

Ninochka had not come for a long visit and the next day she had to go back home to the Russian Far East, where she had grown up in an orphanage.

"The Motherland didn't forget me, it sheltered me and raised me," said Ninochka. "I got married, found my way into safe hands . . . But my brother Mishenka died of typhoid fever in Tobolsk. I'm the only member of the Kuharenko family still alive. And sometimes I suddenly start feeling as if I'm all alone in the whole wide world, within my own huge, united collective of course . . ."

After saying that, she left them, together with her considerate aunt, to go to bed in order not to be late for the morning train.

Three hundred years before the birth of Christ and before the degeneration of biblical character, Aristotle, a contemporary of the late biblical prophets, wrote that without action tragedy could not exist, but without character it could. For instance, the majority of new tragedies do not depict character, since tragedy is not an imitation of individual characters, but of action in life, good fortune and misfortune, and good fortune and misfortune are concomitants of action.

After 1953 a period began in Russia during which, in keeping with Artistotle's ideas, historical action continued, but characters disappeared. Tragedy concludes the life, or a period in the life of an individual or a nation: comedy revives it. Before the eyes of the Antichrist, the emissary of the Lord, character had persisted through the excruciating torment of collectivization, a ruinous war and the hopes of the postwar period; through the second plague of the Lord, famine, the first plague, the sword, and the third plague, fornication... But by the time of the fourth plague, pestilence, character had almost completely ceased to exist, it had become diminished and simplified, although the intensity of misfortune had not diminished, but increased. In fact, if you take a bird's eye view of things, then even earlier than this, throughout the world, just as in Russia, great destroyers with uninteresting, petty characters and great martyrs with petty souls had appeared. It is unlikely that Pushkin and Shakespeare would have taken an interest in the character of Hitler-Schicklgruber or Stalin-Djugashvili. And the characters of the victims of their atrocities, especially during the maximally fiendish period, are scarcely likely to be interesting. Hopeless tragedy is stripped of character, but a lengthy existence without character is impossible. At this point comedy bears fruit and renewal begins through comical character. And so it was. A multitude of comical characters appeared in the late fifties and early sixties. As always happens in comedy, they appeared in strange combinations, with strange aspirations and often without any explanations, in an extremely chaotic fashion, for comedy is the genre most distant from the Lord and therefore the most human.

Savelii returned from the psychiatric clinic transformed from an adolescent with vicious inclinations into a harmless, lyrical dreamer. His path naturally led him directly to the most comical educational establishment that has ever existed anywhere in the world, the Literary Institute of the Union of Soviet Writers. And there he met two individuals from the Volga area, fellow native sons of Bor town in the Gorky Region: the youthful lyrical poet Andriusha Koposov and the satirist Somov. There was also Vasya Korobkov, a strange man whose personal history was a mystery, apparently a late developer from a family of former thieves, or so it was said, with black eyes and eastern features, almost Jewish in appearance, but nonetheless a notorious, rowdy antisemite. Another associate of this group was the erudite Ilovaisky, an old writer who had started talking about Russian Christianity long before religious discussions became respected in society and valued by highly demanding women.

We should note here that in initial conversations this Ilovaisky always showed people his best side: an intelligent man and a capable popularizer of ideas. But that was only for the first half hour of their acquaintance with him. During that initial half hour he usually set forth many intelligent ideas, only to spout absolute nonsense in the course of the years that followed.

The same thing happened when Ilovaisky met the Antichrist and his adopted daughter, the prophetess Pelagia. Naturally, this meeting came about through Savelii, who of course had loved Rufina-Pelagia for a long time, loving her secretly, as he was accustomed to cherishing such feelings. Ilovaisky was disheveled in the manner of Russian disputants, but although his eyes were light in color, they were not Russian, not open, in addition to which he had been rehabilitated from the camps at some time and was drunk every day. Sometimes the impression arose that he liked Alexei Iosifovich Ivolgin's widow Klavdia, Savelii's mother. In any case, Klavdia always put on lipstick when he appeared and in the spot where a portrait of Stalin at work in his Kremlin study had previously hung, she put up an icon of Christ the Savior.

One day they were drinking tea and having yet another tedious Russian conversation about Christ. In general Russian people are capable of doing many things cheerfully and they know how to make cheerful conversation, but they always talk about Christ in an extremely tedious manner and always argue chaotically but assertively. Just try arguing about Christ with a committed Russian Christian. From the very first words spoken it seems that you will easily out-talk him and make him change his mind. His arguments appear too vapid and naïve at first. However the longer the argument continues, the more distinct becomes the impression that although you feel more intelligent than him, he is speaking more intelligently than you . . . In such situations Dan, the Viper, the Antichrist always thought that if his brother Jesus from the tribe of Judah and the house of David, the adopted son of Joseph and a learned Pharisee, were to appear, then even he would not be able to prove anything about himself to a committed Russian Christian in the way that he had skillfully proved his case to the members of his own sect of Pharisees, for although they were men of views hostile to his own, they shared with him a common vision of the world and a common belief in the Law of Moses . . . But here, while the views were apparently held in common, that is, Christ's views, as learned from the Gospels, an entirely hostile, alien worldview rendered your every word unrecognizable and you found yourself powerless against your very own words. This was what gave rise to the essentially atheistic theory that, having created the world, God no longer interferes in its business, for that God supposedly no longer exists, although He did exist previously. This existence of God in the past is the only outward difference that distinguishes theological materialism from ordinary materialism.

But the significance of this quarrel became especially unfathomable when committed Russian Christians started arguing among themselves, all saying the very same thing but in such different words that the quarrel became absolutely irreconcilable. It all became so meaningless, it began to seem that at any moment a glimpse might actually appear of the impossible goal that is sought after in clever, interesting disputes . . . That without even realizing it, an individual lacking in reason would eventually pronounce a word . . . That very word which is the cornerstone of the most un-Jewish of the four Gospels, the Gospel of John . . . This is the best-loved Gospel of the Russian decadent intelligentsia . . . And from this Gospel these individuals lacking in reason reach for the Apocalypse . . . They also love the Apocalypse of John. But is this the same John? The Fourth Gospel is the most un-Jewish piece of writing in gospel literature. The most Jewish is the Apocalypse, a book of hatred and hope . . . That same hatred of the Roman Empire that also filled the heart of Christ. The Apocalypse openly declares that which is stated tentatively in the Gospel of Matthew: the hatred of the builders of the Temple for the builders of the Tower of Babel, which is every empire. As it happens, the Gospel of Matthew, as well as the gospels of Mark and Luke, but especially the Gospel of Matthew, were written with John, the author of the Apocalypse and their brother in spirit, whereas the Gospel of John was written by a talented and skillful foe, moreover talented in a purely literary, not spiritual sense. In the Fourth Gospel the word initially manifested itself and its meaning only became clear afterwards. This is fluent in the Greek style, however it smacks of an attempt to give the divine an image, it smacks of that shift in emphasis at which the division between the Biblical and the Greek, between Judeo-Christianity and pagan Christianity, begins. On the contrary, the Lord sometimes gives us an irrational meaning, but not a word, the meaning is given through that wordless, divine lamentation with which the juvenile martyr Maria wept in 1933 near the Andreevka Junction.

The entire spirit of the Fourth Gospel is Greek and anti-biblical. And yet there are no low heights in the universe. The great is majestic even in its decadence, its mysticism and its degradation. Only in the trivial is there no degradation and no decadence. The acmeist poet Gumilyov declared: "And in the Gospel of John it says that the Word is God . . ." This, of course, is not so, it is unbiblical . . . The word always debases the meaning. In a dialogue between God and a prophet, the divine is debased, in a dialogue between a prophet and the people, the prophetic is debased. The prophets knew that in a great word, God is debased, and in a trivial word there is no God at all . . . However there have not been any prophets for a long time, and over the ages the divine has been repeatedly debased before eventually approaching close to the people through the trivial.

This is why today even an adventitious word is so valuable, even an unbiblical word, a Greek word from the Fourth Gospel. Even a human word that runs ahead of God's meaning.

In the final, heated stage of a Russian argument about Christ, when everybody, even the most mundanely stupid, even Alexei Iosifovich's widow, Klavdia, was speaking cleverly and therefore it was impossible to understand anything and agree on anything, Ilovaisky spoke. After first pawing with rheumatic fingers at his white, blue-rimmed, mass-market teacup that smelled of vodka, he said:

"Look at this chalice . . ." He used the word "chalice" instead of "cup" because he considered himself a learned scholar of antiquity. "Look at this chalice . . . At the moment it is simple . . . But now I'll smash it against the floor and it will immediately become complicated . . ."

And so it was: in Russian, pitiless, anti-philistine style he smashed this object that wasn't his against the floor. There was a crunch, fragments went slithering across the floor and everyone fell silent, for the mass-market cup had indeed become complicated. Then Dan, the Viper, the Antichrist understood that through this individual lacking reason the Lord was giving them a sign, by first allowing a word to be spoken, and only allowing its meaning to be determined afterward. And the Antichrist's adopted daughter Ruth, who was also the prophetess Pelagia, understood this.

And so since 1933 four parables of the Lord have now concluded, and each parable has contained all four plagues of the Lord that were revealed through the prophet Ezekiel. And in each parable one of the plagues has dominated the others and been set in the forefront. Either the second plague, famine, or the first, the sword, or the third, the wild beast of fornication, or the fourth, pestilence, has been dominant. And in the midst of these plagues of the Lord the life of a generation is drawing to a conclusion, and it is necessary to sum it up in a fifth parable.

The prophet Moses summarized divine reality in the blood of the covenant and he poured this blood into a chalice in order later to sprinkle the people with this blood. Moses did not sprinkle the people with river water, but with blood. But now the chalice is broken, and that is the subject of the fifth parable for which the Antichrist was sent to earth.

A Parable of a Broken Chalice

When the orphaned infant, Christianity, lost its Jewish mother as a result of the eternal struggle between the builders of the Temple and the builders of the Tower of Babel, it initially fell into the hands of those who knew everything, or a great deal, about its mother, but were hostile to this. This Greek guardian (for he was, most notably, Greek), a representative of a fundamentally different spiritual culture, tried to ensure that the infant did not know the truth about itself. To this end the Greek guardian introduced eremitism, not as a temporary, creative expedient, in the way that Moses and Jesus had used it, but in the form of permanent, residential monasticism, which created the ideological basis for finally separating the infant from its Judeo-Christian mother, making it forget its genuine spiritual nature, its genuine hopes, its genuine sorrows and sufferings among its own perishing nation. Monastic reclusiveness even gave birth to a new physical image of Christ. And no, this was not the image of a learned Pharisee who, while still at a tender age, astounded the whitehaired, professorial scripturists, not the person who understood the practical significance and strength of the teachings of the prophet Jeremiah concerning nonresistance to the evildoer, from whom, in your own weakness it is possible to take your own soul as your spoils. Nor was this the image of a wise man who had understood that the voice of a prophet is a voice crying out in the wilderness. The prophet foretells the future but the people only apprehend his correctness when the future becomes the past. Therefore the prophet needs power of the kind that Moses possessed. It is Christ the King who is the savior of the people now... He knows how heavy the crown of the King of the Jews is... The bravest and most selfless of them are ignorant, the most intelligent and learned of them are cowardly and avaricious. This is always the case when a people suffers lengthy oppression and this too is clear to him as a learned scholar of the Bible and the prophets. He remembers the words of Moses, he knows that a savior and patriot must also possess cunning, since the world is a den of wolves. He addresses the learned in the incisive, wrathful language of an experienced polemicist and addresses the ignorant in parables, since the path into the darkness of ignorance lies through mysticism and the trust of the ignorant can only be won, provided that they remain completely unaware of what is taking place. If an ignorant individual understands certain particulars he rejects the whole that remains incomprehensible to him. And therefore there must be miracles in the whole and in the part. In both the central idea of salvational human goodness and in trivial healings. For the learned upper echelon of collaborationists, who have seated themselves on the throne of Moses, he is a turbulent young pretender to the throne which, as it happens, is precisely who he is in reality. They understand him and therefore they hate him. For the Roman occupiers he is a destroyer of the Law of Moses, which is a rival to their pagan ideology. They do not understand him and therefore seek to exploit him as a collaborator. In this respect Jesus almost precisely repeats the fate of his spiritual precursor Jeremiah, who was imprisoned in a pit by his own fervently beloved people and rescued from the pit by his abhorred enemies, the Assyrians. For a prophet can foresee and comprehend the fate of a people, but he is powerless against his own fate. And the savior is likewise powerless. The words of those who mocked him while on the cross were true: "He saved others, but he cannot save himself." He is incredibly alone not only on the cross, but even before the time of the cross. Toward the end of his life the Apostles, whom he had always inwardly despised, will become increasingly disenchanted with him, they will seek a means to rid themselves of him. From associating with a great individual the ignorant start to understand particular details and therefore reject the whole that is incomprehensible to them.

Not long before Easter, a direct conflict between Jesus and the Apostles came to a head at the home of Simon the leper in Bethany. The following is from the Gospel of Matthew, the most authentic of the gospels:

"A woman came up to him with an alabaster flask of very expensive ointment, and she poured it on his head as he reclined at table. And when the disciples saw it, they were indignant, saying, 'Why this waste? For this could have been sold for a large sum and given to the poor.'"

Here the apostles are clearly hinting to Jesus that he himself is failing to follow his own teaching that one should give everything away to the poor. Understanding their reproaches, Jesus replied:

"You always have the poor with you, but you will not always have me."

He recalled the words of Moses: "Do not show favoritism to a poor person in a lawsuit . . ." He knew that poverty is illness and woe, but not worthy service . . . It was after this very dispute that Judas Iscariot decided to betray Jesus to the high priest. But what is the meaning of genuine, effective betrayal of someone in the context of observing the letter of the law? It requires demonstrating his guilt in a court. "Now the chief priests and the whole council were seeking false testimony against Jesus that they might put him to death, but they found none, though many false witnesses came forward. At last two came forward and said, 'This man said, "I am able to destroy the temple of God, and to rebuild it in three days."'" To whom did Jesus say this? According to the Gospels he only said this to the Apostles, which means that the two unnamed false witnesses came from among the Apostles. All the subsequent behavior of Judas Iscariot, who in Christian literature and the Gospel of John is represented as the devil incarnate, in reality indicates that this man was only a weapon in the hands of more dangerous and cunning enemies of Jesus among the Apostles, who have remained unknown. Judas was merely the most naïve and straightforward among them, the one least capable of concealing his feelings, and when Jesus suspected a conspiracy among the Apostles, he pointed out Judas simply because, through someone's cunning intent, Judas had undoubtedly become the most conspicuous among them. Although he singled out Judas, Jesus did not trust the others either. On the Mount of Olives Jesus told them: "You will all fall away because of me this night. For it is written, 'I will strike the shepherd, and the sheep of the flock will be scattered.'"

In the provinces, in Galilee, Jesus was a well-known individual, but in the capital few people knew him, and when the Jerusalem rabble came to take him a kiss from Judas was required to indicate which of the twelve outsiders was the blasphemer. And after that we have Jesus's words: "But all this has taken place that the Scriptures of the prophets might be fulfilled." And then all the disciples left him and fled.

Thus did Jesus fall victim not only to the external hatred of collaborators with the Romans, but also to an internal conspiracy of Apostles who had coached Judas and encouraged him to make his doubts obvious. Judas Iscariot was naïve and simple-minded, but the fact that he possessed a real, live conscience is clear from his behavior after the trial. "Then when Judas, his betrayer, saw that Jesus was condemned, he changed his mind and brought back the thirty pieces of silver to the chief priests and the elders, saying, 'I have sinned by betraying innocent blood.' They said, 'What is that to us? See to it yourself.' And throwing down the pieces of silver into the temple, he departed, and he went and hanged himself." In this account we are shown an honest but foolish individual, who did not even understand the significance of what was happening and was surprised that Jesus had been sentenced to death for his reckless talk. Nonetheless in Christian literature and Christian thought Judas is stigmatized as the quintessential traitor, in order to cloak the identities of the genuine, intelligent, secret traitors. And to this day these traitors are numbered among the holy apostles and temples of God are erected in their honor.

Thus slander and falsehood were already demonstrated in the apostolic order's beginning and were further strengthened by the Apostle Paul from the tribe of Benjamin, who had never seen Jesus or heard His living word and had formerly been an enemy of his teaching . . . Therefore there is no cause for surprise that Greek eremitism even brought forth a new physical image of Christ: an emaciated man with tormented flesh who was more reminiscent of Saint Anthony than a son of the House of David.

Later, in the early Middle Ages, during its adolescence, Christianity found itself in the hands of those who were not merely hostile, but knew nothing truthful about its Palestinian mother. Only occasionally in books of sorcery did Christianity read the secret truth about itself, but it was afraid of this truth and punished the most talented individuals for the truth. As it continued to grow Christianity found itself in the hands of people who were entirely alien to Judaism, whereas the Greeks had been hostile to Judaism, but not alien. This was why so much that was simple and effectively clear in the mother's home became complicated, incomprehensible and imbued with metaphysical profundity in the stranger's home. For after all, any human word becomes a cipher in different worlds. Arguably this is why nonresistance to evil as a fundamental Christian dogma was encoded as a metaphysical cipher, not by the early Christians, but rather by the powerful nations of the early Middle Ages, when the hostility of Christianity's initial Greek guardians to its genuine Jewish mother was still felt as living action and not as the mythological element that arose later in the context of Slavic Christianity, while at the same time, in the early medieval period the language of the biblical soul was already lost and had become incomprehensible. When the words about nonresistance to evil lost the genuine savor of the speech of Jesus from the tribe of Judah, addressed to his own passionately loved, stubborn and wayward people, which was perishing in a life-and-death struggle, they became a dictum from the Son of God, who had descended from heaven and conversed in the desert with Greek monks who mortified their own flesh. When the wisdom of a politician and the bitterness of a patriot disappeared from those words, the universal teachings were deprived of a national language and became less and less comprehensible to the living human heart. But why did this happen? From its early beginnings Christianity was hostile to Judaism, but in the world it asserted its faith with emphatic self-abnegation. This is how it came about that excessive assertion of Christ's divine, heavenly origin led to atheism. Do not atheists do exactly the same thing in trying to prove the mythological, antihistorical nature of Christ's personality, in trying to deny him as a national personality, one of the leaders of the national Nazareth movement?

In times long ago the Greek merchant Marcion composed a Gospel in which he denied Christ's affiliation with the biblical Jewish God. "The Biblical God," Marcion claimed, "is the God of the material world, but the father of Christ is the God of the spiritual world." At that time the Ecumenical Council repudiated the Gospel of Marcion. It was too demonstrably mendacious, it distorted authentic reality too greatly and smacked too much of polytheism and paganism. However much later the Council added a fourth Gospel to the three canonical gospels: the Gospel of John. Let me repeat again here that this John has nothing to do with the St. John who wrote the Apocalypse. This fourth, decadent gospel attempts to demonstrate essentially the same thing as Marcion's Gospel, but in a more skillful and eloquent form, and Christ is separated from His biblical God . . . It is interesting to note how the theme of the Apostles' conspiracy against Christ was weakened from one Gospel to the next. In the oldest and most authentic gospel, the Gospel of Matthew, it is given in its entirety, in the Gospel of Mark it is given quite powerfully, in the Gospel of Luke it has already been considerably weakened and in the Gospel of John it is entirely absent. The most tragic episodes preceding the death of Christ are written completely differently. In the Gospel of John, not only has the conspiracy of the Apostles disappeared, so has the ill feeling between the Apostles and Christ, and nothing at all is said about the two mysterious false witnesses on the basis of whose allegations Christ was sentenced to death. However Judas is represented as a solitary traitor, the spawn of Satan. There is no episode in which he renounces the thirty pieces of silver in his grief, on the contrary, his avarice is emphasized by the money bag that he carries around with him. Certainly, Peter's temporary denial of Christ out of his weakness of will is shown, that is simply too notable a fact. However the most important thing, the premeditated conspiracy of a group of Apostles, which is clearly visible in the Gospel of Matthew, is completely concealed in the Gospel of John. And so the conspiracy of the Apostles against Christ was transformed into the conspiracy of Christianity against Christ. The clear, simple divine chalice was mercilessly shattered into metaphysically complex philosophical and religious fragments. Dostoevsky's "Legend of the

Grand Inquisitor" presents a lifeless, anti-national, heavenly-cosmic image of Christ, but the earthly conspiracy against Christ is shown quite accurately. Of course in Dostoevsky's text Christianity is called "Catholicism," but in the fragmented Christian world this is no more than a natural polemical device, which could with equal success be turned against Orthodoxy.

And so, having separated itself from the Bible and the Law of Moses, Christianity embarked on a natural, logical course of segregation and schism. The conspiracy against Moses escalated into a conspiracy against Christ. It is a very long time since Christian ideologues have possessed a shared idea in common. And when there is no shared idea people search for a common, fleshly enemy, who can help them preserve their illusory unity. In fact a common, fleshly enemy was found long ago, back in the time of the first Greek anchorites' monastic withdrawal from the world. Its name was pleasure. Christianity teaches that you should shun the field of pleasures, the field of Satan, and avoid it on your way to the Lord, but the Bible teaches that you should walk through the field of pleasures, the field of Satan, to reach the Lord, for there is no other way, since man is cursed and the Lord drove man out of Eden with its heavenly bread, to eat his own spiritual bread, obtained in the sweat of his brow. If an atheist labors in the sweat of his brow in the field of pleasures for the sake of spiritual bread, he is carrying out the Lord's wishes, but if a man who considers himself to be religious waits in the field of pleasures for heavenly spiritual bread from the Lord, he is opposing the Lord. Christianity, which ruled the world for more than fifteen centuries, is now blamed for the imperfection of the world by atheism, which acquired power less than a century ago. This is the same Christianity that seized power over the world by supporting the secret conspiracy of the Apostles against Christ. It was this Christianity that spent many centuries in spiritual idleness, indulging in a purely Buddhist contemplation of metaphysical truths and replacing doing with malicious arguments about good and evil . . . To this day it still showers curses on those who, in a healthy, sincere, human impulse, flee from these arguments to the field of pleasures, flee to where they should flee according to God's design. But unfortunately for them, those who flee from deranged sermonizing must pass through this field of the Devil, not guided by the intense spiritual efforts of their teacher, but merely obeying their own corporeal instincts. This is why they often perish either at the very beginning of their journey, as a result of juvenile ignorance or, having successfully negotiated the beginning, they are driven by decrepit intemperance past the fruitful core to the opposite extreme, which is dominated by perverted, mystical wisdom. The ruin of these unfortunates provokes only gloating laughter from the Christian spiritual eunuchs sitting at a remote distance in their spiritual idleness. In fact many of these eunuchs have swapped their ecclesiastical robes for the thoroughly secular gown of a professor of philosophy or even the jacket of a man of letters.

This is the truth: whoever knows the Bible knows everything that can be known by man, whoever does not know the Bible does not even know himself . . . Russia is an example of this . . . For more than four centuries they have been building the Tower of Babel in Russia. The Bible warns us that the tower will consume all your strength, all your talent and all your passion, but it will never be completed, and all the strength and talent will be reduced to dust, as happened in Babylon. But the chalice has been repudiated and shattered, clear truths have become the complex metaphysics of fragments. People have striven and strained in their efforts to build. The national architect Dostoevsky arrived and took a look at things. The tower was already approaching the sky by the end of the 19th century. "Well done the Russian people. Anywhere the Russian has set foot is already Russian land. But come on brothers, let's give this tower the appearance of a Temple. Through this we shall be different from Europe. We have a tower and a Temple. The empire is strong and religion is also strong." However the most skillful, selfless builders at the highest levels turned out to be atheists. Then the Christian builders withdrew and now they spitefully mock at those who continue the defiant Babylonian challenge to the Lord that they themselves began, at those whom they themselves taught to accept truths from the heavens, supposedly from the hands of the Son of the Lord, but in reality from the hands of the supreme Greek eremitic monarchs. And history has demonstrated how simple it is in such a case to replace the inhabitant of the heavens and how easy it is to select him . . .

Everything supposedly comes directly from the heavens, for the Gospel of Matthew (and they know that this is the most authentic Gospel, although they delight in amusing themselves with the fourth, decadent Gospel, in which literary talent prevails over spiritual content) . . . the Gospel of Matthew contains verses sixty-three and sixty-four. Christians love to cite these verses as irrefutable proof. What does it say in these verses? Jesus is brought into the court. The high priest, an individual in whom the once-great tribe of Levi attained the ultimate nadir of its degradation, says:

"Tell us if you are the Christ, the Son of God." And Jesus replies:

"You have said so. But I tell you, from now on you will see the Son of Man seated at the right hand of Power and coming on the clouds of heaven."

Then the high priest tore his robes and said:

"He has uttered blasphemy."

But did Christ blaspheme? Let us set aside the fact that this passage is in general obscure and antihistorical. According to the Law of Moses, someone blasphemes if they rail against God. But Jesus does not revile God here. We can admit that the high priest, in collaborating with the Romans, has violated the Law of Moses, but has Jesus violated the Law of Moses? Every Hebrew considered himself to be a Son of God, for since the time of Abraham the people had been the Lord's. Every patriot could sense a messianic force within himself when the people was threatened with destruction. Especially since to the celestial title of the "Messiah" he constantly adds the earthly title of the "King of the Jews": a strange title for an otherworldly, metaphysical, non-national individual. As for the Ascension of the Son of Man to the heavenly heights, this is by no means blasphemy, for in that case the canonically acknowledged prophet Elijah, who was borne up to heaven in a whirlwind of fire, should be accused of blasphemy . . . This is not blasphemy, as the high priest claims in the Gospel, and neither is it a unique phenomenon, testifying to a celestial origin, as the Christian ideologues assert, basing their case on verses sixty-three and sixty-four. It was nothing other than the brilliant state of the soul of a great individual at its moment of ultimate stress. And so, in actual fact, by trying to exalt what is happening, the Christian ideologues debase it, since Jewish history and the Jewish worldview are alien to them. And there is no other path to a genuine understanding of the Bible and the Gospels than through Jewish history and the Jewish worldview, But the chalice is broken.

The chalice is not complicated in itself. In its initial form it does not agitate the mind, but a fragment of the chalice in its initial form, which is also its last, for a fragment possesses its finished form from Alpha to Omega, such a fragment does agitate the mind. The smaller the fragment and the farther it is from the chalice, the more entire it is in itself, and it agitates the mind in this, its initial form. And yet it requires less spiritual exertion to penetrate deep into that which agitates the mind in its initial form. A fragment is immediately disquieting, the chalice is not immediately disquieting, it is clear. But the clarity of the chalice conceals a far deeper meaning than the dark essence of the fragment. A chalice is material and practical in existence and it introduces the material into existence. This is exactly what the Jews have always been accused of. The Jews, they say, introduce the material into the world, and that dooms the world. The Russian national metaphysicians rant these assertions with especial rabidity. Yes, the chalice is practical and dialectical in day-to-day existence, but in eternal reality it is metaphysical; the fragment is metaphysical and mystical in day-to-day existence, but in eternal reality it is dialectical, striving to apprehend the incomprehensible, conferring dialectical meaning on the finite. Conferring an infinite, supreme, eternal, mystical, metaphysical meaning on human passions, human love and human hate, and at the same time striving to apprehend in a dialectical and philosophical fashion such unitary, eternal concepts as heaven and God. The difference between the chalice and its fragments is the same as the difference between faith and religions, between meaning and concepts, between the primary status of intimate feeling and the primary status of public ritual. But God's chalice has been broken and this is the subject of the final and fifth parable of the Antichrist, the emissary of the Lord.

***

As often happens with children conceived by their mother in unbridled passion, Andrei Koposov was a young man with poor health. In fact the child's poor health could have been the result of other causes too, but it seemed as if his mother Vera's morbidly excessive passion had inflamed the boy forever. He grew up to be high-strung and at the same time shy, with a faint smile on his face. Andrei did not know the father after whom he had been named, because he had died many months before his son was born, and that is always bad for a boy. Andrei was not loved in the family. His sisters Tasya and Ustya slapped him, Tasya's sons, Andrei and Varfolomei Vesyolov, fought with him, Tasya's husband, Nikolai Vesyolov, laughed at him, Vesyolov's mother, the old sentry woman Sergeevna, glared at him disapprovingly. Only his mother Vera loved him, but his mother was somehow timid in family matters, her daughters would shout at him and she would fall silent, looking guilty, and was unable to defend her beloved little son. And therefore from his childhood days Andrei had found life burdensome in his native town of Bor in the Gorky Region and, having been repudiated by people, he turned to books and became an enthusiastic supporter of the Bor library. At that time he had reached the age of sixteen and it would have been a miracle if he had not started writing poetry. That miracle did not come to pass and his way forward in life became clear. Somov, a professional versifier at the "Bor Pravda" newspaper, finally set him on the right path.

"Apply to the Literary Institute. You're Russian, a Volga lad with talent, they'll take you."

Somov himself, who was old enough to be Koposov's father, had already applied on several occasions but been unsuccessful. This time around, however, he was sure of his success, since at long last he had acquired a recommendation from the local Department of Agitation and Propaganda.

"They hold a grudge against me for my satirical poem about the war invalid Ivan Prokhorov," Somov explained. "That poem is passed from hand to hand in Moscow now . . . Ah, Moscow! You have no idea what the literary life is like there. And the sex life is pretty good too, all the girls smoke . . . Come on, don't blush, sweet little sixteen . . ."

Andrei's first poem that was published by the "Bor Pravda" began:

"A hunk of bread and a swig of Volga . . ."

"Why, you've got folk talent," said Somov, "that's highly valued these days . . . Everyone's sick of Jewish literature . . . 'A hunk of bread and a swig of Volga,' that's something out of Russian Christianity."

And so at the age of sixteen, for the first time in his life Andrei heard Russian Christianity mentioned as something important and serious, as distinct from his previous youthful Young Communist League ideas and the comical old women on the church porch.

And now as Andrei sat in the Moscow room that he had rented from an old Moscow woman, by a stroke of good fortune as it happened, since she spent most of her old woman's time at her married son's home nowadays, he recalled that initial conversation and felt like a completely different person, which in reality he wasn't, and sitting there alone, face-to-face with only himself, he experienced a searing flush of the shame for oneself that is intrinsic to temperaments like his.

In truth, having moved to Moscow Andrei had remained himself only more so, that is, he had become even more firmly entrenched in his youthfulness, although in a different manner from Savelii, without any shamefaced fear of girls, but simply avoiding them as he did people in general. And then again, he did not really actively avoid people, but he preferred sitting on his own. Having become a student at the Literary Institute, he had lost his love of writing poetry, but had become engrossed in art and started deriving a happiness from it that moved him to tears. He had also developed an active interest in religion, at first from stupid arguments in groups of friends and then through his own ruminations. And in these constant, painful, difficult ruminations, which were frequently mature beyond his age, much was revealed to him. For instance, for some time already he had begun to realize that the humanists' fundamental idea that there are no bad peoples and all peoples are good was as insipid as medicinal food for invalids, containing no meat juices or salt. It was as devoid of talent as the racist idea that some races are superior to others. But the racist idea did at least possess flesh: the porcine, unwashed yet healthy flesh of love for oneself and active hostility toward everything outside oneself. He already knew that the entrance to this maze lay through Christianity's puerile questions about good and evil. That the Christian swamp of metaphysical questions, which was alien to Christ, had robbed western culture of a substantial part of its spiritual strength, by preventing it from approaching those biblical truths that lie at the very foundations of existence. Sometimes his awareness of this was so clear that all the spiritual torments of past geniuses seemed comprehensible to him. He found this both disconcerting and frightening, and it also led him away from clarity to expounders of Gospel truths who were well known and acclaimed in the youthful society of Moscow, and they gained control over him. And again he kept falling into the vicious circle of Christian conversations about good and evil, in which people he regarded as more stupid than himself spoke more cleverly than he did and adduced incontrovertible arguments. But any attempt to protest meant that he appeared to be a reactionary, malicious individual with views that were almost racist, and when one day the high-strung Vasya Korobkov, who happened to be a well-known antisemite, shouted "Fascist" at him, Andrei realized that the Gospel truths, shaped over the centuries, in the form in which they were imposed on people by authoritative interpretations, really did not leave an individual of sound, individual judgment any other choice but to accept these truths in the form that they had assumed over the course of fifteen centuries, or to become a racist. This frightened him and he stopped going to gatherings with spiritual and religious discussions, leaving behind him a confirmed reputation as a reactionary and misanthropist or, as Vasya put it, a reputation as a fifteenth-generation descendant of those very Pharisees who had rejected and crucified Christ. And at the very moment when Andrei had stopped trusting in himself and lost heart, he stumbled across the attitude of Moses to the people. In fact, he had heard numerous times about the tablets of stone that Moses smashed and had even read and reread about how Moses was filled with indignation at his people for betraying God and smashed that first set of tablets and it was only the Lord who persuaded him to write a second set. But Andrei had read this without any of the interest and mental effort that some places in the Gospels aroused in him.

And suddenly at about eleven o'clock one morning, when his landlady was out and he was entirely alone, Andrei read about the tablets of Moses as if for the first time, with a strange feeling of rapturous surprise, as if this time he had not in his usual manner placed the old, dilapidated Bible, bought casually when he happened to come across it, on the dining table covered with the old woman's prewar-style table cloth and had not leafed through the grubby, fingered pages, but had suddenly made a rapid, steep uphill ascent to some place closer to himself and farther away from this communal apartment existence.

The humanists taught that there were no bad peoples. This was noble, but it required an act of violence against his own common sense. The racists taught that there were higher and lower races, moreover by "shuffling the pack" they ranked themselves and their nearest and dearest among the higher ones. This was ignoble, but realistic and in the spirit of mundane reality. But the biblical teaching of Moses, if you thought about it in the state of mind that had come over Andrei that morning, said that there were no good peoples at all. This did not require any violence against common sense and did not impart innate ignoble advantages to anyone. It was a clear, firm point of departure, and by setting out from it you could understand many things about the material history and spiritual life of man. The Bible did not say at all what many of its supporters claimed and did not actually contain that which its enemies denied. Moreover, whereas the Bible of orthodox believers merely haughtily retreated into itself under the furious, protean, street-crowd pressure of Christians enamored with their metaphysical ideology, the living Bible testified to the falsehood and essentially pagan nature of the cult of suffering as a basis for morality, it exposed the substitution of the secondary for the fundamental, it demonstrated that humanism (the deification of man) and racism (the deification of race) were both late brothers, feeble but conceived in passion, of this cult of human, corporeal suffering.

Andrei understood all of this in an instant and wrote it down on a quarter of a sheet of paper in about half an hour. He realized that he would not understand anything more at this moment and would soon start to doubt what he had understood. Therefore he did not tempt himself with hopes of discovering more, hastily closed the Bible and hid what was written in his handwriting, but as if by someone else's hand, not among his papers, but where he kept his money and documents: in a secret pocket of a jacket hanging behind the wardrobe, a jacket that any thief would disdain because it was so old.

It was eight minutes to twelve: Andrei noted very precisely the time on that day when he concluded his genuine life and began his false one. He began his false life by preparing breakfast: he walked out of the room into the communal kitchen with its smoke-darkened walls and individual tables for each of the families living in the apartment, put his landlady's frying pan on the stove, poured several eggs onto the congealed fat from previous fryings and started pondering, glancing now and then at the omelet as it hissed, about the best way he could spend the day in order not to lose sight of or devalue what he had just discovered. If he were to remain alone with himself, that would mean passing the day in a state of intellectual, focused concentration on one thing and that would definitely give rise to doubts and might even render his discovery null and void. But if he were to meet other people on trivial, everyday pretexts, that would mean constantly comparing his secret discovery with the trivial, everyday events taking place around him, which could result, firstly, in his making a bad impression on people and, secondly, testing the strength of his still fragile idea against a well-established, tangible and stable framework of thought, which might also diminish the stature of his discovery, rendering it pale and colorless. Therefore the best thing would be to spend the day with people, but not in an ordinary, everyday manner and preferably not in debates about religion. Then he recalled that an exhibition of the work of a French artist, a former Russian émigré, had opened at the Tretyakov Gallery, creating a sensation and provoking unofficial mutterings. "What a stroke of luck," Andrei thought, "I'll take a look at the Tretyakovka while I'm at it, I haven't been there in ages. I'll call Savelii and Sasha Somov, my Bor town compatriot. And why don't I even call Vasya Korobkov, so there will be different kinds of people? Then I won't be left alone with myself all day long, and with a group of different people there'll be less candid, shallow chit-chat. That's just what I don't need right now."

It was summer, early June, and classes at the institute were coming to an end, the examinations were drawing close and in addition, in accordance with the specific nature of the institute, today was a "creative day," without any lectures. "I won't get another chance to see the exhibition, they say it won't be on for long," Andrei thought. Then he took the frying pan off the stove, turned off the heat and went to the communal telephone: fortunately at this working hour of the day it was not occupied by his neighbors. First he called Savelii. A woman's voice answered, it was either his mother or his neighbor. Savelii was still sleeping and Andrei spent five minutes listening to the crackling and buzzing of the phone. Eventually there was a knock and the sound of distant voices, a man's and a woman's, and Savelii, coughing and clearing his throat, said:

"Sorry, old fellow, I went to bed late . . . Hello . . ."

Andrei told him about the Tretyakov Gallery and the exhibition.

"Of course," Savelii exclaimed enthusiastically, "I'll certainly come, so you definitely wait for me beside that garbage . . . 'Let us beat swords into plowshares' . . . Beside the Vuchetich sculpture . . . But no, better at the ticket office . . . Only I'm not alone . . . I'm with a woman." And Savelii giggled in coy embarrassment.

Somov was at home too and he agreed to come.

"We need to get together, brother," he said. "I want to have a word with you."

After that Andrei started wondering whether to call Vasya, whom he did not like and was a little afraid of.

Vasya Korobkov really was a dangerous and strange person, but not an outstanding individual. He was poor and rootless, no one knew what money he lived and drank on, he lived and drank in a way that was only possible for a man with a literary income in Russia. The volume of such income in the country was very substantial and it fed an entire, extremely miscellaneous social stratum: some with inordinately luxurious extravagance, some to satiety, some frugally, on leftovers, and others only once in a while. However they all lived by drawing on this income: both the grandees and the brigands, who in contrast with the well-fed might not actually have something to eat every day, but always had a snack for chasing a drink. Vasya lived in this way, on a daily gratuitous snack. He wrote strange poetry in Russian and Ukrainian. In Russian he had written this massively popular lyric poem:

I pick up a birch-tree pencil
And the tender-pink verses flow from it
Onto the white page of a snowy field . . .

In Ukrainian he had written these individualistically religious lines:

The Lord made a mistake
And appeared in Kyiv,
And suffered greatly in doing so . . .

"I'm from the Kharkiv Region," he used to say. "Shagaro-Petrovskoe village, the Meadow Farmstead. That is, I was born in Kerch, where my late mother Maria and my grandmother, also Maria, had signed on for work. But all my relatives are from the Kharkiv region. In fact my real surname is Ukrainian, Korobko . . . They added the 'v' later, in the orphanage . . . I was raised in the orphanage until I was ten, and then my aunt took me to raise when she searched and found me after the war. My aunt Ksenia from Voronezh. I don't know my father, but Ksenia says he was a sailor, a Ukrainian from Crimea. And in Crimea every Ukrainian has a bit of Turkish or Tatar blood in his veins, and plenty of Greek too . . . And so

I got my Yiddish-looking features from my father . . . But all my relatives are different, typical Ukrainians. In Shagaro-Pertrovskoe village there's my mother's sister, Shura, and her children, and there was my uncle Kolya, who was killed in the war, and my other uncle, Vasya, who disappeared during collectivization when he was little, which is why I'm named after him. And my aunt Ksenia from Voronezh, you should just see her, she's nothing at all like me, a typical Slavic appearance. I'm the only one with a hook nose, black eyes and black hair. One day a Yid came up to me in the street and started talking to me in Yiddish. And I was drunk of course, but not very, and didn't I answer him by reciting a poem:

> There is nowhere better than our Ukraine.
> There are no Jews, there are no lords,
> And there will be no union . . .

"Oy vey," he said, and I said: "Sorry, it's allowed by the censor, Taras Grigorievich Shevchenko, volume such-and-such, page such-and-such, in a prerevolutionary edition, naturally. And as it happens, lads, I had just been paid a fee and I had followed a glass of vodka in the Ukraine restaurant with some fine Ukrainian borshch and garlic fritters. I turned to the Yid, who had had the insolence to take me for one of his own, perhaps owing to the smell of garlic. "Well now," I said, "not even garlic makes a Ukrainian smell like a Yid. I turned towards him, lifted up my foot and surprised even myself with what I did. That Yid fled from me as I he'd caught the scent of a Cossack that's so terrifying to his unbaptized kind."

Vasya always gurgled as he laughed and was well known in a wide range of social circles for his notable flatulence as well as his passionate, incessant antisemitism. The gas emerged from his intestines in various manners, reflecting his inner condition. Sometimes as a clear, brief word, sometimes as a quiet, lingering lament and sometimes as a wild howl of horror . . .

Andrei Koposov was afraid, body and soul, of Vasya, that is, in his soul Andrei was disgusted by him and in his body Andrei fled from the wrath of an individual who had no reason to spare himself and was therefore dangerous to others. When Vasya expressed his opinion of Andrei by shouting "Fascist" in the course of a religious argument, Andrei had left immediately. He knew that only recently in a religious quarrel Vasya had punched the old man Ilovaisky, a learned scholar of antiquity, in the eye. But there had been other things too.

One day a long time ago, before their quarrels about Christ, in the early days of their acquaintance, Vasya had invited Andrei to his home somewhere on the industrial outskirts of Moscow, where he had a room as a result of a division of living space with his former wife. At that time Andrei did not yet have his own copy of the Gospels and Vasya had promised to lend him one. Andrei found Vasya with his shirt out over his trousers and smeared with paint, holding a brush in his hand. He was adding something to an icon standing in front of him, which appeared to be old. He offered Andrei a seat, poured him some bad tea and set out some stale spice cakes. His initial hospitality was frugal. Later, however, he brought in some bread and a milk can of fragrant rendered pork dripping.

"My aunt sent it from Voronezh," he said. "She spends her money on me, she still doesn't know that I'll come to a bad end." And he smiled.

Perhaps it was because of this incident that Andrei decided to call Vasya too. Suddenly Andrei felt that on the day when he had discovered something that he wanted to preserve, he wanted this individual to be there with him.

"I know, I know," Vasya replied, fortunately in a sober voice, "I'm sure it's a load of empty fuss and bother stirred up by our local Frenchmen, the same way they laud and extol various Maleviches, Tatlins and other persecutors of Russian realism here. But I'll come out of curiosity."

After hastily eating his cold omelet and washing it down with a bottle of kefir, Andrei walked out into a hot Moscow day. He had heard that the public was flocking to the exhibition and people had to stand in line for a long time, so he left much earlier that the time agreed, thinking that the Novokuznetskaya metro station would be absolutely packed. However the Novokuznetskaya station was empty and cool, and although there was a line along the railings of the Tretyakov Gallery, it was only a short one, enough for a twenty-minute wait, no longer. "So what's to be done?" Andrei thought. "I'll go in on my own, and then go in with all the others." After deciding to do this, he set out toward the ticket office and after he had stood in line for twenty minutes someone called his name as he stood beside the railings. It was Somov, his Bor-town compatriot, who had also come early.

"It is he?" said the satirist Somov, glancing at Andrei with a smile. "Do I not recognize him even without the round saucers of his helpful eyeglasses? Hello, certain person, how glad I am that you are alive . . ."

"The lads aren't here yet," Andrei said after first saying hello. He was glad that the most stupid of his friends had turned up first, and not the most morbidly emotional of them, Savelii, or the most spiteful of them, Vasya.

"Let's go in without them," said Somov, "there's something I want to show you . . . I've composed a poem, not for publication of course. It's called 'Epiphenomena of the Reproductive Instinct.' Here it is." And, breathing alongside Andrei's cheek, he started whispering:

"I grabbed my hat and went to samizdat,
The eager editor said: 'Brother, give me that.'
But, tongue-tied, I could only stutter,
Those dreaded letters, 'KGB,' I could not utter.
The angry editor said: 'Oh, go get lost,
What you need right now is a first aid post . . .'"

"I was wrong," thought Andrei, "it would have been better for Vasya to come, if I'm not destined to take a look on my own. At least he would have maintained a baleful silence . . . All in all, I made a mistake . . . I should have viewed the exhibition alone. This friend will be more bother than the others."

The French artist of Russian extraction made an impression on Andrei in spite of the disappointment that he had instilled in himself in advance. The pace of the 20th century has robbed people of one of the main bounties of life, patience. 20th-century people are impatient both in behavior and in understanding. If they have not understood something immediately, they just go striding on.

The exhibition of the French artist with Russian origins was in the two halls farthest from the entrance, so that on the way to it you had to walk past a multitude of pictures, overtaking a multitude of visitors' faces. Andrei was in an agitated and extremely voluble state, only not out loud, but also inwardly, and he liked this condition.

"It seems to me," Andrei observed about the French artist, "that his drawings, especially from the late period, are closer to literature than to a visual artist's work. Something between literature and visual art. Visual perception here serves a merely facilitative function. Like in reading. The colors and forms are the letters of a certain alphabet. You have to learn to read them, and then you can fathom out what is going on, whereas a realistic artist is comprehensible even to the illiterate. This does not make the work either superior or inferior, it is simply different. An illiterate person looks at a picture by Rembrandt or Repin and he sees trees, people, the sky, the things that can be distinguished in a photograph, and at the same time he knows that this is a very famous artist, and he feels proud that he understands all the objects in this artist's work, and he is grateful to the artist for that. It's a different matter if this illiterate person picks up Shakespeare, or even if a literate person picks up Shakespeare in English. He can't even spell it out one syllable at a time. Have you noticed that a book in a foreign language provokes inward irritation? The same thing happens with the work of a non-realistic artist. It provokes open or secret irritation."

Somov felt bored looking at the abstract or surrealist drawings and his face took on that agonizingly stupid hue that betrays the efforts of an individual of feeble intellect to understand something beyond his grasp. But in the other, unfashionable, Russian halls he displayed genuine interest, here he felt more at ease. An early hall with portraits, the age of Catherine the Great. Individuals in wigs, but remove the wigs and their owners could be sitting in the armchairs of directors and bosses of housing construction enterprises or deputy ministers, or be dissolute ladies from industrial directorate offices and wives of members of supreme institutional authorities. They would get into their "Volga" automobiles (or Count Orlov could quite easily be put on a tram or the metro), Catherine the Great would go off to her dacha to make jam in her summer sarafan. These were the people who had built the Tower of Babel and handed it on to reliable successors. After them came Ivanov's huge picture "The Appearance of Christ to the People." There is always a large crowd of gallery visitors, mostly provincials, in front of this picture. Those who are hurrying to get to the French artist did not delay in front of it or did not delay for long. However Andrei lingered there contentedly, examining the picture and the public viewing it. Beside him Somov snuffled, his expression set in the creative tension that appears on the face of someone sitting on the toilet. Mind you, expressions of that kind that can be seen in church too. Andrei saw a woman not far away from him, a little mongrel of about forty, perhaps even younger, but aged by frequent childbirth and premature births. Her face was rural and not urban. Small. Average. Ruddy cheeks, or rather, with an unhealthy flush. A little, upturned nose. Not feminine, with drooping breasts. Such women were devout. And this woman was devout. Such women believed in rumors and trusted the government, if it was their own, Russian government. Standing beside her was a boy of nine or ten, round-faced, with a heavy chin, who looked like a poor pupil from a school in the provinces or the outskirts of the city, but not a mischievous child, to judge from his behavior, he did as his mother said. He was asking questions. He was asking about the picture:

"What's this, Mom?"

"It's Christ," she answered him in a quiet voice. "He wanted all the people to be happy and the Jews killed him for that."

The boy nodded understandingly and moved on to the other pictures. Several lanky, ungainly Russian girls were hovering around a woman, perhaps daughters, or perhaps they had come to the Tretyakovka with her from "the back of beyond." Come to see relatives or to buy groceries. With a list: visit the Kremlin, Lenin's Mausoleum, the Tretyakov Gallery, the big stores GUM, TsUM and Children's World. Of course the food shops came ahead of everything else, in a category all of their own. The woman looked at "The Appearance of Christ." Andrei looked at her and thought: "There you have it, the Russian believer. At the gatherings where religion is argued about many people now say that atheism has lost and a religious renaissance is beginning. Very well, let us concede that atheism has lost, but has religion in Russia gained anything from that? Without having learned any lessons, will it be reborn with the same idiocy instead of feeling, with the same thickheaded arguments about Christ and the common people, who don't argue about Christ, but expect the same things from Him as they do from the Georgian Stalin, the Turk Razin or some other Russian ataman? And if Russia is destined in the future to attempt to save itself through the national-popular consciousness, that consciousness will not be materialist and atheist. The Russian fascist savior will wear a national-religious mask. In the first place, what was called "atheism" has badly discredited itself in Russia, people are fed up with it, it has lost its novelty. And in the second place, in national matters, it has failed to demonstrate the appropriate flexibility, it has proved cumbersome, whereas in the past Orthodoxy has repeatedly proved its willingness to glorify national power and for young people nowadays it also possesses the attraction of novelty."

But now here is a quite different hall. Kiprensky's portrait of Pushkin and Perov's portrait of Lermontov do not make any greater impression than the reproductions of these pictures seen in the journal "Ogonyok." Tolstoy and Dostoevsky are here too. Tolstoy's gaze is simple, but this is natural to him, in the Buddhist manner, since the passion for achieving perfection that intensified among the humanists of the nineteenth century inevitably led, by the shortest possible route, to the spiritual and poetic schematism that is typical of Buddhism. Hanging on the opposite wall is Perov's picture "The Pilgrim." Perov painted Dostoevsky in 1872 and "The Pilgrim" in 1870. They are astonishingly similar. Especially the gaze. As with the "Pilgrim," Dostoevsky's gaze and posture both express an intense self-absorption. As if his gaze is focused on the most profound depths of God's creation, though in actual fact. if you look closely, they are focused on old bast sandals and unpaid debts. But this is eclectically spliced together with great, universal thoughts. It was no accident that Dostoevsky exalted the "Pilgrim" into a saint. A pilgrim, especially a Russian pilgrim, is an eclectic through and through, conflating with mechanical ease his own essential needs and the needs of the world. He dreams of everything coming to pass just as he has arranged things. Perov's "Pilgrim" has an umbrella behind his back and a mug hanging on his belt. Dostoevsky has grasped his knee in his hands. They are both focused on, both pondering on the same thing.

And here is the Frenchman, the Russian émigré. It seems to Andrei that it is an error, a forced error, to view the Frenchman's works in open space, on the wall of a gallery. They ought to be leafed through in an album, like a book. Reproductions lose practically nothing of the original, just as a work of Tolstoy printed at a printing works loses practically nothing as compared with the manuscript. But on the other hand, it is possible to concentrate. Here it was impossible to concentrate. There weren't many "back of beyond" viewers here. Some got carried in occasionally. There were a lot of Jews, for the most part matching the profile of the modern apostate, whether religious convert or lay individual.

To a large extent the prerevolutionary convert was a merchant or shopkeeper, an engineer or doctor, a calculating individual with nothing against Moses, if he would ensure his profit. Nowadays the apostate is an intellectual, a philosopher or a mystic. He is consciously dissatisfied with Moses. "Nothing but prohibitions: you shall not, you shall not, you shall not. But with Christ it's you may, you may, you may." But for the most part what they know from Moses is: "An eye for an eye." And from Christ: "Love your enemy" . . . The Jews are clearly Muscovites, they have seen the other halls many times and do not linger in them, but then neither do other visitors. The composition of the crowd in the hall where the Frenchman's work has been hung is fairly constant, whereas in the other halls it changes and is shuffled about. It's tedious here. But some animation is provided by comments from "the back of beyond."

"And what's that?" someone from the back of beyond asks. "Why is there a little man on that cheek?"

"That's just the way the artist wanted it," replies some woman with a big nose, her eyes gleaming as she secretly chuckles to herself.

"I doubt that," Andrei thought. "Realist painting is far harder to explain, it has more mystery in it. But here everything is set out, like the phrases in a well edited manuscript. There's nothing superfluous."

A certain extremist from the back of beyond, a gaunt, elderly individual with light-brown hair, said to his son in a deliberately loud voice:

"Let's go, after Repin and the other good paintings, it's impossible to look at this."

Nobody reacted to him. There was no squabble, and he had wanted so badly to have his say, as if he were standing in a queue, to defend his Mother Russia . . .

After that comes the Vrubel hall. The well known "Demon" of 1890 seems weaker than the prostrate, corporeal "Demon" lying in a pose of passionate violence, but alone, without a woman. Black, blue, lilac . . . Then comes the Falk . . . with Konchalovsky and the portrait of Yakulov. The jolly little man sitting cross-legged in eastern style, with a little jester's mustache and wearing a tie, seems to be an element of the ornamental design, alongside the yataghans hanging on the wall . . . It is all like a carpet, and everything is on equal terms, a man and a yataghan . . . In Falk's work you sense a weakness. His colors are shamefaced, whereas Konchalovsky's talent has been presented in masterful fashion. It's not a matter of the administrative allocation of places. It's the inner feeling: bashfulness and weakness in Falk, strength and sappy tenacity in Konchalovsky. It's the bashfulness and weakness that are required at night behind locked doors, and the strength and tenacity required during the day in a crowd of one's own kind . . . The weakness develops into an ethereal lightness, not of the flesh but of the essence, that bears you up toward the sky, the strength and tenacity entangle the earth in their roots. Strength and tenacity are inconvenient up in the sky . . . Then come the still life artists . . . Russian bread and meat. And here that Frenchman who was once a young Russian Jew has been been dragged out of the storerooms. Here is "The Honeymoon." He and she rising up from behind the horizon, their long bodies like hazy rainbows . . . The sky covered in bright colors, the earth covered in Belarusian mud. And the goat-like Jewish faces of the enamored couple . . . Then comes the saddest hall. Everything is bright-colored, everything is youthful, and the tears spring to Andrei's eyes. But not for everyone. Somov, his Bor-town compatriot, simply likes it here. He walks around, as cheerful as he was in front of the abstract, surrealist drawings and as unfocused and stupid as he was in front of the realism. He's interested, as if this were a loud drinking party . . . Abstraction and realism are self-affirming art, but impressionism is self-sacrificing art . . . Here the artist is a gladiator who dies in order to move the crowd to rapture. It is not abstraction or realism, but impressionism that is most capable of introducing immature, coarse souls to art, if only it had ever been officially predominant . . . But people feel difficult emotions here, as if they were at some expensive cemetery. Hurry away from here, to the socialist realism that lulls the soul with the substantiality of trifles, to the prosaic clarity of the everyday, congealed forever . . . If Somov was bored in the midst of abstraction, unfocused and stupid in the midst of realism and cheerfully festive in the midst of impressionism then here, in the halls of socialist realism, he feels as if he is in a trolleybus. Everything here is recognizable, everything here is usual, here he leads the way, moves ahead and is lost to sight somewhere in the halls of the academic "people's artists." But Andrei walked outside, to Vuchetich's sculpture "Let Us Beat Swords Into Plowshares."

Savelii was sitting on a little bench beside a café, from out of which there issued, without even a hint of reverence for this sacred spot, the usual public-catering smells. Sitting beside him was a young woman, concerning whom Andrei immediately realized that Savelii often dreamed about her at night, and in a variety of guises. Yes, Savelii was once again in that state when even a whole boiled chicken, set out on a plate with the shanks of its drumsticks sticking up, did not arouse his appetite, but his sexual desire . . . The woman had a simple, plebeian face, only not the round, general-Russian kind, with a hint of Tatar, but a northern Russian face, without any Asiatic element . . . Her eyes were especially unusual. The light-colored Russian eye is usually watery, but here the blueness was dense, shading into darkness.

And when Andrei, a reserved individual, looked at her, there immediately awoke within him some part of his sister Tasya, who had loved the Antichrist with a third form of love, neither carnal nor platonic, and some part of his mother Vera, the Antichrist's ecstatic lover. And Andrei was gladdened by this for, having carried his biblical ideas of the morning through the halls of the Tretyakov Gallery unharmed, he felt his soul fortified even more by this feeling that had suddenly flared up within him, a reserved individual.

"What are you up to?" Andrei asked Savelii.

"We were late," said Savelii, "sorry."

Obviously they had arrived much later than the agreed time, without knowing that Andrei had arrived much earlier and had not waited for them.

"Ilovaisky came," said Savelii, "we got engrossed in talking about Christ . . . Sorry . . ."

"Long life to whoever is sorry," bellowed Somov, who had just appeared "Long life to whoever is sorry, but hello to whoever is blameless."

Somov had walked through the socialist realism halls as if they were a shower room, where he had washed off his boredom at abstractionism, stupidly intense concentration at classical realism and joviality at impressionism, and appeared back in the street exactly as he had entered the gallery, unchanged in any way and ready to carry on living in contemporary reality. The socialist realism halls were like a bath house that washed a person clean of extraneous accretions of the art of the past or the art of an alien reality that was located within the walls of the gallery.

"This is Rufina," said Savelii, "my neighbor, and this is Andrei Koposov, my fellow student."

Thus they were brought together by chance, the chance that in reality is divine providence. In their initial general conversation they realized that they were both from the same town. They realized that in her childhood Rufina had been friends with Andrei's sister, Ustya, and had been acquainted with his other sister, Tasya, and with his mother, Vera. Somov also announced that he was their Bor-town compatriot, that his father worked in the gas-fired boiler house of the Bor Central Hospital and his mother was a bookkeeper, but she had already retired. And that they had to drink to this notable occasion.

In this way what was meant to happen did happen. However there still something missing. Vasya Korobkov wasn't there. He was very late. But when he arrived, everything immediately fell into place. Pelagia saw him from a distance and realized that this was the bad seed of the Antichrist, who had to be eliminated, as Tamar eliminated the bad seed of Judah, his sons Ira and Onan . . .

Vasya was drunk; he walked right up to them and said:

"I'm late, sorry!"

And Somov repeated:

"Long life to whoever is sorry, long life to whoever is sorry, but hello to whoever is blameless . . ."

However Vasya did not like this little verse, just as at one time Pavlov, the war invalid from Bor town, had not liked Somov's poem. At that time Pavlov had struck Somov beside the dance floor in the park. And now in Moscow, in the courtyard of the Tretyakov Gallery, Korobkov whacked Somov hard . . .

Well, the Tretyakovka is a good place, with plenty of militiamen around, and so the entire group ran to get away from the famous Frenchman's exhibition, and when they came together again in a little park square fairly close by, Somov was not with them, he had taken offence . . . The prophetess Pelagia said to Vasya:

"Why did you start fighting?"

And Vasya, who was always jolly after he had hit someone and got away with it, didn't answer: he looked at the prophetess Pelagia and noticed how attentively she was gazing at him:

"Why are you looking at me like that," Vasya asked, "or have you recognized me?"

"I have," said the prophetess Pelagia, better known by the name Ruth. "You resemble my father very much . . . You're incredibly like him . . ."

"Your father wouldn't happen to be a Jew, would he?" Vasya asked sarcastically. "Kike Samuilovich?"

"He is a Jew," the prophetess Pelagia replied, "but his name in Dan Yakovlevich . . . You are mistaken . . ."

"I beg your pardon," Vasya said sarcastically and continued in Ukrainian: "Pardon me, I made a mistake, as they say in Ukraine . . . The Lord made a mistake and appeared in Kyiv, and suffered greatly in doing so . . . Have you ever heard that?"

"You come and visit us." sad the prophetess Pelagia. "You'll see for yourself how much you resemble my father . . . We can drink tea . . ."

And she looked at him again. Her second glance was already fatal, there was very much in it of Tamar, who killed Judah's bad seed, his first two sons Ira and Onan . . .

The face of Vasya from the tribe of Dan contorted and he spoke, repeating the fate of the Shulamite blasphemer from the tribe of Dan:

"I couldn't give a damn for your entire Yiddish gang or your Yiddish God . . ."

Then the prophetess Pelagia spoke inwardly: "Let it be so. A reviler of the Lord's name must die. If a newcomer or a foreigner reviles the Lord's name, he shall be put to death."

She spoke in this way within herself, watching Vasya as he walked away. Andrei and Savelii, who both feared Vasya for his persistence in malign actions, spoke as follows:

"It's a good thing that he has gone," said Andrei.

And Savelii added:

"I only just realized that Vasya looks like Rufina's father."

Andrei said:

"It's my fault, it was stupid of me to invite him."

"The day has started badly," said Savelii, "but it could still end well . . . Ilovaisky is at my place now . . . He has invited us to visit his friends' dacha."

This dacha belonged to a surgeon who had once studied in a theological seminary together with Ilovaisky. The surgeon's name was Vsesvyatsky.

"That's dangerous," said Andrei, "they'll talk about Christ, it would be difficult for me to listen to that today."

"It's all right," Savelii laughed. "These old folk talk about Christ differently . . . They talk about him humorously and cheerfully. And even Ilovaisky talks about Christ cheerfully with them . . . Let's go . . . You and me, and Rufina and my mother with Ilovaisky."

"Yes, let's go," Rufina-Pelagia agreed.

And then Andrei also immediately agreed. For he had already begun to cherish every minute spent in the company of this blue-eyed woman. While Savelii went home to collect his mother, Andrei and Rufina spent more than an hour alone surrounded by a fortuitous crowd of strangers: first of all people walking by, then the passengers in a trolleybus, and then the crowd of people at the Savyolovsky railroad station. They talked about Bor town in the Gorky Region: although the prophetess Pelagia had left Bor as a little girl, she still remembered a lot about it.

"How is Ustya getting on?" Pelagia asked.

"My sister Ustya has two little children," Andrei said, "and my sister Tasya has my namesake Andrei and his brother Varfolomei. Andrei is in the army and Varfolomei works as a driver."

"And how is Vera, your mother?" the prophetess Pelagia asked.

"My mother's a good person," said Andrei, "but she's weak-willed. Everybody shouts at her, she's under everybody's thumb, including her own daughters and her grandchildren, and the old woman Vesyolova, the mother of Tasya's husband, treats her like dirt. My mother's afraid of everything and even when she prays she has a frightened expression, as if even God shouts at her . . ."

They spoke in this way until there seemed nothing left to talk about, but fortunately they still had a lot of time to take pleasure in each other's company and they enjoyed just sitting together without speaking in the way that the prophetess Pelagia sometimes sat with her father, the Antichrist. Pelagia was surprised by this, for she did not yet know that Andrei Koposov was also the seed of the Antichrist, like Vasya Korobkov, although Andrei was healthy seed, even if he was not the primary seed.

An intent gaze is fruitful when the object does not suppress the personality of the person looking, as happens in Buddhism . . . The gaze of a Buddhist includes a cold epic poem, as a result of his merging with nature, something that was an even more powerful influence in the decline of Christianity. However the intent Biblical gaze is lyrical. The wisdom of the law is God's mouth, but the Lord's flesh is exalted lyric poetry. The prophetess Pelagia glanced at Andrei Koposov in the midst of the railroad station's hubbub and she knew him through and through. And she realized that his life would be a lyrical one. For when a life proves to be lyrical, no matter what material it consists of, often even of what is most ignoble and wretched, then God is always present with such a destiny. This man would live a long life, and this life would be tempestuous and dangerous, but it would be the life of a spiritual toiler, and in this life there would not be any punishment from God, only human punishment, which the soul does not fear.

When the prophetess Pelagia had understood all this about Andrei Koposov, there was nothing more for her to be silent about with him, and immediately Savelii appeared, with his mother Klavdia, an old woman who tried to look younger than her age, wearing lipstick, and the old man Ilovaisky, a scholar of classical antiquity. She found meeting old Ilovaisky unpleasant because he thrust forward his unclean old man's lips, set in the unkempt face of a solitary sloven, to kiss her on the lips, and the problem for her was how to dodge the kiss on her lips and offer him her cheek, or actually make Ilovaisky kiss the empty air, by an awkward, apparently unintentional turn of her head. The prophetess Pelagia managed this cleverly and easily, but Andrei was caught out and felt the pressure of the old man's dead flesh against his lips. Moreover Savelii's mother Klavdia, who now imitated everything that Ilovaisky did, also kissed him with a quick jab of her lipstick-painted mouth. Savelii started fussing.

"The train's leaving soon," he said and ran off to buy tickets.

"Savelii's my little son, a true Ivolgin," Klavdia said. "When I see how he fusses, I remember his late father, who always panicking." And she shed a few tears in her habitual manner.

The weather suddenly turned bad. In Moscow this happens more often in summer than in winter. In the middle of the almost cloudless sky thunder rumbled once and then a second time. When they got into the suburban train a cool wind was already blowing, and after they had been traveling for ten minutes the rain started pouring down .The conversations in the suburban train were conducted mostly by people from the suburban areas around Moscow, city folk, but tired of Moscow, so incessantly intrusive when it is constantly there before your eyes, and they were eager to look out at the dacha district through the windows of the train. The exception to this was Ilovaisky, who talked constantly, telling them about various things and giving them no peace.

"Of course," said Ilovaisky, "you young people have not heard about, and have not read the writings of the priest Petrov . . . The Christian philosopher . . ." Ilovaisky giggled. "Love as the foundation of the life of society . . . He rejected private property and economic inequality, and argued that private property is a Jewish invention, not a Christian one . . . Under his influence, seminarians decided to go out into the people with a new Gospel . . . Religious populism has been omitted from the history of the revolution. But Petrov was excommunicated . . . Yes, his stupidity was met by repression, as usual in Russia . . ."

"Quiet, Gavriil," Klavdia said to Ilovaisky.

"Why, what am I saying wrong?" Ilovaisky asked provocatively. "On the contrary, I'm mocking anti-government nonsense."

"Don't say the word 'anti-government'," Klavdia whispered.

"Oh, your soul has turned Jewish from your first marriage with Katz," said Ilovaisky, and a squabble suddenly sprang up between Ilovaisky and Klavdia, testifying to the closeness of their relationship . . .

"I'll go back now," Klavdia whispered at the very next stop. "That's tactless, in front of Savelii . . . And Rufina . . ."

"What's wrong?" asked Ilovaisky. "Rufina knows that I'm not an anti-semite and I respect her father, isn't that so?"

"Yes it is," the prophetess Pelagia agreed.

But Savelii really had turned pale and there was no way of knowing what would have happened if they had not arrived at their destination. Everyone was delighted by their arrival and the change of scenery, including the impulsive old man Ilovaisky, who realized that he had gone too far. He was aware that this was a fault of his, but couldn't deny himself the satisfaction of a little backbiting, if he was sure he would only be berated for it and not struck, as Vasya Korobkov might have done.

The damp Moscow suburbs greeted the city folk with the menace emanating from other people's fences, the barking of dogs, the absence of road intersections with militiamen and several dangerous-looking figures at a beer kiosk. However once they had found the surgeon Vsesvyatsky's dacha and walked into the yard, fending off the dirty paws of a large, affectionate dog, everything immediately became more cheerful. And when they saw a table on the terrace with a plate of apples from the dacha orchard, picked with their stalks attached and some also with leaves, and a plate of fresh raspberries from the same place, this suburban-Moscow charm instantly eclipsed the initial unpleasant impression.

Sitting at the table was their host, the surgeon Vsesvyatsky, a rosy-cheeked old man who took good care of his appearance, and also his wife, Varvara Davydovna, and another old man of the same age, who also knew Ilovaisky. When they were all introduced he said:

"Belogrudov, from 'belaya grud,' meaning 'white-breasted' . . . A folk-tale sort of surname, but more in a mature womanly style than a maidenly one," which immediately indicated that the speaker was a joker. Belogrudov also stated that by profession he was a teacher of literature.

Ilovaisky instantly set about kissing all three of them, first the surgeon, then his wife, then the teacher, and then the surgeon again. A housemaid carried in a samovar and Varvara Davydovna brought in a dusty bottle of homemade cherry liqueur. "Now they'll start talking about Christ," Andrei thought in alarm. But they didn't start talking until they had drunk some cherry liqueur, and after they drank it they started talking in a sweet, pleasant manner, the way old people usually recall the distant days of their youth, dreaming about the past and what might have been.

"Remember?" they said. "Remember?" And their eyes narrowed sweetly, as if they were seeing the kind of dreams that warm the heart, after which you awake with a feeling of regret.

"Remember homiletics?" Belogrudov, the teacher of literature asked, narrowing his eyes sweetly. "Homiletics, the theory of church oratory . . ."

"Liturgics, the church statutes," Ilovaisky put in sweetly.

"Does the church have statutes?" Klavdia asked, gazing at them in owlish surprise. "Gavrusha, does the church really have statutes?" She had also drunk some cherry liqueur and was being coquettish.

Of the art critic Ivolgin's well-provided-for wife, whose severe manner gave her the air of an intelligent, inwardly self-possessed and ceremonious woman, the woman who had once banished her repressed sister's children with a hand of iron, not a single trace remained. Now Klavdia became angry or fussy in the way that shallow, stupid woman do, rapidly forgave everything and made do with the very minimum. She no longer represented any danger to her son Savelii, having long ago ceased to be the strict mother who sought to curb his youthful sin, and he was like a demanding mentor with her, competing with Ilovaisky for her weak soul, although not in order to safeguard this soul, but to demonstrate his manhood to his male rival.

"The church statutes," Ilovaisky said in a patronizing manner, "are the study of the order of conducting a church service."

"And the Gospel texts that were used at home to write the sermon," said Belogrudov, still pursuing his own line, "the study of St. John Chrysostom, remember that, Gavriusha? Remember that, Senechka?" he asked, turning to the surgeon.

"Of course," said the surgeon Vsesvyatsky, "practical training was conducted in the parish churches. But what I enjoyed most of all was theology and medicine . . . We studied that in the senior classes . . ."

"And the proofs that the Catholics use," said Ilovaisky, who was very drunk, "Ah, yes . . . Catholic thought, now that's Europe with all its weaknesses. But, brothers and sisters, in the conception of the Trinity . . ." He attempted to get to his feet, but Klavdia put her arm round his shoulder and sat him back down. "In the concept of the Trinity . . . In our concept the Holy Spirit emanates only from the Father, but in Europe it also emanates from the Son . . . Catholic thought is free . . . But we are enslaved by Judaism, Mosaic religion. It's ridiculous, we're Russians, and Mosaic law . . ."

"Now it will begin," Andrei thought in alarm. If not for Rufina, who was sitting beside him, he would have started feeling very miserable, but his love for Rufina had matured quickly, and the youth, who was only a little over twenty years old, loved the thirty-year-old woman meekly and compliantly, without any element of male coercion in his feeling, and he tried to imitate her manners. And Rufina sat there calmly, looking at the drunken old seminarians.

"Kant identified religion with morality," Belogrudov stated grandly as if speaking from a church pulpit or dais. "For Hegel religion is the initial stage of philosophy, which arose out of savage man's requirement for thought and knowledge: man's self-delusion venerating itself . . . The Godlike nature of the human spirit . . ." Suddenly skipping over something in his exposition, he declared: "At the seminary, forbidden writers included Turgenev, Goncharov, Tolstoy, Belinsky, Pisarev, Chernyshevsky, Goncharov . . . There now, I've mentioned Goncharov twice . . ."

"Look at this chalice," said Ilovaisky, pawing at a beautiful gold-rimmed cup, full of tea, with his rheumaticky fingers, "it is simple . . ."

"Mama," said Savelii, "take the cup from Ilovaisky, or he will break something that doesn't belong to him . . ."

"You, young man, have an Oedipus complex," the highbrow hooligan Ilovaisky said with a turn of his shaggy-haired head.

"If you weren't so feeble, I would have hit you," Savelii said with tears of youthful indignation glinting in his eyes, but on seeing his mother's frightened, anguished face, he contented himself with that and calmed down.

"That's enough!" the Vsesvyatskys exclaimed in embarrassment, speaking over each other, "one little drink and you're like children."

"It's all right, I'm calm," said Savelii, "I'll take a walk in the orchard."

"We have a very nice orchard, I'll go with you," said Varvara Davydovna, and they went out.

"There it is, the Mosaic attitude," Ilovaisky said when Savelii had left, "arrogant . . ."

"Precisely," Belogrudov added, "remember, the revolution . . . The meeting in the seminary . . . An Old-Testament lecturer walked into the classroom, and we said to him: the Bible is our dogma . . . Why, it was asked, do we Russians have to study the history of the Jewish people, chosen by God for some reason or other, and study all the details of this history: study the history of the Jews more thoroughly than the history of our own native land? I wrote to an antireligious journal about this instance of Russian patriotism in the seminary in 1952, but they didn't take it . . ."

"In 1952," said Vsesvyatsky, "an incident occurred that I often recall . . . In our camp hospital an autopsy was performed on a prisoner who had died . . . The physician-in-chief performed the autopsy and all the camp inmates who were doctors were present. The corpse was an elderly man with a large brass cross on his chest. The cross and its cord were handed over to the camp office and the physician-in-chief of the camp, Major Baranov, took the opportunity to ask the inmate-doctors if they believed in God. They all replied: 'Yes, I do.' Only one of them replied: 'I do, but in a philosophical sense.' 'That's the same damned thing,' said Baranov . . . I think," Vsesvyatsky added, "that if they had been at liberty, they wouldn't have said that so boldly: 'I believe' . . . But there, with a sentence of ten to fifteen years, they had nothing to lose."

"Look at this chalice," said Ilovaisky, fingering the cup again, "it is simple, but smash it against the floor, break it and it will become complicated. Remember, the Chalice of Moses . . . Moses is obviously an exaggerated figure," he said, still harping on the same theme, "I'm a historian of ancient times. Sorry, but there's no way you can fool me. The scribe Ezra imputed greatness to Moses in the late period . . . It's a proven fact . . . Moses is not even mentioned by the prophets of the period of Judges and the period of the Kings, and none of the great prophets mention him at all, except for Jeremiah . . . and then merely in passing. The cult of Moses arose in the late period, under Nehemiah and Ezra . . . It was also Ezra who wrote the Pentateuch of Moses and artificially lent it an ancient character."

"But what of it?" Andrei Koposov exclaimed in exasperation, pale-faced and agitated, "What of it? I beg your pardon, but you are using the wrong term. He didn't simply 'write,' he 'wrote down.' I've read a philosophical treatise that attempts to demean the Pentateuch by claiming that it was of later origin . . . But why break down an open door? Even the Patriarchs are not a chronicle. It mentions there, for instance, that Abraham arrived in the region of Dan, although Dan appeared on earth in the fourth generation after Moses, and the region of Dan appeared long after the exodus from Egypt, that is, many centuries after the Patriarchs. Ezra reinforced the figure of Moses at a historically similar moment, after he had left Babylonian exile, repeating the exodus from Egyptian captivity. This is an example of inspired emulation, which Pushkin set on the highest pinnacle of art . . . The emulation of great examples requires far more talent than innovation . . . The lowest stage of artistic creation is feeble imitation, then comes innovation, and then the emulation of great examples . . . This is classicism . . . The greatness of the Bible lies in emulation, in the repetition of God's word . . . Perhaps the brilliant emulator Ezra wrote down a poem from ancient oral traditions for the Pentateuch of Moses and made it the cornerstone, set it in its appropriate place, for the truth of poetry is higher than the truth of history . . . I didn't read that . . . I realized it for myself and only read Aristotle later, and I was delighted to see it confirmed. Aristotle says that the historian Herodotus could be set in verse, but even so it would still be history and not poetry. The difference is that the historian speaks about what has actually happened, whereas the poet speaks about what could have happened. Poetry is therefore more philosophical and more serious than history. Poetry speaks about the universal, history speaks about the specific. The universal consists of what should be done and what goals should be striven for, the specific speaks of what has taken place, what has happened . . . And the biblical creation of the world, about which thick-headed priests argue with scientific and philosophical windbags, is a poem that defies scientific and historical analysis . . ."

Having spoken out at such length, until his throat hurt, Andrei immediately realized that he was trying to say what he himself was convinced of and believed in without the slightest difficulty, but he knew that Ilovaisky would contradict him even more cleverly and irrefutably, in keeping with the ability of Russian disputants to speak more cleverly than their actual meaning. But at this point the housemaid brought in the reheated samovar and the joker Belogrudov, red-faced from the homemade liqueur, also interposed:

"Young people," he said merrily, "My son . . . remember," he laughed, "'Tell me, my son, hast thou not corrupted the milk-loving innocence of thy childhood, dost thou not practice onanism?'"

"'Tell me, my son,'" the tousle-headed intellectual hooligan Ilovaisky immediately put in, "'hast thou not practiced sodomy with anyone or fornicated with a woman?'"

"Get away with you, Gavriil," said Klavdia, blinking stupidly and blushing. "Saying such things in front of the young people . . ."

"'Hast thou not sinned with livestock or with poultry?'"

"The circumcision of Christ on the eighth day of the flesh," old Belogrudov also put in self-indulgently. "On the eighth day do we deign to be circumcised for the salvation of our race."

"And do you remember the fire in the church?" asked Vsesvyatsky, "a box of candle ends caught fire on the gallery . . . The priest was running around with a cross, shouting: 'Put it out, put it out . . .' And then the floor caught fire . . ."

"And we were in the bushes," laughed Belogrudov, "some shouting out 'shit,' some 'catch him,' some 'fool' . . ."

"And the prayer for the foundation of the house," laughed Ilovaisky, "for the digging of the pit . . . 'For Thou dost bless the eggs and the cheese' . . . The prayer for those who bring the first shoots of the vegetables . . ."

And then things became really bad round the table, but the prophetess Pelagia said nothing, for she knew how difficult it was for a Russian person to believe in God . . . If he was offered something serviceable in irreligion, in atheism, he would be happy . . . At first it had seemed that a replacement had been found, and he was happy, but not for long . . . That had passed off very quickly . . . And so he was coming back again, but where to? Can the Russian believe with such vast spaces and such a history? In God, no, but perhaps in "Him, who was crucified for us under Pontius Pilate." The prophet Isaiah spoke words signifying that you should not always search for God, but only when He is near. He is not to be found near a young, irreligious nation when it tires of its tumultuous, merry, free shiftlessness. He is closer to a young nation in its sorrow, in its joy he is far away. A mature nation is seduced in oppression, as the Jews were seduced and deprived of their Father in their Egyptian enslavement, but their joy is the blossoming of God's word and will. Great is the biblical lamentation, the lamentation of the prophets, the lamentation of Jeremiah, but man is closer to God in praise. Not by accident is the Book of Psalms called the Book of Glorifications in its original Jewish source. Will the Russian be able to sense God more fully, not in grief, but in joy, will the Russian faith become mature? Or, without having learned anything, will it come full circle? Russian atheism may have lost, but has Russian faith gained anything from that?

And then the three boisterous old men, the former seminarians, grew tired, and their faces turned pale in their tiredness, and together with the tiredness, piety appeared on them. And now they spoke differently about prayer.

"And do you remember the prayer with three bows to the ground?" Ilovaisky asked. "O Lord, Master of my life, grant me not the spirit of sloth, despondency, lust for power and idle talk. But grant unto me, Your servant, the spirit of chastity, humility, patience and love. Yea, O Lord and King, grant me to see my own faults and not to judge my brother, forever and ever, world without end. Amen."

"And what singing there was in the seminary," said Belogrudov, speaking quietly and pensively now. "The archbishop's choir . . . The choirmaster . . ." And he started singing in a surprisingly young voice, "I believe, Our Father . . ."

The other two old men joined in and the result was euphonious. Coming in from the orchard with a plate of wet apples, Vara Davydovna said:

"Not so loud, you candle-blowers, that's enough prayer services." And then she sat down with a stupid, gentle smile, like the one on Klavdia's face, wiping her eyes.

And all the old men, who up until this moment had been blasphemous, sang with feeling, even the philosopher and scholar of ancient times, Ilovaisky, blew his nose drunkenly as he said:

"And the seminary church had two choirs with their own choirmasters . . . Remember the choirmaster Kolka, who married a rich priest's wife . . . The priest's wife played the piano and Kolka played the violin . . ."

Moving cautiously, in order not to disrupt the beatific, soulful state that had finally descended on the old men, the prophetess Pelagia got up from the table and walked out into the yard, and from there along a path paved with bricks into the orchard. Distracted by the old men's singing of prayers and psalms, Andrei failed to notice Rufina's departure, and when he came to his senses, looked round and didn't find Rufina there beside him, as if he was in a dream he suddenly felt a fear of irretrievable loss, for this was the first time she had not been beside him for the last three hours . . . He drew attention to himself by jumping hastily to his feet, so that the old men even stopped their singing. Then he ran down the steps of the terrace and looked round, not knowing which way to go. Someone came dashing after him and suddenly bumped into him from behind and he shouted out terribly in his fright.

"What's wrong?" Varvara Davydovna asked in alarm, appearing on a step with a lantern, for it was already dark.

Shaggy-haired Ilovaisky dashed out, once again wearing his cunning, malevolent, godless expression.

"Young people, they have their own business . . . It's jealousy . . . He's jealous of Savelii being with Rufina . . ."

"The dog frightened him," said Varvara Davydovna. "He doesn't bite, young man."

"Where's the road to the station here?" Andrei asked, suffering from the suddenness of the change that had come over him, for only a moment earlier he had felt sure of himself in front of these people and defended something dear to him in confident words, he had been so adult and then, by crying out in foolish surprise, he had betrayed the torments of his heart, which in the eyes of these old people appeared childish, so that now the deeply thought-through words that he had spoken in dispute had also become childish . . .

"Wait for a while," said Klavdia, also appearing on the terrace, "perhaps we'll all go soon . . . Or you could go with Savelii . . . Savelii!" she called. "Now where is he? Probably walking with Rufina."

"No, I'll be going," Andrei said hastily, feeling Ilovaisky's mocking, godless gaze on him, "It's time I went . . ."

He walked out through the small gate and set off at random across the wet grass and when he looked round, even if he had wanted to go back, he wouldn't have known the way. In the darkness all the summer houses looked alike. He walked away even further and sat down on a large rock of the kind that often sticks up out of the ground or lies by the road for some unknown purpose in a rural area, and for some reason he started thinking, but not about his love for Rufina, which was strong, and although it had only lasted for three hours so far, had already managed to cause him such suffering and stupid public humiliation. He started thinking about the initial period of his time in Moscow, when everything that was now tense and grueling had seemed festive and agreeable.

On arriving in the capital he had discovered that many of the people he respected at that time were imbued with Russian national-religious sentiment, and precisely this national-religious sentiment had served as the first step of his initiation into the spiritual. It was possible to take various attitudes to what was currently happening, but it had to be admitted that the religious revival among the young generation had begun with mass-produced crucifixes that were made from the same material as moneyboxes in the form of a cat with a slit in its head for the coins. He had also dreamed of obtaining a crucifix like that, as he had once dreamed of obtaining a Finnish hunting knife such as he had seen in the possession of powerful individuals in his world. Since even before this everything worthy of imitation had been Russian and the crowning reward for everything was also Russian, these Russian crucifixes had helped him to set aside the past and change many things, without essentially changing anything. He had started reading the Gospels that Vasya Korobkov had lent him, and in the Gospels everything was Russian too, repudiating everything non-Russian, and of course what was most extremely non-Russian was Jewish and Mosaic . . . What came from Moses was evil, what came from Christ was good. A multitude of well-educated ladies, some of them actually Jewish, having been initiated into the renewed Russian sentiment, reinforced even more the widespread infatuation with the Russian Christ . . . Andrei's joyful honeymoon period of initiation into Russian Christianity was not ruined by spiritual doubts, for which he was still too immature at that time, but by what appeared at first sight to be petty, everyday occurrences typical of the unpleasant disposition of the capital city's Christians. This was not merely unpleasant but familiar, consumerist and more in agreement with national feelings than with sincere efforts to fathom the inner truth of the utterances in the Gospels. And when young people started writing out Gospel texts and handing them out to each other, like proclamations, he finally realized that religion would not save Russia in the future, just as atheism had not saved it in the past. There is no salvation from yourself, and man is defenseless against his own self. National character is a genuine enslaver. It is not given to man to change himself, but it is given to him to understand himself and speak a word of caution to others. God knows what will be, but even man can know what should not be. Excessive hopes should not be placed in religion, as excessive hopes had been placed in atheism. Indeed, now the Christian religion could not even place any hope in itself. Christianity, having begun its historical journey with a conspiracy of the

Apostles against Christ, naturally understands that the most man can expect from religion is solace, for which he is prepared to pay with meek submission. He expects the same thing that a child expects from its mother: If you placate me, I will be obedient, if you do not placate me, I will not be obedient. And this religion placates him with a love of suffering and a reward in the afterlife. However if you replace a love of suffering with a love of heroism, which in principle is the same thing, and if you replace a reward in the afterlife with the glory of the nation, this will serve perfectly well for an earthly challenge to God, for the construction of national Towers of Babel. Apostolic Christianity prides itself on its love for man, but in reality its entire morality is founded on the exaggerated significance of man in God's world, and in this Christians are akin to atheists. No, that is not what the biblical prophets teach, that is not what they promise in order to placate. They placate with biblical truth, God's truth. And truth consists in the fact that man has been a cursed being from the moment of his expulsion from the paradise of Eden. It is open to everyone to understand the truth about himself, but not everyone will agree to understand it. Very few will agree. And yet the truth about yourself will not only make your life easier, but also invigorate it. Every fortunate moment, every occasion of happiness, every good deed will then be accepted as an undeserved and therefore doubly valuable reward, and every calamity and failure will be accepted as a deserved, and therefore less hurtful punishment. Not expecting rewards, which should always be unexpected and accepted as undeserved, and not fearing punishments, which should always be accepted as natural, that is the religious leader's genuine path in life.

There is a famous place in the Second Book of Moses, called "Exodus." In their fear of Pharoah's pursuit, instead of actively struggling, the children of Israel turned to God in prayer and showered curses on Moses for having roused them to active struggle and distracted them from prayer. And the great prophet, whose heart had also faltered, turned to the people with a promise of God's grace for their prayer: "Fear not, stand firm, and see the salvation of the Lord, which he has worked for you today. The Lord will fight for you, and you have only to be silent." And then the Lord taught Moses a lesson. The Lord said to Moses, "Why do you cry to me? Tell the people of Israel to go forward." God's design is not sufficient in itself, without this it will not be realized.

Andrei Koposov recalled that some time previously he had visited a Moscow-region monastery in Zagorsk, the Trinity and St. Sergius Monastery, and had returned from there with a heavy heart. He had always been afraid of graveyards, and there he had seen a kind of graveyard in which the graves had been dug up for viewing. Everything there looked like old, dug-up graves, earning income from the visiting tourists: the monastery walls, the bell towers, the refectory in the gaudy "Russian baroque" style. This refectory was reminiscent of a well-browned bread roll that had turned to stone, the food of the dead, terrifying to a living mouth. And all this was covered in inscriptions like those of graves: church inscriptions in ornamental script, state inscription in severe lettering. Constituting a unified whole with all this were the crowds of old women of approximately the same age, about sixty, and of approximately the same height, and all of them either black or gray. Occasionally a man's face or a young face, more often a girl's than a boy's, could be glimpsed but even they were like the old women's faces and for some reason the thought occurred to Andrei that the faces of all corpses were like old women's faces, regardless of their sex and age. The other visitors glanced at them with apprehensive curiosity, in the way that a live person looks at a corpse. Only the monks, some in full black robes with marks and badges of distinction, chains and crosses, some in gray, belted robes without any marks or badges, walked through the courtyard in various directions with healthy, living, full-blooded faces and spoke calmly with the pilgrims. Something about the monks was reminiscent of gravediggers, accustomed to treating dead bodies as the standard objects of their daily labor. Although it was summer, the day was cold and windy and the pilgrims arranged themselves in railroad-station style on a long row of garden benches under the open sky. Some slept, stretched out on a bench, some snacked on their poor food: bread and boiled sausage, washed down with water from half-liter jars. There were also monastery cats here, who obviously fed themselves on alms from the pilgrims, and clouds of pigeons, who perched directly on the sleeping people and strolled around on them.

In one of the old churches, in front of a famous iconostasis that was the property of the state, a service was taking place. A priest in eyeglasses with a mane of gray hair sat at the head of the silver item with a ghastly glimmer that represented the Holy Sepulcher, God's Bier, and his deep, manly intoning concluded in a womanish "Allelujah!" The pilgrims walked up in single file and pressed their lips against the silver bier. All of this took place in semi-darkness in a crowded space. In the nave, which was just as cramped, there were benches on which pilgrims sat tightly packed together with their bundles and baskets, as if in a waiting room. And despite the "Allelujah" the atmosphere was like a Russian governmental office, with the Asiatic savagery of Russian institutions, Russian equality, uniformity and collectivism. In times gone by the Russian forest-steppe character congealed into a collective and has remained frozen in it to this day. This is why individualism is so weak in it, why this character is atheistic and collective in nature, and even the appearance of a Russian church confirms this. When a Russian individual attempts to coerce himself, taking refuge in hermitages, in asceticism, the temptations that arise within him are especially strong, temptations from which it is only possible to hide in a collective. (Leo Tolstoy, an individual with a rather healthy understanding of life, depicted this amply in his story "Father Sergius.") A little girl of eight, whose tourist mother had brought her to watch the church service, had expressed her reaction in genuinely Tolstoyan terms.

"Let's go away, I'm frightened," the little girl whispered after she had heard too many "Allelujahs" and seen too much kissing of the silver coffin . . .

No, religion will not revitalize the Russian character, because it is itself a creation of the Russian character and it will itself require revitalization. However it is only fair to note that as a result of its Asiatic barbarism Russian religion merely expresses outwardly what is typical of the present-day condition of religion in general. Nowadays Tolstoy's fear of a church that makes faith public and collective is especially easy to understand. All religions took shape when the general mass of people was ignorant and in need of a shepherd, like sheep. But at the same time religion requires intimate privacy no less than love, and perhaps far more. No other man, no matter how good he might be and no matter what title he might have been invested with, should or can violate the intimate privacy of faith. For the public nature of the church's expression of faith, even more so than the public nature of its expression of love, is the path to disillusionment and spiritual ruin. If in the past the public expression of faith was a sad necessity, in the future the intimate privacy of faith will become an unavoidable necessity. The intimate privacy of religion is the only path to its revitalization. People can know that someone is in love, but no one should know how he loves or should even make any suppositions about it. It is the same in religion. The importance of religious ritual, which deprives religion of intimate privacy, should grow less and less, and the importance of intimately private faith should increase . . .

In this way Andrei Koposov, the natural son of the Antichrist from the tribe of Dan and the Russian woman Vera Koposova from Bor town in the Gorky Region, reassured himself. He realized what was tormenting him and clearly determined his road ahead. Concerning himself, he knew that he believed in God and therefore felt entitled to warn against the religious temptation that was advancing on Russia amidst the boredom of the talentless official atheists, to warn that in the future religion would be the greatest danger in Russia. He would be hated for his antireligious stance, he would be hated and mocked in unofficial anti-governmental society, and in official society some would try to exploit him, as Pilate attempted to use Christ's warning about the unreformed Law of Moses, the law in which Jesus Christ, a Jew, himself believed with all the strength of his great soul.

When Andrei, the son of the Antichrist, realized his God-given, antireligious destiny, the prophetess Pelagia, the Antichrist's adopted daughter, who was standing in the dark orchard of the dacha with Savelii, felt this as a gentle stirring in her heart and said with a smile:

"Savelii, I like your friend Andriusha, only he is too young, I am not the right match for him."

The relationship between herself and Savelii had long ago become friendly, frank and open in a feminine fashion, the kind of relationship by means of which an intelligent woman restrains a man she does not love from making any perilous moves. If this continues for too long, the man really does start to understand the woman's every feeling and her life almost becomes his life.

"His love for you is very strong," said Savelii. "He loved you immediately and even if he does meet another woman, he will never be happy now."

"He does not live for happiness with a woman," said the prophetess Pelagia.

"And Vasya loved you immediately," said Savelii, "don't take any notice of his vicious swearing . . . He's an unhappy man."

"I know," said the prophetess Pelagia, "but he won't suffer and be tormented for long."

And suddenly a dark glimmering appeared in her eyes. A dark-cherry red color appeared, the color of iron heated to incandescence or a bonfire as it burns out. It was the cruel color of celestial punishment, which the prophetess had acquired from her foster-father the Antichrist. Any life, good or bad, is terminated by the prepotency of that color . . .

Savelii had never seen anything like it, for the orchard was lit up and the neat apple trees with whitewashed trunks became visible. A normal, healthy man's reason would have been impaired if he had seen a woman he loved do something like this, but Savelli had already experienced a course of psychiatric treatment and he now practiced alchemy with the same passion with which he had practiced the sweet sin of recluses in his early youth. From time to time he had fits, which he experienced without any alarm, at those moments he was simply more stubbornly assertive about the thoughts that tormented him constantly. And so now he started asking Rufina-Pelagia to give him a little bit of her blood.

"Any individual can get their blood analyzed at the polyclinic," Savelii said. "I've arranged things, I'll pay and they'll give me a test tube of your blood . . . Unofficially, of course . . . I have a cousin called Ninochka, I was thinking of taking some of her blood when she came to visit, but then I found out that she was married. I need the blood of a virgin."

In the dacha orchard it was cool and damp after the liberal downpour of rural rain, and there was a rich smell that seemed to be the smell of life itself. "The smell of earthly life at its roots must be exactly like this smell," thought the prophetess Pelagia, "after the late evening rain in a suburban apple orchard."

This smell also inspired Savelii. He spoke about the reason for his sleepless nights, about his obsessive idea of recent months, about his dream of a reformed, contemporary alchemy with the exclusive ability to solve the mystery of everything, the mystery of mysteries, the mystery of life.

The prophetess realized that this man would also not be saved. He had been doomed by a book, as often happens to individuals with impressionable, feminine natures, whose emotional life would be appropriate for a genius, but whose intellectual life would be appropriate for an adolescent. They are capable of the powerful and profound, although one-sided, perception of an artistic image, but a book that requires adult, unifying generalization and synthesis is harmful to them. Of course, Savelii was an individual with a bad mixture of bloods, subject to extreme dangers, but many of his typical features were typical outcomes of young peoples' religious reading. An ardent young man is more likely to discover God in Pushkin than in the Gospels . . . Just as at the beginning of the century there was a universal fascination with clever books about economic materialism, which was the prelude to the downfall of many talented souls, so now a fascination with holy books is a danger that has already been the beginning of the downfall of some, and perhaps of many. Savelii's downfall had begun with the Holy Gospels, that biblical fragment. The Old Testament is less dangerous for such impressionable natures, for it is less attractive to them. "An eye for an eye" is clear, how could you not understand it? But the Gospels—"Love your enemies"—will lead you off and away, promise, entice and hand you on, not to lucid Pushkin, but to mystical books. In this way for the young believer Christian ascetism inevitably becomes transformed into mystical eroticism. This is especially dangerous in the age of spiritual famine that has resulted from the domination of talentless, inconsistent atheism, idealist atheism.

For some time already Savelii had been frequenting a circle of young people who met secretly at the apartment of one of them and joyfully devoted themselves to the Middle Ages, since a fashion had sprung up for singing the praises of the Middle Ages for any possible reason at all. In an aging century Gogol had a right to admire the Middle Ages, he delighted in its youthful, free play of the spirit and thought. However people of our time, who have seen and experienced the inevitably mediocre final outcome of the talented medieval game of the man-God, should not strive to emulate its fruitful, talented beginning in their own talentless final conclusion . . . No children's game should be carried to its boring end, for every child knows that the end is the most uninteresting thing about a game. The Middle Ages are a rediscovered, jolly, temporary childhood that began after a biblical, wise old age. It was precisely in the Middle Ages that the Christian finally became a jolly pagan. Like every broad, popular movement, fascism is a jolly children's game, begun by the geniuses of the Middle Ages. But genius is endowed with the salutary ability to commit the appalling in its own thoughts and soul, thereby protecting the world from the most terrible threat that it faces: the materialization of human fantasies and follies. However when children with bad blood start playing at this game it becomes clear that the fantasies of Shakespeare and Dante have their own exponents and practitioners. The riddle that has tormented the liberal intelligentsia: "Where did fascism come from in cultured Europe?" is quite simple. Fascism is when a multitude of poor children with bad blood become involved in playing the talented games of the Middle Ages, and an adult man, seemingly a representative of an adult nation, blithely joins in these jolly games, casts off the shackles of reason that deprive him of such wild delights, curses the "you shall not" of Moses and endows Christ's "you may" with his own pagan meaning, then becomes frisky and playful, becomes a medieval child of the twentieth century, although now he frisks and plays with pinches and bites, in the way that pimply, half-witted dullards who stink of urine frisk and play. And voluptuous medieval pomp is lent to this game by mystical baubles and trinkets.

At one time in Russia decadent individuals who had forgotten how to believe in God were fascinated with mysticism. What if the children of the tedious atheism of recent years, who have not yet learned to believe in God, now become fascinated with it? What will mass, popular Russian mysticism become? What game will Russian people play out to their own perdition and the perdition of others? The Russian soul bears the burden of many sins, for such is its destiny: a nation that has taken possession of such a vast space cannot avoid inflicting torments on itself and others. But is there not in preparation some terrible future sin that God will not forgive? A sin by which the Holy Gospels will teach immature souls that have lost faith in atheism to do evil . . .

Here are the books that were read in the circle that Savelii frequented: "On the Condition of Man at Death and the Transformation of His Corruptible Body into an Incorruptible Form, as He was Created in Eden and also on the Condition of the Incorruptible Bodies Discussed from the Beginning of Darkness," "The Open Gates of Secret Nature and its Active Properties in Good and in Evil," and also "What is the Essence of Things and for the Attention of all Chemists the First Matter of the Philosophical Universal Medicine that they have Long Desired for the Benefit of Those Who Seek Genuine Medical Knowledge."

However for some time now Savelii had only visited the circle on rare occasions, spending more time sitting at home surrounded by flasks and retorts that he had procured from a pharmaceutical warehouse. He was also pondering the idea of leaving the Literary Institute in order to study biochemistry at the university. Meanwhile he was engrossed in the book "Concerning Philosophical Homunculi, What they are in Reality and How to Create Them." The title page of this book bore a note that Savelii especially liked: "Published in print, decorated with diagrams and communicated to the world." The world was informed about the creation of philosophical homunculi simply and confidently, without superfluous lyricism and with scientific conviction:

"This takes place in the following manner. Take a flask of the finest crystal glass, place in it some of the best dew of May, gathered at the full moon, one part; of man's blood, two parts; and of woman's blood, three parts. But you must mark especially that these individuals, insofar as this is possible, are pure and chaste. Then set aside the glass vessel with this material, after first covering it with a solid lid and keep it in a warm place for putrefaction, and then red earth will settle on the bottom. After this filter off the menstruum that stands at the top into a clean glass vessel and preserve it carefully."

So began the description of the process of creating philosophical homunculi, men and women . . .

The prophetess Pelagia knew that the activity in which Savelii wished to engage was a sin and, having heard on several occasions his requests to give him a small amount of her blood for an experiment, she was trying to think of a way to warn this suffering, ill young man who was in love with her. She knew that words were useless in such a case, but she could not think of a way to warn him by action. She could simply not give him her blood, which was what she had been doing, but that would only reinforce his desire to carry out his plan, he would look for blood somewhere else, living for that purpose and confirming himself in his sin. She could give him her blood, and then he would perform an experiment that would of course come to nothing, or at least not to what had been intended, like any alchemical experiment. Then he would demonstrate genuinely mystical stubbornness, aspiring to and performing further experiments, also unsuccessful, and if he was destined for a long life, he would grow old in his sin. And now, standing among the apple trees in the dark dacha orchard, breathing in the rich, exhilarating, damp smell of life, seeing beside her Savelii's pale face with Klavdia's short nose and the frightened night-time eyes of his father, Alexei Iosifovich, or perhaps even of his grandfather, Iosif Chaimovich, and with an expression on his face of overwhelming love in the Slavic manner, seeing and feeling all this, the prophetess Pelagia decided to fight the sin by allowing it to take place and reveal itself, to fight Satan by meeting him halfway . . .

Incidentally we should note that for a long time the prophetess Pelagia herself had been tormented by womanly urges and had experienced to the full the impact of the Lord's third plague in her own body. It was as a result of the attempt to rape her in the forest near Bor town when she was still a young girl that she had been granted a sign of her status as a prophetess, and she remembered this. She also knew that her heroism in maintaining her virginity as she was now doing for the sake of the Lord was further reinforced by Satan, an inevitable participant in every one of the Lord's perilous dramas . . . At first, when Pelagia was still an adolescent, a sense of shame and daughterly love for her father had helped, and that had been the easiest time of her struggle. But when she had started reading the Bible and the Gospels and praying frequently, for some reason it had become especially difficult for her to keep her vow. She found it easy to reject those who wooed her and no great struggle was involved in that: for the most part these people were members of her own circle, since she and her father, a janitor working for the local housing management unit, did not have a large number of acquaintances . . . But in the period that was the most difficult, from the age of twenty-five to thirty, she had on several occasions encountered men who were dangerous for her . . .

On one occasion the housing management unit sent Pelagia out of the city to work on the potato harvest and the driver who took her to the procurement center in the cabin of his truck attempted to rape her. Obviously there was something extremely feminine about her that could provoke an intemperate individual to violence . . . They fought in a little wood, where they had gone to get a breath of fresh air, and the prophetess Pelagia suddenly felt a desire to allow him to overpower her. And Satan, who was standing close by and had his own plans, saw this and understood everything. This driver was a well-known village hooligan, who had spent time in jail for stabbing someone with a knife, but he was handsome. He had already raped several women in the village, but they had been afraid to report him. He didn't like simply to rape, he liked to frighten and mock first, and especially so this time, when this woman was entirely in his power, alone with him in the wood in the evening. Of course he did not see Satan standing beside the prophetess. However when the driver struck Pelagia in the face and grabbed hold of her, Pelagia did not want to use her powers as a prophetess, she preferred to use her own human strength. For when Pavlov had tried to rape her she was still a weak, young girl, but now she had filled out and become a sturdy woman of the Russian north. She kicked the driver in the belly and walked away in her torn blouse, covering her exposed breasts with her hands. That was how she escaped from temptation the first time. On the second occasion everything ought to have gone amicably, she had taken a liking to a good man who was handsome, although he was a war invalid. Everything happened quickly this time too, indeed the main danger lay in the quickness of it. Everything about the wooing was fine, that was all in good order, and her vow of chastity stood strong in the face of that good order. She was only afraid of disorder and chance occurrences. And a chance occurrence began at someone's wake that she attended with her father the Antichrist. Her father Dan, the Viper, the Antichrist left early to deal with his janitorial duties and Pelagia went to accompany this invalid home. At the wake, of course, there had been tears and although the dead person had not been a close acquaintance of hers, her soul had been mollified. She was in this condition as they walked along, and he was not escorting her, but she was escorting him, since there was black ice and he had an artificial leg and a stick. They reached his house and he started asking the prophetess to come in:

"Come on, Rufina, let's take some tea after the cold . . ."

Then there was everything that men usually do in this kind of situation . . . She went in and he started showing her his photographs of himself with the dead man at the front. He wept as he showed them to her, his face became absolutely like a child's, she felt sorry for him because he had sacrificed his male youth to the war and now didn't have all the attributes of a complete man. And once again she wanted to let herself be overpowered. And Satan was there beside her just like the other time. They put the light out beforehand: the invalid obviously felt embarrassed by his disfigurement and his stump in front of the young woman . . . The prophetess Pelagia had already lain down and suddenly in the darkness her hand snagged the invalid's stick and it fell with a clatter, and this noise brought the prophetess back to herself from the place where she had gone to for a minute or two as she lay on a pillow beside somebody else's tense body, which she had to rescue from this state of tension while also rescuing herself . . . She instantly got up off the pillow, for now everything that had happened had already taken the form of a complete story before anything irremediable had happened. And as soon as it all took the form of a complete story, order was restored, and as soon as order was restored, the vow of virginity that she had sworn to the Lord was restored. The prophetess got dressed, apologized to the invalid and left, only she asked him not to turn the light on until she had gone and she made her way out by groping. She was twenty-seven at the time and since then it had seemed to her that her chastity was especially secure and not susceptible to temptations. However temptations had recently started appearing again, first in her dreams and then in waking life. And that was why, as she stood in the dark orchard beside a sinner who was in love with her, the prophetess decided to fight against sin by meeting sin halfway, by meeting Satan halfway, but nonetheless without breaking her vow of chastity.

"All right," she said, "I'll give you some of my blood for an experiment."

Then he asked if he could kiss her hand. And she permitted that too. But he did not dare to go on to ask anything more and they walked out of the orchard.

"Rufina, perhaps we could stay the night here," Savelii said. "It's a big dacha and they could find a room for you."

"No," said the prophetess, "my father is at home alone . . . And I miss him . . ."

"Then I'll go too, we can leave without saying goodbye, my mother will understand, and otherwise she would only delay us. But how can we call Andrei out?"

"Andrei left a long time ago," Rufina-Pelagia said. "I saw him go."

"He's suffering," said Savelii, "I feel sorry for him."

"But you don't feel sorry for Vasya," Rufina-Pelagia said unexpectedly, "and after all, he's suffering too."

"Vasya?" Savelii echoed in surprise. "You know, I've known him for a very long time. He's dangerous, he lives a strange kind of life, it's as if he's reproaching everybody else for offending him in some way. I'm afraid of him," Savelii admitted, "he's an antisemite, he's a terrible, sick, disturbed kind of antisemite."

"But he really does look very much like my father, doesn't he?" asked the prophetess Pelagia.

"Definitely," said Savelii. "I've been thinking about that myself. It's probably because southern Ukrainians have a very large admixture of Turkish blood. By the way, he knows how much he resembles a Jew and suffers very badly as a result. If his appearance was different, perhaps he would be a goodhearted young man and a calmer antisemite. Today near the Tretyakov Gallery he was too agitated and the way he hit Somov was too stupid. He could have hit Somov more intelligently, he deserves it. Vasya isn't stupid all the time, after all: when he gets carried away with something and seems to forget about himself, then his kindness shows through and he's pleasant to be with. But today he really did go too far."

And this was true. Ever since they parted at the Tretyakov Gallery, after he shouted about the Yiddish gang and the Yiddish God, Vasya had been unable to settle down and he had walked and walked, hoping to get tired and become calm. But he hadn't got tired and he hadn't become calm. And he couldn't understand what was wrong with him: whether his hatred of Jews had driven him to a nervous breakdown or he had fallen in love with the blue-eyed Jewess. Vasya had always regarded women more calmly and rationally than Savelii and Andrei, and he thought of being in love and heaving heartfelt sighs as unmanly, Jewish, weak things. Vasya used to have a wife, a scullery maid, from whom he had got divorced and now he had a girl who was an English teacher at the school located opposite his house . . . And now this morning disaster had struck. Vasya knew where Savelii lived and he had heard that the Jewess whom he couldn't get out of his mind lived in the same apartment.

"I'll go," Vasya decided, "I should have gone a long time ago. I'll raise hell at that Yiddess Rufina's place, calm down and forget about her."

First of all Vasya called in to the famous restaurant at the Writers' Center, where the privileged literary fraternity was permitted to breathe the piquant aroma of decomposing meat and stale, sour tomato sauce . . . Seating himself at the table of a rich Jewish songwriter, who was very much afraid of Vasya's scandalous escapades, and whom Vasya had actually struck during the May Day celebrations the year before last, he drank three hundred grams of gratuitous vodka and ate a single gratuitous sprat. Vasya did not eat much. From the Writers' Center to the boulevard where the Jewess lived was only a stone's throw and Vasya walked quickly, but three hundred grams of gratuitous vodka worked even more quickly to disassemble and distort God's world in front of his eyes. And so Vasya arrived at the house on the boulevard. It was an old, genteel, prerevolutionary house and Vasya thought there was a sweet Yiddish odor on the staircase. However, one floor higher up people were crudely making merry, reciting rhyming ditties loudly for all the world to hear, and that reassured him, it meant the Yids were under pressure, they weren't being allowed to prevail . . . With eyes that were watering for some reason he located the apartment he needed and rang the bell. Someone opened the door.

"Can I see Rufina? . . . Is Rufinochka at home? . . . The girl Rufinochka?" Vasya began, slurring his words, and immediately stopped short.

What he saw in the doorway astounded him. He saw his own image, grown old, illuminated by the feeble yellow glow of the light bulb in the corridor. Vasya saw himself as an elderly Jew with gray hair and a stooped Jewish back. It was Rufina's father, Dan, the Viper, the Antichrist who had opened the door.

"Rufina's not at home," said the Antichrist, glancing at Vasya and recognizing him too.

This was his firstborn, conceived on the seashore near Kerch with Maria, the kind soul and juvenile fornicatress from Shagaro-Petrovskoe village in the Dymytrov district of the Kharkiv region. Then the Antichrist opened the door wider and Vasya from the tribe of Dan, the bad seed, walked in. Father and son sat at the table, facing each other, and looked. And the longer they looked at each other, the more they recognized each other.

"Well now," said the Antichrist, "tell me, son, about how you have reviled your own Jewish God."

"You're lying, you Yid," Vasya shouted. "My father's a Ukrainian . . . A Ukrainian with an admixture of Turkish blood. And my mother came from Shagaro-Petrovskoe village. And my God is the Orthodox God. And I hate the Yiddish God. And I hate your filthy Yiddish bread." He grabbed a piece of bread that was lying on the table and flung it onto the floor.

And that bread really was the impure bread of exile bequeathed by the prophet Jeremiah. And then the Jewish eyes of the Antichrist were transformed as a light was kindled in them, the light that destroys, the light that the prophetess Pelagia had acquired from her foster father. And at the very same time that her father's eyes lit up, her eyes also lit up many kilometers away from that place, in the darkness of the dacha's apple orchard. When the Antichrist's eyes lit up and the room was illuminated by a nebulous flickering light, now cherry-red, now crimson and as dark as the rays from a cloud in the late evening sky, Vasya was frightened, and his heart, which only an instant earlier had been self-assured in the Slavic style, started trembling as it felt for the first time the genuine, the only Jewish guilt before this fallen world, the name of which is Defenselessness. Vasya got up and started walking away, but his father did not accompany him. He opened the door of the apartment himself and walked out onto the landing. At that moment a door swung open on the floor above, where they were making merry in crude fashion, and every one of the rowdy, red-faced boors who were there strolled out onto the landing. This was the maneuver known as "the men have gone out for a smoke." And one of the boors said to Vasya:

"Where are you going, Yid, have your eyes fallen out of your head?"

Vasya didn't answer and he didn't remember how he got home after that. But when he got home, he started looking for something to hang himself with. At first he was going to hang himself with the belt from his trousers, but then he realized that the belt might break under the weight and in the dust under the bath he found a washing line that had been lying there for goodness only knew how long, perhaps it was left over from the previous occupants of the apartment and had been waiting for Vasya in order to fulfil its destined purpose. He formed the rope into a noose and started searching for a hook, but he couldn't find a good hook either in the room or in the kitchen, and there wasn't a firm nail either, or a hammer, because Vasya lived in a haphazard, unorganized manner. He lived with dirty bottles and jars on the windowsill, with dirty socks on the steam heating radiator, with heaps of garbage swept into all the corners and apart from two icons, "Christ the Savior" and "St. Nicholas the Wonderworker," Vasya didn't have any objects of value.

"They'll bury me with the money from these icons," Vasya thought, "if they go for a good price, probably to foreigners, and they'll be able to put up a cross. I'll write a note to Aunty Ksenia asking her to sell the icons to pay for my funeral and the cross on my grave."

Vasya sat down at the table with the washing line coiled onto his arm and wrote a note to Ksenia, and then immediately wrote a request for whoever might discover his death to send a telegram to Voronezh to Ksenia Korobko, married surname Gusakova, and added the address. And also a letter to the Dymytrov District in the Kharkiv Region, to the Meadow Farmstead at Shagaro-Petrovskoe village, to Alexandra Korobko, married surname Nalivaiko. After adding a crumpled three-ruble bill to complete his preparations, he started looking for a hook again. Not finding one, he decided to simply throw himself off the balcony, but felt ashamed at the idea of provoking the merry clamoring of idle gawkers and attracting a stupid crowd. Then he carried on searching and found a hook after all in the corner by the window: it was enveloped in cobwebs and had been painted over when the walls were whitewashed. The previous occupants had obviously used this hook to support a rail on which they had hung heavy curtains. After making sure that the hook was firm, he wetted a piece of soap under the tap, lathered up the rope and dropped the soap right there, in the middle of the room. Vasya prepared the noose, set a rickety stool in place, felt severe cramps in his belly, got up onto the stool, urinated on the floor and as he jumped with the noose round his neck he stepped on the edge of the stool, making it fall over. The noose instantly drew tight, Vasya croaked and started wheezing and died squalidly, emitting a crude Kharkiv region fart from his entrails.

In this way was the rotten seed of the Antichrist, the Lord's emissary, rejected.

Vasya was found three days later by his neighbors and of course he frightened them. It is impossible in any case for a hanged man not to frighten people, but in this case the fright was reinforced by the following occurrence. After the neighbors had already shouted out and gasped and phoned the militia and called an ambulance without touching the dead man, suddenly, before the authorities arrived, right there before the eyes of the jostling crowd of people from various different apartments, the rope snapped, Vasya fell onto the floor and a thin little sprocket wheel, like one from a large pocket watch, seemed to roll out of him before describing a semicircle, then trembling and trembling before finally settling dolwn and lying flat. The strangeness of Vasya's death ended with that. Ksenia and Shura arrived, having been summoned by the telegrams, ordered a coffin and booked some musicians.

As quite often happens to women who are dissolute in their youth, Ksenia had turned into a kind, warm-hearted, childless old woman. She was a rich widow, who lived on the financial resources left to her by her husband in her own little house with a garden on the outskirts of Voronezh. For Vasya she had always been a kind of guardian. Remembering his mother, her sister

Maria who had come to live with her as a young girl in the hungry year of 1933, but whom she had sent back to her village because of a family scandal, Ksenia had tried her best to do good for Vasya. Ksenia organized the funeral at her own expense, and Shura didn't give a single kopeck. But then Shura didn't even have a single kopeck. Shura still lived as she had done before, almost never leaving Shagaro-Petrovskoe village, and she was poor, with a large number of children who had grown up and done poorly in life, and her glance was still as angry, stupid and tormented as ever. Vasya's old coat, Vasya's patched sandals, Vasya's blackened kettle: she bundled it all up and took it away with her to her home in Shagaro-Petrovskoe. Ksenia took only the two icons of Christ the Savior and St. Nicholas the Wonderworker for herself. She was going to take them home with her, but on the advice of one of the neighbors she sold them for a good price to a man with a beard, naturally paying her adviser a fee for his help.

The moment came when Vasya was carried out. And when Vasya was carried out, the ignominy of a poor death was immediately apparent. In the early working hours of a summer day the strains of a funeral march played by several musicians who had been hired suddenly rang out amidst the workaday tedium. The wreaths were carried out, and also the coffin lid, which was not balanced on the bearers' shoulders, but on their heads. Finally they carried out the dead man with an unintelligent expression on his face, like most people who are lying in a coffin. If people say: "The deceased had an intelligent expression," then they are deceiving themselves, remembering the time when the person was still alive and dear to them.

There were not many people at the funeral. A few old men and women and some young people, obviously neighbors. There amongst them was Andrei Koposov, who had learned about Vasya's death and come to see his brother off. For while he did not know, in some strange way he sensed that Vasya was his brother, although a shameful, unsuccessful brother . . . And that was indeed the case, of which he would be convinced later. But the father of Vasya and Andrei, the Antichrist, and his adopted daughter, the prophetess Pelagia, watched the funeral from a distance.

Vasya's funeral was jolly, which was the work of jolly children. There was a school located opposite Vasya's house and he was known there, perhaps because on several occasions he had visited it when drunk to see the English language teacher Ekaterina Anastasievna . . . This teacher was either not in Moscow just at the moment or she had taken a dislike to Vasya because of one of the wild escapades for which he was notable when alive. It was clear that the street knew about his escapades and the young pupils found them amusing. And so now the young pupils joyfully flocked to the funeral. Adolescent girls joined hands, jumped up and down and shouted:

"They're burying Garlic, they're burying Garlic . . ."

Apparently Vasya's nickname here was "Garlic." A mischievous boy, wishing to amuse the girls, ran up close to him and then recoiled, screwing up his face and said:

"Yuck, he stinks."

The children ran to and fro across the street.

"There's a coffin over there," they shouted, enjoying themselves.

After all, children are not sensitive, for they have not yet been worn down by a consciousness of reality, they have to grow, their hearts are still strong and crude, like the roots of young plants growing into the ground. But two female workers in white coats came out of a laundry close by and, listening to the strains of the funeral march, they looked at someone else's coffin and wiped away their tears. To them life no longer seemed to be endless, as it did to these young boys and girls, and for them every death was a threat. They were feeling wounded and sorry for themselves.

Then the Antichrist, the father of this firstborn rejected by the Lord, spoke these words from the sixth psalm of David:

"Turn to me, Lord, and deliver my soul, save me for the sake of your grace."

And the Antichrist's adopted daughter, the prophetess Pelagia, continued:

"For in death there is no remembrance of you; in the coffin who will give you praise?"

However the Antichrist did not yet know that his daughter was a prophetess, he thought she had studied the Psalms well. And he praised her.

In the meantime the late Vasya was loaded onto a truck and driven away to be buried. Only a few people accompanied him to the cemetery; Ksenia, and Shura, and several people hired by Ksenia for money, who held the wreaths. The only person who saw off his brother Vasya without payment was Andrei Koposov, the son of the Antichrist and Vera Koposova from Bor town in the Gorky Region. Vasya's funeral was poorly attended and humiliating, but only several days later people suddenly started speaking about Vasya as a literary talent who had died tragically before his time. Lunches and dinners in the literary restaurant were transformed into wakes, everybody's hearts were mellowed and for several days they treated each other considerately.

However there were people of a different kind too. Vasya's death also affected them, but in a different kind of way. They retreated even more determinedly into their pose of "Who is trying to destroy Russia?" with their cheeks propped on their hands, occasionally clenching their jaw muscles and gazing at the wine-soaked tablecloth. Andrei Koposov also glanced round, looked at these various individuals, who had achieved everything, or at least very much, and he realized that in the natural way of things, sooner or later he would see these individuals in the obituaries too. "Whoever lives, will die," he thought, "but I am not living, and neither shall I die." He simply impressed that on himself: "I shall not die, and that's that." He impressed a sinful thought on himself. For he already knew a great deal about himself. He knew that he was the son of the Antichrist, the emissary of the Lord, although he realized this obscurely, as if in his sleep. And soon his mother, the pious old woman Vera Koposova, informed him of it.

After the passions that had erupted in her life, she had taken to reading the Gospels and aged quickly, and now looked much older than her fifty-something years. Ten years older, if not even more. When she put on her cheap old-woman's eyeglasses with a metal frame and picked up the Gospels her face took on a foolishly solemn expression, and her nape was like the back of a domestic animal's neck as it peers curiously at some human object or other.

The face of a thinking individual reading a profound book is very beautiful. On the contrary, however, the face of a non-thinking person reading a book that genuinely agitates them irrationally, according to some external impulse, often loses all its human features and the features of an animal, always unpleasant on a human face, show through on it. Something monkey-like showed through on Vera's face when she read the Gospels. But at the same time, while being stupid in her thoughts, Vera could sometimes be surprisingly intelligent in her words. When she came to visit her son, Andrei decided to take his old mother to Red Square, a place to which former provincials often take their provincial relatives in order to inspire them with respect for their present situation.

On that day Andrei had a pre-examination consultation at the Institute, so he and his mother arrived at Red Square early, when the sun was still rising. In the daytime the center of Moscow is irritating and noisy, but the quiet dawn over the Kremlin is more festively solemn than any church prayer services. The early pink radiance of the heavens lies on the old stones of the Kremlin. Rus is pensive in these moments and the human soul feels at ease there, as comfortable as if it is in its own ancestral home, and whoever comes to Rus at such times sees her as a mother for whom there are no friends or strangers, a mother who will take compassion on everyone, like the Mother of God . . . These minutes of spiritual peace and unity in the summer dawn on Red Square are brief. The pealing of the bells of the clock in the Kremlin's Savior Gate Tower rings out high in the crystal-blue, ceremonial sky and soldiers marching in close formation over the echoing cobblestones as if they are under under the high vaults of a church, perform the ritual of changing the military guard of honor at the Marxist Holy Sepulcher, Lenin's Mausoleum.

Andrei Koposov and his mother stood and watched as all this was taking place. Looking round, Andrei suddenly saw tears in his mother's eyes, the tears that flow without a person realizing or noticing them.

"What's wrong, Mom?" Andrei Koposov asked, "this is the changing of the guard at Lenin's Mausoleum. It happens several times every day."

"What great honor for a man," Vera Koposova said quietly with tears in her voice: she was constantly oppressed by her own sin and and the sins of all people, "what honor for a man." And she spoke these intelligent words without thinking with her reason.

This is how genuine national character manifests itself. In Rus the term "national character" had long ago become an idol. Its meaning had been canonized by the Slavophile intelligentsia: national character is the common people. The Slavophiles also have their own Bible, which they study with the meticulousness of fanatical monks, in which they believe unconditionally, and which they vainly boast about and counterpose to the Bible of the Jews in disputes.

"You have the Bible, but we have the Russian village: there, that is our Bible. And you cannot possibly understand our Bible."

Here we see the influence of that same old mystical dream of the Slavs about halting history. Here is that sharp mind Herzen with his absurd hopes for the *obshschina*. Here is that prophet of the dependent Russian intelligentsia, Dostoevsky, who supposedly discovered national character in its finest form among convicts. However what is national character, not according to Dostoevsky, but according to Pushkin? According to Pushkin, "national character" is not the common folk, but what is truly national. National character in a writer is a virtue that can be thoroughly appreciated only by his compatriots. According to Pushkin, the aristocrat Racine is national for a Frenchman, but not national for a German. As always, Pushkin expresses himself with the clarity of genius, however even his prophetic genius could not grasp what had not yet been said by the Lord through the passage of time. For time is the Lord's language, in which he speaks with man. In Pushkin's time the national question was not yet a tragic question. In Pushkin's time there was no such tragic conceptualization of the people's problems as exists now. And genuinely national character also existed in great amounts, it seemed to be available on tap, like the mineral resources of our planet. Then who drained it all, who exhausted it? It was emptied out by national consciousness, through which the people started rising to become the leaders of history. The popular instinct is fruitful: that massive, eternal reason of our grandfathers and great-grandfathers in which a man seems to act in his own way and speak in his own way, but in reality his great-grandfather spoke in that way and his grandfather acted in that way: a reason in which man does not speak his own thoughts, but what is general and eternal. As soon as a man starts speaking his own thoughts, while being devoid of culture, he immediately becomes fruitless. The people cannot teach, but it is possible to learn from the people, in order afterwards to explain the people to themselves. This is the sacred duty of the individual personality. The people are not capable of understanding their own fruitful instinct with their own fruitless awareness, if only because in order to understand their own national instincts, they would have to possess a supranational, panhuman consciousness. When the people attempt to understand their own profound instincts with their own low level of awareness, this produces the bast-sandals-and-rhyming-jingles philosophy that is worshipped by the Slavophiles in Russia. And the end product of such popular consciousness is the roguish bandit and rascally politician or oppositionist. But it is even worse when culture, which is duty-bound to serve the people by explaining them to themselves, that is, by explaining national character to the people, attempts in a cowardly, slavish fashion to learn from the people the truth about itself, about culture and about the individual personality. In so doing, it corrupts the people and by paying homage to the people's fruitless awareness it destroys the people's inherent instinct. Not much of it now remains; it has only been preserved here and there, where shared sacred words are born out of individual unawareness, where a person thinks stupidly but speaks intelligently . . . If Russia succeeded in creating a great culture in the 19th century it was thanks to the fact that the reforms of Peter the Great tore the intelligentsia away from the people, and that, while drawing upon the fruitful ocean of national instinct, culture was not enslaved by the people's level of awareness. It was only later, near the end of the century, thanks to the efforts of non-gentry intellectual dissenters, that the people's awareness started to enslave culture and the disciples of these denouncers carried this process through to its extreme limit.

This was what Andrei Koposov thought as he sat in his consultation and recalled his mother's words. In the Literary Institute, which was formerly Herzen House, the house of a man who advocated the rural *obshchina* as the savior of Russia, the summer refurbishment was already in progress, there was a smell of paint, the corridors were cluttered with furniture and the floor was covered with newspapers. The conference hall, where the educational process of training disciples of socialist realism continued, as yet remained untouched. After thinking for a while about something of his own and cursorily jotting down a few notes and remarks on a sheet of paper, Andrei tried to listen to what people around him were saying, but so much that was being said on all sides was spoken in that self-same spirit of Slavophilism and national consciousness and the well-known poet who was leading the consultation, a man with a purely Russian pseudonym, spoke so loudly in his indigenous Ryazan manner that Andrei's attention wandered and he started looking around himself. The conference hall was decorated with pieces of literature from all peoples of all times, exactly like separate organs extracted from a body. For a long time Andrei had wondered what they resembled, all these book jackets displayed on the stands that completely covered all four walls: classics of the past and books that were called classics nowadays, and simply first-rate, second-rate and third-rate books. There were profiles and silhouettes on every side. And Andrei realized that this was a literary dissecting room, a morgue for separate parts of the body: quotations and bindings preserved in alcohol, like livers, lungs, hands and feet pickled in glass jars. Parts of the body preserved in alcohol have less in common with a human being than a stone in the street or a branch of a tree. A stone or a branch of a tree bear a greater resemblance to a man than his own liver or lungs that have been extracted from him. These pieces of literature in the literary dissecting room were just as distant from literature. And in general there was something medical and scientific about this entire institution, where literature was like a creature subjected to experimentation, a guinea pig tormented by researchers, where the role of literature was to be sacrificed in the name of human wellbeing, in accordance with the humanistic principles of socialist realism.

Having finished his classes, Andrei Koposov hurried home, since he and his mother still had to visit many more places where provincials obtained commodities that were in short supply. For Varfolomei Vesyolov, his sister Tasya's son, they had to buy a pair of jeans: for Tasya, the former beloved of Andrei's father, the Antichrist, concerning which Andrei knew nothing, they had to buy a slip: for the old sentry woman Sergeevna, the mother of Tasya's husband, they had to buy natural lump sugar for tea, which was impossible to find in Bor town: for Ustya's children they had to buy underwear and treats and also, if they could, canned meat for reserve supplies and oranges and lemons, sacred fruits for a real indulgence. However when Andrei got back home he discovered that everything had already been bought, neatly packed in white, gray and blue wrapping paper or colorful paper bearing a shop's trademark and tied round with string. And there was a string bag full of the sacred fruits, oranges and lemons. And his mother Vera, dressed in a clean little white dress, was sitting and reading the Gospels, with a cunning, joyful and mysterious look on her face.

"Now son, guess who was here and helped me do the shopping . . ."

"Why, do you actually know anyone in Moscow, Mom?"

"Yes I do, and they know me," said Vera. "I didn't want to tell you about it straightaway, I felt awkward. But the Old Believer Chesnokova, the very old woman who lives at house number 30 on Derzhavin Street, happens to write to her old lodgers. She gave me the address of Dan Yakovlievich and his daughter Rufina. And I asked your neighbor, such a very nice woman, to call them on the phone . . . Rufina came in a jiffy. And she invited me to visit them, here's the address . . ."

"I know this address," he said, "and I know Rufina too, I love her, Mom, and I can't hide it any longer."

At this point the cunning look on his mother Vera's face disappeared and a solemnly stupid expression, like the one with which she read the Gospels, appeared in its place.

"Well now, you're in an awkward situation, son," said Vera, crossing herself with short, swift movements, "You're so restless and unpredictable, how can you possibly love your own sister? Your sin will be forgiven, because you didn't know, but my sin is that I didn't tell you. Oh, I am mired deep in sin."

"What on earth are you saying, Mom?" asked Andrei, surprised and frightened. "Is she really your daughter?"

"She's not my daughter, but she's your father's daughter . . . Your father is Dan Yakovlevich, a Jew . . . That means you're not Russian . . . It's no accident that our relatives through Tasya don't like you, the Vesyolovs are an old Volga region family, they don't like Jews . . . Especially Sergeevna, she has a forest creature's nose for Jews, even though she's so advanced in age. So I confess my fault to you, son, and ask you to forgive my grave sin."

And she tried to go down on her knees in front of her son, but Andrei caught hold of her in time and said:

"Don't say that, Mom. It doesn't matter whose son I really am, I'm just afraid I need a bit of time to get used to it. Come on, Mom, let's sit and hold each other, perhaps I'll get used to it sooner that way."

They put their arms round each other and sat like that until the evening. In the evening Andrei Koposov said:

"I'll go to see my father."

"Thank you for that, son," said Vera. "And I'll go with you, although he's not my husband in people's eyes, he is in the eyes of God."

When they arrived Rufina met them in the hallway and said in a quiet voice:

"Our father is marking a sad occasion today. The Jewish fast of Shivah Asar B'Tammuz has begun, the fast to commemorate the smashing of the tablets of the covenant..."

When they walked into the apartment and Vera Koposova, the prayerful old woman, saw the object of her last passion, grown old and gray, with a back stooped by the centuries, her head started spinning as if she was still young and she said:

"Is this you, my darling, here I am, your sweetheart... And this is your son Andrei, not named for you, but born to you..."

The mother and father, who had not seen each for a long time, embraced; the son and the father, who had never seen each other, embraced; the brother and the sister, who had seen each other, but had not known how they were related and had almost committed a sin because of it, also embraced... And then the time came to light the candles. For the lighting of the candles on the eve of a religious date always takes place at a strictly determined time.

And so Dan, the Viper, the Antichrist, the emissary of the Lord met the fast in the company of his earthly family. Here is the listing of this holy family. By her anonymous mother, who was being dispatched into German slavery in a railroad freight car, the prophetess Pelagia, who was born in Bryusany village near Rzhev town, was handed to the Antichrist as an infant girl. Through fornication, the third plague of the Lord, Vera Koposova became part of this holy family, as Tamar became a member of the holy family of Judah through fornication. And in Bor town Vera gave birth to the Antichrist's son Andrei, his good seed. But his bad seed, his firstborn Vasya, conceived with Maria

Korobko close to Kerch city, was renounced and rejected and became a lost brother for evermore . . . For not all the fragments of the Chalice shall be glued back together, some shall be rejected, although through the power of God the Chalice shall be as new . . .

The fast of Shivah Asar B'Tammuz, the fast of the 17th day of Tammuz, was one of the saddest, for it was an occasion of mourning, not for external coercion, of which there had been much in Jewish history, but for internal wrongdoing committed by the people against their own selves when they rejected their own God and insulted their prophet Moses, who in his wrath and anguish disavowed the irrational nation and smashed the tablets of the covenant. Then there had followed an intense dialogue between the Lord and Moses. Every time Moses attempted to disavow his ungrateful people, the Lord sought to persuade him to overcome his righteous wrath, not in the name of the people, who were as depraved as other peoples, but in the name of fulfilling the prophecy of the prophet. And when the Lord wished to disavow the people, Moses sought to dissuade Him, again not in the name of the people, but in the name of God's plan, which was connected with this people. In this way, during the interval between the first set of tablets and the second, a highly authentic and simple relationship was firmly established between Moses and the people. And it was declared: "The tablets were the work of God, and the writing was the writing of God, engraved on the tablets."

When Moses and Joshua the son of Nun approached the camp, Joshua said:

"There is a noise of war in the camp."

But Moses said:

"It is not the sound of shouting for victory, or the sound of the cry of defeat, but the sound of singing that I hear."

This was the way, with singing and dancing around a golden calf, a pagan idol, that the people disavowed God. And in this way art, the gift of God, was turned against Him who had given it. This was a double sin, for apart from art man has nothing divine. Science is a human business, essential and necessary for the provision of human comforts. It has no need for God, there cannot be a religious science and there should not be. Philosophy is also a human business, like science, and the reason for its existence is clear: philosophy is necessary to a rational being for intellectual exercise. Just as a squirrel in a wheel achieves the useful result of preserving its muscles through the pointless activity of running, so does philosophy preserve the strength of the intellectual muscles necessary for the provision of human comforts and the struggle for existence. Therefore religious philosophy essentially serves the same purpose as atheistic philosophy and any coherent attempt to apprehend the nature of God via philosophy inevitably leads to atheism. Nor is it possible to apprehend the nature of God via morality, since every consistent moralist, even one like Leo Tolstoy, must answer the notorious questions concerning morality: "Why is man mortal and why is evil triumphant in God's world and within the limits of human life?"

But there is something that is not necessary for or comprehensible as a means for the provision of human comforts and the struggle for existence, quite the opposite in fact, for it often counterbalances the effect of science, reducing physical capabilities, and counterbalances the effect of philosophy, not always increasing intelligence and obscuring the eternal questions by exploiting morality to oppose them. It was born on the seventh day of Creation, when the Lord asked man to give names to everything that He had created . . .

In this way the Lord began his game with man, and man called this game art. What is art, if not the instinctive imitation of the Creator? Of course, it is not possible to see God and comprehend His nature through art either. For after all the Lord told Moses: "You cannot see my face, for man shall not see me and live." But art is the tongue of flame that Moses saw in the burning bush, deep in the desert by Mount Horeb, when he was still a totally unknown shepherd. Not even great art can apprehend the nature of God, but it is a sign, like the tongue of flame in the burning bush. A sign that God is present. When the human soul is amazed and enlightened by art it means that God is nearby and you should not waste your opportunity, as the shepherd Moses did not waste his own amazement. In these moments the Lord allows you to speak with him directly, tête-à-tête, for the prophet Isaiah said: "Do not always speak with the Lord, but only when the Lord is nearby . . ." However, in order not to miss your moment when God is nearby, you need to have at least a particle of the talent that Moses possessed when he said: "I will turn aside to see this great sight, why the bush is not burned . . ."

And in the holy family of the Antichrist, the emissary of the Lord, everyone was endowed with such a particle of talent, no one missed their moment. Neither the prophetess Pelagia, nor Vera Koposova, nor Andrei Koposov. But the bad seed Vasya, born of Maria Korobko, was repudiated.

When they were saying their farewells before leaving, Vera Koposova raised her eyes to look at her husband and suddenly asked:

"Is that you, Lord?"

He replied:

"Do not call me Lord, for we have only one Lord. We shall all come and go. For what difference does it make how we are banished to the next world, whether it is by hopeless external circumstances or by our own cunning wiles."

And having spoken in this way they said their farewells. And each of them started living their own life. Vera, the wife of the Antichrist, having become even more stupid in her thoughts and more intelligent in her words, took with her to Bor town the bundles of things that had been bought and the sacred fruits, the oranges and lemons; Andrei, the son of the Antichrist, completed his course of study and went to take a break from his musings in the capital beside his mother; the prophetess Pelagia set about fulfilling the promise she had made to Savelii, who was dreaming of using her virginal blood in an experiment to create philosophical homunculi; the Antichrist, awaiting instructions from the Lord, continued working for the housing maintenance office as a janitor and Vasya, the rejected seed, lay in the cemetery, surrounded by the flowers that had been heaped on his grave by the numerous admirers who had suddenly appeared.

And so Pelagia gave a blood sample for analysis at the laboratory of the local health clinic and Savelii bought a test tube of her blood, illegally of course, from a nurse working as a laboratory assistant there who drank. In an equally illegal fashion he bought a test tube of his own blood, which he intended to mingle with the blood of the woman he loved, if only in a retort. Now he could attempt the experiment a second time. For he had concealed from the prophetess that he had already carried out a first attempt that had proved unsuccessful: he had bought from the dubious nurse in the laboratory the blood of a man and a woman whom he didn't know, mixed them together in the required proportions, added pure dew of the month of May, collected on Tverskaya Boulevard at dawn, covered all this with a solid lid and set it in a warm place to putrefy. However after he had filtered off the film that formed on top of the mixture, the menstruum, and transferred it to a different, clean flask, the bubble that should have testified to the conception of an artificial philosophical life had failed to form. And although Savelii was distressed about one thing, he was gladdened by another. No he wasn't gladdened because he had decided to abandon this fruitless and sinful activity. He was gladdened because he had had doubts in any case about the perilous idea of taking the blood for the experiment from people he didn't know. For it was written: "If the blood from which the Pater was prepared and from which the man and the woman grow was taken from unchaste individuals, then the man will be half a beast and the woman will also have a horrible appearance from below."

Now he was repeating the experiment after locking himself away in his room, for in his mother's room the scholar of antiquity Ilovaisky argued about Christ first with one, and then with another of his friends. Ilovaisky had recently moved in with them and become Savelii's stepfather, and now he argued about Christ while dressed in casual domestic style.

The scholar of antiquity Ilovaisky was barefooted, and in the course of the debate he walked to and fro, planting his geriatric white feet with a red flush on Klavdia's parquet flooring. His toes were not all afflicted with calluses to the same extent, but they were all unhealthy. He was wearing short, wide trousers of an indeterminate color and a salad green singlet with wide shoulder straps that kept slipping off his white, bony shoulders when he gesticulated. The singlet's armholes were so large that they exposed his sides and scraggy ribs and the singlet was shorter at the front because Ilovaisky's belly bulged out like a balloon from his skinny body.

"You see this chalice," he shouted, grabbing hold of a cup that smelled of vodka from the already half destroyed tea service that had been bought in Ivolgin's time. "But now I'll smash it against the floor and it will immediately become complicated . . ."

Savelii took a thermos flask of tea, some sandwiches with cheese and sausage, and locked himself away for the whole day, only emerging when he needed to relieve himself. Neither his stupid mother nor even the tactless Ilovaisky disturbed him. However as evening was falling someone knocked on his door.

It was a difficult, anxious evening. The experiment was approaching the stage at which it had ended in failure the last time. The blood had already been mixed in the proportion of two parts of his to three parts of Rufina's, it had already settled in a warm place under a tight lid, it had already been moistened with dew, although not dew of the month of May, which was rather worrying: the red earth had already sunk to the bottom, the menstruum had already been separated off and placed in a clean flask, and part of a tincture from the animal kingdom, a raw egg, had already been placed in this flask, but the embryonic bubble had not yet appeared.

When the knock on the door came, Savelii was sitting with his head clasped in his hands, feeling as if worms had infested the back of neck. He was about to cry out angrily and abuse his mother when he suddenly heard

Rufina's voice, the voice of the woman he loved, whose blood had participated in the experiment together with his own. His heart started pounding and his breathing quickened. Savelii unlocked the door.

"How stuffy it is in here," Rufina said as she walked in, beautiful and blue-eyed. "The window's closed . . ." And she opened the window wide.

The warmth of a moonlit July evening flitted gently into the blazing hot room like a bird and seemed to whisper something incomprehensible in Savelii's ear . . . In the center of stone-walled, sterile Moscow the scent of an apple suddenly appeared in the air, not the scent of a musty apple on a street fruit stall, but a living apple watered by the night rain. That is how life smells. And when this scent of life coincides with the glance of a beloved woman, this is already the insanity without which it is impossible to bear fruit. This insanity lifted up Savelii, tormented since his late childhood by his shamefaced, boy-recluse's sin, and bore him toward the woman with his arms outspread. However in the cramped room cluttered with flasks and test tubes, his foot caught on some object that he was unable to identify later and he fell, striking his knee hard. Rufina laughed and ran her sweet little hand over his hair, making him come out in goosebumps all over, as if he was standing in a cold wind, and walked out of the room. Savelii lay down on his bed without getting undressed and fell asleep, exhausted, without closing the window. He awoke suddenly, as if he had heard a shot. It was the scholar of antiquity Ilovaisky, who had slammed the front door. Having quarreled drunkenly with Klavdia and finding himself in a Voltairean condition, Ilovaisky had gone out to wander round the city. He walked into a metro station and took a seat in a train. No sooner did the train set off than Ilovaisky started furiously shaking his gray-haired head first to the left, then to the right, clutching his eyeglasses in his fist without their case and frightening the peaceful population around him with his yellow face. After getting out at the final stop, he set off, walking unsteadily in the crowd, but didn't get as far as the exit: he cast a sheep-eyed stare, moving his eyes down from the above to below, at some women sitting on one of the benches, sat down beside them in the narrow space at one edge and propped up his head, which seemed ready to tear itself off his neck, on his open hand.

However Savelii was not awoken for long and he sank back into a deep sleep. He had a dream that was appallingly comical at first and then simply appalling. First he dreamed that he was walking along a street and he saw the words: "I'll slit your throat" written on the fence in chalk. He walked round a corner and saw more words written in chalk: "Believe it, he'll slit your throat." Then he dreamed that he was vomiting a substance that looked like cotton wool and little pieces of this cotton wool were flying around him as he vomited. Making an effort and forcing himself to wake up, in the way that a drowning man forces himself to rise up to the surface, Savelii really did feel a wave of nausea surging upwards from his abdomen. He turned on the night lamp, got up and hastily walked over to the flask with the menstruum in it and the flask with the particle of a chicken's egg sprinkled with the menstruum of blood and dew. An embryonic bubble had risen upward, and there was not only a bubble, but something that had developed during the night, with veins. Then, with trembling hands and stiff fingers, numbed by his fear of dropping the flask, Savelii unsealed the menstruum and poured a small amount of it into the flask with the embryo, after first warming it on a little spirit lamp.

From that moment on Savelii's life lost all meaning for him except for the experiment. Adhering strictly to the instructions, he tried not to disturb the tightly sealed flask. He never left the building and turned pale-faced and put on weight because of his lack of physical activity. He watched as the mixture in the flask fermented and the bubble grew larger and larger. In the course of a month he poured in menstruum four times, each time increasing the dose. And then there came about what was foretold in the alchemical book. "After this time, when you hear something hissing and whistling, approach the flask and to your great joy and amazement you will see living creatures in it. If they are from chaste blood, you will take delight in them and look on them with heartfelt merriment. For they will be no taller than seven inches, and yet they will bestir themselves and move and walk to and fro across the flask. At the center a little tree will grow, hung with all kinds of fruits."

And all of this happened. From that time on Savelii added the menstruum through a little tube with a rubber clamp, for he knew that the air beathed by an ordinary person was harmful for the tiny man and woman living in his flask. Many herbs and trees grew around them, from which they fed themselves, and they regarded Savelii with fear and respect. Savelii decided to take advantage of this fear and respect to find out from the philosophical homunculi what he wanted to know. Savelii asked:

"What are the main ideas of the world?"

The little philosophical man replied, while the little philosophical woman sat beside him and caressed him affectionately.

"The main ideas are the idea of time and the idea of space. The idea of time is religious, the idea of space is atheistic. The idea of space gave birth to philosophy and science, the idea of time gave birth to religion and art. Later, however, incestuous mingling occurred. The idea of space is contemplative and in it man is capable of achieving the illusion of equality with God. The idea of time is active and in it man feels his weakness in the face of the future, his subjection to the future, and is in need of the help of God. Buddhism and antiquity are ideas of space. The Bible is an idea of time. After the chalice was smashed, the Christian world became less and less temporal and more and more spatial. In the idea of space, the idea of the real, the idea of beauty, genius achieves greatness, but nonetheless it attains to its true limit in the idea of time, the idea of the future."

Then Savelii asked:

"What is the philosophical world and what is the religious world?"

The man in the flask replied:

"The philosophical world is a world of unity, the religious world is a world of polarity. In the philosophical world everything emerges from Singleness and returns to Singleness. This is the world of the man-God. In the religious world the fundamental reality is forever divided by an abyss. This is God's world: heaven and earth, God and man, life and death . . . What is on this side of the abyss is accessible to understanding: what is on the other side of the abyss is accessible to conjecture. But the connections between God and man, heaven and earth, life and death are not accessible either to understanding or conjecture. The mingling of religious and philosophical concepts is an arbitrary method that is scientific and fruitful in particulars but obscures the essence . . ."

Then Savelii asked:

"What are the paths to God?"

The philosophical homunculus in the flask replied:

"The three paths to God are belief, disbelief and doubt. Belief is the simplest, most widespread and least secure path. It is the path of the church. Disbelief is the most dangerous path, although it is also fruitful. This is the path of those earthly geniuses who on their personal path to God sow atheism among the weak. The path of doubt is the path of righteous individuals, the path of Job. This the most laborious path, traveled in daily spiritual effort. It is a slow but secure path."

Then Savelii asked: "How can we distinguish good action from evil action, for in the world evil often wears a mask of good and good wears a mask of evil."

The homunculus in the flask replied:

"If what you do and what you teach is difficult for you, it means that you do good and teach good. If your teaching is easily accepted and what you do is easy for you, it means that you teach evil and do evil."

Then Savelii asked:

"What is truth?"

The homunculus replied:

"There is not one truth for man, and neither are there three truths. There are two truths, the genuine truth and its mirror reflection. It is not given to man to distinguish which of them is authentic and which is legendary: however you have to make a choice and in seeking the authentic truth not switch over to the legendary truth, and in seeking the legendary truth not switch over to the authentic truth. You must not disavow your own truth or seek a third, for it does not exist . . ."

At this point Savelii's conversation with the philosophical homunculus in the flask was broken off, since his mother called him to dinner and Savelii could not refuse, because he suddenly felt very hungry. As he left the room he saw the woman in the flask nestle against the little man, who was tired from all his talking, and start caressing him.

In the time of Alexei Iosifovich Ivolgin, whose portrait used to stand on the writing desk, but had now been hung on the wall, Klavdia had never been a good cook. Of course she could roast beef quite well, but the borshch she made was the army kind, with tough cabbage, and the main course was most often large saveloys or meat patties with macaroni. But Klavdia spoiled her new husband Ilovaisky, whom she adored, although she squabbled with him because of his bad character, with delicious food, saying as she did so with a a tear in her eye:

"And in the concentration camp he gorged himself on salted fish, he was half-starved."

She pampered him with various kinds of food, but she had had her greatest success with the national cuisine of Belarus. Sour cabbage soup with mushrooms or boiled buckwheat, Gomel-style liver, braised meat loaf with pork fat, onion and root vegetables, potato pancakes with pork, raw potatoes with pork, flour and root vegetables baked in the oven.

The food was delicious this time too and Savelii ate heartily in spite of his intense intellectual labors, and his headache eased off somewhat. However he remembered that he had not understood everything in the explanations of the little man in the flask and had not asked him everything. And therefore Savelii ate hastily, wiped his lips with a napkin after such a heavy, greasy meal, went back to his room and locked himself in.

"What is a kind man?" he asked the homunculus in the flask.

"A kind man is not a man of God," the homunculus replied. "There is nothing godly in kindness, it is too petty a feeling for God, but it is absolutely essential for sinful little man. Far more essential than truth and spiritual riches. The good and kindness are different things. A genius cannot be a kind man, for he serves God, a kind man cannot be a genius, for he serves man. A kind man rarely brings good into the world, for bad people gravitate to him, people who have dissipated themselves and lost themselves, and the kind man is not like a healer for them, he is like a sick-nurse for the spiritually incurable. A truly kind man is an anonymous righteous individual who is willing to practice complete self-renunciation and therefore the genius and the prophet cannot be kind men, for they would thereby sin against God by rejecting the divine quality that they have been granted from on high for the sake of imperfect and transient human matters. The appearance of good in the world is in no wise connected with kind people, but with the prophets, those healers and geniuses who are the accumulators of spiritual riches. The bitterness of truth and the pitiless clarity of genius heal the world, kindness does not. Kindness does not heal the world, but it comforts the sinful and rescues them from their loneliness, and therefore it reinforces the fallen world, it will not permit people to destroy themselves in the body, for kindness is not a spiritual feeling, but a corporeal one. It groans together with the sick, thirsts together with the thirsty, hungers together with the hungry and lends an ear to other people's repining and afflictions. People are drawn to it and make unconditional demands on it, especially since it is giving by nature. The world remains evil, but thanks to kindness they carry on living and are not destroyed by their own evil. The genuine Christian is a kind person of any religion, but the genuine Hebrew is a genius and prophet of any religion. Analyze any genius and you will discover a Judaic principle in him, even if he repudiates Judaism. Judaism is much closer to God than Christianity, and Christianity is closer to man. But a truly kind man, like a genius, is a rare phenomenon, and therefore there are few genuine Christians, just as there few genuine Hebrews. The majority of people merely call themselves something, most often by virtue of their birth, more rarely by virtue of their circumstances. The most important untruth of Christianity is its claim that you can serve God by serving man. It is a different matter that in the face of human sins the Lord approves this path too, although it is far from the divine. For after all the Lord has Himself changed His decisions several times, He created man without foreseeing the consequences. When He had created man and seen how that turned out, He decided to destroy His own creation. First he expelled man from the paradise of Eden, then He saw that this had only increased sin and decided to destroy life altogether. But after the first righteous man, Noah, the first Savior, whom God did not venture to destroy, and because of whom He saved the rest of the world too, the Lord realized that man's inability to love Him was not the result of his evil intent but of his paltry nature. Only geniuses and prophets are capable of such love. Then he decided to send a Messiah, Christ, in order to change the ideal of love for the sinful: if they cannot love God, let them at least love each other, And civilization was built on this ideal, which is not founded on geniuses or prophets, but on the kind man, who does not serve God. Being blind and irrational, he gives of himself to all equally, but the evil take from him more skillfully. And thus kindness propagates evil, for it does not obey God, but its own blind heart. Those who are most in need of kindness are the most cheated by it. Christianity built civilization because it deviated the most from God: thanks to the ideal of kindness it was able to entice into following it the most tenacious, strong, hungry and malign, that is, those who were short-changed most of all by this ideal. Only geniuses did not participate in this game, which is founded on the falsehood that by serving man you serve God. A man living by God's commandments, which are extremely simple, has no need of Christianity.

"But since a sinner is incapable of complying with 'You shall not murder,' 'You shall not steal, 'You shall not commit adultery,' he takes refuge in the vaguenesses of Christianity. The masses live according to habit and for the masses Christianity is a boon. But it is a tragedy for someone who tries to be a conscientious Christian. Although even here the tricksters find a way out: "I strive, but I am not ready." Christianity is an extremely dexterous game on the brink of atheism. Judaism is not capable of such a flexible game, it is too serious for that. In Christianity it is possible to believe strongly while being a nonbeliever and exploiting the advantages of this, for the Christian faith is extremely dialectical. Strife and searching in the eternal and the immutable, precisely where there should not be any strife or searching, such is the drama of the Christian life. At first glance it might seem that Christianity is an idealistic teaching that does not take human nature into account: man is evil, and it preaches idealistic good. In reality this is not so. An idealistic teaching is capable of creating a religion or a culture, but it is not capable of creating either mighty empires or earthly civilizations. And it is precisely Christianity that has exploited true human nature with immense skill. For the primary element of man is after all not evil, but frivolity. Extreme frivolity is the basis of Christian feeling, and it corresponds to a fallen world. It is clear that Christ was not a Christian and never even heard this word in his lifetime, but He understood what frivolous human nature required. It was not Christ but Christianity that built civilization. Christ Himself was a keen-minded, profound individual who associated with God. Christ considered himself a Jew and he was a Jew from the sect of Pharisees. But the serious accomplishment of Christianity is to have created the appearance of total change while essentially not changing anything at all in the evil, pagan world that He hated. And social atheism learned this lesson from Christianity at the moment of its rise to dominance. It was able to maintain order in a fallen world by changing the form of many things while not changing anything in essence. Judaism could not have done that, the gulf between it and paganism and idolatry is simply too great, the mutual repulsion is too powerful. God is great and man is sinful, that is why Judaism, a religion of the genius and the prophet, preserves God for man, but Christianity, a religion of the anonymous, irrational, kind man, the voluntary martyr, who renounces himself for the sake of ungrateful others, saves man for God in a frivolous fallen world: saves him, if not in the spirit, then at least in the body. The world has not only become used to Christianity's corporeality, it has come to love it. Christian corporeality does not need to be changed, however today the essence of Christianity needs to be understood and transformed. But for fifteen centuries its essence has consisted in fighting against its Biblical root."

Savelii saw that the little man in the flask was absolutely exhausted, as he was himself. However he knew that the little man was obedient to him and so he carried on asking questions.

"Tell me," Savelii said, lowering himself wearily onto a chair and closing his eyes, "why can't I believe in God with my intellect, although I have read many intelligent books that seek to prove the existence of God?"

"Because," the homunculus in the flask replied in a quiet, weary voice, "God is not in the intellect, but in the instinct. Man is born with the instinct of God just as he is born with the instinct to eat, drink and reproduce. But those instincts are simple, concrete, and susceptible to experiential corroboration by reason. The reason of the savage was not capable of apprehending even the physical phenomena of the earth and the sky that are susceptible to reason but lie outside of physical experience. The reason of civilized man finds itself in the same position with regard to the instinct for God that lies outside of physical experience. If you imagine the fantastical situation in which the desire to drink is not corroborated by the availability of water, then the existence of water would be exactly the same kind of problem for the reason as God is. Thirst would force you to search for and imagine water, but reason would find it easier to prove its absence than its presence. If you imagine to yourself a man who has never seen a woman, a world without women, then desire and lust would force him to imagine woman, but reason would find it easier to refute her existence than to prove it; the desire would be strong and it might perhaps torment rational individuals more than irrational ones, because many rational books would be written about the existence of woman. But while reason would be tormented by these attempts to find woman through analysis, one or two equally rational, far more honest and consistent, clear and intelligent books would prove the absurdity of believing in the existence of woman simply because of the existence of lust, or of the existence of water simply because of the existence of thirst. And if it were taken into account that thirst and lust arose in primitive times, then it would be easy to declare them a result of those primitive times, which have not yet been outlived. 'I believe because it is absurd,' the early Christian writer Tertullian exclaimed in despair. He was intelligent enough to realize the powerlessness of reason in the apprehension of God, but not intelligent enough to abjure reason in the apprehension of God, for the absurd is a rational, scientific con cept. Only a man of art can hear God's voice from a blazing thorn bush, like Moses. Reason demands rational proof, but the only proof in instinct is need. The need for God is the only proof of the existence of God, just as thirst is the only proof of the existence of water, even if it might not exist on earth, and lust is the proof of the existence of woman, even if God did not create Eve."

Following these words silence fell in the room and Savelii suddenly heard something hissing and whistling like at the beginning of the process of germination. He opened his eyes in fright and saw that the man and the woman in the flask were partaking of the fruit of the tree that had grown and blossomed first, and a mist like a cloud had accumulated under the lid of the flask. This cloud grew denser literally as he watched and then it turned as red as blood. Savelii quickly warmed up the menstruum on his spirit lamp, although it was not the right time to pour it in. And no sooner did he pour in a large dose of the menstruum that maintained the lives of the small people in the flask than there was a blinding flash from the bloody cloud and both of the little people started crawling about, trying to hide from the flames, Pain stabbed at Savelii's heart as before his eyes the colors in the flask faded, the plants withered and the trees shriveled as if during a drought. Then the earth in the flask gaped asunder, there was a powerful flash of fire and both the little people, the man and the woman, fell and lay motionless and were consumed by the eruption that was taking place. Savelii started sobbing in horror, it was no longer his heart that was in pain, but his soul, something much larger that filled all of his chest from his belly up to his throat. He heard his mother and Ilovaisky knocking on the door but he did not unlock it, he watched as four layers were formed in the flask, settling on top of each other. He could not look directly at the upper part because it was shining too brightly. Below it there was a crystal layer, followed by a layer as red as blood and at the very bottom there was black smoke, incessantly swirling.

"Savelii," his mother shouted, "unlock the door my boy, we'll help you."

But Savelii knew that he shouldn't unlock the door until everything was all over.

"Don't be stupid, old man," he heard Ilovaisky's voice say, "you should only pretend to be insane when it's in your own best interests."

"Gavriil," said Savelii's mother, "go and bring the janitor, we're going to break in the door." And she started crying loudly.

Savelii could hear that there were already a lot of people on the other side of the door. Someone moved something up, someone tried to force the door with his shoulder, something metal clanked. And at that moment there was a loud explosion and Savelii was scorched, he felt something sharp tear at his left cheek and left arm, for his left side was turned toward the flask. He stood there, feeling the pain growing until blood started pouring from his cheek and his palm, then he fell and lost consciousness. The explosion had occurred because the flask was not strong enough, he had made a bad choice in using a long, rectangular flask whereas he ought to have used a round, spherical one.

When they ran into the room Ilovaisky, Klavdia, the locksmith from the housing management unit and the prophetess Pelagia, taking her father's place, saw a terrible sight. Everything was swathed in ominous, toxic blackish and yellow smoke, the floor was awash with some kind of slippery, greasy solution and there were splashes of it on the furniture, shards of glass from the exploded flask crunched underfoot and a shapeless mass of something that looked like river silt and smelled like a swamp had tumbled out of the flask. Savelii was lying in the middle of all this chaos, bleeding from his lacerations.

There is no need to speak of the grief felt by Klavdia, the wounded madman's mother, there is no need to speak of the alarm and dismay felt by everyone who saw what had happened. Fortunately an ambulance arrived promptly and Savelii was given first aid. They moved him to the couch in the sitting room and treated his wounds, which proved to be superficial, although they were bleeding copiously. Savelii opened his eyes.

"What happened to you, my dear son?" Klavdia asked, going down on her knees.

"Mom," Savelii said in a quiet voice, "I feel as if my head has shrunk so that it's smaller than the head of a pin, and someone's trying to push something really big through it," and he pressed his bandaged hand against his forehead.

Soon they took Savelii away. And when they had taken Savelii away the prophetess Pelagia regained her composure, went down on her knees and said:

"Lord, I have sinned against Your servant Savelii . . . How can I atone for this sin?"

And the prophetess realized that she would not have done this if Satan had not been there beside her. But previously Satan had always approached the womanly side of her nature, and now he had come not only to her womanly side. Suddenly she understood why Satan had arrived and she felt afraid. But she remembered Lot's daughters, who made their father drunk and slept with him in order to continue their family line after the destruction of sinful Sodom. She remembered how the great Moabite woman Tamar dressed herself as a harlot and slept with her father-in-law Judah, thereby continuing the tribe of Judah and creating the House of David, which produced the wise Solomon and the Messiah Christ. And this was a portent to her to realize her idea through violation with the help of Satan, for there is tenderness in the love of a daughter for her father, and there is cruelty in the passion of a woman for a man, and the Lord cannot be cruel.

Her father Dan, the Viper, the Antichrist came back from somewhere and they sat down to have supper. For this supper the prophetess Pelagia had followed Lot's daughters in making ready a bottle of homemade wine infused with forest herbs, which Vera had brought to her from the Old Believer Chesnokova in Bor town. Pelagia had been thinking of saving this bottle for the cheerful feast of Simchat Torah, the joy of reading the Torah, but she realized that now was the time, it was necessary for the idea to be realized. And it was for this that Satan had already partly revealed himself. For Satan is in the habit of appearing by parts, it is as if you are gradually glancing further and further round a door. At first Satan's hooves appear, then they are followed by a hirsute torso, which is later joined by the wise goat's face of the wily pessimist.

The old woman's wine infused with herbs of the forest was good. The Antichrist drank like Lot from Sodom and he saw his beloved daughter's ripe body that she had been saving, neither expended nor exhausted by use in womanly matters. Her arms were rounded and her shoulders were broad, but not broad like a man's shoulders, there was no hard man's bone to be sensed in them, no wiry muscle, but the tenacious strength of a bearer of children. The Antichrist knew that this woman was physically strong in the way that beautiful northern peasant women are strong. She was no longer a young girl, and as the beloved father of a beloved daughter who trusted him in all things, he knew that she was still untouched. There are old maids who wither without bearing fruit. However she had not withered, this was a miracle of long blossoming, just as some lives are long. But even the long-lived die and every miracle has its limits. Through the sly pessimist Satan the Antichrist realized that he, the father, was destined to set the limit to his daughter's unfruitful blossoming. She was not his blood daughter, but she was his soul daughter, he had taken her as a little baby from the arms of her mother on the very threshold of death and raised her, and now it was incumbent on him to perform an act that was unthinkable without the help of Satan. He did not see Satan, he only smelled the acerbic odor of a moist, warm body, a bad, musty, acrid herring-like odor, the odor of something always kept well hidden away, putrefying in the warmth, that had now been laid bare . . . This was the odor of Satan the tempter, for Satan appears by parts, gradually, in order to prepare you and accustom you to himself.

Dan, the Viper, the Antichrist realized that there was no way back, behind him there lay only a curse: he realized that he would destroy his dream if he now embraced Rufina in a paternally affectionate manner and did not seize her forcibly like a man prepared for manly action. And if, after grabbing her, he delayed and did not fling her down immediately, then he would destroy his hope forever. But he, the Viper, was cunning, he decided to allow his daughter to turn her back on him so that he could seize her. When she turned away toward the sideboard it was precisely the right time, but even so he delayed and grabbed her at a moment that surprised even him. She had gone to the far end of the room to get something, and it was a long way to the beds, to her maidenly bed behind a screen and his folding bed, and so he flung her down on the floor right there. However what happened then was what he had expected least of all. He had thought that she would resist with her arms and knees, but she sank her teeth into his open hand, not biting it in the way that a person, a woman does, but in the way that a wild beast does, unhesitatingly, to bite right through, ignoring the person who has been grabbed by its teeth. The Antichrist groaned in physical suffering, caught by surprise, his hand and wrist immediately went numb, and the Antichrist was no longer thinking about anything but how to save his hand. But at the very moment when he decided to back down, Satan helped him to stop focusing on the appalling pain in his hand and understand that this was only limited resistance on the part of Rufina, who could not submit so easily in womanly matters to her beloved father. And meanwhile her strong knees, a woman's foremost defense, were acquiescent and yielding. And then with his free hand, the one not grasped in Pelagia's teeth, the Antichrist helped himself to do everything he wished for and had dreamed about.

And so it was done and the moment came when Satan appeared completely, with all of his parts, and the cruel sweetness of doom washed over their bodies in a wave of hope that their hearts would simultaneously give out and they would both die happy. But no matter how hard they sought to remain in this ruinous sweetness, the same power that plunged them into this transhuman condition banished them from it, returning them to life, to pain and to the fear of death, and their hearts instantly made this steep ascent, abandoning the bliss of eternal sleep . . .

Something glimmered one final time in the darkness of their room: it was Satan's face disappearing, handsome and sad, and not at all maliciously satirical as it is in temptations when a person fights against him.

The clock struck two in the morning. They both felt thirsty, as if they were ill, there was very little saliva in their mouths and it was thick and sticky. Rufina got up off the bed without turning on the light and her clothes rustled in the darkness. they had been crumpled by the Antichrist and perhaps even torn in places. She undressed and lay back down on the bed. The Antichrist also took off his shirt and lay down beside her.

"What will happen now?" he asked anxiously.

"Be quiet, father," said Rufina, for even having become his wife, she still called him "father."

The Antichrist did as the daughter whom he had raped said, since they had no other path to the idea. They lay there and the night, as usual, lived and worked and strove towards its own end. At first the night strove towards its end invisibly, imperceptibly, not changing in any way, and then by becoming paler and whiter and starting to move.

"What will happen now?" the Antichrist asked again when a tentative reddish glow entirely alien to the peace of night appeared. This was no longer the night, but the dawn.

"Be quiet, father," his daughter, who had become his wife, told him.

And now they both lay there amid the frantic, hasty labor of the forces of morning clearing the sky and the earth to the mounting clamor of the birds. When everything had become bright and clear and there was nowhere to hide from the light, he asked for a third time:

"What will happen now?"

She did not answer. She was sleeping with a beautiful, kind expression on her clear, morning-fresh face. And only then did the Antichrist learn from the Lord that his daughter Rufina was really the prophetess Pelagia from Brusyany village near Rzhev town.

As the Lord gave over Job into the hands of Satan so that, having suffered torments, he would be reinforced in his faith, so had the father and daughter been handed over, for the sake of God's works, to Satan, a constant and essential participant in the Lord's tragic dramaturgy. Then Dan, the Viper, the Antichrist recalled the prophet Isaiah: "Then Isaiah said, 'Hear then, O house of David! Is it too little for you to weary men, that you weary my God also? Therefore the Lord himself will give you a sign. Behold, the virgin shall conceive and bear a son, and shall call his name Immanuel. He shall eat curds and honey until he knows how to refuse the evil and choose the good.'" Further on Isaiah says: "And I went to the prophetess, and she conceived and bore a son." Like his brother, the Antichrist was a well-educated Jew and he knew that this was not that son, but it was a son who was a sign. And without a sign none of God's works can be accomplished. And now, following the House of David, it had been given to the House of Dan to be glorified, proclaiming: "For to us a child is born, to us a son is given."

When the Antichrist understood this and it had been accomplished, he started pining for his past and for his own land. He had only pined in this way at the beginning, when he appeared as a Jewish youth, almost a boy, together with the Lord's second plague, famine, in Shagaro-Petrovskoe village in the Dymytrov district of the Kharkiv region. At that time, thinking of his beloved Holy City he had repeated especially often the age-old oath and curse: "If I forget you, let my tongue stick to the roof of my mouth."

A man's genuine homeland is not the land on which he lives, but the nation to which he belongs. Neither Russian, nor Jewish, nor English, nor Turkish, nor any other land. All land is the Lord's and the Lord is the only indigenous dweller on earth. And the genuine right to one or another piece of land is not procured by historical conquests or historical displacements or the fact of centuries-long possession, but by whether or not a nation makes a piece of the Lord's earth fruitful and the customs on it just or, like Gogol's Pliushkin, a nation oppresses the Lord's wide expanses that have fallen into its hands. The Lord will hold such a nation severely to account for His property. But the Lord will reward a nation that preserves the Lord's property.

And now the Antichrist saw the city, but it was different, not flourishing, but returning to life after the four plagues of the Lord. According to the Book of Nehemiah it had been like this after the Babylonian exile, for unlike the period following the Egyptian exile, when there was only Moses, during the revival following the Babylonian exile there was Nehemiah, who led the people out of Babylon, and also Ezra, who taught the people the law. "Then Eliashib the high priest rose up with his brothers the priests, and they built the Sheep Gate. They consecrated it and set its doors. They consecrated it as far as the Tower of the Hundred, as far as the Tower of Hananel. And next to them the men of Jericho built. And next to them Zaccur the son of Imri built. The sons of Hassenaah built the Fish Gate. They laid its beams and set its doors, its bolts, and its bars. And next to them Meremoth the son of Uriah, son of Hakkoz repaired. And next to them Meshullam the son of Berechiah, son of Meshezabel repaired. And next to them Zadok the son of Baana repaired. And next to them the Tekoites repaired, but their nobles would not stoop to serve their Lord. Joiada the son of Paseah and Meshullam the son of Besodeiah repaired the Gate of Yeshanah. They laid its beams and set its doors, its bolts, and its bars . . ."

In this way, with the antlike stubbornness of weak human hands, they restored the eternal.

"Malchijah the son of Harim and Hasshub the son of Pahath-Moab repaired another section and the Tower of the Ovens . . . Hanun and the inhabitants of Zanoah repaired the Valley Gate . . . and repaired a thousand cubits of the wall, as far as the Dung Gate . . . Malchijah the son of Reshab, ruler of the district of Beth-haccherem, repaired the Dung Gate . . . And Shallum repaired the Fountain Gate . . . And he built the wall of the Pool of Shelab of the king's garden, as far as the stairs that go down from the city of David . . . After him Nehemiah the son of Azbu . . . repaired to a point opposite the tombs of David, as far as the artificial pool, and as far as the house of the mighty men . . . Next to him Ezer the son of Jeshua repaired another section opposite the ascent to the armory at the buttress . . . After him Palal the son of

Uzai repaired opposite the buttress and the tower projecting from the upper house of the king at the court of the guard . . . Above the Horse Gate the priests repaired . . ."

However in a fallen world in addition to the builders there are always the destroyers, and they should also be understood. The present-day liberal and humanist will always be more apt to understand the great truth of the destroyer than the narrow truth of the builder. It is no coincidence that since the end of the 19th century the gilded words of the liberal have always preceded the knife of the murderer. For indeed the builder egoistically labors for himself, whereas the destroyer self-denyingly strives for everyone. The destroyer is always cheated, even though he has plenty of everything. He is always to be pitied, he always loses. For in a fallen world not to find means to lose . . .

"Will they ever really finish? Will they really resurrect the stones from a heap of dust that has actually been burned? They will not know or see anything till we come among them and kill them and stop the work."

However an experienced builder always knows what should be expected from the sufferings of a destroyer and how painful other people's wellbeing is for a destroyer. At that time the destroyers were Sanballat the Horonite and Tobiah, who lived on extensive lands that they had acquired for gratis after the Babylonian invasion. Here are the words of Nehemiah, the son of Hachalia, the former cupbearer of the Persian king Artaxerxes, the Nehemiah who led those who built:

"So we built the wall. And all the wall was joined together to half its height, for the people had a mind to work . . . And I looked and arose and said to the nobles and to the officials and to the rest of the people, 'Do not be afraid of them. Remember the Lord, who is great and awesome, and fight for your brothers, your sons, your daughters, your wives, and your homes . . .' From that day on, half of my servants worked on construction, and half held spears, shields, bows, and coats of mail . . . Those who carried burdens were loaded in such a way that each labored on the work with one hand and held his weapon with the other . . . So neither I nor my brothers nor my servants nor the men of the guard who followed me, none of us took off our clothes; each kept his weapon at his right hand . . ."

The Antichrist remembered all of this very often and was constantly pensive. From the day when through Satan the Antichrist had become the husband of his own daughter, the prophetess Pelagia's love for her father had not declined during the day. But at night a passionate desire for her husband had also appeared. And so Pelagia conceived and by her own calculation she would be delivered of an infant in early spring in time for the feast of Purim, a happy festival. After Pelagia conceived, she went everywhere with her father, for she knew that he would not always be with her. Her father took good care of her and, knowing that a mother-to-be needs country air, he often went a long way out of the city with her, to the autumnal suburban woods, for the autumn had already arrived.

One day they arrived in a sparsely populated area with numerous ravines and an elevated hill overgrown with trees. Also with them was Andrei Koposov, who already knew who his father and his sister really were: his sister, who had also become his foster mother, had conceived a child from his father. When they walked up onto the hill Dan, the Viper, the Antichrist, the emissary of God spoke to them through the Gospel of Matthew, the most veracious Gospel, in the words of his brother from the tribe of Judah:

"Do not think that I have come to abolish the Law or the Prophets; I have not come to abolish them but to fulfill them. For truly, I say to you, until heaven and earth pass away, not an iota, not a dot, will pass from the Law until all is accomplished."

And then Andrei Koposov who was following the most difficult, third path to God, not through belief and not through unbelief, but through doubt, like the righteous man Job, opened the little pocket New Testament that he always had with him and asked:

"Father, why does your brother Jesus from the tribe of Judah say directly in the seventeenth and eighteenth verses of the fifth chapter of the Gospel of St. Matthew that he has come to fulfill the Law of Moses, but from verse twenty-one he starts saying something different, and in verse thirty-eight and verse thirty-nine he says: 'You have heard that it was said: "An eye for an eye and a tooth for a tooth." But I say to you, do not resist the one who is evil. But if anyone slaps you on the right cheek, turn to him the other also.' In verses thirty-three and thirty-four it says: 'You have heard that it was said: "You shall love your neighbor and hate your enemy." But I say to you: love your enemies and bless those who persecute you, do good to those who hate you and pray for those who offend you.'"

"It is all truly spoken and there is no contradiction here. As a pious Jew, as a genius talking with God, he preserves and fulfills the Law of God, in order to preserve God for man, as it says in the seventeenth and eighteenth verses. This is his first truth, the truth of Moses. But as a sage, the Savior and Messiah, He knows that a sinful man in a fallen world is not capable of loving God according to the Commandments of the Law of Moses and is not capable of fulfilling God's simple commandments: You shall not murder, you shall not steal, and you shall not commit adultery. Neither are God's prophets capable of making evil sinners believe this, their voice is the voice of one crying out in the wilderness. This is why, for the salvation of a fallen world, He has not invoked God's law as revealed by the prophets, which is alien to the world, but the precepts of the kind man, which are comprehensible to every sinner and through a kind man's self-denial and self-sacrifice the sinner lives like a worm in an apple. In this way the fallen world is saved for God not by divine works but by human works. This is what my brother Jesus from the tribe of Judah speaks of. These are not commandments for the many, but they save many. This is his second truth. And there cannot be a third truth... And in concluding his Sermon on the Mount, Jesus, my brother says: 'You therefore must be perfect, as your heavenly Father is perfect.' Such are the words of Him who apprehended the will of God, spoken for those who in their sin are not capable of apprehending God's will and must be saved by a different, human perfection, for kindness is also perfection."

Then the prophetess Pelagia, the adopted daughter of Dan the Antichrist, and also his wife asked:

"Father, for whom did your brother Jesus bring salvation? For the oppressed or for the oppressors, for those who are remain invisible or those who hate?"

And Dan, the Antichrist replied:

"Of course, it was for the oppressors that Christ brought salvation and for those who hate, for their torments are terrible. Terrible is the suffering of the evildoers and oppressors."

"Father," the prophetess Pelagia asked, "then how can the oppressed be saved and how can the oppressors be saved?"

And Dan, the Antichrist replied:

"For the oppressors Christ is the Savior, for the oppressed the Antichrist is the Savior. For this I have been sent from the Lord. You have heard that it was said: 'Love your enemies and bless those who persecute you, do good to those who hate you and pray for those who offend you.' But I say to you: do not love your enemies, but the hatred of your enemies, do not bless those who curse you, but their curses against you, do not pray for those who offend and persecute you, but for your suffering and persecution. For the hatred of your enemies is God's seal, which is your blessing. If the hatred is centuries-long and all-encompassing, if the passion of this hatred is sincere, if it is not the hater himself who hates, but rather something within him that hates, if sometimes the hater's reason cannot control his hatred, if ideologies and empires are created around this hatred, it means that through this hatred the Lord is sending an invisible sign. The hatred of people for each other is not such a rare thing in a fallen world and very frequently it is as trivial as a fallen world. But only the Lord's people is worthy of being hated with a universal fruitful hatred, constantly for more than two thousand years and for the duration of more than ten empires, those Towers of Babel. It is in no way marked out from other peoples and in no way better, except that it is marked out through this constant hatred and through this constant hatred it is better."

With this Dan the Antichrist, the emissary of the Lord, concluded his reply, already knowing that his time here would soon be ended, for the present four plagues of the Lord were over and only the Lord knew when new torments would be sent. Of course, these plagues are always present in the fallen world, but there are sinful periods when they are renewed and acquire exceptional strength. Then the Antichrist might appear again, or he might not appear, that will depend on what God plans. And therefore the prophetess Pelagia knew that she would be separated from her father and husband for a long time, if not forever. However she did not know when the leave-taking would happen and she beseeched the Lord that it would at least happen after the birth of their child. And so they lived until Christmas in love and trepidation.

This year Christmastide was not very frosty, but it was windy and restless. Dan the Antichrist celebrated the birth of his brother modestly, with only the prophetess Pelagia, his daughter and wife. He celebrated it in thoughts about his brother and in conversation with his daughter, who was due to give birth to his child. He said:

"All people are born spiritually poor, born foolish and spiteful. But while they are reasonless infants, they live in God's paradise. However when the rudiments of awareness appear, they are instantly banished from paradise to fend for themselves, to where poverty, stupidity and malice lie in wait for them. How can you return to God, living by your own efforts, fending for yourself? Against poverty there are geniuses, against stupidity there are prophets and sages, but against malice there are kind people, anonymous people. These are not the earthly genius Pushkin, not Shakespeare, not God's Moses, not the prophet Jeremiah and not the prophet Isaiah. They are merely those who are willing to expend themselves wholly and completely in the present and of whom nothing will remain in the future. And if a kind man does leave something after him, if he achieves prominence and becomes famous, if they say about him that this man was kind, then it means that he did not dispense genuine kindness, did not carry his plans through to their conclusion. Only the anonymous, righteous man who receives no thanks performs his good works to the very end. And for that my brother from the tribe of Judah was born, for He is the only consolation and reward of the anonymous righteous, who live for the salvation of the oppressors. But I came to reward the oppressed."

That night the Antichrist awoke, raised himself up on his elbow, remembered his words about himself, which the Lord had put in his mouth, smiled, looked at his daughter, who was sleeping beside him, warm and large, with beautiful yellow patches from her pregnancy, looked at the night through the window, beyond which the Christmas stars were shining, and one star among them was brighter than the multitude of all the rest: he looked and gently bid farewell to God's world, bid farewell to his daughter, touching his lips cautiously to her forehead in order not to wake her. And then Dan, the Viper, the Antichrist carried on living for a little more than three hours in his sleep and died at dawn, instantly forgetting all earthly events that had happened to him, as people sometimes completely forget their night-time dream on awakening in the morning.

Even after her father awoke from the earthly realm his daughter, the prophetess Pelagia, carried on sleeping beside the cooling body that had once belonged to her father. She dreamed of a funeral, as Annushka Emelyanova, the unrighteous martyr had also dreamed of a funeral in a German pigsty. But Annushka Emelyanova dreamed of her mother's coffin standing in the pouring rain in the yard of the building with the address: Barracks Building 3, Sector 3, Rzhev town. In the prophetess Pelagia's dream the location was not shown, although she and Annushka Emelyanova were practically from the same place, for Bryusany village is not far from Rzhev town. And the prophetess Pelagia did not see rain, but a sunny day. A dense crowd of people was walking along, carrying four coffins. The crowd with the coffins walked onto a bridge that was narrow, but long. It walked on for a little distance and set down one coffin on the bridge, then walked on farther and set down a second coffin. When the people walked off the bridge, they lowered the third coffin into the water and after walking along the riverbank a little farther they lowered the fourth coffin into the water too. But the coffins did not float away downstream, they bobbed and swayed close to the bank. Suddenly a strong, healthy young woman tumbled out of the coffin that was closer to the bank. She fell and then stood up, with the water up to her throat. Then a youth got up out of the coffin that was swaying farther away from the bank, walked across the water to the young woman, led her by the hand out to the people on the bank, then went back and lay down in his own coffin, which started slowly floating away downstream. But no sooner did the young woman emerge on to the bank with water streaming off her than she started speaking very loudly, speaking like a madwoman, but not in the language she had spoken before her death, not in Russian. And she changed, growing darker, her hair became black, the rounded plumpness of her body disappeared and her gestures became rapid, in the southern style. The people standing on the riverbank took her cautiously and respectfully by her wet hands, led her away and brought her to a room of some kind. There the young woman was already wearing a dry dress, which left her knees uncovered, and carrying a small white purse embroidered with beads. But her monologue continued, although it no longer sounded so insane and was not as loud as before. This monologue was in an incomprehensible language, perhaps a primordial, barbarous language, and it sounded quite unlike any other. But even so every now and again a familiar Russian word fleetingly appeared in this torrent of incomprehensible, guttural words. However it was impossible to ascertain or divine anything from this word. But the people listened avidly and watched the gestures of this young woman. Those who had not managed to get into the room peered in through the windows, peeped through the narrow crack of the door or jostled around the entrance. They listened for many hours, although they did not understand anything. At first the prophetess Pelagia was wary of entering the room and then she thought: "What can it do to me?" and walked in. She walked in and said to the deceased young woman:

"Hello . . ."

"Hello, Pelagia," the deceased woman replied in Russian and once again launched into her torrent of foreign volubility, among which from time to time a Russian word fleetingly appeared.

Meanwhile the longer the people listened to the deceased young woman, the less they understood and the more often they expressed their agreement:

"Yes . . . Oh, you don't say . . . Well I never . . ."

And there seemed to be a different crowd around her now, not mournful or funereal: a lot of young people with colorful clothes and faces that were not gloomy or brooding.

And so Pelagia awoke from her deep sleep with her heart lightened and saw Christmas morning outside the window, frosty, sunny and cheerful. She put her arms round her father in order to wake him and tell him about her strange dream, but immediately recoiled in revulsion. For an instant before her mind was petrified by human grief at the death of a loved one, she felt a genuine biblical abhorrence for the dead body. She knew that in every word her father had spoken and she had remembered, and even in every object that he had touched, there was more of him than there was in this empty body that he had left behind forever. It was for a good reason that in ancient biblical times the Nazarenes, people who had devoted themselves to God, were forbidden to touch a dead body. While the body remains here, no living memory of the deceased is possible. The body must be committed to the earth as quickly as possible in order for that which was dear to be resurrected.

And that was what she did, modestly and inconspicuously, and her brother Andrei Koposov helped her to do this. At a public cemetery accessible to all, the children buried their father, who had died of heart failure, in a modest, inexpensive coffin. However even as they walked away from the cemetery, their hearts were revivified. Their father was with them again. From that moment on they were rarely parted from their father or from each other, but even so they were never a burden on each other and they never tired of each other.

Pelagia gave birth early in March, exactly on the festival of Shuran-Purim, the fifteenth of Adar in the Jewish calendar. This festival celebrates the deliverance of the Jews from the threat of total extinction as envisioned by Aman the Greek, a foreign official in the Persian empire, who attempted to resolve the Jewish question thirty-seven years before the birth of Christ in order that, as it said in the decree: "These people should not hinder us in times to come from leading our lives in peace and tranquility to the end."

However thanks to the efforts of Esther the Jewess, a woman, peaceful humankind was not rescued from the birth of Christ. Aman, the rescuer, was himself hanged on the orders of the king. And so the first Greek conspiracy against the as yet unborn Christ was a failure. But the second Greek conspiracy, which was active after Christ's death, was partly successful. The chalice was smashed. And after the four grievous plagues of the Lord had passed, this conspiracy was once again opposed by a woman, the prophetess Pelagia from Bryusany village near Rzhev, who had given birth to an infant who was a sign from her father the Antichrist, the brother of Jesus Christ.

This infant, named Dan in honor of his father, took after his father in his Jewish appearance, but he had his mother's northern eyes, Rzhev-town eyes. Like all healthy infants, he dwelt in God's paradise, however it was already clear from certain subtle signs, which only his prophetess-mother Pelagia was capable of reading, that after leaving God's paradise of infanthood, Dan would distinguish himself from the many, and on becoming a youth would distinguish himself from all others. He would quickly pass through the time of searching and when his search was rewarded, he would be quick to believe in what he had found. He would love the biblical prophets with all his soul, but most of all he would love the prophet who has remained forever anonymous, who was arbitrarily included in the book of the prophet Isaiah and arbitrarily named Deutero-Isaiah, each word of whom, as if in manifestation of the divine meaning contained in it, blazed without burning up, like the thorn bush of Moses.

"Behold my Servant, whom I uphold, my chosen, in whom my soul delights: I have put my Spirit upon him; he will bring forth justice to the nations," read the prophetess Pelagia, mother of Dan. "For a long time I have held my peace," she read, "I have kept still and restrained myself; now I will cry out like a woman in labor; I will lay waste and devour everything. I have given my back to those who strike, and my cheeks to those who pull out the beard; I hid not my face from disgrace and spitting."

So said the unknown prophet Deutero-Isaiah fifteen hundred years before the star of Bethlehem. And he also said: "But the Lord God helps me; therefore I have not been disgraced; therefore I have set my face like a flint, and I know that I shall not be put to shame. He who vindicates me is near. Who will contend with me? Let us stand up together. Who is my adversary? Let him come near to me."

Such is the short fifty-second chapter of Deutero-Isaiah, consisting of only twelve verses. The entire spirit of the Gospels, the drama of the Gospels and even to a large extent the basic theme of the Gospels, in this little chapter written by Deutero-Isaiah fifteen hundred years before the Birth of Christ. Everything creative that there is in the Gospels is given to us in this chapter. It lacks only the pagan decoration and pagan meaning with which the Gospels were later debased by their Greek guardian. This is the Gospel of Deutero-Isaiah, the most ancient, fundamental and poetic. Not a chronicle-Gospel like the others, but a prophetic Gospel.

"Who has believed what he has heard from us? And to whom has the arm of the Lord been revealed? For he grew up before him like a young plant, and like a root out of dry ground; he had no form or majesty that we should look at him, and no beauty that we should desire him. He was despised and rejected by men, a man of sorrows and acquainted with grief; and as one from whom men hide their faces he was despised, and we esteemed him not. Surely he has borne our griefs and carried our sorrows; yet we esteemed him stricken, smitten by God, and afflicted. But he was pierced for our transgressions; he was crushed for our iniquities; upon him was the chastisement that brought us peace, and with his wounds we are healed. All we like sheep have gone astray; we have turned, every one, to his own way; and the Lord has laid on him the iniquity of us all. He was oppressed, and he was afflicted, yet he opened not his mouth; like a lamb that is led to the slaughter, and like a sheep that before its shearers is silent, so he opened not his mouth. By oppression and judgment he was taken away; and as for his generation, who considered that he was cut off out of the land of the living, stricken for the transgression of my people? And they made his grave with the wicked and with a rich man in his death, although he had done no violence, and there was no deceit in his mouth. Yet it was the will of the Lord to crush him; he has put him to grief when his soul makes an offering for guilt, he shall see his offspring; he shall prolong his days; the will of the Lord shall prosper in his hand. Out of the anguish of his soul he shall see and be satisfied; by his knowledge shall the righteous one, my servant, make many to be accounted righteous, and he shall bear their iniquities. Therefore I will divide him a portion with the many, and he shall divide the spoils with the strong, because he poured out his soul to death and was numbered with the transgressors; yet he bore the sin of many, and makes intercession for the transgressors."

Such is the Gospel of Deutero-Isaiah, the only prophetic Gospel. Despite the fact that it is prophetic, that is, written long before the events related came to pass, it contains more essential substance and meaning than the Gospels written considerably later than the events occurred. Its final phrase indicates who Jesus is: an intercessor for the malefactors, who are in the majority. Not, however, an intercessor for the victims.

Of course, in the world of philosophy, in the world of unity, in the spatial world of general concepts, the malefactor and the victim are inseparable, and therefore Christ the philosopher is an intercessor for all. However in the religious world, in the world of polarity and of fundamental concepts, in the fluid, temporal, biblical world the malefactor is clearly distinguished from the victim in every concrete moment and in religion Christ is only an intercessor for the malefactor. It is the Antichrist who intercedes for the victim. And that is why in the spatial world of Greek antiquity Christ and the Antichrist are as it were amalgamated into one, for in the world of antiquity the victim cannot be separated from the malefactor.

Deutero-Isaiah speaks not only about Christ, but also about the Antichrist: "And I will lead the blind in a way that they do not know, in paths that they have not known I will guide them. I will turn the darkness before them into light, the rough places into level ground. These are the things I do, and I do not forsake them . . .": so said not only the intercessor for the malefactors, Christ, but also the intercessor for the victims, the Antichrist: "When you pass through the waters, I will be with you; and through the rivers, they shall not overwhelm you; when you walk through fire you shall not be burned, and the flame shall not consume you."

Through the Antichrist, His emissary, the Lord addresses the victim: "I, I am the Lord, and besides me there is no savior . . . Thus says the Lord, your Redeemer, who formed you from the womb: 'I am the Lord, who made all things, who alone stretched out the heavens, who spread out the earth by myself. Who says to the deep: be dry!'" But to the oppressors, for whom Christ is the intercessor, the Antichrist, the intercessor for those who are currently oppressed, says: "I will make the oppressors eat their own flesh, and they shall be drunk with their own blood as with young wine. Behold I have taken from your hand the cup of staggering; the bowl of my wrath you shall drink no more; and I will put it into the hand of your tormentors, who have said to you, 'Bow down, that we may pass over'; and you have made your back like the ground and like the street for them to pass over."

So says the Antichrist, the father of the prophetess Pelagia and the father of her son, the Antichrist, who in the philosophical world, in the world of unity, is the enemy of Christ, but in the religious world, in the world of polarity, is the brother of Christ and complements him in the realization of God's equitable justice. This was how the prophetess Pelagia read Deutero-Isaiah and understood him.

When the infant had grown strong, the prophetess Pelagia began taking him often to the thinly populated area outside the city with numerous ravines and a hill overgrown with trees, on which Pelagia's father had taught her and her brother Andrei Koposov. Her brother Andrei Koposov also went there with her, and so did her neighbor Savelii Ivolgin who, according to an official medical note, had practically been cured of his mental illness. And indeed his face had now lost its former dangerous animation, which testified to an internal hubbub of many voices, its expression had become less lonely and it looked out at the world with greater trust, no longer suspecting that the world was plotting against him and concealing something from him. And the question of cognition was no longer an ironic question for him. He already knew that there was no unity in the world, and therefore the question of cognition was mundane, not tragic and fateful, as it would be in the case of a comprehensive unity of phenomena and conceptions. He also remembered the fundamental religious commandment of the anonymous prophet Deutero-Isaiah, with which his revelation concluded. Here it is, from chapter fifty-five, verse six: "Seek the Lord while He may be found; call upon Him while He is near."

And so, thanks to the latest methods of treatment, thanks to his rejection of the search for the unity of the world, which he had been taught by the little man in the flask, now deceased, and thanks to the prophet's great commandment, Savelii had acquired calmness of soul and had become pleasant to be with, and the prophetess Pelagia gladly invited him to go on her country walks.

When the first anniversary of her father, the Antichrist's departure came around, precisely at Christmas, the prophetess Pelagia took her infant child to the country and her constant companions, Andrei and Savelii, went with them. Pelagia swaddled her little child warmly, for although this Christmas was not tempestuous and windy like the previous one, it was frosty and thick snow had been falling constantly since first thing in the morning.

In winter, especially in the country, two colors are dominant on a snowy day, white and black, for against a background of whiteness everything dark seems black. That is why, if you look at the trunks of trees from the side from which drifting snow was swept up against them earlier, perhaps during the night, then all the tree trunks are like white brothers, thickly plastered with snow, but from the opposite side they are all like black brothers. These two colors lend the winter forest its aura of sanctity and you walk through it with your soul transfixed, as if you are in a house of God. There is a sacred severity in the white and black, and all other colors seem secondary and ordinary. The winter forest is sublime under its white canopy, until the sun peeps through and awakens the earthly colors and an earthly, frivolous, joyfully female glimmering and glinting appears, together with the joyful, bright blueness of the sky. This is beautiful and pleasing, but it is restless in a womanly fashion. There is a momentary flash of a summery dissipation that is pleasing to the body, of a boisterous, summertime expenditure, when you feel that every day departing from life is your loss. But with a fine, snowy, country winter, God seems to give man a respite, minimizing the vain bustling of life and maximizing a sense of tranquil immobility, rendering the days pleasantly alike, and man does not feel the loss of his days. Even among the birds, those creatures that enliven nature the most, the most frequent sight is an unhasting, black winter bird on white snow, a crow or a jackdaw. A bright bullfinch comes flying in like something insubstantial, like a flash of gaudy, feminine color among the whiteness, like a secular note in a sacred temple . . .

With feelings like these, as if they were entering a house of God, Andrei Koposov, Savelii Ivolgin and the prophetess Pelagia with her infant son Dan walked into the winter forest. Dan had already demonstrated the first shoots of awareness, delighting his mother, but was still far away from expulsion from God's paradise. They set out with their feet sinking into the snow to the place on the hill where in the previous autumn their father Dan had taught Pelagia and Andrei. They looked round and saw that everything low and earthly all around them was sacred, and there was nothing higher, neither the sun, which the heliolaters worshipped, but Abraham refused to do the same, nor the pagan idol of the sky, which had now been extinguished by the earthly holy day of Christmas, nor the boundless expanse of the stars, possibly the culprits that bear the greatest responsibility for polytheism, the stars, whose many-faced beauty had long distracted ancient man from the One True God. But now He was close and this was that holy moment when He could be found, for the black winter forest was ablaze with His whiteness, as once in the desert the thorn bush had blazed before the shepherd Moses. And Andrei Koposov, the son of the Antichrist, Savelii Ivolgin, a sinful alchemist, and the prophetess Pelagia, the wife of the Antichrist, heard the voice of God more clearly than ever before. However the infant Dan, lying in his diapers in the arms of the prophetess and gazing up with his blue, northern, Rzhev-town eyes into the overhanging, snow-covered, fresh, fragrant branches, heard the Lord as if He were standing in front of him and holding His hand on his face. Of course what he heard will remain hidden from him in his heart for a long time, but when the time comes it will be revealed to him, if he lives the life that was conceived for him by the Lord and created by his father.

In the biblical poem about the creation of the world it says that the Lord created and man invented names for what had been created, for to assist human incapacity the divine had to be debased through the word and through naming, that is, through art. In this way also the fathomless thoughts of the Lord are debased though the great words of a prophet for the sake of their comprehensibility to man. But the word of a prophet is debased many times over if it sounds forth without a sign of the kind that the sacred winter forest had now become for these people. It is said in the book of Isaiah: "Ask a sign of the Lord your God; let it be deep as Sheol or high as heaven." This is what the Lord said to these people in the sacred winter forest through Isaiah: "If favor is shown to the wicked, he does not learn righteousness. For behold, the Lord is coming out from his place to punish the inhabitants of the earth for their iniquity, and the earth will disclose the blood shed on it, and will no more cover its slain."

The people in the winter forest understood that the evildoer can put his hope only in Christ and he will be forgiven and consoled by Christ for the blood that he has spilled. But the Lord will not forgive, for Christ is the Savior, but the Lord is the Creator.

When it is past, every life and every destiny, even a bitter life and a harrowing destiny, must be transposed into a psalm: a song of praise to the Lord for it's having happened, as opposed to lives that were never born and destinies that were never lived. Every life, even a bitter one, is a gift and a privilege. Therefore by his very birth a malefactor and forswearer deceives the Creator. But Christ is the Savior, pure-hearted, for a heart that does not know the torments of creation is pure, Christ was sent by the Lord in order not to abandon those whom the Creator himself, the Lord, has abandoned. The essence of the Lord is eternal and incomprehensible to man, but in this eternity there is one single aspect, perhaps not the principal or most significant one, that is comprehensible to human understanding; the Creator.

"Behold, the days are coming," the Lord declares through Amos, the oldest of the prophets and the founder of prophecy, "when I will send a famine on the land, not a famine of bread, nor a thirst for water, but a thirst to hear the words of the Lord."

These times are approaching now, and the hunger for the word of the Lord may perhaps be the fifth plague of the Lord, and the most terrible, foretold through the prophet Amos, as the previous four were foretold through the prophet Ezekiel. The evildoer, forgiven by Jesus, was saved from the first four plagues: from the first plague, the sword; from the second plague, famine; from the third plague, the beast of fornication; from the fourth plague of sickness. But the evildoer will not be saved from the fifth plague of hunger and thirst for the word of the Lord, and the intercessor for malefactors, Christ, will not save him. The evildoer will die in torment from hunger for the word of the Lord, from thirst for the Lord's consolation. But the righteous man will be sated with the word of the Lord. As it says in the book of the prophet Isaiah:

"Before they call I will answer; while they are yet speaking I will hear . . ."

And it has been said: "Come, everyone who thirsts, to the waters, and who has no money, come, buy and eat! Come, buy wine and milk without money and without price. Why do you spend your money for that which is not bread and your labor for that which does not satisfy? Listen diligently to me, and eat what is good, and delight yourselves in rich food. Incline your ear and come to me, hear that your soul may live, and I will make with you an everlasting covenant, my steadfast, sure love for David . . . For as the rain and the snow come down from heaven and do not return there but water the earth, making it bring forth and sprout, giving seed to the sower and bread to the eater, so shall my word be that goes out from my mouth; it shall not return to me empty, but it shall accomplish that which I purpose, and shall succeed in the thing for which I sent it."

In this way genius repeats genius and the book of the prophet Isaiah repeats the Deuteronomy of Moses, in which the following is stated concerning the word of God:

"May my teaching drop as the rain, my speech distill as the dew, like gentle rain upon the tender grass, and like showers upon the herb . . ."

The people in the forest understood through the sign of the black trees blazing with the sacred, snowy whiteness, that after the four grievous plagues of the Lord a fifth and most terrible of the Lord's plagues was approaching: thirst and hunger for the word of the Lord. And only a spiritual toiler could admonish the world and save the world from it by giving the world the food and drink of God's word. Then they also understood the essential meaning of the prophet Isaiah's vehement entreaty:

"O you, who call the Lord to mind, do not be silent!"

October, November, December 1974; January 1975

Afterword

The Soviet Jewish *Haftarah*: Friedrich Gorenstein's *Psalm*

> In Magdeburg, on a little poster of international readings . . . I was labelled a Jewish Ukrainian. . . . I was asked in response to my inquiry about this peculiar interpretation of my ethnicity, "What should it have said?" I responded, "A Jewish Jew."
>
> —Friedrich Gorenstein

> Everything that I write
> is in essence commentaries . . .
> And where is the Canon?
> Where is—Borukh Ato,
> Adenoi Eleheine,
> Adenoi Ekhod?
>
> —Ian Satunovsky

-1-

Friedrich Gorenstein (1932–2002) is a major figure in the history of 20th-century Russian literature—and a most curious one. On the one hand, his novels blend fiction with religion, philosophy, and politics in a way that is quintessentially Russian. On the other hand, throughout his voluminous body of work, he defiantly tackles those selfsame issues as a Jewish writer, a Jewish thinker, and an uncompromising Jewish voice. Until now all but unknown in English, this daring and complex author was brought to the attention of

American readers with the publication of *Redemption,* his first major novel, in a masterful translation by Andrew Bromfield in 2018.[1] Bromfield's equally masterful translation of Gorenstein's second major and most controversial novel, *Psalm,* is an event of utmost cultural and literary significance.

Gorenstein's life story replicates the grim travails of Soviet history. His father, a prominent academic in Kyiv, was arrested in 1935 and sent to the Gulag where he soon perished. At the start of World War II, his mother died unexpectedly during the family's evacuation to Central Asia, leaving Friedrich in an orphanage and later in the care of his aunts in Berdychiv, Ukraine, where he returned after the combined atrocities of the war and the Holocaust had done their worst. Haunted by past trauma, the youthful Gorenstein learned to remain in prolonged obscurity. He thus came to literature relatively late. His first and only "official" publication—"House with a Torrent," a beautiful short story about his mother's death—saw the light of day in 1964, at the end of the Thaw period. Having studied screenwriting at the famed Moscow state film school, Gorenstein made a living by writing scripts, most famously and consequentially for Andrei Tarkovsky's *Solaris.* In 1980, seeing no future for himself in the Soviet Union, he emigrated to West Germany and remained in Berlin until his death in 2002 at the age of seventy. His works, which, in addition to *Redemption and Psalm,* include an 800-page novel spanning the generations of Soviet history, *Place* (Mesto), the play "Berdychiv," which offers a portrait of the Jewish Pale of Settlement in its post-Holocaust Soviet days, and a 1,500-page play about the reign of Ivan the Terrible, were published in various émigré venues and widely translated into French and German. His last novel, a poignant and haunting *Traveling Companions,* which brings together Russian, Jewish, and Ukrainian traumas, has been available in an imperfect English translation since 1991.[2] Not until the Perestroika reforms did his works finally come out in Russia and Ukraine. In the past decade, many of them have been reissued while a critical interest in his biography and legacy has grown.

From the early 1960s on, Gorenstein desperately sought recognition for his prodigious talent. He was indeed deemed a genius by many who knew him or of him, but when that no longer sufficed, he began to cultivate an image

---

1 Friedrich Gorenstein, *Redemption,* trans. Andrew Bromfield (New York: Columbia University Press, 2018).

2 Friedrich Gorenstein, *Traveling Companions,* trans. Bernard Meares (New York: Harcourt, 1991).

of a bitter and quarrelsome outcast who found no home in either the liberal or the conversative camp, sympathizing neither with those who opposed the regime nor with those who lived by compromise. Most importantly, he also wore his Jewishness on his sleeve, putting off potential friends or allies by, for example, deliberately pronouncing his certainly impeccable Russian with a Yiddish intonation. To this day, many fans of his writing feel the need to explain away his "provincialism."

To Gorenstein himself, however, Jewishness was anything but provincial, as he was always proud of his Pale of Settlement lineage. Even as he places his work in the Russian literary tradition, he uniquely insists upon his distinctive Jewish voice. Moreover, what makes him a Jewish writer is not merely the preponderance of Jewish themes and characters in his novels, stories, plays, and essays, but precisely his polemical stance toward Russia's (and Ukraine's) history, language, literature, and religion—and toward the concomitant Russian demand for Jewish assimilation to those norms.

As he put it in one of his essays, "If I knew Yiddish, I probably would have become a Jewish writer and written in Yiddish. But I write in Russian, hence I'm a Russian writer whether anybody likes it or not."[3] Irreverently, Gorenstein speaks here to the undeniable fact both of his origins (Jewish) and of his actual language (Russian), chosen not so much by him as for him by the destructive and capricious forces of history. He regards Russian simultaneously as a tool and as a piece of cultural property that is enriched by his use of it:

> I use it without right or permission from those I've insulted. I didn't ask for it on a church steeple—I took it myself without any solicitations. "With such opinions," [they say], "what right do you have to write in Russian?" What right? And what right do *you* have to use the Jewish Bible and the Jewish Gospels?[4]

To call such a worldview unusual for an acculturated Russian Jewish writer of the Soviet era is an understatement. It flies in the face of both the assimilationist or conversionary ethos of Russian-Jewish cultural and literary history and the anti-Jewish animus prominently present in the Russian letters.

---

3 Friedrikh Gorenshtein, "Tovarishchu Matsa literaturovedu i cheloveku, a takzhe ego potomkam," *Zerkalo zagadok* 5 (1997): 42.

4 Gorenstein, "Tovarishchu Matsa," 41.

But Gorenstein's stance does resonate with a certain central strain in modern Jewish literature in both Yiddish and Hebrew. His is a vision of a modern Jew speaking with an ancient voice, through which he reclaims his hereditary dues and graciously shares them with others.

Gorenstein's notion of the "Jewish Gospels" is paradoxically a part of this vision, a stumbling block for many of his readers. Coupling his artistic credo with his revisionist theology, he viewed the Hebrew and Christian Bibles as a single Jewish document and the later Christianity as a usurpation and betrayal of the Jewish lineage. *Psalm* is the fullest and most radical expression and delineation of this idea.

-2-

Gorenstein considered *Psalm* to be among his three most important works, the other two being *Redemption* and *Place*. He wrote *Psalm* fairly quickly in 1974–75, having initially conceived of it as a *povest'*—a novella or a long short story. It was first published in the West in Munich in 1986, and in the Soviet Union in 1991. *Psalm* is a unique text, a metaphysical and theological tour de force which dumbfounded practically all of its critical readers and commentators. Divided into five parables, it takes place in Ukraine, Belarus, and Russia proper, stretching from the Holodomor—the famine in Ukraine orchestrated by Stalin in the early 1930s—to World War II and the Holocaust, to the post-war antisemitic anti-cosmopolitan campaign to Moscow of the late 1960s and early 70s. As Gorenstein explained to John Glad, "The Soviet Radio Committee was helping people find relatives who had disappeared during the war. A search was announced, and listeners were encouraged to write in letters telling of their lives. Some of the letters were read on the air. But the most interesting were given to me."[5] These stories transformed into the novel's characters: sinful and downtrodden little people, caught up in the historical horror they were destined to live through and often perish in. And while the historical markers provided by Gorenstein are easily recognizable, there's a sense that we're dealing with some remote hellish planet where the language spoken by its inhabitants is only ostensibly Russian. With

---

5 John Glad, *Conversations in Exile: Russian Writers Abroad* (Durham, N.C.: Duke University Press, 1993), 190-191.

this radical sense of defamiliarization Gorenstein is following in the footsteps of Andrei Platonov, a writer he deeply respected, whose Russian, in Joseph Brodsky's formulation, "reveals a proclivity for dead ends, a blind-alley mentality in the language itself."[6] Andrew Bromfield is to be commended for capturing the strangeness of Gorenstein's Russian in his translation.

The novel's daringness goes beyond its style, however. Gorenstein creates a theological mystery novel—what he calls *razmyshlenie*—translated by Bromfield as "reflection," but it is also contemplation or even here deliberation. The wickedness and brutality taking place in the Soviet empire is God's punishment—the plagues—for its people's offences, and a fulfillment of the prophecies of Ezekiel, Jeremiah, Isaiah, and Amos. The executor of God's will is a Jew from the tribe of Dan—the Antichrist, whom Gorenstein envisioned at first as simply the Devil. He is an observer of the unfolding historical and cosmic drama; both a witness to it and an actor who initiates the divine plan into motion. The main outcome of Dan's presence on earth is him begetting a child with his stepdaughter who becomes a prophetess. Thus, he brings into the world a new Antichrist messiah.

What is behind this theologically heretical mishmash which at first seems to smack of the worst of antisemitic lore? Resolutely not a postmodernist writer, Gorenstein offers not a parody, but an earnest theological vision with far reaching historical implications, whose intent is to figure out the mechanism by which Jews have survived for millennia in an irrevocably hostile world. His Antichrist is God's messenger and Jesus's blood brother. "You, the antisemites, are right in claiming that the Antichrist is a Jew who came to destroy Russia," Gorenstein seems to be saying, and continues, "but you haven't discerned the most important thing: he is from God and his plagues are God's scheme incarnate." Gorenstein returns Jesus to the Jewish camp as well. In doing so, he goes farther than such notable modern Jewish thinkers, as Martin Buber and Franz Rosenzweig, who redefined Jesus as a Jewish prophet. Gorenstein's Jesus is not merely a Jewish renegade, whose image was forcefully distorted by Paul and the later Christian theologians. On the one hand, Gorenstein reads the Gospels literally and concurs that Jesus was God's son. On the other, his Jesus is the King of the Jews, but in a strictly nationalist sense: as another Maccabee who reminded his broken people of

---

6 Joseph Brodsky, *Less than One: Selected Essays* (New York: Farrar Straus Giroux, 1986), 286.

the fearlessness of their spirit. With this reimagining of the New Testament, Gorenstein is reviving the spectacle of public disputations between Jewish and Christian theologians in medieval Europe, most of which ended in the shaming of Judaism. Gorenstein is certain that he is restoring the historical truth: he does not merely establish the link between Christianity and Judaism but proclaims Judaic preeminence. He does so brazenly both as a Russian writer and a Jewish provocateur suffering from the surplus of Jewish memory.

This memory, however, is highly selective and of a special kind, since it goes without saying that this theological scenario has very little to do with either Rabbinic Judaism, which has no need for either Christ or Antichrist, or the redemptive precepts of Christianity. In *Psalm*, Gorenstein divides humanity into two unequal halves: the sinners who are incapable of fulfilling God's commandments and accepting his justice, and those against whom they sin—the Jews. Christianity offers a watered-down morality and absolution—"kindness"—to the greater half—the sinners—while Judaism remains the only option for the select few. It is this chosen minority who are comforted throughout history by Dan the Antichrist. To quote from the novel's last chapter which serves as its theological coda:

> The good and kindness are different things. A genius cannot be a kind man, for he serves God, a kind man cannot be a genius, for he serves man. . . . The appearance of good in the world is in no wise connected with kind people, but with the prophets, those healers and geniuses who are the accumulators of spiritual riches. The bitterness of truth and the pitiless clarity of genius heal the world, kindness does not. Kindness does not heal the world, but it comforts the sinful and rescues them from their loneliness, and therefore it reinforces the fallen world. . . . The genuine Christian is a kind person of any religion, but the genuine Hebrew is a genius and prophet of any religion. Analyze any genius and you will discover a Judaic principle in him, even if he repudiates Judaism. Judaism is much closer to God than Christianity, and Christianity is closer to man.

Gorenstein does not so much preach as he provokes and *razmyshliaet*—contemplates and deliberates, incessantly formulating and reformulating to himself his theses. As he writes in one passage, "This is so important that

I feel the need to repeat it in rather different words." Despite the utter lack of actual Judaism in this portrayal of "a Judaic principle," his deliberation is reminiscent of the logic (or rather, the illogic) of the rabbinic pilpul—a Talmudic analysis of Scripture and relevant philosophical and moral issues—whose "mind . . . zigzags . . . but at the end succeed[s] in disentangling itself," to quote from Abraham Joshua Heschel's musings on pilpul.[7] In the case of *Psalm*, such a disentangling results in bold insights which have to do with both Gorenstein's vision of Jewishness and the aesthetic make-up of this cumbersome yet fascinating and profound text.

Gorenstein thus formulated his intent regarding *Psalm* in the same interview with Glad:

> I decided to look at Russia and its history through the prism of the Bible. I have been reading the Bible for a long time now, and each time I learn something new. We can learn from its style as well as from its merciless courage in the revelation of human failings. . . . This kind of courage can't be found in most popular folklore. This may be why Jewish folklore grew into the Bible . . . here we see man in his complexity of the good and evil resident in him. Evil often grows out of good, and good out of evil.[8]

Gorenstein is very astute both in terms of his portrayal of biblical heroes and in fact providing a rabbinic view of human nature as impregnated with both good and evil inclinations which each individual has to learn to balance. In light of the Hebrew Bible's moral honesty and a realistic assessment of human nature, Gorenstein's idea of Jews as humanity's spiritual geniuses does not lead him to glorifying actual Jews. He states, "As people, Jews are just as bad as all the rest of humanity. But as a specific historical formation, as a Biblical phenomenon, they are a people close to God, and man intrinsically hates God, therefore he also hates Jews, and therefore many Jews, as people, hate themselves and their own Biblical destiny." Thus, most crucial and painful for him is the abyss which separates the chosen people's eternal spirit from the realities of embodying this spirit in the everyday. Gorenstein

---

7 Abraham Joshua Heschel, *The Earth is the Lord's: The Inner World of the Jew in East Europe* (New York: Jewish Lights, 1995), 54.

8 Glad, *Conversations in Exile*, 190.

reproaches Jews—Soviet Jews, in particular, represented in *Psalm* by the servile and fearful Alexei Iosifovich Ivolgin—for their constant inability to cleanse themselves of the stench of what he calls in the novel "the fleshpots of slavery" which leads to "defenselessness"—the main Jewish sin in front of God. Gorenstein's obsessive crucial idea throughout his oeuvre is the historical pathology of this sin which causes Jews to seek approval from others, grovel in front of them, and be grateful for every morsel of mercy.

The roots of Gorenstein's evaluation of the exilic Jewish condition point undoubtedly to Zionism. Though he never visited Israel, he was an avowed Zionist and penned in his essays some of the most astute and convincing formulations of the derangement and perniciousness of anti-Zionism and the threat it poses to both the Jews and the West. In proclaiming in *Psalm* that "a man's genuine homeland is not the land on which he lives, but the nation to which he belongs" because "all land is the Lord's and the Lord is the only indigenous dweller on earth," he was arguing for the importance and value of remaining a Jew even outside of Israel. At the same time, in adding that "the genuine right to one or another piece of land is not procured by historical conquests or historical displacements or the fact of centuries-long possession, but by whether or not a nation makes a piece of the Lord's earth fruitful and the customs on it just," he was pointing to the modern return to the Land of Israel and the establishment there of the Jewish state. Notably, he prefaces these ideas by quotations from the Book of Ezrah about the return from the Babylonian exile and the restoration of Jerusalem, the Jerusalem Dan the Antichrist pines for.

In the context of Zionist thought, Gorenstein's idea of "defenselessness" is also closest to the writings and philosophy of his fellow Ukrainian Russian-speaking Jew, Vladimir Jabotinsky. Like Jabotinsky, Gorenstein insists on the Jews' self-sufficiency, independence from others and refusal to apologize for their perceived sins. In *Psalm,* he powerfully brings this vision back to the Bible and its dynamic of slavery and freedom as the poles of Jewish existence, which touches directly on the novel's poetics.

The unparalleled uniqueness of *Psalm* is that large chunks of the text consist entirely of quotations from the Hebrew Bible which the narrator then comments upon through his speculation/deliberation. This idiosyncratic commentator is the novel's only true voice; whether it's also a reliable voice is for the reader to decipher. The title—Psalm—is misleading, for most of the biblical quotes come from the prophets, mainly Jeremiah, Isaiah, and Ezekiel, all prophets of exile, destruction, but also messianic premonitions.

Psalms—poems of supplication and praise—are out of place here despite the notion at the very end of the novel that "every life and every destiny, even a bitter life and a harrowing destiny, must be transposed into a psalm." Another major genre employed in the text—a parable—invokes the Gospels rather than the Hebrew Bible. What this play with genre suggests is that Gorenstein emphasizes and clings to the *secondary*, the *post*—an addendum to the canon. In Judaism, there's a concept of *haftarah*—additional readings from prophetic books to the weekly Torah portions recited during a synagogue service. The usual explanation for the development of this custom is that in response to persecution, when Torah readings were outlawed, the haftarah became the replacement. Whether Gorenstein was familiar with this practice and tradition or not, I would see *Psalm* as a haftarah novel, a response to historical horror and trauma and a substitute, often an uneasy one, for the actual Torah—the canon.

Psalm, which luckily exists now in English, will certainly inspire its readers and force them to contemplate and deliberate, but it can also, as I've argued, repel and puzzle. I would like to offer two venues which will hopefully illuminate its cumbersome complexities: *Psalm* as speculative fiction or what the Soviets termed *nauchnaia fantastika*—the scientific fantastic genre—and *Psalm* as not just a Russian Jewish masterwork, but a Soviet Jewish one, the product of the now bygone Soviet Jewish civilization.

-3-

It seems rather obvious, at least to this author, that a novel which features the Antichrist residing as a Jew in the 20th-century Russia, and where many of the main theological pronouncement regarding Judaism and Christianity are propounded by a philosophical homunculus created by one of the characters in a crystal glass, belongs in the genre of speculative fiction. In the Soviet Union, all of speculative fiction fell under the category of science fiction, although at least one critic in the 1960s distinguished in it between "scientific" (*nauchnaia*) fantastic and non-scientific (*nenauchnaia*) fantastic. Approached as science fiction, the novel's strangeness and outlandishness fall into the markers and byproducts of the genre.

Gorenstein was drawn to science fiction. In 1969, he wrote a short story, "A Counterrevolutionary," which he specifically designated as a science fiction text. Its protagonist is a professor introduced to a graduate student obsessed with the idea that all of humanity's problems stem from the fact that people walk on two legs. Once they discover the "third point of support" which would allow them to position their bodies at a proper angle toward the horizon, human civilization would revive itself and overcome mortality. The professor sees the student as a modern day prophet: "And the professor understood that such were the ancient mad preachers who were followed by the crowds of the sick and the hungry."[9] Terrified at the prospect of the student's ideas gaining traction, the professor destroys the document with his calculations. He yells to "the false prophet," "Let's imagine that you will create your life spans of millennia on three feet under the biocybernetic angle toward the horizon. . . . But who will need this life if there won't be in it a new Pushkin or imperfections since happiness in it will be not transitory, but eternal. . . . Your ideas can only attract the hungry, the sick, and the physically deformed."[10] In *Psalm*, Gorenstein would also present Christianity as a false prophesy for the hungry and the sick, and describe Pushkin as a Jewish genius in essence. The story was never published, though it's unclear whether he ever submitted it anywhere. He would return to sci-fi in *Place*, which presents alternative histories about the assassination of Trotsky and an attempt on Molotov's life after Stalin's death.

I would conjecture that Gorenstein, who felt unwelcome in whatever club he tried to join, be it his attempts to get published officially or participate in the semi-official or unofficial venues, would have been accepted by the world of Soviet sci-fi. Future biographies of Gorenstein are yet to shed light on his entreaties with sci-fi and what precluded him from taking on the title of a sci-fi author. Science fiction underwent a renaissance in the Soviet Union and parts of Eastern Europe in the 1960s, achieving a huge popularity with the free-thinking intelligentsia. Relying on the metaphysical and avantgarde roots of the 1920s, it often became a place of subversion where religious questions could be explored in a camouflaged but also at times explicit fashion. Most interestingly, sci-fi in the Soviet Union was also a Jewish artistic space for both the authors and the readers. Many of the major sci-fi writers, critics, and translators were Jewish—the Strugatsky brothers, Gennady Gor, Ilya Varshavsky, Rafail Nudelman, Aleksandr Mirer, Boris Shtern, among others; even the non-Jews, such as Ariadna Gromova and

---

9 Fridrikh Gorenshteyn, *Dom s bashenkoi i vse rasskazy* (Leipzig: Isia Media Verlag, 2005), 238, 240.

10 Ibid., 243.

Mikhail Emtsev, were preoccupied with the Holocaust and the Jewish fate. Broadly, sci-fi became a place where antisemitism, the Holocaust, Jewish history, memory, language, Scripture, and spiritual concerns were presented and debated, again often in a subterranean and fragmentary fashion, but also occasionally unambiguously. Gorenstein would have had a decent chance of fitting right in.

There are two or rather three figures who are especially relevant in thinking about Gorenstein as a sci-fi author in relation to *Psalm*: Stanisław Lem and the Strugatsky brothers, Arkady and Boris. There's an explicit connection with Lem and a more tenuous one with the Strugatskys. Gorenstein wrote a script for Andrei Tarkovsky's adaptation of Lem's novel, *Solaris*. Notably, Tarkovsky wrote in his diary in January 1979, seven years after the release of *Solaris*,

> Read Gorenstein's *Psalm*. It is a stunning book. Of course he is a genius. He writes of a man and of his God with such passion, such persistence; pain finally overcomes by purification, by an understanding of the divine role. It is a book that has to be read. The first three parts are less successful. . . . However, the closer we go to the end, the more remarkable it becomes.[11]

What is remarkable and even paradoxical is that Tarkovsky, who was deeply and personally invested in Christianity and to an extent Russian nationalism, admires Gorenstein's revisionist Jewish theology. Lem, as is well known, disliked what Gorenstein and Tarkovsky did with his novel. He felt that they completely misunderstood it. At the same time, when it comes to Gorenstein the novelist, Lem and he appear to be on the same wave length, even if they come to seemingly divergent conclusions.

Both Lem, a Jew from the Ukrainian city of Lviv, and Gorenstein, a Jew from the Ukrainian city of Berdychiv, carried the trauma of the Holocaust and survival within the entirety of their lives. Lem had an enormous impact on Russian sci-fi authors and was worshipped by the Soviet readers. Though it has been rarely discussed, he viewed the fissures of human memory and the cosmos through a biblical and exegetical lens. Central to Lem's oeuvre is the

---

11 Andrey Tarkovsky, *Time Within Time The Diaries 1970–1986*, trans. Kitty Hunter-Blair (London: Seagull Books, 2018), 178–79.

impossibility of establishing contact with an interplanetary force that might be transcendent—the radical Other—and this invariably brings to mind the Hebrew Bible's concept of the divine. Lem always pits his characters against the ineffable, whatever that might be, which leads to their traumatic and revelatory experience of the Mystery. In his works, humanity understands its inconsequentiality while the human condition becomes fundamentally a tragic one at the cosmic level. The horror of the war and the Holocaust are a manifestation of this state, yet Lem largely chooses not to frame it in a personal way for philosophical and aesthetic reasons.

In *Solaris* specifically, which tells of a mysterious planet-ocean that generates the phantoms of memory for the scientists stationed on it, the protagonist Kelvin comes up with the idea of "an imperfect god," "the only god," he says, "I could imagine believing in, a god whose passion is not a redemption, who saves nothing, fulfills no purpose—a god who simply is."[12] Such a god would not be centered on humanity, would experiment with it for his own sake, and then abandon it as a useless toy. A belief in this god results from a never-ending sense of trauma and metaphysical realism.

Similarly to Lem, Gorenstein views the human plight as deeply fractured, traumatic, and inconsequential. In *Redemption*, written in 1967, a professor of literature hounded by the regime, who is the novel's philosophic and theological voice, points to the notion of a biblical "boundary" that humanity will cross once the cup of its inequity and suffering has at last overflowed. Beyond this apocalyptic boundary, he posits, "lies either universal life or universal death."[13] The professor dies, leaving behind writings that argue for the basic comedic insignificance of human existence, "our invented little earthly meaning of life" and the false idea that man is "himself and is unique, distinct from everything."[14] *Psalm* offers a "biblical" corrective to this vision which does not cancel, however, the terror or human existence. Though Gorenstein abides by the idea of all-powerful God who communicates with those among humans who dare to hear him, in the terms of the novel, this God is also erring and imperfect as are his messengers, Christ and Antichrist. Kelvin's beguiling words at the end of *Solaris* are "I knew

---

12 Stanisław Lem, *Solaris*, trans. Joanna Kilmartin and Steve Cox (San Diego, CA: A Harvest Books, 1987), 199.

13 Gorenstein, *Redemption*, 165.

14 Ibid., 194.

nothing, and I persisted in the faith that the time of cruel miracles was not past," which contain an absurdist element of hope.[15] The same absurdist hope in future miracles and justice permeates *Psalm* and the conclusion of *Redemption,* where "a naïve, unpretentious, human dawn was beginning, and God's agonizingly wise, soul-crucifying night was ending."[16] My hope is that Lem and Gorenstein were careful readers of each other. Certainly to read Lem through Gorenstein and Gorenstein through Lem is an enriching experience.

The Strugatsky brothers provide another instructive and fruitful parallel to Gorenstein's philosophy and mindset in *Psalm*. The most cult of Soviet sci-fi authors of the 1960s and 70s, who wrote a script for Tarkovsky's other sci-fi film, *Stalker,* the Strugatskys also present the human-centric view of the universe as fundamentally flawed. Human history is nothing but "a picnic on the side of the road" in the wider cosmos, to use the title of their most well-known work, making perennial human challenges not merely insoluble but also insignificant. In their masterwork, *The Doomed City* (beautifully translated by Andrew Bromfield!), written very close to *Psalm,* in 1971–75, and published for the first time in 1988–89, they describe a city with "infinite Void to the West and infinite Solidity to the east," where the sun is extinguished and reignited at will.[17] Some unknown power is conducting an experiment, importing people from all over the post-World War II globe. The city constitutes a matrix, an explicit parallel mirror dimension to the Soviet Union. This speculative setting allows the Strugatskys to condense different Soviet epochs—the Stalinist period, the liberal Thaw period, and the stagnation period of the 1970s—into one place and time. Throughout the novel these periods do not follow each other chronologically but are jumbled up and interwoven, symbolizing the unchanging vicious circle of Soviet history. Thus, both Gorenstein and the Strugatskys arrive at a bird's-eye view of this history; he via his biblical speculation/deliberation redolent of sci-fi, and they explicitly via sci-fi.

A preoccupation with Jewish history and destiny unites the three authors as well. The brothers, sons of a Jewish father and a Russian mother,

---

15 Lem, *Solaris,* 204.

16 Gorenstein, *Redemption,* 199.

17 Arkady Strugatsky and Boris Strugatsky, *The Doomed City,* trans. Andrew Bromfield (Chicago: Chicago Review Press, 2016).

were always fascinated with Jewishness, an interest manifested prominently in their works through characters, tropes, and allegorical constructs. *The Doomed City* features a protagonist, the Jew Izya Katsman, transported to the City in 1968, after the Arab-Israeli Six-Day War, which played a crucial role in reawakening the Soviet Jewish self-consciousness. He acts as a Jewish Socrates, an eternal sceptic and trickster, never satisfied with any status quo yet fully comfortable with his Jewishness, even proud of it as the source of his wisdom. "A unequivocal Jew . . . an ostentatiously provocative Jew," to use Boris Strugatsky's description, he resembles Gorenstein himself and Dan the Antichrist in *Psalm.*[18] At the end of the novel, Izya, presented now as a true sage, develops a theory of the "Great Temple" of culture. The temple, "the heritage of the minority," is being built by the select few—writers, artists, thinkers—whether the majority wants it or not;[19] at best, history can provide conditions that do not irreversibly hinder the construction. Izya recognizes that the temple's builders are not immune from the impurities of life, yet they are humanity's only positive sustaining source. Their "minority" status emphasizes the temple's Jewish underpinnings.

There are absolute parallels between Gorenstein's idea of Jews as history's "geniuses" and the Strugatsky's builders of the "Great Temple" of culture as actual and symbolic Jews. In fact, Gorenstein told Glad that for him, "the Bible is a textbook of culture."[20] Writing in the context of the Soviet 1970s with their ubiquitous antisemitism and overall absurdism, Gorenstein and the Strugatskys produce unpublishable works which strive to salvage Jewish uniqueness and uphold Jewish dignity. The fact that they do so via speculative allegories and radical new theologies speaks to the specificity of the Soviet Jewish mind and the dynamics of Soviet Jewish culture. Thus, my final proposition is that *Psalm* is best to be viewed as a Soviet Jewish creation.

-4-

It's curious that writing in the mid-1970s, when a Jewish religious and Zionist underground was in full swing in Moscow and other cities and the first

18 Strugatsky, *The Doomed City*, 461.

19 Ibid., 449.

20 Glad, *Conversations in Exile*, 191.

major aliya to Israel from the Soviet Union took place, Gorenstein remained outside of these circles and movements. Perhaps his insistence on not joining any club that would have him as a member, to recall Groucho Marx via Woody Allen, accounts for this oddity. Despite the fact that both Gorenstein and his novel were clearly radically outside of normative Soviet literature, *Psalm* speaks to his embeddedness within what I call the Soviet Jewish bookshelf, the bedrock of Soviet Jewish culture or even civilization. As I strove to demonstrate in my book, *The Soviet Jewish Bookshelf: Jewish Culture and Identity between the Lines,* Soviet Jewish culture after the Holocaust and Stalin's death was rich and complex while at the same time fragmentary and precarious.[21] This culture was a cautious triumph of the spirit that allowed Soviet Jews to assert their identity in a deeply hostile environment and form a canon of officially published books, consisting of everything from the Russian classics to translations of Yiddish and Hebrew literature to science fiction, from which they derived the "salvaged fragments" of Jewish knowledge and learned the meanings and expressions of Jewishness. Gorenstein was a product of the Soviet Jewish bookshelf and ultimately a contributor to it: a model Soviet Jewish reader and the creator of his own artistic and philosophical universe.

The core of the Soviet Jewish canon were the writings of the German Jewish author Lion Feuchtwanger. Published in the 1960s, his collected works became for Soviet Jews the primary source of Jewish historical, literary, and mythological knowledge, enveloping the entirety of Jewish history from the biblical era through the golden age of medieval Spain to the crises of modernity—both due to their content and the critical apparatus supplied at the volumes' end.

Particularly important for the Soviet Jewish reader was the Josephus trilogy about the great Roman Jewish historian and traitor, begun in the 1930s and completed during the war. Feuchtwanger's imagination paints him as the quintessentially modern Jew, stranded between the antagonistic and yet complementary worlds of Rome and Judea. Undoubtedly, Gorenstein was a careful reader of Feuchtwanger—in a photograph from 1986, Gorenstein is captured holding the first edition of his just-published

21 Marat Grinberg, *The Soviet Jewish Bookshelf: Jewish Culture and Identity between the Lines* (Waltham, MA: Brandeis University Press, 2023).

Gorenstein with his newly-published *Psalm*; photo courtesy of Yuri Veksler.

Psalm, and behind him are his bookshelves on which the most visible volume is that of Feuchtwanger.

Gorenstein embeds Josephus in his Dan the Antichrist. In *Judean War,* the first part of the trilogy, Josephus accompanies Titus through the besieged and devastated Jerusalem: "They came to a ravine into which the people in Jerusalem now flung their dead. A terrible choking stench rose from it: the bodies lay piled up in a loathsome heap of corruption. Titus paused. Joseph halted obediently."[22] Published in 1932, these images appear eerily prophetic of the Holocaust ravines of Ukraine, depicted in Gorenstein's *Redemption* and *Traveling Companions.* Titus wonders if Josephus is a spy and how he can endure seeing his people's catastrophe: "Here, looking down at the ravine filled with corpses, he tried to find some sign of repugnance or of grief on Joseph's face. But Joseph's face was impassive and Titus was overcome with a cold and strange sensation: How could the Jew endure such a sight?" The narrator explains, "It was as though a torturing impulse drove Joseph to the place where the horrors of the siege were to be seen at their worst. He had been sent here to be the eye that should witness all these horrors. It was easy to be shocked by them. To stand still and contemplate them because one must was far harder."[23] Dan the Antichrist is also sent to witness the devastation, to contemplate the

---

22 Lion Feuchtwanger, *Josephus,* trans. Willa and Edwin Muir (New York: The Viking Press, 1932), 399.

23 Ibid., 399–400.

injustice done to his people and ultimately reaffirm their glory, which is what Josephus will eventually do with his writings as well. Feuchtwanger's types were often the main sources for the Soviet Jewish artistic imagination; Gorenstein's character is a vivid example of that.

Notably, extensive commentaries to the Josephus trilogy, included in the collected writings, were written by Shimon Markish, a classicist and son of the great Yiddish poet Peretz Markish, murdered by Stalin in 1952, who would become the pioneer scholar of Russian Jewish literature after leaving the Soviet Union. Markish was also an astute reader of Gorenstein and saw *Psalm* as the "main height of Gorenstein's artistry," because in it, Gorenstein's "renegade, heretical, his own unique Jewish spirit was concentrated like in no other work. . . . The character of Dan is the product of the most curious and refined fantasy, which provides an incredible insight not only into the meaning and thought of the Hebrew Bible, but the very intonation of its Russian rendition."[24]

Markish's last comment brings us back to the question of Gorenstein's "biblical" style and via it also the Soviet Jewish bookshelf. Gorenstein clearly did read the Bible in Russian which he somehow was able to obtain. There's a cryptic note in his notebooks right next to the entries about *Psalm*, about a book in the US which costs $10-15. Perhaps it's referring to a copy of the Bible he was promised which could be smuggled from the US. In terms of how Gorenstein approached the biblical style, which he strove to capture in his novel, he relied, I would propose, on the few existing Soviet scholarly translations of various biblical books and the commentary to them. Such volumes were an integral part of the reading lists of Soviet Jewish intelligentsia.

In the interview with Glad, Gorenstein emphasizes the idea of "rhythm" as the most important element in prose, and in the biblical text in particular: "I tried to write parables in a biblical rhythm. All prose has a rhythm."[25] In 1973, right as he was about to embark on writing *Psalm*, an authoritative volume was published, *Poetry and Prose of the Ancient Near East*, in the prestigious *Library of World Literature* series. It included translations of various biblical books and a commentary to them and the Hebrew Bible at large which stated, "Rhythmic prose occupied for a long

---

24 Yurii Veksler, *Pazl Gorenshteyna: pamiatnik neizvestnomu pisateliu* (Moskva: Zakharov, 2020), 326.

25 Glad, *Conversations in Exile*, 192.

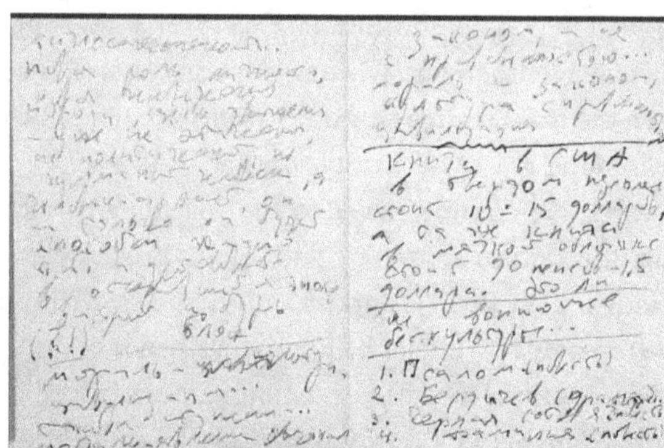

A page from Gorenstein's notebooks mentioning *Psalm* as a novella, and a book from the US; photo courtesy of Elena Frolova.

time an important place in ancient Hebrew literature. The most important works of rhythmic prose belong to the art of oratory—the 'prophets'' sermons. A 'prophet's' speech can descend to simple 'conversational' speech or, at the height of inspiration, include purely poetic sections or, finally, be almost pure poetry—such are the many sections from Isaiah, Jeremiah, Ezekiel."[26] In writing *Psalm*, Gorenstein was following meticulously in the footsteps of the biblical prophets, as described in this officially published Soviet commentary. His style also combines lowly conversational speech of his characters and biblical poetry, all to create the novel's special rhythm.

When it came to quotations from the Bible and how he quoted them, the Soviet Jewish bookshelf came into play as well. As perceptively noted by Joel Weinberg, Gorenstein comes close to or even replicates how the authors of the Dead Sea scrolls quoted from Scripture, often from the same prophetic books.[27] There were a number of volumes about the Dead Sea scrolls published in the Soviet Union in the 1960s and 70s by Iosif Amusin, one of the few Soviet Jewish scholars of the Bible to have survived the Holocaust and Stalinist purges. Joel Weinberg was his student. In the 1971 volume on the scrolls, Amusin emphasizes how their scribes "actualize the biblical text"—in

26 I. Braginskii (ed.), *Poeziia i proza drevnego Vostoka* (Moskow: Khudozhestvennaia literatura, 1973), 549.

27 Joel Weinberg, "Peshar kontsa XX veka: Vetkhii Zavet v romane razmyshlenii F. Gorenshteyna 'Psalom'" in *The Bible in a Thousand Years of Russian Literature*, ed. Wolf Moskovich (Jerusalem: The Hebrew University of Jerusalem, 1994).

other words, apply it to their own historical moment, and see the prophets' messages as a "mystery which applies specifically only to the Qumran community."[28] Ditto for Gorenstein: he radically and heretically actualizes the prophets' curses and premonitions through Soviet history and present, uncovering in them a special meaning and mystery, which for him holds the key to the entirety of Jewish existence. Thus, a model Soviet Jewish reader, Gorenstein pieces his comprehension of the Bible from various fragments, which necessarily makes his knowledge fractured and incomplete, but also supremely imaginative. It is this fragmentariness that accounts for *Psalm*'s daring and insight, outlandishness and idiosyncrasy.

The last book of Feuchtwanger's Josephus trilogy, *The Day Will Come*, published at the height of the Holocaust in 1942, ends with Josephus, no longer an apologist for Rome, but a polemicist against attacks on Jews and an archivist of their ancient and recent history, returning to the Land of Israel only to be killed upon arrival by a Roman legionnaire. Feuchtwanger writes:

> Now the region in which this happened was a high plateau, barren, covered with only a few bushes; but in the spring those bushes bore yellow blossoms. So Joseph lay in the mild, bright sunshine, and with blurring senses he absorbed the yellow-speckled desert and the mild, cheerful sun. The Joseph who had come to Rome to impregnate Rome and the world with the Jewish spirit.[29]

Gorenstein's Dan the Antichrist serves exactly the same purpose in *Psalm*—to impregnate Russia and the world with the Jewish spirit. The last and fifth "most terrible" plague, mentioned in *Psalm*, is "the hunger for the Word of the Lord . . . foretold through the prophet Amos." In Amos 11, the idea of the curse is clear: ready to repent, the Israelites will want to hear God's word, but "shall not find it" because there's still too much inequity around. Gorenstein presents this condition as perpetual, remedied through the presence of the Jewish genius—a "spiritual toiler"—in history. The spiritual toil is impregnating the world with the Jewish spirit. Such was also the mission of Gorenstein the artist who named his own son Dan. *Psalm*'s last line is "the

---

28 Iosif Amusin, *Teksty Kumrana* (Moskva: Nauka, 1971), 87.

29 Lion Feuchtwanger, *The Day Will Come* (London: Hutchinson & Co., 1942), 255.

vehement entreaty" from Isaiah 62:6—"O you, who call the Lord to mind, do not be silent!" It is chiselled on Gorenstein's gravestone in the Jewish cemetery Weissensee in Berlin.

Marat Grinberg

Gorenstein's gravestone; photo courtesy of Yuri Veksler.

www.ingramcontent.com/pod-product-compliance
Lightning Source LLC
LaVergne TN
LVHW011656100826
845155LV00004B/10

* 9 7 9 8 8 8 7 1 9 8 8 5 9 *